Under The Saltwater Moon

A Millie Myles Mystery Series
Book 1
Christa Hickcox

Christa Hickcox

Published by Christa Hickcox

Website: https://www.christahickcoxbooks.com

Edited by Sara Elisabeth and Laura Quill at Two Girls One Book Editing

Copy Edited by Sara Elisabeth and Laura Quill at Two Girls One Book Editing

Blurb by Skye Erikson

Cover Design by Sarah Earnhart

Edition 1

Dedication

In memory of Trae Michael Young

7/25/2000 - 7/25/2000

I don't know what type of man you would have grown up to be, but

I have no doubt you

would have put the forever in someone's best friend.

Forever the keepsake of my heart.

Land Acknowledgment

I acknowledge that my stories take place on traditional land of the first people of Seattle, the Duwamish People past and present and honor with gratitude the land itself and the Duwamish Tribe.

I acknowledge that the land I live and write my stories on are the traditional homelands of the Puyallup and Nisqually Tribes, and on lands with deep significance to other Coast Salish tribes. Coast Salish people have lived on and stewarded these lands since time immemorial and continue to do so today. We recognize that this land acknowledgement is one small step toward true allyship and we commit to uplifting the voices, experiences, and histories of the Indigenous people of this land and beyond.

Trigger Warnings

Reading is for enjoyment, so as you turn each page, I encourage you to take care of yourself if you are triggered by any of the following topics: panic attacks, OCD, homophobia, physical assault (off-page), death of family members, murder, blood, gore, vomit, religious cults, descriptions of cult activities, mentions of child labor, and difficult family dynamics. Please note that all intimate acts are consensual.

Your mental health is more important to me than your purchase. Please return this book for a refund if any of these topics are triggering.

CHAPTER 1

Oh, hello! I didn't even see you there! I do apologize.

I've been so busy planning for my next murder that I can barely focus on anything else.

But now that you're here, I imagine you have so many questions. Questions like how will this story end? Will the detectives catch me? Will I die in the end? Intriguing right?

Oooh... now I bet you are wondering who I even am? Who this serial killer possibly could be? Your neighbor? A coworker? The stranger sitting across from you at your local coffee shop? Or, how about what makes me tick? Isn't that the million-dollar question everyone wants to know?

People have been fascinated by serial killers for decades. Why do we kill? Is it because we love the sight of blood? Maybe. Is it for power? Possibly. Or is it about notoriety? The last is always my favorite theory.

If you believe what the psychologists say, then you will buy into their ideology: "we were starved for affection, abused by our loved ones, or *bullied at school." Yes, I am doing air quotes right now, in case you were wondering. They think this is our way of getting the attention we never received as young children. All of these are common threads for sure, but many people come out of the same horrible and disgusting situations and enter society as relatively normal adults. So, how do you really explain how or why someone becomes a serial killer?*

I won't keep you wondering because you have been very patient already. It's not complicated really.

Why do we do it? We do it for love. That's it. Nothing more and nothing less.

The power, fame, blood, or to finally feel extraordinary—all of that just comes with the brand "serial killer." But haven't we all found a love so strong that it has created the ultimate shift within our minds and souls? Love. Now that *is why we do it.*

I get it. You're invested now, and you want to know more about me. What made me different? What made me trip the line? What made my internal fuse fizzle to the end of the bomb that finally exploded inside me and made me take my first victim? And then my second?

Or maybe the real question is what will make me decide I am done? Will it be when I'm caught? Maybe I will just get bored and decide to open a little bookstore or coffeeshop and live out the rest of my days in peace.

I mean, it certainly won't be because the police catch me. I sound cocky, don't I? You are probably thinking, all the great ones think they will never be caught. But they are not me.

I am here to tell you that I have created the ultimate plan. No, more like a strategy. Yes! A strategy. You see. I am not a monster. Truly, I'm not. I am a builder. A creator. An artist. I believe in mercy; I don't want to hurt anyone. I want to give them peace, you see. I am a savior.

Keep following me. I promise you won't hate me by the end of this story. You might actually love me a little.

CHAPTER 2

"**B**rake! Brake! Agggaaah! Hit the *fucking* brakes!" I threw a forearm in front of my eyes while pointing at the biker over Lorraine's shoulder with my other hand. The rider appeared out of nowhere in my peripheral vision and scared the hell out of me. "Are you kidding me? You almost killed that guy, Lorraine." I lowered my hand to calm my racing heart.

Okay, Millie. You can clearly see that the biker is okay. He is leaning on his bike, spinning his pedals backwards, waiting for the light to change.

I could still hear my heart pounding in my ears as the terrifying images began to burst into my thoughts, one after another, like someone threw firecrackers into an unexpected crowd. I had no escape from this moment, so I dropped my head into my hands. My energy shifted quickly from a seemingly calm morning bus ride to a chaotic thought loop that was quickly spiraling out of my control.

Bus speeding... Biker crossing... Biker... Bus...

My stomach started to turn as the bile entered my throat from the gruesome images that flashed into my mind.

Please don't throw up. Please, not on this bus. Bus speeding... Biker crossing... Biker... Bus... Bus screeching... Biker hit... Screaming... Blood... Biker dead.

Stop. Stop it Millie.

I could feel the temperature in my body start to rise. I rubbed my hands down my jeans to dry the sweat.

I need to call Mickey.

I checked the time on my watch. 7:48 a.m. *Too early.*

"I can't look. Is he dead? Is he going to be okay? Lorraine? Lorraine!" I raised my voice to get her attention. I needed her to tell me that man was going to be okay.

Lorraine's booming voice shook me back to reality. "Millie, yes, he is completely fine. He is twenty feet away from us. Now will you please take your goddamn seat, girl. I will not tell you again. Sit your ass down. This is a city bus, and I don't take kindly to passengers who don't follow my bus rules. Especially the ones who have been riding my route for the past twenty years. Besides, these bikers have their own lane these days. It's even painted green with a concrete barrier between us. What is your damn problem today?"

I tried to regain my composure when I looked from the biker to Lorraine. Then I wrapped my arms over my stomach to settle the churning and took my seat.

I attempted to downplay my sudden outburst. "I'm sorry. I'm running late for my private investigator test, and you're driving like a maniac! Plus, I don't have time to explain to a traffic cop that my bus driver is more interested in texting with her wife than keeping these potential road rash rebels safe." I pointed anxiously to the biker, who was now taking a swig from his water bottle.

That went well. Note to self: when trying to downplay an outburst, don't call your bus driver a maniac.

Lorraine calmed her voice and looked at me with sympathetic eyes. "What kept you from getting to my earlier route this time, honey?"

I hated these kind of questions. It's hard when everyone who was close to me knew I had OCD because when I messed something up, they always had a recommendation on how I could have done something different to fix myself. I decided to answer her honestly anyway.

"I wasn't sure if I turned off the coffee pot or unplugged it after I got to the bus stop, so I had to go back to the condo to make sure it was, in fact, off and unplugged." I paused and tapped my chin. "Okay, I had to go back a couple of times, and by the time I got back to the bus stop, your bus had already come and gone, so I had to wait for the next one." I opened my backpack to double check the coffee pot was still in there.

Wait for it... wait for it... and here it is.

"You know honey, you could take another bus. I am not the only bus driver in this city. Also, have you thought about making yourself a list to check off before you leave the house so that you wouldn't forget to do anything?"

Brilliant! The solution to all my problems. It's not like I haven't tried everything under the sun to make this overwhelming feeling go away.

"I've told you a million times, you are my one and only bus driver, but otherwise great idea, thanks for the advice, Lorraine." I smiled at my friend.

"You're welcome, honey. Now stay in your seat." Lorraine's eyebrow raised with a nod.

My head dropped lightly against the cool metal bar in front of me, I took a deep, calming breath. I alternated between looking out the window and staring at my watch while I waited for the time to turn from 7:59 a.m. to 8 a.m. At the top of the hour, I leaned forward and pulled my phone out of my back pocket, went to my call log, and selected my brother's name from my recent calls. He answered on the first ring.

"Still kicking," Mickey mumbled with a big yawn. "Hey, be on time, I want to talk to you about something tonight. It's important. We need to talk about Mom and Dad. This conversation is long overdue, and you know it, Millie." Mickey sounded serious.

I ignored his comment, and replied, "Just making sure you're still alive. I'll see you for dinner this afternoon." I tapped End on the call.

I glanced up when I heard Lorraine say my name. She was talking to me through her own reflection in the oversized mirror above her head. "Are you seriously still trying to become a private investigator?"

Here we go again. Always a lecture about my life.

"Come on Millie, do something real with your life! You're a smart girl. You have a college degree in all that computer stuff, a family who loves you, and great friends. Why not just find a real job and a nice young lady, and stop with this nonsense? Honestly, how many times have you taken that test?" Lorraine shook her head.

These conversations made me feel more defeated with every second, I shrugged instead of responding to Lorraine. I let her voice fade into the background and turned my attention to the passing buildings as I pondered her question. I honestly couldn't remember how many times I had taken this test, but I knew today would be the day that I passed. Lorraine was right, though. I had a lot going for me: family support, friends, a college education to lean on when the right job came available. But I still had dreams of my own that no one seemed to understand.

I looked back at the front of the bus, and I took a chance with my question. "Lorraine, what if I pass the test today? Have you considered my offer?"

"Millie, I've been doing this bus thing for a long time. I have good benefits. I don't think I can quit and be your administrative assistant for your PI business. Sweetie, I love that you have all these dreams, and you know I have supported all of them since you were a little girl." She giggled. "Remember when you first started riding my bus? You were twelve and you wanted to be an archaeologist, and you spent all summer at that camp in Montana?"

"Yeah, I remember that. I found dinosaur bones. Then, when I found out that they planted them, I wrote to the governor, the FBI, *and* the President of the United States. The camp director finally gave us our money back."

Lorraine laughed at the memory at the same time she turned the big steering wheel clockwise onto Cherry Street. "Right, and you've tried every part-time job while you were in college to figure out who you wanted to be as an adult. You've been a bank teller, a scuba diver, a train conductor at the zoo, a rat catcher, a food critic, a junior park ranger, a professional mourner, and a spider-safe slayer, whatever the hell that is. I think my favorite was when you were seventeen and you met your first girlfriend, what was her name? Jenna? You two decided you were going to open a tiny town just for lesbians. I told you I would be your city bus driver." She cracked another smile.

"I told you before, there aren't enough eco-friendly exterminators in the Seattle area; spiders are a very important part of our ecosystem and deserve to live. Anyway, you're still going to do that, right? Be my bus driver for my lesbian city?" We locked eyes. I wasn't smiling.

She shook her head and broke eye contact. "Are you serious? Look Millie. I want to support everything you do. I really do. When you graduated college, I thought you were going to do something real with your life. You had plans to change the world. Now look at you. You have probably waited every damn table at every damn restaurant in this city. Millicent, it's time. You are thirty-two. It's time, honey."

Whenever Lorraine called me by my full name, I knew she was serious. It's not like I didn't try to get a job in my field. Forensic computer specialist roles weren't exactly a dime a dozen. I still applied every time one came up. Me and one-hundred other applicants. I had a job. Waiting tables wasn't using my degree, but it was steady work and the tips were really good. I wasn't ashamed of the work I did. It just didn't feed my soul.

What she didn't seem to understand was that I had wanted to be a detective, just like my grandpa, my dad, and my brother. So far, I spent my entire life doing what everyone else expected of me.

My brother told me it was too dangerous and that women were more likely to get killed in the line of duty. Sexist. I think he just doesn't want his little sister to outshine him.

We came from a long lineage of strong, proud Italians. Michael, or Mickey as everyone calls him, is really a big softy. And I will deny I called him that if ever confronted. He is good at his job, but he's also part of the boy's club. Well, sort of. More like they let him think he's part of the boy's club. It doesn't matter either way because that club doesn't have room for Mickey's little sister, Millie. So, I am going to get my PI license and make a difference my own way.

If I could just pass the damn test.

My stop was in one block. I reached up and pulled the line to signal for Lorraine to pull over, even though she knew where I needed to be dropped off. We'd done this routine thousands of times, and she'd never missed my stop. I just liked to make sure it stayed that way.

I looked out the window to see the little sparks flying from the friction of the electric bus cables like a small fireworks display. When the bus stopped, I shuffled past some seated passengers and skipped down the steps.

"Get a real job, Millie." Lorraine called as I jumped onto the concrete and ran toward the hotel where my test had surely already started.

I'm trying. I really am.

There was something about stepping off Lorraine's bus into the crisp November air that immediately made me feel rejuvenated. I took a deep breath and watched my breath form into a light fog as I exhaled.

I am safe.

Stuffing my hands in the kangaroo pocket of my hoodie, I looked both ways before rushing down the street.

"Brrrr..." I mumbled. Turning the corner, I bumped into a police officer, spilling his coffee down the front of his shirt.

A cop. A sign. A definitive sign that I am going to pass the test this time.

"What's your hurry, young lady?"

"Sorry officer, I am on my way to outrank you." I saluted him, spun around, and slammed into a woman handing out fliers. Her fliers flew into the air, floating back to the pavement. I didn't even look at her. I grabbed a flier, slid it into my bag, and kept going. "Sorry lady. I am running late to change my future."

"There is no future. It's all happening soon; the King Tides are coming. Help..." Her voice became softer as I put more distance between us.

Pretty sure she was one of Noble Pines's followers from that group out on Blake Island. They have been around for years. Harmless people, but annoying as they were constantly asking for donations of money, food, or something else for their cause. But whatever the cause,

I wasn't interested. These religious groups needed to stop preying on others. It was getting a little ridiculous.

Blake Island was 1,127 acres of densely wooded land and five miles of saltwater beach that was only accessible by boat. Not many people went out there unless it was to camp. I think the isolation was why they chose to set up their little village there. The state tried and failed for years to push Noble Pines and his followers out, but for one reason or another, they found a way to stay.

I wasn't interested. These religious groups needed to stop preying on

"Millie, the test has already started. You can't go in there," commanded the officer, who quickly swiped away the sign-in sheet before I could put my name on it.

"I am only seventeen minutes late. Come on, let me in," I pleaded.

"No." he stood up behind the sign-in table, holding the clipboard close to his chest.

"I'm going in there, whether you want me to or not."

"You are not going in there, Millie."

I walked backward toward the door. "You wouldn't want me to scream, would you?" I reached behind my back and turned the doorknob.

"You know, you might actually have a bright future in this line of work if you could just pass the test."

I narrowed my eyes at him and pushed the door open with my hip. "Jerk."

Nobody looked up from their papers when I entered the room. I walked over to the desk quietly and grabbed a test off the top of the pile. I strolled down the aisle to find an empty seat at a table next to another person who was concentrating so hard that they didn't even notice when I sat down. They were chewing on the end of their pen, still on their first question. I nudged their elbow.

"Good luck." I smiled. They turned toward the window and covered their test with their arm.

I studied the exam. There were fifty questions, and I had about one hour to finish. I contemplated going against my morals and answering the questions according to the way the government *thinks* I should answer them or answer them the way I knew was right.

Here we go! I firmly settled into my seat.

    1. Can private investigators arrest people? *Yep, lock 'em up!*

    2. Can private investigators access private information? *Yep. How else will I lock 'em up?*

    3. Can private investigators wiretap or bug a person? *Yep. See answers to questions one and two.*

It was important that I had the freedom to do my job as a private investigator with little interference from the police or anyone else. So, in similar fashion, I answered the next five questions.

"Thirty minutes remaining, folks. Thirty minutes," the overseeing officer called out.

I leaned over to speak to my deskmate, Cinnamon Haskins, according to the name on the test.

Interesting name.

"Cinnamon, what would you do if someone was cheating on their wife? Would the PI a, follow him into the hotel, b, wait for him outside, or c, confront him before he goes into the hotel?"

"Shhhh! I will not help you cheat, lady."

"It's not cheating. We are partners on the same team," I reminded Cinnamon.

"What the fuck are you talking about? Leave me alone."

I turned away and blew out a deep sigh.

Okay, I don't need help. I totally got this. Let's think this through. Logically, if the said husband is thought to be cheating on his said wife, then, of course, you would want to gather all the FACTS and all the EVIDENCE. I would obviously follow the said husband, break into his hotel room, hide in his closet, and record everything. Then I would share all the evidence with the said wife. Case closed. No matter the outcome."

I didn't even realize I was mumbling until my desk partner hushed me.

I raised my hand and cleared my throat to get the test proctor's attention.

"Yes, Ms. Myles?" She asked with two fingers placed firmly on the bridge of her nose.

"I have a question. May I ask it?" I continued to keep my hand raised.

"No Millie. This is a test. There are no questions. I tell you this every time you are here."

"Oh, okay, then I am just going to pick the first option because I am pretty sure the husband did it." I smiled proudly and went back to my test.

"Millie, please keep your answers to yourself. Fifteen minutes left, people. Fifteen minutes," the test proctor yelled out.

Shit, I have well over half the test left. I started to color in the little circles.

I am going to fail this test again.

When the test was over, Cinnamon gripped the metal around the rubber wheels of their wheelchair, pushed back from the table, and jetted out the door. I dropped my test off at the front of the room and ran to catch up.

"Cinnamon! Cinnamon!" I called out. "Wait up! I just want to talk to you for a minute."

I stopped abruptly as I saw the wheels whip around and race back toward me. "It's Cici. I don't go by Cinnamon. Yes, it's my legal name, but please don't call me that. It's triggering." They gave me a hard look. "I just feel like a Cici. I'm just me. Look, what I am trying to say is that I am non-binary. I go by they/them, okay? I hate my legal name."

I moved back slowly to show I was a safe person, which seemed to calm Cici a bit. I smiled as I took in the details of their appearance. I could see what they were saying. I admired their long pudgy nose, rocky brown eyes, and long brown hair, which was pulled back in a ponytail. I felt the beautiful uniqueness and energy that defined them as a person, not a gender.

When they stopped speaking, they turned their head to see me still standing there. I was hoping they would find some comfort that I didn't bail on them, but despite my best efforts to exude a calming vibe, they became even more irritated.

Cici threw their hands in the air in frustration. "Why the hell am I telling all of this to you? I am trying to get my name changed, but everything costs money. Getting my PI license is my biggest priority right now." Cici gave an expressive exhale. "Again, why am I telling a complete stranger all of this?" They snapped, shaking their head and turning to wheel away again.

"Cici wait. It's okay. I think we could really benefit from each other. I am trying to get my PI license too."

"Really? Is that why you were here today? I thought maybe you were selling rain squeegees for driveways. Not interested." They continued to wheel down the street.

I stood there, stunned at their temperament and sarcasm, but then I realized they gave me a great lead. "Is that a thing? Squeegeeing driveway services?" I called out after them.

CHAPTER 3

"Mickey!" I burst through the old rusty screen door.

Startled by my explosive entry, Mickey jumped out of his recliner and raced over. "Millie, what the hell is wrong? Are you okay? Are you hurt? Bleeding?" He started to assess my forehead and then my arms.

"Huh? No, I'm not hurt. Well not physically, anyway. But my feelings are charred to little burning bits of ash." I hurried through the living room into the kitchen, hoping if he knew I was dying inside, he would go easy on me for failing my PI test again and then maybe he wouldn't bring up our parents.

"Look, Soda Pop. If you are going to tell me you didn't pass your test or that another girl broke up with you, save it. Just save it all. I have zero empathy. I keep saying this is a waste of time, all this PI business. Detective work is a man's job. I have seen so many women get hurt in the line of duty. I don't know why I can't get this through your head.

You should be behind the scenes in technology or research, like in a lab where it's safe." He walked back over to the stove to stir his spaghetti sauce.

I could feel the redness creep through my cheeks. In an attempt to remain calm and not snap at my brother, I reminded myself that we'd never seen detective work in the same light. His misogynistic views had always held me back from exploring my dreams.

Sometimes I hated that people could tell we were related. "I can't believe how much you look just like your brother" the teachers would always say in school. I knew it was true. We both shared the same dark amber eyes and thick head of dark, raven-black hair, although Mickey sported a bit of salt and pepper in his these days. To say it kindly, we're a bit soft in the middle, which came from our love of the amazing bread that Mickey liked to make every Sunday. We affectionately called them our bread bellies, and I wouldn't give mine up for the world. Take me as I am, I say. I stood a good head taller than my brother, but I wasn't sure which side of the family I got my height from. Someone out there definitely did me a solid because I had nowhere near as much body fuzz as him.

Mickey said I took more after Mom's side while he took after Dad's. He thought I mostly looked like my sister. I wouldn't know, I guess. I never met my parents or sister. Well, at least I don't remember meeting them. It made Mickey sad when I said things like that. He took it so personally, like I spat on their graves. He wanted me to remember them like he does. I only wished I could.

Mickey raised me after our parents and older sister died on a trip to Italy. I was only two years old, and Mickey was eighteen. Mia, our older sister, who was four years older than Mickey, was attending college abroad in Milan, where we had family ties. My parents went to visit her and while traveling, they were in a horrible car accident. Mickey stepped up and raised me. If it wasn't for him, I would have ended up in foster care. I owe him my life.

It was the mid-nineties, and his entire world just imploded with one phone call. "Your parents and sister are dead," the voice said on the other end of the line. He said that Dad had called at eight that morning, but Mickey was dealing with me. I was crying because I didn't want to get dressed, and he claimed that if he had answered the phone, he might have prevented the accident. Maybe he would have delayed them from leaving the hotel, and they never would have died. Two hours after the missed call, Mickey got a phone call from a stranger telling him our family was gone. Suddenly, he was an eighteen-year-old boy with a mortgage in West Seattle and his two-year-old little sister to raise on his own.

Now, I have to live with the fact that because I was throwing a fit that morning, my parents and sister were dead. I started calling Mickey every morning at eight sharp to make sure he was still alive because I could never live with myself if I was responsible for him dying too. 8 a.m. is the time Dad called Mickey, so 8 a.m. is the time I will always call Mickey too. No one else in my family can die because of another missed call.

Mickey had just graduated high school and was starting college for his criminal justice degree to become a cop like our grandpa and dad. Even though it was a lot of work, Mickey got his college degree and a job with the Seattle Police Department, all while raising me. Mickey had no social life; he spent all his free time with me. We had no money, so he gave me our older sister's 1980s toys: a Cabbage Patch doll, a Glow Worm, and some My Little Ponies. But my favorite toys were a Strawberry Shortcake doll and Grumpy Care Bear.

On weekends, we played Atari video games like Pac-Man, Donkey Kong, Q*Bert, and my all-time favorite, Frogger. Mickey would always let me win. For movie nights, Mickey would gather the blankets and pillows, and we'd watch the same three movies while eating popcorn and candy: *The Karate Kid*, *The Terminator*, or his most treasured, *The Outsiders*. Mickey said our lives were like that movie because the parents also died in a car hit by a train and the big brother had to raise the younger siblings, just like us. That's why he started calling me Soda Pop; it was the name of one of the boys from the movie. I haven't seen it in years.

I strolled down the narrow hallway toward my old bedroom to call my roommate and best friend, Trae. The house felt so eerie, like I was walking through a time capsule. Mickey never bought new furniture so everything was exactly the way our parents left it. The only new additions were my school pictures that lined the long hallway.

I tried to call Trae twice, but he didn't answer, so I left a message. "Hey there bestie, I'm spending the night at Mickey's but will see you when you get home from work tomorrow." I tapped End on the call.

I will give him four minutes to call me back.

There was a familiar pit in my stomach when Trae didn't answer. I bet he was mad at me. I could feel it. He was probably letting his phone go to voicemail. I checked my watch.

Okay four minutes is up.

I called a third time. My knee bounced rapidly while I listened to his recorded greeting again and waited for the beep.

I felt slightly more panicked this time. "Hey Trae, I know there must be a hundred reasons you're not answering your phone. One, you decided to work, two, you are on a date, three through nine-ty-eight, you are mad at me. Please call me back."

I let out a long, nervous sigh.

I hope he's not mad at me. He always answers my calls. Why didn't he answer? Seems odd. Maybe I left the kitchen a mess, and he is super pissed. Wait! That's it! He knows I didn't pass my test, and he is mad about that. Breathe it out Millie. You aren't thinking logically. How would Trae know you failed your test? Fuck, he knows. He knows, and he is going to kick me out, and I will have to live with Mickey. I really don't want to live with Mickey again.

Logically, I knew Trae was with his boyfriend, Jeremy, and his friend, Beth, tonight. It was weird that he didn't answer my call, but he was fine. Right? When I closed my eyes, I could see him laughing with Jeremy and Beth while they ate dinner.

"Soda Pop!" Mickey's voice snapped me back to reality. "Trae just called the house phone. He said he's at Jeremy's and his cell phone only has one percent battery and he will call you later. Dinner is almost ready."

I closed my eyes and nodded my head.

Of course. Trae never takes his charger over to Jeremy's. I'm going to buy him an extra one to take with him next time.

I placed my hand on my chest and took a few deep breaths to slow my heart rate. It took me a few minutes to gather myself before walking back down the hall to the kitchen. I didn't tell Mickey when I spiraled like that. He would just want me to go back on those awful meds or see another therapist who would tell me the same things I've heard a million times before.

I passed the family room that Mickey pretty much lived in. I think he slept on the stained yellow couch because you could barely make out the floral patterns and most of the stuffing had gone flat. He had moved the old grandfather clock, which left a reverse shadow on the green shag carpet.

Almost to the kitchen, I shut the creepy basement door that led to the laundry room. I don't go down there. It's just full of our parent's and sister's boxes. Mickey doesn't get rid of anything.

I offered to help him go through all that stuff. It would be nice to donate some of it, but he kept saying "maybe next summer when it's warmer." Then summer came and he said, "it's too hot down there so we can tackle it in the winter when it's cooler." I eventually quit offering.

When I entered the kitchen, Mickey was setting plates and glasses in our normal places at the table. He still owned our parent's same steel-legged kitchen table that once had a bright white tabletop, now chipped and dingy. The red vinyl chairs had duct tape covering the cracks. I often wondered why my brother never married or made more of a life for himself. He said he was too busy raising me, which made me feel guilty that he thought he still had to take care of me. I've had my own life for years. He was making excuses not to move on.

"Trae told me when he and Jeremy arrived at Beth's apartment for dinner, she wasn't there. He said to feel free to eat the chocolate turtle cake he made in the fridge. He sounded upset." Mickey tossed a broken piece of bread in his mouth as he arranged the garlic bread in the basket. "How is Trae doing? Has he heard anything from his parents?"

Odd, that doesn't sound like Beth at all. Why would she ditch Trae like that? They had been friends since college, and they almost never missed a Sunday night dinner together.

"Yo! Earth to Millie." Mickey snapped his fingers in front of my face.

"Stop it!" I swatted at his hand. "I don't know why you keep asking me that. You know Trae's parents kicked him out of the house when he was fifteen. If it wasn't for his grandma taking him in like she did, he would probably be unhoused or worse," I reminded him.

"Well, he did get that nice condo when she passed away." Mickey set the bread basket in front of me. The savory smells made my stomach growl.

"And we got this beautiful mansion when our parents died," I teased, picking at a piece of the purple floral wallpaper that was curling from the wall.

Mickey sat across from me, so I quickly made the sign of the cross, grabbed a piece of bread, placed the buttery garlic side onto my tongue and bit down.

"Millicent, what the fuck?" Mickey said in his thick Italian accent.

"What?" I garbled and turned my palms up, shrugging my shoulders.

"You know we pray before we eat. Put the fucking bread down and say grace." He pointed to my plate.

"Sorry. Bless this food; let's eat. Good? You good? We good? Can we eat now?" I pointed to my mouth still full of food.

With a big sigh, Mickey surrendered. "Yeah, we can eat. So, how did the test go today? How is work going? How's your girlfriend doing?" Mickey rapid-fired all his questions.

I followed suit and, in rapid succession, I answered. "I'm pretty sure I failed the PI test again, the restaurant is great, and my girlfriend broke up with me. Anyway, what was that about Mom and Dad?"

"Seriously, Millie," Mickey whipped his napkin onto the table. "What happened this time? You know what? Don't answer that." He threw his hands in the air. "I don't even want to know. You just sit there with what happened. Actually, no, you go to your room and think about why you can't pass a test or keep a relationship and don't come back out here until you come up with a solution on how to fix this."

We stared at each other.

"You know I'm not going to do that, right? Go to my room and think about what I just did? That is not going to happen, because I'm THIRTY-TWO FUCKING YEARS OLD, MICKEY!" I shouted the words in my thickest Italian accent. A glob of spaghetti slid off my fork and down my front. "Shit, every fucking time!" I wiped the red sauce from my white shirt.

"Okay, okay." He pushed the air down with his hands, signaling me to calm down. Then he stood and went into the family room. A minute later, he returned and slapped a printed copy of a job posting down on the table.

"What is this?" I picked it up and looked at the job title which read, Property and Evidence Control Specialist.

"It's an opportunity to do something a little behind the scenes and get you out of waiting tables someday. I got you an interview tomorrow if you want. I know the manager. She's a friend of mine."

Looking over the job responsibilities, I knew this was my dream job. I could feel the excitement building as I read each duty description.

Calm down, Millie, you don't have the job yet. Let's check these off and make sure I'm qualified. Of course I'm qualified! I am a Myles!

Property and Evidence Control Specialist Job Responsibilities:

- Sign in/out evidence to lab staff for testing – *So basically, I need to know how to sign my own name and make sure others know how to sign theirs. CHECK.*

- Sign in/out evidence to be submitted as court exhibits –

Same! Sign, sign, sign.

- Maintain accurate physical and digital copies of evidence inventory – *I do have a computer science degree.*

- Must follow all laws, rules, and guidelines of the unit, department, and state. "Who's a rule follower? This girl." I said, pointing at myself.

Job Qualifications:

- May have to climb, walk, stand, jog, bend, crawl, but mostly sit for long periods of time. – *Sounds like an agility course. Fun.*

- Must be able to lift 50 lbs.– *I was a farm hand for a day, throwing bales of hay for horses. Maybe I could demo that?*

- Must take a polygraph test. – *Shit! Need to practice.*

- Must pass a drug test. – *Easiest test I will ever take!*

- Must wear a uniform. – *Promise?*

Desired Qualifications:

- Exceptional Computer Skills – *Again, degree.*

- Be willing to testify in court – *Just doing my part.*

- Touch items of an unpleasant nature – *Ask more questions.*

- Drive a forklift – *Oh, hell yeah!*

"Mickey, what time should I be there? I really want this job. This job has my name written all over it."

"It's very part time, Soda Pop. It's only a couple random overnight shifts during the week, so you will still need to keep a couple of shifts at the restaurant. You will be on probation for ninety days. If you do a good job though, they might hire you on and then who knows. It could lead to something full time with benefits and a pension."

I didn't want to disappoint Mickey, but this wouldn't be a permanent gig. It was just until I got my PI license and started my own business. When I had graduated, I couldn't find a job because no one was hiring. Mickey told me he would help me find something but never did. Trae landed a job before he even graduated with the same degree as me, only he was a senior software engineer. He coded video games for a living, but his true love was being an amateur inventor, building robots for fun. I loved seeing all his inventions. I wished he could do it full time. Maybe someday we would both be able to live out our dreams exactly how we were meant to.

I rolled my eyes at myself. Really the only thing Mickey was missing was a little house in the burbs with a wife and kids. "So, what time should I be there?"

"Be there at four. The day manager, Officer Palmer, is doing a split shift. She will meet you in the lobby. Now, how about some dessert?"

Mickey collected our plates and put them in the sink. Next, he grabbed the milk out of the fridge, then the Strawberry Quik canister from the cupboard. "You deserve a special treat after the day you had. I will make us some strawberry milk."

I shook my head as I watched him grab a spoon to pry the lid off the old tin canister. I don't know why Mickey kept using this old metal box when they offered nice, clean recyclable plastic ones, which I guess he did buy, but he transferred the powder back into that old rusty one.

And he thinks I'm the one who isn't willing to grow up.

After our dessert, I went back to my bedroom and shut the door. I sat in the squeaky old swivel chair that didn't match my little white desk and made me feel like a giant now that I was in my thirties. I swung back and forth while listening to the whining sound with every turn of the chair's metal springs. As I twirled, I reminisced about that seventeen-year-old girl who found her true self in this very room.

The first time I kissed a girl happened right here. Her name was Jenna, and she was my girlfriend. I thought we would be together forever. This room was like our little house, and we decorated every inch of it together, including the purple walls. I did a full rotation in my chair, taking in the entire room until I stopped in front of a faded rainbow flag. I smiled, turned to the left, and got a little teary staring at a glow-in-the-dark mushroom poster. I giggled when I saw the sign next to the poster that said, "Eve was framed." Damn, we were good together. Jenna was happily married to her wife and living down in California with their two kids.

The old chair wobbled when I aligned my body in front of my desk. I closed my eyes and inhaled the smells of old musty wood as I opened the desk drawer. A piece of splinter wood poked my finger when I stretched my arm deep into the space. The pain was worth the reward when I pulled out the small red tin box. There wasn't a lock on it or anything. It's not like Mickey ever came in here. As far as I knew anyway.

I opened the creaky, rusty lid slowly, exposing my prize possessions. On top was a little baggie of rolled joints. I kept them in case I had a weed emergency. I set the baggie aside. Next, was a necklace that was my mom's. It had a dark red ruby with diamonds wrapped around the outside. Mickey said it was very expensive. Then there was my dad's pocketknife. Ironically, it had a train carved in the ivory bone.

I stood up and took the box, leaving my parent's stuff and emergency weed on the desk, and plopped onto the bed. There was also another necklace called a *Cornicello*. I held the trinket in the air and let the little gold pepper sway back and forth. It was my sister's and supposed to be good luck. I could probably use some good luck. I sat forward and snapped the clasp around my neck, laying my hand flat over the necklace. I felt her presence with me for a moment. It was nice.

Lastly, one by one, I pulled out my collection of Garbage Pail Kids playing cards, each wrapped carefully in airtight Ziplock baggies. I placed Hip Kip, Sticky Ricky, and then my favorite, Leaky Lyndsay, onto the bed. I set aside the rest.

"Millie, come out here. You have a visitor," Mickey yelled from the family room.

Ha! Trae could tell I was having a bad day. Best friends can always tell when you need them without you even having to say the words.

I chuckled, walking down the hallway, but then I stopped dead in my tracks. "Cici?"

"I need your help." They didn't look happy.

CHAPTER 4

"Cici, are you okay?" I rushed over to them.

"I'm fine. I just need somewhere to stay tonight and maybe a bit of whatever smells so hella delicious." Cici wheeled themselves towards the kitchen.

Mickey and I looked at each other with shock and curiosity. Then, we shrugged and followed them into the kitchen. He went to the fridge and pulled out the leftover containers while I created a space at the table for Cici's wheelchair.

"Seriously, what's going on? How did you find me? I mean, don't get me wrong, I'm not knocking your PI skills. I mean, sure they're probably great. Outstanding, in fact. It's just, I'm not an easy person to find—"

"Your address was on your test paper. I copied it down while we were sitting together. You seemed harmless for the most part." Cici looked me over, possibly questioning their first assessment of me.

”I *am* harmless,“ I mumbled when I heard the microwave beep, so I hurried over to take the hot plate of food from Mickey. I nodded toward the family room, signaling for him to leave us alone.

Mickey gave me one of his stern big brother looks and whispered, "We are going to talk about you using my address, Soda Pop. No more. I told you. We are going to talk about Mom and Dad too, you hear me? No more excuses." He pointed his finger at my chest before he turned and walked out of the kitchen.

I set the plate in front of Cici. "So, what's going on? Why do you need a place to stay tonight?"

"Oh, it's really no big deal. There is a minor rat infestation in my apartment building, and we aren't allowed to stay there while they are taking care of it."

Cici was shoving food in their mouth like they hadn't eaten for days. It certainly made me suspicious. I was starting to wonder if there might be more to this story. I decided to tread lightly on what could be a very sensitive topic. Very lightly. "How long have you been unhoused and without food or drink?"

"Oh, so it's like that? Okay, so I show up here with a duffel bag, in a wheelchair, needing a place to crash for a while and shoving food in my face, and suddenly, I'm an unhoused starving person? Screw you, Millie."

"Well in my defense, you did show up here with a duffel bag, in a wheelchair, needing a place to crash... wait, for a while? I thought you said just for tonight. Cici, I don't live here. This isn't my house. I live in a two-bedroom condo with my best friend, Trae. We live in downtown Seattle, in the Pioneer Square neighborhood."

"Great. I can't wait to see our condo. Are we sharing a room? Are you sleeping on the couch?" Cici put their fork down to wipe their mouth with a napkin.

I thought about this for a minute. "We do have a little den-like room with a futon. I guess you can sleep in there. Trae used to game in there, but now he uses it mostly for his herb and vegetable garden."

The garden was an amazing room. I only went in there when Trae had something new to show me because I was afraid of accidentally breaking one of his robots or killing one of his plants. Even though the room got a decent amount of light, he had these purple grow lights that he rigged to turn on automatically when the natural light went too low for his plant babies.

Trae had a passion for cooking breakfast foods, dessert, and sometimes dinner, so he grew all his own veggies, herbs, and fruits. He built and programmed tiny robots that he called his "bot boys" to take care of the garden. He mentioned something about machine learning. Apparently, the more they gardened, the more they learned. The little robots were obsessed with the plants. It was actually a bit concerning.

Cici seemed excited by this prospect. "I love plants! We are all going to get along great. I will even help with the rent. I'm not a freeloader. When can I see my new place?"

"Er, tomorrow, I guess." All I could think about was how pissed Trae was going to be that I was bringing home another unhoused person.

For some reason, I was struggling to make eye contact with them, so instead I chose to continually flick the broken piece of plastic that circled the outside of the kitchen table. "So, you have a job?"

"Of course I have a job. I'm an investigative journalist for *The Seattle Times*. I told you my apartment is infested with rats, and I need a place to sleep. Look, I'm new to the area. I just moved here from Portland six months ago, and I don't know anyone. When we met earlier today, you seemed like a fairly normal person who wouldn't murder me in my sleep. I've seen a lot of stuff over the years in my line of work. I have to be careful."

"I *am* normal." I reminded them as I picked up Cici's dishes from the table. "Would you like some dessert?"

"Sure, I have a huge sweet tooth. I will eat about anything when it comes to desserts."

Cici didn't disappoint when I placed the same dessert Mickey made for us in front of them.

"Oh my gosh, Strawberry Quik. It's been forever since I have had one of these, and I love this Smurfs glass! I used to watch old reruns of this show as a kid." Cici turned the glass to see all the different characters. "Look! There is Papa Smurf, Brainy Smurf, and Grouchy Smurf. Look, look! There's Smurfette! Man, I had such a crush on her."

"Really? You did? A little blue gnome? A crush?" I felt a little concerned for my new friend.

They backtracked. "Well, I was like eight. How big of a crush can a kid at that age have, really?"

We shared a long stare until I decided to break the awkward silence. "Right, not big." I changed the subject. "So, your job sounds amazing. Do you like, help the police catch murderers and drug dealers?"

"Well, no, not yet anyway. That's why I'm trying to get my PI license. I want bigger stories. I keep getting assignments that involve boring stuff like tax evasion and money laundering. The closest I got to drugs or murder was an accountant who shot his partner when we leaked the story about them giving illegal tax breaks to city officials. But of course, that story got pulled right from under me with the first drop of blood."

"That sucks, Cici. I'm really sorry. Do you think you passed the test?"

"Probably. It wasn't hard. You?"

"I don't think so. I never do." I grabbed Cici's empty glass and put it in the sink.

"Why haven't you passed it? It's a pretty straightforward test."

I thought hard about how to answer Cici's question before I responded. "Because the multiple choice answers are not aligned to how we must dutifully resolve the crimes that are placed before us."

"Yes, they are. The answers are exactly the way we are to resolve situations that are presented to us, according to state law," Cici confirmed.

"Yeah, no Cici, not really." I shook my head and gave them a stern look.

"Okay, this could be why you haven't passed the test yet. Look at it this way: they are giving the test again in a few months so that gives you more time to study. The right way. I'll help you," Cici offered.

"Do you want to join my PI business?" The idea just popped in my head and out of my mouth with little to no consideration that it might be too forward.

"Look, Millie. Like I said, I'm getting my license for my job. That's it. I have full-time work. I mean, you don't even have your license, a business location, a business name, or what every PI needs: clients."

I made a mental checklist of everything Cici just said so I could write it all down later. "Thanks for the advice. I'll show you where you'll be sleeping. You can have my room after I clean up a few things. I will take the couch tonight. I'm glad you found me, Cici."

"I might regret saying this later, but I'm kind of glad I found you too." Cici backed their wheelchair from the table. "Now show me my room."

Mickey stopped us in the family room. "I don't mean to interrupt, but Millie, I just got called in. There was a, uhm, a situation downtown." He was being purposely vague to not alarm Cici.

I looked over at Cici, who seemed confused but didn't ask any further questions. I knew what he meant. There was a murder downtown, and my brother, the big, bad homicide detective was called in to investigate.

"Okay, be safe. I will call you tomorrow," I promised before showing Cici to my room. I decided to take Mickey's room since he'd be gone.

I stood in the hallway staring at my phone, waiting for the minutes to tick by. Once the time turned from 7:59 a.m. to 8 a.m., I went to my call log and selected my brother's name from my recent calls. He answered on the first ring.

"Soda Pop," Mickey said quickly followed by the biggest blow off ever. "Look, I can't talk now. I will call you later." The phone went dead.

Cici and I entered the kitchen to find that Mickey left out breakfast for us before he went to work. There was a choice of three cereals sitting on the kitchen table: Captain Crunch with Berries, Corn Flakes, and Apple Jacks.

"Hungry?" I handed Cici the Tony the Tiger bowl and kept the Captain Crunch bowl for myself.

"Oh my gosh, it's like living in some eighties childhood home here." They giggled while checking out their bowl.

"What do you mean?"

"All this old stuff. It's like I entered an eighties time warp."

"Mickey just doesn't feel the need to buy new stuff when the old stuff isn't broken." I felt a little judged.

"It's not just your brother. I slept in your room last night, remember?"

"Oh, you're talking about the Cabbage Patch and Rainbow Bright dolls in the closet? Yeah, same story. Mickey gave me all that stuff. He just likes things the way they were when my older sister and parents died. They died in a car wreck with a train overseas. It all happened when I was two years old, so I don't remember any of it. Mickey raised me."

"Damn, rough start to life. I'm sorry."

"Like I said, I don't remember any of it. It was a lot harder on my brother. Mickey thinks I'm traumatized and wants to have this big emotional talk about it. I avoid the conversation at all costs. I don't know why he suddenly feels like it's a good idea. Well, I kind of know why, but I'm fine." I poured cereal into my bowl and continued.

"Mickey's a homicide detective with the Seattle Police Department like my dad and grandfather. I think that is why he doesn't want me to follow in his footsteps or to even get my PI license. Mickey thinks it's too dangerous, so I got my computer science degree with a minor in forensics, but I can't find a job around here, and I can't leave Mickey. So, I have been serving tables until I find a job."

Cici sat there and took this all in. "So, this is why you stay around Seattle? To take care of your brother?"

I finished drinking the milk from my cereal bowl, which slid down my chin and onto my blue shirt. "Every fucking time," I mumbled. I stood up wiping my face and headed to the sink to rinse my dish. I stood there for a moment, blotting the milk off my shirt with a kitchen towel, not exactly sure how to answer that question.

"I think so, yes. I mean, he never married. As far as I know he never dates either. He just goes to work, comes home, and watches old reruns of *Knight Rider* and *MacGyver*. Mickey doesn't drink or smoke like other detectives. He just sits at home, waiting to retire. Kind of sad, don't you think?"

"Super sad. I can see why you stick around." They said with a pouty lip.

"Not to change the topic, but we should figure out what our plan is for the day. We can take the forty bus across the West Seattle bridge into downtown. Then, I typically take Lorraine's bus to my condo in Pioneer Square. Which bus do you take to work?" I pulled out the bus schedule from the drawer.

"I'm not working today. I called in because of the rats so, I'm all yours today. What do you want to do?" Cici took another bite of their cereal.

"You know, I have a bit of training as a rat catcher. I might be able to lend you a hand."

Not convinced of my skill set, Cici replied, "Yeah, no thanks. I think I'll leave that to the professionals."

"Well, just so you know, I could take care of your little situation a lot quicker than those so-called professionals." I made air quotes with my fingers, before taking Cici's empty bowl. "We can just head over to my condo. I will get you settled in and then I have a job interview at four."

"For what?" Cici grabbed their backpack and zipped it closed.

"Property and evidence control specialist at the evidence warehouse. It sounds so cool! I will be checking in and out evidence. I'll have to take a polygraph test and testify in court, but none of that should be a problem. I'm a Myles. Everyone knows me around the police department and courthouse. After all, my family has been in the police force for years."

"Sounds boring." Cici started wheeling toward the front door.

"What? Why do you say that?" I dropped the bowl in the sink.

"It will be just like my job. You think you'll get to see all the cool stuff, but you won't. All that will happen is an officer will drop off a bag full of broken headlights from a car accident or, at best, some dirty clothes. What fun is that? It will already be in boxes or bags, and you log it in a computer and then it goes on a shelf. Done. Boring."

"Have you done this job before?" I grabbed my beanie and jacket from the brass hooks by the front door and tossed Cici their coat. I held the door open for them to exit before I turned to lock the front door behind us. Cici wheeled down the ramp and I went down the steps.

We continued up the street, then turned down the hill toward the bus stop where we both noticed the clouds thickening and the rain turning from a mist to a sprinkle. Cici looked suspiciously to the sky. "It's going to be a gross day; I can feel it in my bones."

"Yeah, I think we are in for a hard winter this year. Mickey said it is supposed to be a colder and wetter winter than last year. If these first couple of weeks of November are any indication of what we are in for, we're screwed." I snugged my beanie tighter over my ears.

Cici backtracked to my last question. "To answer your question about whether I've worked at a warehouse job before, no. But I have gone to the warehouse to get story leads. While I waited for someone to come talk to me, I watched this same routine for over an hour before I realized no one was coming. They were making me wait it out until I got bored enough to leave. Which I did."

It took ten minutes for the bus to arrive, so instead of sitting in silence I told Cici about the West Seattle neighborhood I grew up in. I first pointed over the hill towards Alki beach.

"Look, that is where my brother keeps his fishing boat and that is where I used to go to the beach with my girlfriend, Jenna, in the summers. Over that way..." I pointed down the road. "Was an abandoned building where Jenna and I used to go and get high then kiss a lot."

Cici gave a concerned look.

"Oh, I don't really smoke weed anymore. I couldn't care less if people do. In fact, I keep emergency weed in my old bedroom, just in case, but I know I'll have to take a drug test once I get my PI license and for this warehouse job, so I'm clean."

Cici looked away, and instead of responding, started to smooth out the blanket that laid on their lap. I was about to explain the purpose of emergency weed, when I smelled the burning oil of the city bus coming up the road.

I typically just jumped on the bus and off we went. This was the first time I waited for the wheelchair ramp to come down. As Cici loaded themselves on the bus, some people seemed irritated about having to wait, which made *me* irritated. I wondered if I had ever been irritated in the past, having to wait for a person in a wheelchair to be loaded.

"Do you need help, Cici?" I went to grab the handles of their wheelchair to guide them to the ramp.

"Fuck off. I'm not handicapped. This is just the way I move, like your legs. I don't grab your hand to walk you across the street, do I?"

"Got it." I threw my hands in the air to surrender, smiling at them.

I really liked my new friend. They were independent, strong, and kind of an asshole. I only hoped they would get along with Trae, who could be sensitive sometimes.

We got to our next stop and waited for Lorraine's bus to arrive. When it did, I was surprised that I wasn't her first greeting.

"Cici, get your ass up here and give me a hug. It's been like three weeks since I've seen you! Millie, move out of the damn way." Lorraine shouted.

I stepped off the curb and moved to the side to allow Lorraine to lower the ramp for Cici. Once the beeping confirmed the ramp was locked in place, Cici reluctantly rolled onto the platform to give Lorraine her hug.

"I know, it's been crazy. Work has been so busy. I got a story down south, so I haven't ridden your route." Cici leaned in for a half hug. "Oh, and get this, I got rats in my apartment building. I'm going to stay with Millie and her roommate until my landlord gets rid of them."

"Millie and Trae?" Lorraine looked confused.

"Yes, me and Trae. Can I get on the bus now?" I started up the steps.

We all sat quietly the rest of the ride. We were in the vicinity of my condo when I realized that I probably shouldn't show up empty handed.

"We need to stop by the store really quickly to buy an extra phone charger for Trae. I want to bring him a gift. I think I'm going to have some sucking up to do."

"I get it. You're bringing home a lot."

I was nodding my head in agreement when my eyes grew huge as we passed Trae's office building. There were tons of red and blue flashing lights and Mickey was bent over, puking all over the ground.

I immediately pulled the line. "Lorraine, STOP!"

CHAPTER 5

I fought my way through the crowd and under the police tape to Mickey's side. "Mickey, what the hell is going on? Is Trae okay? Is he in there?"

Mickey was hunched over in the pouring rain with one hand resting on the building and the other on his knee. He tried to scold me between dry heaves. "Get out of here, Soda Pop. Go home!"

Holding a handkerchief to his mouth. "You have no business being here, he fumed. "I don't know what to tell you right now." He put the cloth in his pocket while he stood up. "Just get the hell out of here!" he snapped at me. Mickey had a fearful look in his eyes that I don't remember ever seeing before.

Mickey's partner walked up interrupting us. He patted Mickey on the back. "Your big brother has a bit of a hard time with the sight of blood. Such a sensitive man. Maybe I will introduce him to my little sister. She could use a sensitive man." He laughed and walked away.

Mickey pushed past me while dabbing the spittle from his chin with his jacket. "I'm not going to tell you again. Go home, Millie."

Suddenly, I felt someone grab my arm. I looked over to see an officer pulling me away from the building. "Ma'am you need to get behind the yellow tape. This is a crime scene."

I didn't argue. I walked back to the bus where I found Cici taking pictures with their camera.

"Millie, check out these pictures." They scrolled through the pictures on their camera. The shots were so raw and told a frightful story of the horror that had unraveled at Trae's office building without the need for any words. One image captured an officer trying to calm a woman down as they tried to cross the crime scene tape. There were other photos of the forensics team taking multiple boxes of evidence out to waiting vans. Cici had a real talent for photography.

I pointed to the crowd which drew Cici's attention in that direction. "Is that person the same person who was trying to cross the line? I think that is Trae's friend, Beth's mom. I've seen her at one of Trae's company picnics."

Cici nodded to the picture on their camera then to the women in the crowd. "Yep, same woman. That's really sad. I hope she is okay."

"Come on you two," Lorraine barked. "It's freezing out there and you're getting soaked. You'll catch a damn cold. Get in here. I can't keep the bus here all day." Lorraine lowered the ramp.

"Here, will you hold my camera while we get back on the bus?" Cici requested.

I took Cici's camera and waited while they went up the ramp. I took one last look to see if I could find Mickey, but I couldn't see him, so I hopped up the steps to find Cici.

I sat back in my seat as the bus started to move again. "One. Two. Three. Four. Five. Six. Seven." I recited my numbers so that Trae would be okay. I need Trae to be okay. I will die without my best friend.

I could feel the vibrations of my heart pounding against the seat of the bus as grisly images began to flood into my thoughts, one after another, like a tsunami drowning each innocent soul with the swallow of its massive wave. My energy rapidly intensified into a chaotic thought loop that was quickly spiraling out of my control.

The heat rose so quickly in my body that tiny beads of sweat started to form on my forehead. I tried to shake my head, desperately trying to release these thoughts.

Stop it, Millie! Stop it! Stop it! I began to rock back and forth.

Trae stabbed... Trae shot...

Was Trae dead in his office building? Oh my God. I rocked harder.

Trae stabbed... Trae shot... Trae bludgeoned... Screaming... Blood... Trae dead.

My skin started to tingle, which made me feel lightheaded.

I can't pass out on this bus.

"One. Two. Three. Four. Five. Six. Seven."

"Okay, what the hell are you doing? Why are you counting to seven?" Cici sounded annoyed.

Lorraine spoke up before I could answer. "Cici, leave her alone, honey. She doesn't need to answer that right now."

"Yeah, she kinda does," Cici snapped back. "Listen, I don't know what that was, but maybe you should consider therapy. It might help you stop doing that."

I looked between Lorraine and Cici. I didn't mean to get angry, but I snapped. "Been there, done that. Mickey had me in therapy for...You know what? Fuck you."

"Fuck you!" Cici quipped back.

"You know what *you* need therapy for? For having fantasies about a blue gnome in a mushroom house. Oh Smurfette, ohhhh Smurfette," I lashed back at them.

"Do you two want to find your own way home?" Lorraine interjected. "Because I will pull over this goddamn bus right here and now to let you both off in the middle of the damn street if you don't knock it off. I *will* do it. Shut the hell up."

Cici looked down at their phone, and I shakily rose up to walk toward the front of the bus. I needed Lorraine to tell me Trae was going to be okay. "Thanks for sticking up for me, Lorraine. I have to say, Mickey didn't look good at all. I think something pretty bad must have happened in that building. I just really need to get home and make sure Trae is okay. I can't breathe very well right now. Would you hurry please? I'm scared."

"I understand honey, and I do think Trae is okay, but lashing out at your new friend isn't the answer. If Cici is going to be staying with you, you might want to think about opening up about your condition." Lorraine certainly doesn't mince words.

"They aren't exactly super approachable, but I will think about it." I walked back to my seat.

Cici's eyes widened, as they turned their phone around to show me the message on their screen. "Millie, you need to see this! Look what just came through on the wire."

I stared at the alert: *Mass murder at the new Stone Water Games building.*

"I'm going to email my editor right now and ask to be on this story. If you don't ask, the answer is always no, right?"

I sat back down next to Cici to read the story. Cici tilted their phone so I could see the screen. "I'm going to submit the pictures along with my request for the job."

I tried to distract myself from completely breaking down in front of Cici by throwing rapid-fire questions: "Is this how investigative journalism works? You take pictures and write stories to go along with them? Do you submit all the photos at once? Or just some of them?" My stomach was spinning, and I started to rock slowly back and forth, trying to soothe myself.

Cici replied excitedly, oblivious to my mental state. "That is only a small part of it. I also go undercover, interview people, and work with law enforcement, drug dealers, unhoused people, sometimes psychics, you name it. And yes, I take photographs and write stories. I'm not picky how I get the story or who I work with to get the truth out there."

"Makes sense. So, getting your PI license gives you that little extra access you need sometimes?" My palms were sweaty. I could feel my heartbeat quickening as visions of Trae's body lying in a pool of blood flashed across my mind. I desperately tried to refocus on what Cici was saying.

"Yeah, access for sure. People will see me as a professional, and the more stories I get like this, eventually I might be up for a promotion to senior investigative reporter, which would mean I will be making the big bucks."

The bus stopped, and I didn't bother responding to Cici's last statement. I jumped to the sidewalk before Lorraine could lower the ramp and impatiently waited for them to reach the street.

Like a mom to her children, Lorraine called after us, "You two take care of each other, you hear? I am counting on you both."

"We will," we said in unison, then awkwardly looked at each other.

The journey from the bus to my condo only took a couple of minutes. Neither of us had much to say on the trek over, likely because we were thinking about what had just happened at the Stone Water

Games building. Cici was probably thinking about what kind of story they would write if given the opportunity.

Me? I really needed to know that Trae was okay and honestly, if Mickey was as well. Mickey was probably so embarrassed that he got sick in front of his peers and the public. The crime scene must have been so horrible. Even though my brother wasn't super tough, I never would have pegged him as a queasy guy either.

The fifteen-second elevator ride to the fifth floor seemed to take an hour, but we finally arrived. I unlocked the door, and to my utter relief, I found Trae sitting at the island eating a sandwich, twisting one of his short, dark locs between his fingers.

He looked up. "Bestie!" he squealed in a high-pitched voice.

I slammed the door shut without entering or acknowledging Trae and turned to Cici in the hallway. "Wait here. I will come get you in a minute."

I opened the door again, stepped inside, and shut it quickly. Trae's tall, lanky body came skipping over with the poise of a basketball player and the excitement of a toddler. I was instantly sad when my eyes met his dark copper ones. It killed me knowing that I was about to turn the big smile that stretched across his dark complexion into heartbreak when I told him about the murder. He stopped and started to say something, but I cut him off, slamming my body into his and wrapping him in the biggest hug. Tears started to slide down my cheeks.

"Thank God you're alive! I was so scared!"

"Oh geez, this isn't awkward." Trae sounded perplexed. "We don't always do the long hug thing. You okay, baby girl? Are you crying? What is going on and what the hell are you talking about? Why wouldn't I be alive?"

While I turned my head slightly to the side against his shoulder to wipe my eyes on his shirt, I immediately started to interrogate Trae. "Why are you home in the middle of the day? You didn't go into the office? Obviously not, you're standing right here. But it's Monday. It's a workday. And we are still hugging?" Relaying my last statement with a curious tone. I looked Trae in the eye as I released him. "Wait, oh my God, Trae, so you really haven't heard. I was worried about that."

"I didn't feel like going into the office, so I called out sick today. I spent the night at Jeremy's and decided to sleep in. Hey, wait a minute, what are you doing at home? I thought you had breakfast and lunch shifts on Mondays. Millie, what the hell is going on? You're freaking me out! Haven't heard what?"

I answered as calmly and sympathetically as I could. "Trae, there was a murder at your office building. People died, but no one knows who it was."

Trae's face dropped as his head turned toward me. "Wait, was it the new building or the old one?"

"That's right, the new building isn't fully open yet. It was the new building. Who would have been there?"

Trae's voice started to tremble as he gazed off into the empty space in front of him. "Umm... only a few people are going over there right now. Our network team, security, managers, and people like that. Oh no, Millie. My friend Beth is on the network team. Do you know if Beth was there? Millie, was Beth there? Has anyone reached out to her roommate? This can't be real. Do you know what happened?" His jaw started to shudder as a deep frown formed along his lips. Tears burst from his eyes, streaming down his cheeks.

Trae turned away, and for a moment laid his head on the island. I could see his back shaking violently with sobs. "I need to call Beth and work." Trae grabbed his phone and started to make call after call, all of which went to voicemail. I wrapped my arms around his shoulders to hold him when we heard a knock on the door.

I looked back, knowing it was Cici. "There is something else I need to tell you."

"What is it, Millie? I don't know if I can take anything else right now." He leaned back against the island and inhaled a long deep breath. Trae looked up and wiped his eyes with the heels of his hands.

I opened the door and in wheeled my new friend. "Hi roomie!" They exclaimed with a wave and a smile, clearly not taking in the temperature of the room.

Trae's mouth dropped. "In my room. Now, Millie."

We walked to his room. Trae shut the door behind us, and we sat on the bed. "Millie, what the hell is going on? We don't have extra space for a roommate."

"Cici is only temporary. Their apartment is full of rats, and they can't stay there while it is being exterminated."

"Did you tell them you are a professional rat catcher?"

"I did."

"And?"

"They declined my services."

"Ugh. How long, Millie?"

"I really don't know how long these things take. Maybe a week? Two, max."

"Where will they sleep?"

"I figured in the garden on the futon. With the bot boys." I pressed my hands together to form a begging plea.

"Ughhh, Millie. Okay fine. But if the bot boys have any issues with them, they are moving out of the garden. Got it?"

"Yes, got it. Thank you so much, Trae. You are the bestest friend ever!" I hugged him.

"You're welcome. I have a date again tonight with Jeremy. We're supposed to go see the opera, but I'm going to cancel. None of this feels right."

"Yeah, you hate musicals anyway," I reminded him.

We both looked behind us when we heard the door creak open and Cici rolled in.

"Can I come in? I just wanted to introduce myself... holy potions and eyeballs, this room looks like a mad scientist lives in here. I'm digging all the orange and green lighting. I promise I won't touch anything, but Trae, what are you up to in here?"

Cici wasn't wrong. Trae's room had every piece of technology that you could imagine. In one corner were six different monitors of varying sizes, not including the fifty-five-inch TV on the wall. I had no idea what he used them for. In the other corner, was a well-organized science lab of bins, shelves, and cabinets, filled with wires, screws, bolts, and computer chips. No potions or eyeballs like Cici eluded to though.

I stood and headed toward the door. "I have to get ready for my interview at four. I will see you both later this evening." Trae stood up so I could give him another hug, which he held a bit longer. I pulled away and wiped the wetness from his tears on his shirt. "We got this, Trae. Mickey will find out who did this. I know he will." I walked out of the room but paused just outside where I could still see them through the crack in the door frame. I wanted to listen just in case Cici made it weird.

Cici wheeled a little further into Trae's room. "I know it's odd having me here, a stranger, but I know how it feels to lose a friend. Someone you love. If you want to talk about it, I have all night to listen."

Trae attempted a smile and nodded. "Thanks."

Cici looked around the room, then pointed to one of Trae's bot boys. "These little robots are really cool. They look like LEGOs but made of metal. I like that you painted each of them a different color. What made you start building these little guys?" Cici seemed genuinely curious.

Trae picked up the little orange bot boy and smiled. "When I was about seven my dad started to put a lot of pressure on me to play sports. He wanted me to play basketball like he did. Then, for my eighth birthday, he got me a build-your-own-robot kit and a basketball. I never touched the basketball; instead, I perfected the robot. When I told him I wanted to go to college to be a computer scientist, he took a hammer to the robot. I was devastated. It didn't stop me though. I started building these little bot boys. I tried to make them look like LEGOs, because I figured if he thought they were LEGOs, he wouldn't smash them too." Trae handed Cici the little orange robot.

Cici took it and admired all the small details when suddenly the little bot boy kicked her finger. She laughed. "Ouch, that kind of hurt." They giggled uncomfortably.

Trae continued. "As a teenager I taught myself to code, so I could teach them to talk. I didn't have any friends. I was just this tall, scrawny black dude, with thick glasses and an amazing fashion sense already, I might add. They were my only friends, and I told them everything. My dad hated my hobby in general but hated it even more when he found out I programmed them to answer questions like if I should ask a boy on a date. That's how my dad found out I was gay. My parents kicked me out of the house when I was fifteen, and my grandma let me come live with her. And here we are today." Trae splayed his arms around the room.

Cici admired the little robot in their hand while it kicked its feet and turned its head back and forth. "It's so cute. Millie said they talk and garden." Cici tried to tickle the bot boy, who produced a small farming tool.

"Yep, they are programmed to pull weeds, hoe, and turn the water on and off." Trae beamed with pride.

"Where did you and Millie meet?"

"At an LGBTQIA+ ice cream social in college. I was sitting at a table by myself being shy when Millie walked up and asked if I wanted a drink. I told her I was gay-gay. She laughed and said she was also gay-gay, but I looked like I needed a drink or a hug but offering a hug when we just met might be a little weird. She wasn't wrong. A hug would have been a little much. We talked all night and became insta-BFFs." Trae chuckled at the memory.

Trae had a way with people and, between the two of us, he had always been the one who humans naturally gravitated toward. He would smile, and people would smile too. He laughed and people laughed with him. Trae gave the best hugs, like the kind of hugs where you felt safe. He was a big, tall, gay teddy bear who never got mad at you but whose disappointment was one hundred percent worse than him being mad.

I started to walk to my room to get ready for my interview.

I think they are going to be just fine.

A smile crept across my face as I realized that it had always just been me and Trae. Now, my little chosen family was expanding. My heart was full.

CHAPTER 6

Did you know that statistically, there are no hard numbers on how often a killer stands at their own crime scene and watches investigators gather the evidence? At least none that I can find, anyway. But, then again, I think we all have our own unique rituals after a big kill. For example, one thing I like to do is position myself right behind the officer guarding the crime scene tape perimeter. I can hear what they say when updating other officers as they come and go, and if I hide just right, it also keeps me from being photographed by the media.

Cops are so loose-lipped, it's not even funny. They give up so many details to the public without even knowing. Technically, I don't need any of the details because it's all my own art. That's right. I am the Artist. The Builder. The Ultimate Creator and Savior. I'm so fucking amazing.

I don't want you all to think I'm a horrible person because I'm not. In fact, every single one of my victims received a proper send off. The way I see it, every person deserves to be told they are loved before they die, and I do that for each of them. I told them, 'I love you,' and I gave them each a hug, one by one. They all cried. Hell, even I cried. It was such a beautiful moment. Ugh... goodbyes are so complicated.

Oh my gosh, I just heard a detective tell the officer standing in front of me that "it's a fucking blood bath in there," as he walked by.

I can't help but grin because I do love a good blood bath. The deep crimson color really goes great in any setting, don't ya think? It is always so beautiful and especially at this office building and particularly in the basement, which is the room I chose. Mmmm... it was like a room full of candy canes—freshly painted white walls spattered in blood. I did so good, and it will just keep getting better. My first two kills were somewhat lame. Boring, in fact, but necessary. They are all necessary. But this one was special. I'm really proud of this one.

I mean, look around at this crowd! They all came here to see my work. Thank you! Thank you!

I want to take a bow, but I don't want to be obvious. Wow, look at all my fans! You just wait folks... the best is yet to come!

I just heard another officer get pissy with my cover officer, yelling at him to, "quit standing there and go get that woman. She's not supposed to be behind the fucking line!'"

People are fucking idiots.

I mean, look at that young woman with that cop puking on his own shoes. Interesting.

Oh wait, now she is talking to someone who just took my picture. Did they just point at me? I'm not sure I like that. The person in the wheelchair just gave the camera to the girl who was with the puking cop. Oh... no... no... no... we can't have this! I need to get my hands on that SD Card.

What do you all think? Will the girl be a pawn or a fawn for me? I'm going to have to keep an eye on this one.

Welp, now I lost my cover so that is my cue to leave. On to my next murder. God, I love saying that!

CHAPTER 7

I arrived at the evidence warehouse ten minutes early because Mickey always told me if I was on time, I was late. I walked up to the door to find it locked. There was a large video screen that reflected an image of me standing there staring at myself in the camera.

"You got this, Millie," I said to the woman on the screen.

"Are you going to ring the buzzer? Or just stand there talking to yourself?" The voice called out from the call box.

I straightened immediately and saluted the camera before pressing the button for entry. Once I heard the buzzer sound, the door clicked and started to open slowly. I pulled on the handle to make it open faster, but that didn't increase the speed, so I just tried to be patient, continually looking back to the camera to give the officer behind the lens a thumbs up.

The first door led into an entryway where I was stopped by a second door that also slowly opened into a large, cold lobby. The room was completely empty, besides a sign on the wall that stated this was the evidence warehouse and a folding chair in the corner. At the furthest end of the room was a desk with an officer sitting behind a computer and a phone. That was it.

"Name, purpose for your visit, and who are you here to see?" The officer shoved a clipboard in front of me.

I scribbled my information down at the same time I also introduced myself. "My name is Millicent Myles, and I'm here for an interview with Officer Palmer."

He shook his head. "Have a seat over there." The man pointed to the corner chair.

Before I even made it to the folding chair, I heard my name called.

"Millie? Hello. My name is Officer Palmer. Your brother has told me so much about you." A woman in a police uniform who looked to be close to fifty years old greeted me as she walked toward me with an extended hand. Her strawberry blonde hair was tied up in a tight bun. Her voice boomed off the empty walls, which made her sound all the more authoritative. She certainly had my attention.

I accepted Officer Palmer's handshake. "It's great to meet you as well, ma'am."

She turned quickly and I fell in line as we left the dimly lit lobby. "It's so nice to finally put a name with a face. You know Mickey talks about you all the time. He is so proud of you," she mentioned as she punched in a code and swiped a badge to open the double doors into the warehouse.

As we walked through the doors, I was amazed how large the facility was. "This place is much bigger than I expected. I thought it would just be like the size of a basement or something."

"Nope. It's about twenty-six-thousand square feet. We even have a massive freezer where we hold all the DNA samples. Want to see it?"

"Uhhh, yeah!"

I was getting excited. I felt oddly at home, like this is exactly where I was meant to be. We walked around the warehouse. I was in awe of the tall aisles filled with an assortment of evidence. The first aisle had the end of what appeared to be a baseball bat poking out the top of a banker's box, while overstuffed manila envelopes full of papers were stacked on another shelf a few bays down. Every one of the boxes and envelopes had case numbers written on them, which piqued my curiosity.

"How old are some of these cases?"

"I think the oldest case file we have on record is about fifty years old and is still unsolved, unfortunately. We will never stop looking for the bastard who killed that poor woman." Officer Palmer was so passionate about her job, and it was inspiring. I could tell that she was dedicated to the evidence and what it meant to solving these cases.

"So, Millie, I know you have computer experience, but do you have experience standing for a long time? We often stand or walk for hours. Do you think you can handle that?"

"Yes, ma'am; I'm also a waitress, so I stand around doing nothing for hours when we don't have customers and walk around a lot when we do. This job will not be a problem for me."

"Great, before I go through the rest of my questions, do you have any questions for me so far, Millie?"

"Where are all the broken headlights?" I asked when a garage door opened suddenly, and a van pulled in, then another, and another.

What the hell was going on?

"Millie look, I know I said this would just be a couple of random overnights. But could you start sooner? The hours could reach full time for a while. We have a really big case hitting us here at the 'house' as we speak, and I don't have time to interview anyone else. I need someone now, and you seem like a good fit. Plus, I know your brother, so I know whose ass to kick if you don't work out. What do you say? You want the job?"

"Yes! But what about the drug test? And the forklift test? Oh, and the polygraph test? I was really looking forward to the polygraph test. I have been practicing for that one all day." I lowered my head in disappointment.

"You will still have to do all of those and will be on probation until the results come in. But with everything coming off these vans, we are drowning in evidence that needs to be logged and shelved immediately. I need you to start right away."

"Okay! How soon is right away?"

"How about right now? There are temporary badges and uniforms that you can change into in the locker room just off the lobby where you entered. Nothing fancy. Just white jumpers, so just grab your size and anything else you need off the shelves. Your locker will have your name on it by tomorrow, so it will be easy to find. On your way out, leave your size with the officer at the front desk and we'll get you some duds of your own. I sure hope you have a stronger stomach than your brother." She turned and walked away.

I found the locker room right where Officer Palmer said it would be. I changed quickly into one of the uniforms, but before I went back to the floor, I sorted through the biohazard gear. I grabbed a face shield, gloves, and a hair net.

I hurried back out to the warehouse to find a short, round man sitting at a long wooden table with a clipboard counting banker boxes.

"Hi! I'm Millie. Millie Myles. I'm the new—"

My introduction was stopped mid-sentence when the officer shoved the clipboard into my chest.

"I know who you are. You're Mickey's little sister. He's a good guy. A bit of a wuss, but a good guy. Follow me."

What the fuck?

I knew my brother wasn't the toughest guy around, but it was weird to hear he had this reputation of being so weak. I really didn't believe it. I refused to believe Mickey was this big of a wimp.

"What can I do to help? Where should I start?" I put the tip of the pen to the clipboard and started trekking behind the man.

One of the crime scene investigators shouldered their way past me with a box full of bags. "Oops, sorry," she apologized.

It was intense here. Every time I turned around, there was another person with boxes coming at me. It was like the old days of playing Frogger with Mickey. I kept dodging the crime scene investigators until we got to the other end of the warehouse.

We stopped at a station, and he turned and pointed to his name tag. "Eddie's the name. You can start by creating a new evidence sheet and logging each item. Then simply put the item you logged into a box, then write the box number at the top of your log sheet. Got it?"

Pausing, Eddie looked me up and down. "You know, you don't have to wear biohazard gear. It's all bagged already."

"None of these bags are vacuum sealed, nor do they have any documentation stating they have been cleared of airborne pathogens and/or diseases that could be infectious. What if I were to have an accidental exposure and something infectious makes contact with my skin? What is your protocol, Mr. Eddie?"

Eddie locked eyes with me as I returned his hard stare, hoping he would just drop it. I really didn't have time to explain the importance of good hygiene to him.

"Mickey mentioned you had your own way of doing things. I tell you what, if you find this murderer, we will let you personally test him for all the diseases you can think of. Sound good?"

I felt the redness creep up the sides of my neck and stiffly responded. "That won't be necessary, sir." We walked back to my workstation. "So, what happened?"

"Besides the obvious, that there was a murder?" Eddie chuckled. "It was the whole damn network team in the basement of the new Stone Water Games building in Pioneer Square. They were setting up servers and security cameras. The weird thing is that the bodies are missing... again." Eddie started to walk away.

"Wait, what do you mean again?" I jogged to catch up with him.

Eddie stopped and turned toward me with a confused look. "Don't you watch the news? Seattle has a serial killer on the loose."

"Well, actually no. I try not to watch the news," I admitted.

"Well, if you did you would know there are three crime scenes in total, the Stone Water Games building being the third. The reporter who was at the scene today said they got word from a reputable source that the murder scene was super gruesome, and the bodies were gone. The killer took them. Cops had to tell the public something, so they admitted that this was true, but they are not releasing any additional information."

"That sounds horrible. I can't believe Mickey didn't warn me that a serial killer was on the loose."

A person randomly approached with a brown bag. "Where do you want this?" I pointed to the other boxes and bags that were quickly piling up.

"The news said the other two crime scenes were missing one body each. The police claimed they are still investigating leads. In other words, they have no idea why this creep is killing people and taking their bodies. This killer wants these bodies for something. As soon as I told Mickey that I think this guy is eating these people, Mickey's face turned as green as Kermit the Frog."

"Who?" I asked as if I was confused, even though Mickey made me watch those Muppet shows for years.

"Kermit the Frog? You know, and Miss Piggy?"

I shake my head. "Nope. Cousins? Friends of yours?"

"Get your ass back to work, Myles. Now!" Eddie walked off mumbling something about this generation of assholes.

I couldn't believe I was looking at evidence from the murder of Trae's coworkers. I couldn't stop thinking about how heartbroken he was when I left home this afternoon.

I spent the rest of the night logging more than seventy boxes and paper bags. Each sealed plastic evidence bag had a label stretched across it that was noted in permanent marker with what, when, and where the evidence was collected, then placed in a paper bag or a box, depending on weight or size.

I know I wasn't a full-blown private investigator—not yet—but maybe someday. So I wanted to try and find a common theme in all these things. It appeared that none of these puzzle pieces seemed to create a clear picture, at least for now.

Most of the items were covered in blood. There was a piece of plaster, a square of maroon-soaked carpet, a fraying rope, and a hammer. Was the hammer supposed to be the murder weapon, or did it just happen to be at the crime scene? I logged flash drives, which I guessed were from surveillance cameras. I also logged a piece of clean candlewick, a flyer, broken pieces of colored glass, pieces from what looked like a pottery bowl, and a piece of torn vintage-like paper with handwritten lines drawn on it from what appeared to be a graphite medium.

I took a closer look at the blood-soaked flyer. "Holy shit! This is the same flyer I got from the woman from the Keepers of the Pines the other day." I mumbled to myself while I inspected it through the evidence bag. The label said that it was found in the pocket of a pair of jeans at the crime scene. I slid my phone from my pocket and looked around to see if anyone was watching before I snapped a quick picture, then I logged the items and tossed them into the box.

Some may think this type of work would be boring, but not me. This was important work. I started to imagine busting through the front doors of the killer's house, throwing him to the ground, and placing him under arrest. I needed to get this right for the victims. If I screwed up, their murders would go unsolved and a killer would remain free. Families wouldn't get closure, and bodies would never be found. Evidence would—

"Myles, what the hell are you doing?" Eddie yelled, interrupting my thoughts.

Cranky, I thought as I drifted back from my daydream.

I got back to work. This had to be the coolest and grossest job ever! I was so invested. This was my calling, my duty.

I am Millie Myles, property and evidence control specialist at your service. I saluted no one in particular.

"Myles, I'm not going to tell you again," Eddie snapped.

I stopped, finished with my quick salute, and wrote down the last piece of evidence: Item: Clean Candle Wick. Box 45. Then I sealed the box and moved on to the next one.

CHAPTER 8

I tugged my beanie over my ears so the misty chill of the morning air wouldn't feel so damp. I was two blocks from my bus stop when I looked at my watch and noticed it was 8 a.m. on the dot. I retrieved my phone from the inside of my rain jacket pocket and quickly zipped it back up to my neck. I went to my recent calls and selected my brother's phone number. Mickey answered on the first ring.

"Still kicking." Mickey yawned. "What are you up to this morning?"

"I just got off work."

"You got the job! That's awesome, Soda Pop. I'm proud of you. Now you can—"

"Bring something for Sunday dinner, you say?"

"Okay, I see how you are going to be this morning. No, I've got it all covered. You know you don't have to call me every morning. We've talked about this. Which reminds me—"

"About what? Welp, at my bus stop. See you Sunday!" I quickly tapped End, so I didn't have to talk about our parents.

Before I put my phone back in my pocket, I noticed I had multiple text messages from Cici and Trae, worried about where I was all night. And an odd one from an unknown number: "You have five days."

"La de da," I chuckled. I have five days to forward this message, or I will have bad luck forever. I hate these chain messages. I deleted the text. Clearly, that was for some chump who believed in that hoodoo. I also noticed I had two missed calls from an unknown number as well.

Desperate.

Since I was getting home in the early hours of morning, I turned the key slowly so as not to wake Trae or Cici. I opened the door only wide enough for me to slide in sideways. I took a whole ten seconds to shut the door, then I turned around to tip toe into the kitchen to grab something to eat before taking a nap only to find Cici and Trae at the island eating cereal.

"Where the hell have you been?" Cici demanded.

"Where?" Trae repeated wide eyed with his arms crossed.

"I was at work. Geez, got the morning grumps, Cici? Is this how you always wake up in the morning?"

"Actually, yes. I typically do wake up a bit grumpy, especially when I have nine little robots with pitch forks surrounding me discussing if I should live or die. But that's beside the point. We have been worried sick about you all night! You haven't answered any of our text messages. I mean, come on Millie. There was just a murder in our neighborhood, and you didn't come home from a job interview?" Cici looked pissed.

"Um-hmm..." Trae mumbled in agreement.

"Oh wow, okay. Yeah, I'm super sorry. I didn't even consider letting you both know. Surprise! I got the job!" I smiled, throwing my arms in the air with a bit of spirit fingers to capture the moment.

Cici crossed their arms but then turned their palm out to suggest I should continue my story. Trae mimicked Cici by holding out his palm as well.

"Ok, so I was interviewing for the job, when suddenly all these vans started pulling into the warehouse. Officer Palmer was like, 'Millie, you're amazing, the only one for the job. We must have you and no one else. Please say you will accept the position.' Everyone was cheering and clapping—"

Trae and Cici gave each other a bullshit look, but I continued with my story.

"Anyway, I told her, of course I would accept the job as an ode to my family name and for the citizens of our community. I will serve and protect all who come under the care of—"

Cici cut me off. "So why the fuck are you strolling in at eight-thirty in the morning, Millie?"

"Why?" Trae repeated, placing his hands on his hips.

"Fine, they had over seventy boxes of evidence to catalog, and they needed to hire someone immediately to help. Since they know Mickey, they thought I was trustworthy enough and hired me on the spot. But I'm working on a probationary status until my drug, forklift, and polygraph tests all come back clean and clear. So, I stayed and worked my first shift and forgot to let you both know. I'm so sorry."

"You scared us. Don't do it again. We were freaking out all night. We almost called your brother earlier but decided to call him if you didn't show up by nine."

"Detective hottie." A naughty little smile crept across Trae's lips.

I rolled my eyes, but my annoyance dissipated. I had increased energy about what was happening, especially with what this new job meant for all of us.

"Thank you for not calling Mickey. He has enough on his plate. But you two are not going to believe this! Trae, the case I got last night is the Stone Water Games murder. I'm literally seeing all the evidence from your coworker's murders. And it gets worse. My supervisor told me there is actually a serial killer on the loose in Seattle and that this isn't the first murder."

"Yeah, Millie, we know. That is half the reason we have been freaking out all night. It's been all over the news." Cici threw their arms in the air.

"Well, then you also know that this is our chance to be a part of something bigger than ourselves. I don't know about the two of you, but I have been thinking all night about this, and I truly believe that between the three of us, we have what it takes to catch this guy. I'm close to the evidence. Trae, you can do anything with technology. And Cici, you can get us access to places that we might not be able to typically get into. I'm serious. The police have nothing, and people are dying. We need to help! Not only for Trae's friend, but before anyone else dies."

Cici remained silent, not their typical response. "Cici, did you hear what I just said? There is a serial killer running around the city and the cops have zero clues, except for a bunch of bloody, random things that make no sense. I should know, I logged the evidence myself last night. We can't keep letting this happen. We need to help."

Trae was obviously done with the conversation because he started scrolling through TikTok. "I think I'm going to shower and get ready for work. Now that I know you are alive, I'm going to pretend I didn't hear the rest of this. It is all very scary, and I don't like to be scared,

Millie. But as long as I don't have to touch or see anything gory, I will help however I can, as long as my bot boys and I can do it from my room."

"It's okay, Trae. I don't like being scared either. We will get this bastard and find Beth's killer." Trae kissed on the top of my head and walked toward the bathroom.

Is he patronizing me? Holy shit, he isn't taking me seriously. Fucker.

I could see Trae standing at the mirror while his bot boys stood on their platforms, one shaving his face and the other brushing his teeth. I shook my head and turned my attention back to Cici.

Cici looked pale. "What are you thinking, Cici?"

"I got the story, Millie." Their scared eyes met mine.

"Cici, that's great! Congratulations! We need to celebrate this. I used to be a party planner. I can totally—"

"Millie, no. I don't want a party. Do you know what this means? I'm the reporter on a serial killer story for *The Seattle Times*. I didn't know that was what I was getting when I asked for this. I thought it was just one office murder when I took those pictures from the bus yesterday. But now in a matter of hours it's grown into something much bigger than any of us ever imagined."

"But it's what you wanted, right? I mean, you asked for this case, so I don't understand. Are you having imposter syndrome or something? Because if you are, just shake that shit off right now. You are going to write the *best stories ever*."

Cici shook their head. "No, it's not about writing the stories. I can write the stories. It's my legs. How am I going to chase down a serial killer with you and Trae? Maybe I should just stick to fraudulent accountants."

Trae came out of the bathroom plopping down at the table. The whites of his eyes were bloodshot like he had been crying. His voice cracked as he started to speak. "We just received an email telling us who were murdered. Beth was one of them. I can't believe she is gone. So, if we are going to catch this motherfucker, I'm all in. Tell me what to do. I want justice for my friend." Trae started to pace quickly around the room.

He paused and took a seat next to Cici. "Okay, Cici, hear me out. I know you are worried about not being able to contribute as much because you are in a wheelchair, which is not the case at all. If we are going to make our up-and-coming private investigator company a success, we each need to consider how and where all our different skill sets best fit."

Trae's energy was notably starting to shift while I watched him attempt to convince Cici that to find Beth's killer we needed to work as a team. We needed Cici. They would be an important part of this team.

He really is starting to buy into my PI company idea!

Trae continued. "My point is, there are things I can't do and things Millie can't do. So, we will just fill in each other's gaps. For starters, I don't do blood, guts, or girls. I do tech and robots but maybe new robots only. I will *not* put my bot boys in any danger. So, that's my list. Millie, what's on your list?"

I thought about this for a second. "Well, I also prefer not to do blood and I don't mess with bots and for sure no boys. Cici, anything on your list?"

Cici looked at me, then at Trae, and they shrugged their shoulders. "Well, nobody likes blood or guts, but otherwise I'm flexible."

"Oh... Cici, are you telling us that it's not the part, but the heart that you love?" I made a heart sign with my fingers.

Trae seemed confused. "Wait, are we still talking about my bots?"

"Moving on…" Cici's phone buzzed as they looked down at the screen. "Holy shit. I have just been given what we journalists call 'the key to the city.' It means I have full access to ask for whatever I need or want to get the story. Do you know what this means? It means I can go undercover. I can get resources. It means they will give me a credit card."

They seemed so excited that I squealed. "That's awesome, Cici! What are you going to do first?"

"Not me, us! It means we are going to the crime scene!"

"We? Uhhh… no." Trae crossed his arms over his chest. "I'm not going anywhere. I'm going to sit my pretty little black ass right here and wait for you all to need something from me."

CHAPTER 9

Trae hoisted Cici's wheelchair into the back of his 1977 Volkswagen van. It was originally his uncle's old work van that he bought for five hundred bucks. He restored it with all the coolest features and technology. Trae painted the outside with a sunset over a river, a rocky shore and trees.

Once Trae opened the door, the inside illuminated a light blue color, and a sexy male voice spoke. "Hello handsome human, would you like me to start the vehicle?" The van voice never shut up. It was always complimenting Trae. "Can I play you a song, gorgeous human? Can I roll down the window, hot human?" Trae was still working on perfecting the technology.

In the back there were leather bench seats along either side. With the push of a button, they folded down into a bed for Trae and his boyfriend Jeremy's camping trips. Today, it made a perfect space for Cici's wheelchair so they could sit comfortably. Now that we were buckled in, we were officially ready to go on our first assignment.

"Trae, turn right. The building is just around the corner." I pointed toward the street we were approaching as if he didn't know how to get to his own office building.

Trae pulled over, parked, and gave me the side eye. Then he crossed his arms and refused to get out of the van. "I'm going to wait right here. Text me if you need anything."

"Sure buddy. You just wait right here," Cici muttered under their breath as we smiled at each other knowing damn well he was coming with us whether he liked it or not.

Trae held the front door open as Cici flashed their credentials to the officer on duty, who stepped aside to let us move past him into the lobby. We headed to the elevators, and I pushed the button to go down to the basement.

"Twenty minutes is all the time you are allowed down there. Don't make me leave my post to come get you," the officer threatened.

As soon as the elevator doors opened, we walked into a room that had clearly been cleaned out by the evidence team because it was empty except for a few materials left behind. If I had to guess, we were looking at an area the size of your average bedroom. The networking team had obviously been installing security cameras because there was a very large wheel of coaxial cable on the floor to the right of the cart, an empty toolbox to the right of the cable wheel, and some empty cardboard boxes randomly strewn around the room. The lighting was dim despite the bright white walls, which now looked dirty with reddish, brown splatters.

We pinched our noses in response to the rancid stench, but it tasted metallic as I inhaled through my mouth. It was the same smell from last night at the evidence warehouse. The smell of blood.

We stared at the scene, still as statues, astonished at what we were witnessing, and it was obvious that none of us had ever seen a crime scene before.

Trae was the first to follow the evidence. "It is undeniable that a murder happened here."

"Yep, looks *and* smells like it," Cici agreed.

Now in detective mode, I broke into action. "Let's get to work." I set my backpack on the ground and pulled out a medical mask, a face shield, and gloves. "Here, put some of this under your nose. You won't be able to smell all this blood." I tossed Trae the container of Vick's VapoRub to share between the two of them. I learned this trick from all the coroner shows I used to watch. I methodically donned each item, when a particular area caught my attention. "Trae? Cici? Besides the obvious, what do you see? What is still in this room that shouldn't be?"

Cici did a full spin in their wheelchair. "It looks like the crime scene investigators took everything. There is nothing left in this room but blood, Millie."

"Wrong. Trae?" I snapped my finger and pointed at him.

He considered his answer before cautiously responding. "Cameras mounted on the wall?"

I shook my head with disappointment. "Nope. I logged the flash drives into evidence last night at the evidence warehouse, so the cameras are irrelevant. Any other guesses?"

They both shrugged their shoulders.

"They left behind a witness!" I pointed to the center of the room where the cable wheel sat in a puddle of water.

Trae and Cici looked in the direction I pointed where a pair of eyes were staring back at us. A beautiful white long-haired cat peered over the cable wheel, but then they quickly lowered their head. I could immediately tell that this cat had quite the story to tell us because they were covered in blood.

I stretched one arm out with my palm facing Trae and Cici to indicate that they should stay still. Then, I brought my finger to my lips as I inched forward.

"It's okay, kitty. We aren't going to hurt you. We just want to talk to you, ask you a few questions. What's your name, sweetie? I see you have a collar, so you must have an owner. How did you get here? Did you see anything yesterday?"

"Millie, it's a cat. It doesn't know what you are saying. It's probably just a stray." Cici slowly created distance between themselves and the cat. "I'm *not* a cat person."

The cat peeked timidly above the cable wheel again as I leaned down to see eye to eye with them. I reached out and whispered, "Aww, hey sweet baby kitty, looks like you are a girl by your cute little pink collar."

The kitty gave a soft meow and then *whack, whack, whack*! The cat hit me along the side of my head as she jumped from the wheel and ran across the room into Trae's arms. I could hear her rumbling purr from several feet away as she nuzzled Trae's chest.

"Hey there, kitty," Trae said as he looked at me and then back at the cat. "She sure is pretty... and wet... and...bloody. Ummm... she has blood all over her paws, Millie. I don't do blood, Millie. Help me. Millie! Come get this cat!" Trae exclaimed, gasping for air.

As soon as I started to walk toward him, the cat hissed at me. I took a step back putting my hands up. The white furball rubbed her head under Trae's chin, smearing blood across his neck.

"I'm sorry, Trae. I think you are her safe place. I think she loves you. We *need* this witness, so you have to try and be okay with this for just a little bit longer. Just until we get home," I pleaded. "There doesn't appear to be a tag on her collar, so how about we let you name her? It will help you bond."

Cici chimed in. "Hurry it up! We can't take all day. Trae, name the damn cat so we can collect the witness and go. So, what's it going to be? What is her name?"

Trae held her up in the air in front of him, trying to control his breathing. His bottom lip quivered as he smiled weakly at the cat. "I think that will be easy enough considering I already know her name. I recognize the collar. This is Beth's cat. Her name is Mozzarella."

"Hey, are you guys ready to wrap it up down there? I said twenty minutes, and I meant it!" The officer made us all jump when he exited the elevator doors.

"Yep! Just finished. Heading out now. Thanks for your patience, officer." Cici wheeled up to the officer to distract him, while Trae and I stuffed Beth's cat into my backpack.

After we had Mozzarella safely tucked away, Trae and I ran to the elevator. "We should get back, Cici," I called out to them.

"Thank you for your time, officer. I hope your replacement is on time today so you can get to the game tonight." Cici wheeled into the elevator as the door shut behind them, leaving the officer in the basement to complete his final rounds before the end of his shift.

We arrived home after stopping by the pet store to get all the necessities to welcome Mozzarella home: cat litter, toys, food, shampoo, and a multi-level cat condo with perches and cubbies. She had probably just witnessed her mom's murder, so she needed all the kitty comforts.

We unloaded our purchases on the kitchen island and met in the bathroom with a feather toy and prayer. If I had to do that moment over, those are the last two things I would bring into a bath with a cat.

Giving Mozzarella a bath was like wrestling an alligator in a kiddie pool. None of us came out of the experience the same. There were words uttered that could not be unsaid, friendships were tested, and feelings were damaged. Afterward, when Mozzarella was as dry as we could manage while protecting ourselves from her claws, we had to spend time alone to regain our balance and composure.

Logically, with time, we understood that we would recover from the physical and emotional wounds caused by the bathing incident. I choose to use my alone time writing each of my friends a letter to apologize for the hurtful words I yelled in response to the feline fire demon attaching her claws to the sides of my face while biting my forehead. I would hand my letters out at breakfast. Now, I laid down to sleep.

Ouch, not on my left side.

I will need to sleep on my right side tonight.

I was grateful for the night off work to get a good night's sleep. The next morning, we all decided to collaborate in the living room to talk about our next steps.

"Okay, so now what? We have a cat for an eyewitness and a bunch of evidence under surveillance at the warehouse. I honestly think we might be in over our heads. We have no idea *what* we are doing!" Trae plopped down on the couch, looking completely defeated.

"We need to interview the cat." I dropped down next to him.

Trae and Cici turned to each other and shared a look like they thought I was losing it.

"Look, I know what you're thinking. You're thinking I sound crazy but hold on and hear me out. I believe this cat holds the answers to the murders and we just need her to talk to us... uhm, meow I should say."

Trae crossed his arms. "Okay, I'll bite. How are you going to get a *cat* to help us with a murder investigation?"

"Watch and learn my friend. Watch and learn." I walked over to where Mozzarella was sleeping peacefully on her perch and reached my hand toward her.

Snap!

Mozzarella's fangs pierced my finger, and blood started to drip down the side of my arm as I yanked my hand away. I hurried to the kitchen to clean my finger and get a bandage while yelling back to my friends. "Owie! Why does she hate me?"

Mozzarella flew from her cat condo onto Trae's lap, then snuggled deep into his side like she'd known him her whole life. There was obviously something about Trae that made her feel safe. Something to note.

Where should I log this? On a piece of paper, a sticky note, or... damn it! Of course, every private investigator has means of tracking all their information!

I looked over at Cici, who was writing this new development down in their leather-bound flip top notebook. "Okay, gay man and cat find love," Cici commented. Then they put the pen to their lip thinking about what that might mean.

"It could be my winning personality, Cici. I'm more than my sexual orientation and gender." Trae seemed offended.

Suddenly a long line of bot boys marched out of the garden room. "Cat. Free. Zone. Cat. Free. Zone," they all chanted.

"Boys, there is room for all of you and Mozzarella in our lives. She needs us right now." Trae bent down to address his robots, but they had no desire to hear him out. The bots turned and marched back into the garden chanting. "Cat. Must. Go. Cat. Must. Go."

Cici shook their head as they dismissed the bot drama. "Let's move on. "I wrote my first story for the paper. I'm not sure if you have seen it or not." Cici slapped a newspaper on the coffee table in front of us. They returned to assessing what they knew: "So basically, we only know what the cops have, well mostly. I say we go over everything we collected to date and decide what to do next. Trae, are you ready for this? I know these were your friends and coworkers so it might be hard."

Trae looked at Cici. "It's been all over our work chat groups. Whatever details you have doesn't change that I already know my friend and coworkers are never coming back." Trae pulled Mozzarella up to his neck and closed his eyes as he continued. "Besides, Mozzarella knows me because I have probably been to Beth's apartment a hundred times at least, which is why she feels safe with me. Not because I'm gay, but because I'm a very handsome familiar face, thank you very much."

Cici rolled their eyes and continued. "Okay, well here's the first newspaper article I wrote. Give it a read, then we will figure out our next move."

Seattle is on edge as the city learned in today's police conference that the community may have a serial killer on the loose. Investigators stated they have enough evidence to confirm that on Monday morning, four individuals were murdered and their bodies were taken by an unknown suspect or suspects from the new Stone Water Games building in Pioneer Square. Police are not releasing many details at this time; however, a source close to the investigation said there were two other murders in the past six months that have similar patterns, which led detectives to believe these cases are connected.

Liza and Tim Lewis, the owners of Stone Water Games, are not commenting at this time other than to share their thoughts and prayers with the families and friends of the victims. Tim is also chief librarian at the Seattle Public Library. The Lewises have recently purchased the building and are in the middle of renovations due to Stone Water Games's expanding workforce. Both Liza and Tim grew up in the Seattle area and donate to many humanitarian causes, and are big supporters of the Washington Midsummer Renaissance Faire.

The victims' name have been released: Stacia Petersen, a 39-year-old network engineer and single mother of three children who loved sewing and quilting; Stanley Smith, a 37-year-old business analyst who started with Stone Water Games when he was just eighteen in the mailroom and was an avid woodworker and recreational softball player; Darrin Russel, a 61-year-old software engineer and recent widower who was looking forward to retiring in Texas where his family resides. Beth Weber, a 41-year-old technology project manager with a love of geology.

A security guard discovered the crime scene while on routine rounds. He was interviewed by police and ruled out as a suspect. Based on the amount of blood found at the scene, there was no chance any of the victims could have survived this brutal attack.

"An inside source told me that there was also a significant amount of dirt in the area as well as on several articles of clothing found at the crime scene. A janitor also saw a person running from the building but did not see anyone enter. The janitor admitted they had been cleaning on multiple floors and may have missed them entering. Also, Gloria, Beth's roommate, had a falling out with Beth and was looking for a new place to live. That's all I got," Cici finished.

Trae got up and ran into the bathroom slamming the door behind him. Cici and I could hear him gag and then begin to throw up.

I hated seeing Trae like this. My heart was breaking for him.

Trae came out of the bathroom and sat next to me, looking drained and tired.

"You okay, buddy?" I put my hand on his shoulder.

He gave a curt nod. "I'm having flashbacks from the crime scene. I don't think I can go there again."

"You don't have to. I will do the gross stuff from now on. I know you have a weak stomach. I'm sorry we made you go to the office building. That was really insensitive of us. It will never happen again."

"I'm sorry too, Trae." Cici took the newspaper from the coffee table. "Other than that, I don't have much else to offer, but I think our next steps are pretty clear, team. We need an insider at Stone Water Games and since you already work there, Trae, it's going to have to be you," they declared.

"Yes, I agree. We are really doing this aren't we? We are going undercover. Like real detectives?" I was nervous, excited, and scared.

"Okay, good. Trae, you up for snooping around a bit?"

"As long as I don't have to do any more blood. But keep in mind, I do work there for my day job, so I have to perform my actual job too."

"Trae, I will provide you with a list of evidence you should collect from your job, along with people you should try and talk to. I will leave it for you on the kitchen counter, so you can grab it before you head into the office tomorrow."

Cici used their best teacher voice. "Millie, I worry about you the most. You have a lot of energy around this. We have to be careful."

Trae pointed to Cici and nodded in agreement.

"Do I need to remind you both that I'm a—"

"A Myles... yes we know. "They finished my sentence in unison.

CHAPTER 10

I'm going to prove them wrong. I'm going to prove everyone wrong. I'm the best almost private investigator in Seattle. I went into the kitchen, made myself a sandwich, and grabbed a notebook. Then I headed to my room to make a list of evidence to gather for Trae before my night shift at the evidence warehouse. I closed my bedroom door and laid on my bed.

I glanced at the list. Our trip to the Stone Water Games office building had been useful, so Trae had a big job to do when trying to slyly interview Beth's boss.

I decided I should pack my backpack first, so I didn't forget anything. A private investigator should be prepared for any scenario. I threw my backpack onto my bed and put in my notebook, wallet, earbuds, and my pen and pencil case. I studied this arrangement for a moment before realizing that I didn't leave room for my lunch.

My heart started to pound as I took a deep breath. I unpacked my bag and started over.

Damnit! If the pencil case lays flat, then my lunch can go vertical, but the salad dressing might leak and mess up my notebook or zap my earbuds.

I took everything back out. I put my lunch bag on the bottom and my pencil case on top followed by my earbuds and then notebook only to realize my wallet had fallen to the floor.

What if my pencils fell out and got in my lunch bag, and I didn't notice it all day? The tip of the pencil could literally sit there and soak into my sandwich for hours and give me graphite poisoning, I know it's a thing. I just know it.

Beads of sweat formed on my forehead. I unpacked my bag again and then collapsed, exhausted, onto my bed. My hands shook and a tear dripped from the tip of my nose as I begged the universe to not let anyone die.

I hate this so much.

My eyes grew heavy as I stared at all the items. They resembled a large puzzle that I couldn't solve. My energy was being quickly sucked from my soul, so I decided to put just the list into my backpack. I placed my earbuds beside the bag to put in my pocket in the morning. The rest of my backpack would remain empty tomorrow. It was just easier.

I closed my eyes for only a second, or so I thought, when I was jolted awake an hour later by something hitting my window. I hurried to the window to see what hit it, but instead turned back toward my bedroom door when I was distracted by a loud crash and a scream.

I turned away from the window and ran into Cici's room to find them bleeding, while Trae and his boyfriend Jeremy looked very confused.

So much for getting a decent nap before work tonight.

"Get off of me, you creep! It was the green one. That one right there!" Cici pointed at the little green robot who stood on their lap with its arms up in the air as a sign of surrender.

"I. Did. Not. Do. It. Color. Green. Innocent."

"You stabbed me in the cheek, you little asshole. I'm bleeding." Cici clenched their teeth as they held out a bloody tissue.

"Okay, Cici. Tell us what happened." Trae picked up the bot boy from Cici's lap and started to comfort him before setting him on the edge of the garden.

Pressing the tissue back to their wounded cheek, Cici said, "I entered my room—"

"Not. Cici. Room. Color. Green. Room," the robot interrupted.

"Shut up, you little bottle cap!" Cici erupted as they wheeled towards the bot. Trae stepped in front of his bot protectively.

"All I did was pick up one of those plants to look at it." Cici pointed to the plants.

"Ohhh nooo," Trae and I moaned.

Jeremy took Cici's side. "There is a reason these little metal men aren't allowed in our bedroom when I stay the night. See this missing part of my ear, yeah? Courtesy of the purple bot." Jeremy whipped his head around to give Trae a dirty look. "Honey, I'm going back to bed where it's safe." He turned on his heel and left.

I loved the dynamic between Jeremy and Trae. Trae towered over Jeremy's five-foot six frame. Jeremy was Pacific Islander descent with adorable chubby cheeks. And as much as they enjoyed the same movies and food, they had the complete opposite tastes in hobbies. Jeremy couldn't stand his bots and Trae hated musical theater, but there wasn't a love more pure than theirs.

"Yeah, you really shouldn't touch the plants. The bot boys are very sensitive about their plants, Cici," I reminded them.

Before Cici could argue, Mozzarella zoomed into the room, grabbed the pink bot, and raced away. "Nooo, Mozzarella! You drop him right now!" screamed Trae as he bolted after her. Cici and I followed.

In the living room, I spotted Mozzarella and cornered her between the couch and the coffee table. She growled and took a swipe at my leg, and I went down faster than an imploding building. I grabbed my shin, which was now swelling with red welts.

Trae hopped over the couch, barely missing my head with his foot. The white furball slid to a stop and was trapped—or so we thought.

Mozzarella's glowing yellow eyes darted around as she looked for another escape route. "Release. Color. Pink. Now," demanded the pink bot as its little legs dangled and kicked anxiously in her mouth.

"Mozzarella, you drop my bot boy. You hear me girl? Drop him *right now*," Trae instructed.

We could hear the light vibrations of Mozzarella purring as the room fell silent, and she flicked her tail slowly back and forth. Trae cautiously approached her, and she opened her mouth allowing the bot to fall to the floor.

Trae reached for his robot but before he could pick it up, Mozzarella grabbed it again and took off running with a little *too* much gusto.

Wham!

She slammed right into the side of Cici's wheelchair and dropped the bot. Cici grabbed the robot off the ground and handed it back to Trae.

We were all speechless for a good thirty seconds while trying to make sense of what just happened. I broke the silence. "Good times! Can we all go back to bed now?"

"Please," Trae said, wiping the cat spit off the pink bot as he walked to the garden to assess it for any damage.

"I'm supposed to just go back in there and sleep with these murderous metal minions?" Cici sounded genuinely concerned for their life.

"I. Love. Her. I. Love. Cici," the pink bot announced.

"What did your bot just say, Trae?" I was confused. They were trained to tend to the garden, not emit feelings.

Trae placed his hand over the pink bots chest. "I'm not sure, but the bot is very warm to the touch. I will have to check him out."

I drew my attention back to Cici. "Look, you'll be fine. There is only one rule in the garden." Everyone in the living room, including all the bots from the Garden, repeated the one rule together.

"Do. Not. Touch. The. Plants."

I walked back to my room, shut the door, and laid back on my bed. That was enough excitement for one night.

My phone vibrated with an unknown number. I pushed the side button to ignore the call. My phone buzzed again with the same unknown number. I decided to answer.

"Hello?"

I listened to the silence, then I heard light breathing.

"Hello?"

"You have something I want? Leave it behind the picture in the unisex bathroom at the library. You have five days, or I will take something from you." The caller sounded like they were using one of those voice distortion thingies. Then they hung up.

That was fucking weird. I hate prank calls. The other day someone called and told me it was so nice having dinner with me. When I told them they must have the wrong number because I didn't have dinner with them, they asked me if I would like to have dinner with them. Creep.

This seemed different though. Very specific details. I needed to go with my gut, so I decided to call Mickey and tell him about the phone call.

I went to my call log and selected my brother's name from my recent calls. He answered on the first ring.

"Hey sis, what's up?"

"I just got a super weird call. Probably just a prank, but I thought I should let you know."

"Okay, what did they say?"

"They said, I have something they want, and I should leave it behind some picture in the unisex bathroom at the library and if I don't give it to them, they will take something from me."

"Millie, that sounds like a threat. What was the number?"

"It was unknown. You don't think it was a prank? Mickey, you're scaring me."

"Millie, you are working on a big case at the warehouse, and I'm a detective on the same case. I'm always going to take everything, no matter how small it seems, seriously. I need you to think really hard. You didn't take anything from the evidence warehouse, did you?"

"Of course not. I would never take anything from there."

"Okay, Millie, did you talk to anyone about what you've seen or heard from there?"

"Well, no, not really? What are you getting at Mickey?"

"We've seen this before. The serial killer starts to taunt the police. I do find it concerning that you are not part of the force, so that gives me a little hope that this might be just a prank like you think, but Millie, I'm not going to lie, it does put me on edge. I need you to stay as far away from this case as possible. I know you are going to see the evidence but just go to work and go home. We will solve the case. Just stay away. Got it?"

"Yeah, sure, of course. I wouldn't go near it. I'm going to get some sleep before work. Night, Mickey."

"Night, Soda Pop."

We hung up and I sat there weighing the facts. If there was a person who's connected me to this case, then they know they are up against a Myles and a private detective... well almost... maybe someday.

Wait, a realization had me sitting up and sprinting to my window, *before I heard Cici scream, something hit my window.*

I raised my blinds slowly, and I sighed with relief when I didn't see anything but cars and the empty bus stop across the street.

I lowered the blinds, but I kept my eye on the bus stop. That's when I caught sight of a pebble hurtling towards my face. Before I could react, the rock hit the glass with a *pling*. I dropped to the floor and sat underneath the window with my arms wrapped around my legs. Another one hit. And another one.

Pling! Pling! My body jumped with each strike of the pebble against the glass.

What the hell? Who is throwing pebbles at my window? They seemed to stop. I waited for a minute before standing up. But as soon as I stood, it happened again. *Pling!*

I crouched back down.

I guess I will just stay down here forever. Fuck! What the hell is going on?

My fingers found the blinds string, and I pulled them shut and ran to my bed.

I'm just going to hang out here until it's time to go to work. Probably just some stupid punk-ass kids.

CHAPTER 11

After a long night at the warehouse processing evidence from the Stone Water Games crime scene, I started to notice some odd patterns. Maybe nothing, maybe something. I knew that Cici and Trae were at work, so it seemed like the best use of my time would be to create a murder board. The condo could serve as our living space and our investigation home base.

I entered the office supply store and immediately took in all the wonderful smells: new office furniture, notebooks, markers, and crayons. If I closed my eyes, it was like walking into my first day of elementary school.

I grabbed a cart from the corral.

Okay, just get what you need, Millie.

My first stop was the whiteboards. Obviously, I would need an extra-large one, and it would have to be mobile, so I would need to buy the huge whiteboard on wheels. I grabbed one of the tickets to purchase it at the register. Then, I went to the accessory aisle for sticky notes in every color.

I spotted the animal-shaped pads, and grabbed a handful.

What if we need animal representation, after all?

Ohhh, and it's very possible that food might be involved.

I snagged the veggie-shaped ones from the shelf.

I continued to the next aisle. The expo markers were easy: rainbow, pastels, primary, grays, and blacks, all in washable and scented.

I will get us each a pack.

I tossed them into the cart and went looking for whiteboard tape and magnets. I geeked out when I found little magnetic push pins shaped like knives. I tossed fifty of them in my cart.

Last, but not least, I went looking for the one accessory that would tie everything together, literally: string.

At the cash register, I loaded my supplies onto the conveyor belt and pulled out my credit card.

"That will be $798.39." The cashier didn't even look at me as she started bagging.

I slipped my card back into my wallet, pulled out another card, and handed it to her.

"Thank you, Mickey. Have a nice day." The cashier read my brother's name off the receipt as she handed it to me, along with my shopping bags.

🔪🔪🔪

After the murder board was finished, I showered, dried, and dressed at warp speed. I wore what I believed to be typical detective attire:

black slacks, black socks, black shoes, a button-down shirt, and a black jacket. Today's shirt color was electric blue.

I headed to the stairwell to do my morning walk down the four flights of stairs. This was my preferred route as the stairs helped me avoid the awkward conversations that occurred in small spaces such as elevators. I only took the elevator in the evenings because most people were too tired from their workdays to care about pleasantries.

With a push, I opened the heavy steel door at the bottom of the stairs and walked out onto the sidewalk on the north side of our building. I headed across the street and down a couple blocks to a little coffee shop called The DeCafé. I had been coming here for so many years that it almost felt like a second home. There was something about your neighborhood barista that felt like family. The name of the place was a mystery to me until one day, I worked up the courage to ask the owner, Hans. Fortunately, Hans answered my question in just a few words: "It's a spoof on decaf coffee. Funny, right?" He slapped his hand on the counter.

The bells on the wooden door jingled as I pushed it open. I was immediately tormented with the aroma of fresh pastries and brewed coffee. Hans's place was a tourist stop since it was so close to Seattle's Underground Tour and the sports stadiums, so it was always busy.

The biggest draw to Hans's coffeeshop was the small roaster on display where customers could watch the coffee roasting process and participate in a free monthly tasting. Hans was also known for only sourcing his ingredients for his baked goods from local vendors within a twenty-five-mile radius.

"*Guten Morgen*, Millie!" Hans greeted me.

"Good morning, Hans. How's the morning shaping up?"

"Not too bad. Do you want the usual or can I tempt you to try one of my new blends?" Hans asked in his thick German accent while pointing to one of the burlap sacks.

"Nope, the usual: grande dark roast with two creams and two sugars, in that order, and before you pour the coffee." I paused to study the menu board behind Hans. "Oh, but maybe I will get a little wild today and have one of those blueberry muffins sliced in half with two pads of butter spread evenly corner to corner, then put back together and in a bag."

"Tis is not wild; you do that every day," Hans teased, opening the case to grab my muffin. "I also have a little surprise for you. You won two free tickets and to the Underground Tour for being today's one hundredth customer. It's our thirty-year anniversary."

"Congratulations Hans and thank you. Trae will be so excited. He loves history." I took the tickets and the brochure and put them in my backpack.

Handing over my order, Hans leaned across the counter, looking around to see if anyone else could hear him. "*Ja*, did you hear about the murders a couple of blocks down the street?" he whispered. "*Morgen* paper told the story: a whole machine team dead. Dead. DEAD!" Hans made a slitting motion across his throat. "All people in suits. My customers that work in other suits at other companies are fracking out. A breakfast killer murdering machine people, Millie. You should ask your brother to tell *ja* murder man to stop it. Scaring my customers."

"I will tell Mickey, Hans. I guess I will take one of those papers as well then," I said, pointing to the rack of newspapers behind the counter. "And it's *freaking* out, not *fracking*. Fracking is when oil... umm, never mind." I raised my elbow to tap Hans's elbow as our way to say goodbye, which is a German tradition that he's forced on me for years. "I need to hit the road, *tschüss.*" I grabbed my purchases and waved over my shoulder. I pulled open the heavy wooden door, trying not to look back as I exited. I'm terrible at goodbyes.

I passed a couple of unhoused people sitting outside the café entrance and dropped a dollar in their basket. The new Stone Water Games office was just across the street and on the way to the old office, which is why I decided to walk today. Plus, I preferred to walk when I could. I put on my ear buds to look preoccupied even though nothing was playing.

There were still barricades in front of the new Stone Water Games building. Susan Spruce, the news reporter for KRHG News, was on the scene preparing to report live, so I joined the crowd and tried to blend in so I could listen.

The camera turned on along with a bright light that shone on her face. "Susan Spruce, KRHG News, reporting live from the scene of the alleged quadruple murder of a technology team who was installing networking equipment here at Stone Water Games's new office location. Police have not released any further details of the crime or their investigation, but we have spoken with two unhoused citizens who claim to have seen someone running from the building in the middle of the night. The police dismissed this information as unreliable due to the man and women being intoxicated at the time they gave their statement. In other news, the urban version of cow tipping is hitting Seattle neighborhoods. Join us at noon to hear how Smart Car tipping has become the new headache for both city officials and local police." Susan closed out her news spot with a promise to be the first to report any breaking news on the murders as it became available.

Interesting. The janitor also said they saw someone leaving the building. I will have to make note of this when I get to work.

"Millie Myles?" I heard footsteps jogging up behind me.

I turned to see Susan walking up to me. Confused, I looked around to verify it was me she was actually addressing. "Yes, that's me. How do you know my name?"

Extending her hand, our palms came together as I felt a small twinge of nerves in my stomach. I pulled my hand away quickly. "You are Detective Mickey Myles's sister, right? I'm an investigative reporter and have been following your brother's cases for years."

"Yeah, but I don't know anything about what's going on down here. He doesn't talk to me about his work. It's all confidential. Sorry, but I can't help you." I turned to walk away.

"No, Millie. That wasn't why I asked. I was wondering if you knew why they pulled him off this case?"

"Pulled him off the case? I don't know anything about that either. I should go. Nice to meet you, Ms. Spruce." I hurried off, fumbling through my backpack to find my phone so I could call Mickey.

I looked at my watch.

7:57 a.m. Come on. Come on. 8 a.m., hurry up. I can't call until 8 a.m. or he will die.

My heart was pounding. I looked at my watch again as I walked down the street and started to cry.

7:59 a.m. Please. Please!

As soon as the time on my watch flipped to 8 a.m., I punched the Call button on Mickey's contact. The phone rang and rang before going to voicemail and a lump immediately formed in my throat while my heart pounded.

Mickey always answers on the first ring. What the hell is going on?

I called again, and this time he picked up.

"Still—"

I cut him off. "What the fuck, Mickey? They pulled you off the biggest murder case in Seattle. Why?"

"Millie, what? Where did you hear that? That's ridiculous." He sounded equally surprised.

"Susan Spruce just told me. She was reporting outside the crime scene and asked me if I knew why you had been pulled. What is happening, Mickey?"

"I don't know, but I'm pulling into the precinct right now. I have to go. The chief's calling in."

"Mickey, call me—"The phone went dead.

I walked back over to Susan. "Um, hi Ms. Spruce. Can I ask you a question?"

"Please, call me Susan."

"Okay, Susan, you said you were able to talk to the two unhoused people. Are they still around?"

"Yes, they're over there in front of DeCafé. I had to buy them cinnamon rolls to get them to talk." Susan rubbed her fingers together to suggest I would be shelling out some money. "So, if you're thinking about asking them about it, don't be surprised if they make you cough up something too before they talk."

"I don't mind buying them a cup of coffee or something. It's hard out here on the streets." I nodded to her as I turned back toward DeCafé.

As I approached them, I stopped to read their sign: *Not going to lie, we just want money for the pastries.* I dropped a couple more dollar bills into the croissant-shaped basket. "Hi, my name is Millie. What are your names?"

The woman made eye contact, then looked away and didn't respond. The man smiled and reached out his hand. "My name is Roy, and this here is my little German gem, *El-suh*. But like I told that news lady, if you are going to spell it for the papers, make sure you spell it E-L-S-E, the German spelling. We are very particular about this." Looking away with a quick nod, Roy pointed to the cash in the basket.

"Thanks for your donation."

I raised my elbow for a tap instead and responded, "I'm not a reporter, Roy. Just here to have a chat is all. What kind of pastries do you like?"

"Ah, ya German too, are ya?" Roy bumped elbows with me.

Else started laughing, which made Roy laugh, so I started to laugh with them because I didn't know what else to do. "Did I say something funny?"

"Yeah, you asked what kind of pastries we liked, like you didn't know it was a little piece of heaven coming out of the DeCafé. Look little lady, if you came over here to insult us like two idiots just because we don't wear the latest fashion, well, you can just walk back across that street and get yourself a rock-hard donut from one of those chain bakeries."

"No, I didn't mean to insult you about your choice of pastries, or your attire, I was just asking..."

Else jumped up and came within an inch of my face. "Well, if you buy us one, you can find out for yourself now, can't you?" I took a step back. I could smell her peppermint schnapps or mouthwash breath.

"Sure, then would it be okay if I ask you both a couple of questions about what you saw the night of the murders? The person running out of that building over there?" I pointed toward the Stone Water Games building.

Else and Roy exchanged a look. "We already talked to the police and the news lady. Told them everything we saw."

"Yeah, my questions might be a little different though. How about I throw in a couple cups of hot cocoa or coffee?"

"Cocoa! I want hot cocoa with extra whip and chocolate syrup on top and, of course, one of those famous pioneer croissants." Else was right back in my face.

"You got it, three pioneer croissants and three hot cocoas coming up," I said as I opened the door.

When I returned with our food and drinks, we sat on the sidewalk. I sunk my teeth into my buttery croissant, tasting layers of bacon, ham, cheese, and egg. This wasn't a normal breakfast sandwich. One does not simply eat this heavenly pastry; one savors bite after bite. None of us spoke until we had finished.

"I told you!" Roy tossed the last bite into his mouth. "Now, what did you want to know?"

"I only have one question. Did they look back at the building?"

"Yeah, a lot. But more like you would look back at your new car than looking to see if someone was following you." Roy paused and looked thoughtful as if he just realized something new himself.

"Thanks, that actually tells me a lot." I stood up and brushed crumbs off my clothing. "I appreciate you talking to me."

Else tugged on my pants. "When will we see you again?"

"Aww, Else, you are so sweet. I love having new friends too. I pass by here every day on my way to work. I will stop and say hi." I patted her on the shoulder.

"I just want your money for pastries," Else said as she pointed to her basket.

"Oh, of course." With a half-smile, I tossed in another dollar.

CHAPTER 12

"Millie, what are you doing at my office? How did you get past security?" Trae sounded annoyed.

"I brought your lunch and you forgot your evidence list I wrote up for you. The security guard let me up when I told him I was your BFF."

He peered into his lunch sack. "Ohhh, sweet! I love it when you make my sandwiches in robot shapes."

"Trae, who is your friend?" I nodded at a short, thin man with a bread belly and a long blond ponytail. He wore khaki shorts with a striped pink and yellow button-down shirt. Seems like I was the only person that dressed up today.

"Oh Lamar, this is my friend Millie. She was just dropping off my lunch."

"Hi Millie, nice to meet you. What do you do for work?"

"I process evidence at the police evidence warehouse in Seattle," I responded cautiously. I was new to having a real job, and I wasn't sure if I should be telling people what I did for a living.

"Millie is working on the serial killer's evidence," Trae blurted out.

I gave him a dirty look and tried my best to downplay his admission. "I don't get to really see much to be honest. It's all in evidence bags and boxes. I just log stuff. Mostly admin stuff. Anyway, I'm really sorry to hear about the loss of your coworkers."

Lamar gave me the oddest look. "Yeah, thank you, we are all devastated by this loss. We can't even imagine why someone would want to hurt such wonderful people for absolutely no reason."

"Lamar was the network team's manager," Trae again blurted out.

This time Lamar tried to downplay his role. "Yes, and it was an honor, but it was them who brought all the glory to the team. I was just a mere witness to their success."

Lamar and I were clearly getting a strange vibe from each other. Before I could ask anymore questions, Lamar said goodbye and abruptly left.

"He is an odd man, Trae."

"He's alright. Keep in mind, his whole team was just murdered."

"I get that, but he didn't seem too upset just now. I'm going to add to your list of evidence to keep an eye on him. Something is off. I know how people tick."

Trae rolled his eyes. "I get off work in a half an hour. Do you want to do something?"

"You know what? Hans gave me free tickets to the Seattle Underground Tour. How about we go be tourists for the afternoon?"

"That sounds horrific, Millie. I hate the dark and bugs and there are probably rats down there."

"Please? I have never been. It will be fun, plus we could use a break from all this stress," I pleaded.

"I don't think so, Millie. Sounds dirty."

We started the Seattle Underground Tour in a small room with our guide explaining the history of how Seattle was named after Chief Seattle, who was chief of the Duwamish and Suquamish tribes. We sat and listened to the story of the Great Seattle Fire of 1889 that burned over twenty-five city blocks. The city saw the fire as a blessing because every time it rained the streets would flood, so the blaze gave the community an opportunity to start fresh with new ideas to solve their swampy streets problem. However, some city leaders didn't want to wait for the many years it would take to build higher structures, so they continued to build new businesses, streets, and sidewalks even though they knew at least two stories of their new construction would eventually be buried underground.

"See? No rats, it's probably like a normal city down there." I looked over at Trae, who was nervously chewing on his nails.

I was so enthralled by all the history. I couldn't believe Trae didn't find it even a little bit entertaining that these people would climb down ladders to access shopping while the new higher city was being built above them. He didn't even giggle when they told us that when residents wanted to cross the narrow street, they would lay ladders down as makeshift bridges, sometimes dropping their shopping bags onto people's heads below. I couldn't wait to start the tour.

"Let's go!" I yanked on Trae's sleeve to get in line with the tour group.

The tour started on the city streets above ground where our guide pointed out the glass skylights on the sidewalk where we stood. Now stained from years of decay, the chunks of dirty glass were added over one hundred years ago to provide more daylight to the underground.

"Wow, Trae, we've probably walked over these a thousand times and never knew a whole ass city was below us. Who knew!"

"Yeah, wahoo. Who knew." He was clearly unimpressed.

Our guide led us down a series of steps and unlocked a door. We entered a large room that looked like an old salon where we learned more history. Next, we were led into a long passageway along a long wooden pier. The scent of mold and dirt filled my nostrils. The tour company had hung antique light bulbs to give the underground streets a late 1800s aesthetic. Every now and then our guide would bang a stick on the wall or a random item as we walked through the space, probably to let the ghosts know we were here.

"I guess this isn't so scary, Millie. It's just dirty." Trae seemed a bit more confident now.

I tried to keep him interested. I explained that we were literally walking on original sidewalks and streets that were built over a century ago. I pointed to the old wooden pylon holding up the streets above. He did seem more interested and asked a few questions about the brick building and shop windows that were lined on each side of the thin streets.

"Why are some of the store windows filled with cement and others are boarded up?" Trae nodded at the boarded-up one.

The tour guide stopped the crowd. "That's a great question. Some of these buildings still use these bottom floors as basements so they boarded up the windows for privacy. Others were filled in years ago for structural support."

We continued our tour when the whole vibe started to feel a bit eerie as the paths became stone and dirt tunnels. There was an old busted up elevator shaft filled with broken pieces of machinery as if one day it just crashed right there.

"Trae, did you see that?" I pointed just past an old wooden sign that said, *Tellers Cage.*

"See what? I didn't see anything."

"Just past the old banker's vault. I swear I saw a light blink on and off." I started to walk toward the vault.

"Rat! Rat! Rat!" Trae took off running to the front of the line. "Rat! Rat! Rat!"

I immediately went into action. "Folks, please do not panic. I'm a professional rat catcher, I know what I'm doing. If everyone would kindly move to the end of the passageway, I will begin my assessment of the area—"

"Ma'am that's not necessary. We know there are rats down here, which is why I've been banging this stick on the walls." He directed his attention back to the group. "Everyone, follow me. We will end our tour at the gift shop."

"Can we just go get some coffee or something?" Trae sounded exhausted.

"Of course. We should probably thank Hans for the tickets anyway."

"Trae, Millie, my *freunde,*" Hans came around the counter to greet us.

"Hi Hans, thanks for the tickets to the Underground Tour. It was—"

"Dirty and full of rats," Trae interjected.

"It was fun." I finished.

"*Ja ja*. Coffee? Treat? Gloria just baked some fresh muffins."

Trae and I glanced at each other with wide eyes.

"Gloria who?" Trae asked.

"Awww. I hired Beth's roommate, Gloria. She need money. Good baker."

Gloria pushed backward through the swinging steel kitchen doors with a tray full of muffins. "Trae? Is that you?"

"Oh shit, this is going to get awkward," Trae mumbled to me.

"Why?"

"You'll see." Trae turned and smiled at Gloria.

He started to fidget with a napkin dispenser. "Yeah, hi Gloria. I'm sorry I haven't reached out. It's been so hard for all of us."

"That's okay, butter knuckles. I'm always glad to lay my eyes on you."

"Ha." Trae gave a nervous giggle.

"What the hot butter knuckle fuck is going on here, Trae?" I whispered to him.

He ignored me. "I'm not hungry. I'm going to find us a table, Millie."

I turned and ordered for myself. "Grande dark roast with two creams and two sugars, in that order, and before you pour the coffee, and I will also have one of those blueberry muffins sliced in half with two pads of butter spread evenly corner to corner, then put back together and in a bag. Thank you."

Gloria gave me a dirty look while Hans took my order, which was confusing, so I tried not to make eye contact. After paying, I walked to Trae's table and sat down. "Okay, what gives? Obviously, you know Gloria better than you let on."

"No, I don't. But she has a weird crush on me, and no matter how many times I've tried to tell her that I'm gay-gay or have shown up to Beth's parties with Jeremy, she still flirts with me. It's so awkward, Millie."

"I'm your BFF, and I will always protect you. I promise. I got you, Trae. But this little obsession might be useful for us. Remember what Cici told us about Gloria and Beth having a falling out and Gloria looking for a new place to live?"

"Yeah, I remember."

"Well, maybe she will give you some information if you're sweet to her."

"No."

"I think, yes."

"Nope."

"Think of it as going undercover."

"Okay. No."

"Trae, I will buy you a vanilla bean plant."

"Two plants, and I will only talk to her in a public place while she is working."

"Deal." We shook hands.

Trae slowly made his way back up to the pastry case where Gloria was restocking the baked goods. "How have you been holding up, Gloria?"

"Oh, my tall dark stalk of sugar cane, it's been so tough. I can't talk right now. How about you come over tonight and I will make you some of those mint chocolate chip cookies that you love. Then we can talk about it... in private." Gloria winked and snickered.

"Ummm... sorry, but as fun as that sounds, I have a date with my *boyfriend*, Jeremy. Remember Jeremy? My *boyfriend*? Maybe I will see you around though."

"Jeremy? No, it doesn't ring a bell, but alright then. I will see you soon." Gloria winked again, closed the case lid and walked back into the kitchen.

I was watching the interaction from afar, when Hans approached me with an envelope. "I found this sitting on the table outside with your name on it."

I took the envelope from Hans and without thinking ripped it open to find three words: *Rat! Rat! Rat!*

Trae came back to the table. "That was a complete waste of time. She can't get past my incredibly good looks."

"Trae!"

"It's like she only sees me as a hot man muffin."

"Trae!"

"I keep telling everyone that I'm more than a beautiful face, I am—"

"Trae, shut your pie hole, and look." I shoved the note in front of him.

"What is this, Millie?" Trae looked concerned.

"I think the serial killer was on the tour with us today."

CHAPTER 13

Oh my gosh! Here I am always bragging about all my murders. I forgot to tell you about my other news! I got a pet. Yes, my very own pet. Her name is Millie, the little sister of the Seattle detective who was assigned to my case. She is adorable, so quirky and carefree. Not sure what my plans are for this one yet, but I know that I need to keep her close. I'm going to need her... well, at least until I don't.

I have given her two warnings. She has pictures of me. She is holding onto said evidence and is purposely not releasing them to the media. She is teasing me with them, waiting until just the right moment to release them. Why? Because she is playing the same game I am. But I play this game better.

I saw her today with her little friend. Now I know there are three of them. It is obvious that my Millie is the one who is leading them all. "Rats! Rats! Rats!" that is what the young man screamed. Yes, that is exactly what you all are. Rats!

I will give her one last chance, one final message, and if she doesn't give me what I want, I will take everything she has ever loved because I cannot risk losing everything I've worked so hard to build.

One day, she will see that I'm not the monster here. Truly, I am not. I am a builder. A creator. An artist. I believe in mercy; I don't want to hurt anyone. I want to give them peace. She will see. I am a savior. I just hope I don't have to remove someone Millie loves before it's too late.

CHAPTER 14

"What do you mean someone called you accusing you of having something they want? For Christ's sake, Millie, you can't keep these things from us," Cici scolded me.

Trae called Cici immediately after I showed him the note that Hans found.

"Did Hans catch this person on camera?" Cici asked.

Trae shook his head. "No, Hans's camera doesn't capture the far edge of the sitting area where the note was left."

I sat on the chair outside of Hans's coffee shop while I watched each one of my tears make a splatter pattern on the sidewalk. "I fucked up our investigation, and it's not even dinner time."

Trae chimed in. "You actually didn't. Because of your evidence list, I was able to get some information about a few of the victims at work. I overheard two people talking about how they thought one of the murder victims was into some weird shit. They would have candle-making team building events at work, and Millie you said that stuff was found at the crime scene. Someone also said they saw Darrin Russel, the software engineer, talking with a group called Keepers of the Pines, who were handing out fliers in Westlake Center. You also said one of their fliers was found in a pair of jeans at the murder scene. Millie, you are piecing things together. I think you should check out this tree group."

I scrapped my sneakers against the sidewalk while I thought back to a couple of days. "I do know that group. I ran into them the other day and took one of their fliers. I bet I still have it somewhere at home." I wiped the tears from my cheeks. "So, really, you two aren't firing me from our private investigator company?"

Cici chuckled. "I don't think firing you is a thing. We aren't a real company, but we are a team, remember? I'm going to head back home to finish my next story for the paper. If I hear anything else from my end, I will be in touch. Millie, start researching this Keepers of the Pines group and let me know what you find out." Cici wheeled away, leaving me to my despair.

Trae started to follow Cici. "I'm going to head home too. Be careful, Millie. Stay in the public eye."

I sat there for a while, wondering if I was cut out for detective work.

Maybe I should just go back to catching spiders. I was good at that, and it was feel-good work. This doesn't feel good.

I pushed off the concrete wall and started to walk. I felt like complete shit for letting things get out of control already.

What does this person want from me? Someday I'm going to make this PI gig work, and I will be the best investigator in all of Seattle.

Which reminded me: I had to be at the warehouse in a few hours. But, since I had some time to kill until then, I might as well head down to Westlake Center to check out those pine tree people.

"What a beautiful day," I acknowledged to no one in particular as I bounced along the busy street. It was nice seeing the city alive again. During the pandemic there weren't a lot of people downtown. Many businesses had been boarded up and the only occupants were unhoused people, the police, and of course, members of Keepers of the Pines, who were handing out fliers.

I pulled my phone from my pocket and Googled their group to see what I could find before I arrived at Westlake. Turned out there was quite a bit of information about them online. Their group was in the news a lot during 2020, trying to rebrand themselves a humanitarian group by promoting food and clothing drives for the unhoused.

Back in the earlier nineties the Keepers of the Pines were accused of targeting unhoused children, some as young as eight years old, with the promise of food, clothing, shelter, and love only to force them into child labor at their commune in the woods, which, at the time, was closer to the Cascade mountains.

The claims were unfounded, but the locals drove them away. For years, everyone believed the Keepers of the Pines had disbanded, but the group resurfaced during the Covid pandemic shutdown. What was once a cult of more than two-hundred members, had now dwindled to about seventy-five, according to *Wikipedia*. And it looked like they were living out on Blake Island in Elliot Bay the last few years.

I slid my phone back into my pocket and hurried across the street where I walked up to a young man holding a stack of fliers. "Hey buddy, my name is Millie. What's your name?"

He just stared at me and shoved a flier in my chest.

"Ummm… you don't have a name? Or you just don't feel like sharing it today?"

"He's mute," I heard a voice call out behind me.

I turned around and stopped. There was a flutter of tingles that stormed my entire body when I saw a beautiful woman with honey-colored eyes staring back at me. She wore a smile on her lips, but I wasn't sure if she was happy or sad. It was a chilly day, but she must have been working hard because she looked warm. Her dark wavy, bobbed hair was pulled back in a ponytail, and I could tell she was a bit taller than me. She walked toward me, and my eyes traveled down her long torso and over her curvy hips before I quickly snapped myself back to reality and into detective mode.

"Hi, I'm Millie." I extended my hand to greet her, only to trip over a crack in the concrete. I stumbled head first into her chest. Then, I fell to my knees. The woman leaned over to help me up at the same time I stood, knocking my head into her chin. She fell back, biting her lip, and blood gushed all over the sidewalk.

"Hurry, get me a towel. Quick!" she hollered to the boy.

"I'm so, so very sorry! I'm truly sorry to have fallen into you. What's your name?" I hopped side to side while trying not to touch any of her blood but also patting her on the shoulder as she tried to stop the flow with her cupped hands.

"Juniper, my name is Juniper." She sounded irritated as she grabbed the offered towel and sat down on the ground.

"Is everything okay over there, Juniper?" a man asked.

"Yes, Father Noble. I'm fine," Juniper yelled over my shoulder. She pulled the towel away from her lip to assess the damage.

I turned around to verify that she was indeed talking to the one and only Keepers of the Pines leader himself, Noble Pines. I was even more shocked to find him chatting with Tim Lewis, Liza Lewis's husband.

"What the fuck?" I whispered.

"What's wrong? Does the sight of blood make you woozy?" Juniper looked up at me from her sitting position.

"Can I talk with you? I don't want to be a bother or anything, but I feel like I owe you an explanation of why I was introducing myself, although unintentionally aggressively."

Juniper laughed and waved her hand over the empty space at her side in invitation. "Be my guest."

I sat down crossed-legged beside her while being careful to avoid any of the blood on the ground. "Thanks. So, it seems like you can feed a lot of people. Where do you grow all this fresh food?"

"Are you a reporter or something?" She sounded suspicious.

"No, just passing by. I have actually passed by a few times and every time I think it's super impressive that your community is able to feed so many people in need."

"Hmmm... do you now? Well, you will be even more impressed when I tell you that we also take volunteers to serve food. Would you like to help serve food? Or maybe you would like to hand out fliers? Or better yet, maybe help us tear down, clean up, and load up the trucks when we get kicked out of here at night?" Juniper seemed irritated.

"I seem to have upset you. I honestly didn't mean anything by it. I'm just curious." I tried to sound sincere.

"Sorry, I guess I just get frustrated when people think all we do is stand here all day and hassle everyone to donate to our cause. Which, I guess, at first glance, we do, but it goes so much deeper than that. We put every penny of those donations back into feeding, clothing, and sheltering the unhoused. We work year-round to grow food to feed who we can. We make clothes for the unhoused, and we build tiny homes wherever and whenever the city officials will let us. We do all of this while we live mostly off the earth on Blake Island. None of this is easy, Millie."

"I can see that it takes a lot of work. It also looks like you get a lot of influential support out here. Isn't that the chief librarian for the Seattle Public Library over there, Tim Lewis?"

"Oh him? Yeah, he drops off books for the unhoused."

"Why does that guy over there keep staring at us? Did I do something wrong? I mean besides accidentally injuring you."

"Father Noble is a kind man who just doesn't trust easily. Can you really blame him? The way people always seem to have it out for us. We get called all sorts of slander: pedophiles, cultists, sinners. You name it. We've heard it all." Juniper lowered her head.

Without thinking I grasped Juniper's chin, tilting her head back up. "Hey, how's the lip?" A bolt of electricity shot through my body when our skin made contact.

Her skin is so soft. Wait, no. Millie, those are professional tummy tickles you're feeling. You're just excited to be on your first assignment. This is completely normal.

She looked up at me without a smile and my eyes grew huge. "Holy shit, Juniper! That doesn't look normal. I mean, it looks swollen. I think you should get some ice. I can't believe I made your lip so big." We started to giggle.

"We will always have the ultimate first date story." Juniper winked.

I blushed and smiled.

Millie, you're undercover and not supposed to feel anything. But why did I like how this felt?

No matter how hot she was, I couldn't allow anything to happen between me and Juniper. I'm a professional. I needed to get back to my investigation—why I was here in the first place.

"Seen much of Darrin around here lately?"

"Who?" Juniper looked confused.

"Darrin Russel. You surely know Darrin, right? Older guy, maybe in his sixties? Seen him around?"

"Oh yeah, Darrin. He helps us shuck corn. Says it reminds him of when he was a boy helping his grandma. Darrin comes by maybe once or twice a month. Do you know Darrin? If you stick around, he might show up tonight." Juniper seemed pleased by Darrin's contributions.

So sad that she doesn't even know her friend is dead yet. I'm not going to be one to tell her.

"I wish I could, but I should probably head out. Juniper, it was so nice to hang out with you, and, again, I'm really sorry about your face." We gave each other the same curious look as I fought the overwhelming urge to kiss her swollen lip.

That was weird. What the fuck is wrong with me? I'm a professional.

"Okay then. Yeah, off I go."

I pushed myself from the concrete, then wiped my hands on my pants. I extended my hand to help Juniper up, but she declined.

"I think I'm going to hang out here a bit longer. I have a headache right now." She gave me that same closed lip smile from earlier.

I wrote my number on an extra flier and handed it to her." I understand. Here is my phone number in case you ever want to chat or, I don't know, talk about anything. I hope to see you again really soon, Juniper." Our fingers grazed. I really hoped she would use my number. For professional reasons, of course.

I waved before turning around to find Noble and Tim staring at me. I repeated the wave for them, which was not returned. Noble creeped me out with his long white hair, pulled back into a ponytail and beard. He had these piercing steel grey eyes that drilled holes into your soul like he knew every move you were about to make. I didn't like that. I understood being suspicious of people, but it felt like he knew exactly why I was snooping around.

For the entire walk back to my condo, I tried to deconstruct what I had just experienced: meeting Juniper and also seeing Noble and Tim talking while unloading the van full of donated books. It made me wonder why Tim would make donations to a group with their reputation. This was risky for a public figure. He could have donated to hundreds of other shelters or group homes.

So why this one? What drew him to support Keepers of the Pines?

Oh, and Juniper. Sweet, beautiful, Juniper. I didn't want to use her or lead her on, but I needed an in, and she might very well be the only way I could get a foot in the door. Hopefully, one day she would forgive me. This wasn't personal; it was work and no one ever said going undercover would be easy. Sometimes I had to break hearts to save lives.

Oh my gosh, that is what I will tell her when this is all over. I will sit her down, take her hand, and say, "Juniper, this truly wasn't personal. Sometimes, I have to break hearts to save lives." Then, I will kiss her on the cheek and wipe away her tears before I walk into the sunset toward my next case. Why? Because I'm a Myles. I am Millie Myles, private investigator. Well, almost. Maybe someday.

I slid my phone from my pocket and selected Mickey's name.

"Hey Soda Pop. I'm glad you called."

"I feel honored, but I don't have time for family bonding. I have a few questions about the Keepers of the Pines cult."

"Me first, Millie. When you come on Sunday, we are going to sit down and talk about Mom and Dad. You can't avoid this any longer. Neither of us can. You are not getting better. You made me a promise to get help. I think for you to start healing, you need—"

"Mickey, stop, one of Trae's best work friends just died and you want to talk about people that died thirty years ago? His friend was murdered."

Mickey sighed. "Millie, I told you and your friends to stay away from this murder. These people are dangerous. I saw you down at Westlake today. I don't want you anywhere near Noble Pines. You hear me?"

"Mickey! Were you following me? Is Noble Pines a suspect?"

I knew it. I knew we were on the right track.

Mickey took a deep breath. "I don't know why I'm telling you this, but right now, we have some odd connections between some of the victims and the Keepers of the Pines. But nothing that screams cold, hard evidence. Please stay away from this. Let the police, the professionals trained to solve violent crimes, do our job. Okay, Soda Pop? Now Sunday, we are going to talk. I'm not letting you off the hook this time."

"I knew it. Thanks bro. See you Sunday." I tapped End on our call.

I arrived at my condo and typed in the door code. As I started to open the door, I paused and took a good look around before deciding to investigate where I thought the location of last night's rock thrower might be. I crossed the street to inspect the bus stop, but there was so much garbage on the ground that it was hard to tell what might've been left by the suspect versus the average person waiting for the bus. There was nothing of note, so I walked along the buildings nearby. Same thing. Nothing of note.

I hurried back across the street and returned to the condo building's front door. I was about to enter the code again when I noticed a pile of small pebbles on the ground directly under my window, which was four stories up.

I bet these are it! They probably tossed them at the window, then leaned against the building where I couldn't see them when I looked out. Nice move, asshole. What did they want from me? Maybe it's time I told Trae and Cici.

I looked around again and saw Hans waving at me from his coffee shop across the street.

CHAPTER 15

*T*he phone on the other end hadn't even rung when the woman answered, "Nine-one-one. What is your emergency?"

I'm telling you; it was so hard to keep a straight face and not laugh my ass off as I tried to keep my composure on the phone.

"Dispatch, this is ambulance three on highway eighteen, two miles east of Auburn. We have a multi-vehicle accident with multiple injured patients. Reporting one patient with severe lacerations to lower leg with a suspected tibia and femur fracture, and another patient with chest pains after airbag deployment. Requesting a helicopter for transfer to a trauma center due to the severity of the leg injury."

I clicked off my voice disguiser and ended the call. Have any of you even used one of these little voice distorters? So, fun. You can make your voice sound like a cartoon character too.

Hilarious, I can't stop laughing!

Okay focus.

That will kick off the series of dispatch events necessary to get my helicopter in the air. I love technology. Who knew a few simple hacky-hacks here and hacky-hacks there and BAM! Nine-one-one thinks a paramedic is calling from my fake car accident scene in need of air support.

I really hope this works. Of course it will work! I am the artist. The builder. The creator and savior. We need to hurry because we don't have much time to get to the other side of the highway and back to the stolen car before the cops get here. These burner phones are the greatest invention of all time!

I snapped it over my knee and tossed it in the ditch. I don't normally break ritual, but we have our next set of victims to greet.

The helicopter should be crashing right... about... now. Come on, get in the car. According to my watch, we have about ten minutes to get to where we need to be. My heart is pounding with excitement.

How about yours?

The anticipation is exhilarating! We have a five-mile drive out to the clearing where I made sure everything would come together...ever, so, carefully. I can't stop grinning.

Seatbelts people! We follow laws around here!

What do you think the city will say about this one? Weird, I don't normally get nervous. But what if they didn't make the connection? I want them to know it was me. They haven't even given me a proper name yet. I must ensure they make the connection between all these murders. I will be more famous than Jack the Ripper or the Zodiac Killer! They were never caught, and I won't be caught either.

The difference between me and other serial killers is that I'm leaving them with nothing. I take everything from them. No one will bury their loved ones or say goodbye because their families don't deserve it.

I have a question for you before we get there. If a killer's goal is to be famous in the moment but not in the end, what is their true goal?

Don't you love a good riddle?

Chapter 16

I clocked in right on time at the warehouse, which meant I was late. Eddie was standing at my table waiting for me, and he didn't look happy.

"Millie, we follow a few rules here at the warehouse. One of those rules is that we are a family. And family keeps each other informed of what happens in the world outside of this warehouse. We do this because it helps us keep the cases we protect safe from police and witness tampering. So, that means we don't talk to the police if they come in here or if they're asking questions on the outside. Ever. You come get me if a cop shows up here asking questions. That includes your brother. We don't talk about anything we see, collect, hear, smell, or taste. Capiche?"

"Yes, but one question. What in the world would I possibly ever have to taste?" My stomach churned at the thought of tasting anything related to a murder scene.

"Just covering all the bases, kid."

"Okay, but why are we so secretive?" I fiddled nervously with some papers at my table.

Was he on to me? Did he know me and my friends were also trying to solve this murder?

"Well, we've been given strict instructions from the chief to prevent any evidence leaks or tampering. Just routine stuff, nothing to worry about. Sometimes this happens with bigger cases." Eddie had a neutral expression, so I figured he wasn't on to me.

"Are there any other rules I should keep in mind?"

Why do I feel so nervous? Maybe because I know I'm breaking some rules to help my friend, but all in the name of justice.

"Just one. We all eat lunch together. You'll see why."

"Okay, I did bring lunch. So that sounds nice... I guess."

Fucking weird!

Eddie walked away and I got right to work. My boxes were still in the same place I left them from the night before.

Did I miss anything?

I decided to take a picture of the candle wick, pottery bits, and pieces of colored glass to send to Trae and Cici. Other than that, I kept going back to the old vintage paper. It had lines drawn all over it. I finally put it back in the bag to file away, then immediately took it back out, snapped a picture, and sent it to my team.

I spent the next three hours going back through each box, pulling out each tag, and logging it into the computer. Suddenly, I dropped my scanner and looked closer at the pieces of plaster I was about to log. There was blood splatter all over them.

"What the hell is that?" I said out loud as I grabbed a magnifying glass from my drawer. "Oh, wow, is that what I think that is?"

A single pine needle was stuck in the blood. This couldn't be a coincidence, I understand pine needles were everywhere in the Pacific

Northwest, but not in a pristine new office building. Trae said a murder victim was seen talking to members from Keepers of the Pines. I'm probably overthinking this.

Before I could take a picture of the pine needle, the lunch horn sounded, which was immediately followed by Eddie yelling, "Lunch time!"

We gathered in the lunchroom, pulling our food bags out of the fridge before sitting at the table. There were only six of us on the overnight shift.

Like clockwork, everyone threw a cookie in the middle of the table. One of the ladies threw in an extra Oreo. "The case I'm logging tonight is a kid with an arm blown off while popping off illegal fireworks in the park."

Another person threw a few cookies on the pile. "Ha, amateur! I raise your blown-off arm with three chocolate chips and a marijuana bust during a fire that got the fire department so high that they are being sued for making sandwiches in the guy's kitchen."

A third person tossed a monster cookie on top of the others. "I raise your firecracker kid and your lit firemen with a mega monster cookie and a drunk priest and nun from St. Mary's Catholic Church robbing a 7-11 with a fake gun before trying to get married at the court house."

Eddie pushed the cookies toward the man who upped everyone's bet with the priest and nun bid, and then they started to eat their lunch.

"Sounds like everyone gets some pretty intense cases around here." I looked around the table.

One of the ladies, whose badge said Bernice, shook her head. "Night shift can be pretty boring. We have to keep ourselves entertained somehow. Plus, the day shift leaves the most gruesome, messed up cases for us. If we can't laugh, we would all end up going insane."

When I got back to my station after lunch, I immediately texted pictures of the pine needle. I was hoping Trae would be able to identify the needle type. Since it was three-thirty in the morning, I knew I wouldn't get a response anytime soon. I didn't know what all this evidence meant, but I had a feeling that between the vintage paper, the candlewick, the pottery, the pieces of colored glass, and the pine needle, we had a little more to go on than we did yesterday. Not that any of these items made sense together.

No wonder Mickey never solved any cases!

Eddie yelled from across the warehouse. "Myles, you got more boxes coming in! Should be here in five minutes. Suit up. Err, never mind, you've already done that. Just be ready."

"Always ready, Eddie. What's going on?" My curiosity was piqued.

"There's been another murder. Or I should say murders."

Box after box started coming through the garage doors, dropping onto my table in a single-file line. I stood there, bewildered that they were trusting me with the biggest serial killer case in Seattle history.

Why me? They could have put someone else on this and gave me the fireworks kid.

As if reading my mind, Eddie chuckled. "It's not like we are trusting you with Seattle's biggest serial killer case. But none of us wanted to do that much work." He slapped me on the shoulder lightly before heading back to his own station.

I caught up with one of the crime scene investigators unloading boxes. "What's the story here? It will help me log the evidence," I lied.

"Oh yeah, this was so messed up. A Medical One helicopter was headed to a car accident call when they reported engine trouble. They went down, but when the rescue crew arrived on scene, they found the helicopter lightly damaged, a lot of blood, and no bodies. On the other end of the call, when the police and a second ambulance arrived at the car accident scene, it was obvious it was a fake call. Traffic was moving normally and there were no signs of any disruptions. It was like this sick son-of-a-bitch was sending us a message that he can pull angels out of the sky."

"So... no ransom, no messages from the killer, nothing?" I walked him back to his van.

"Nothing so far. But these idiots will eventually mess up. They always do." Slamming shut the van's back door, he hopped into the driver seat and pulled away.

He said Idiots. Plural. I wonder if the police think there is more than one killer.

I walked back to my station and looked at what had to be well over a hundred boxes and bags of evidence. I took a deep breath, trying to maintain my composure. I felt overwhelmed.

I'm so out of my league. What was I thinking? We can't take on a serial killer. Maybe we should back off before one of us gets hurt. But I want to help Trae get justice for his friends. No! What am I thinking? We have to do this.

I opened the first box as I fell back into my chair. I pulled out a Ziplock bag that contained more bloody pine needles. I snapped a picture and then continued through the rest of the boxes.

It was amazing how similar this crime scene was to the office space. There was just as much evidence as the first murder scene, but once again, none of it told an obvious story.

Three victims this time: a pilot, a nurse, and a doctor. They were all women.

So sad.

I hadn't yet found the box with the report, which would be interesting to read. It was going to be a long morning.

When I arrived home, I sat down at the kitchen island and waited for the time to turn from 7:59 a.m. to 8 a.m. At the top of the hour, I picked up my phone, went to my call log, and selected my brother's name from my recent calls. It went to voicemail.

Odd.

Mozzarella watched me and then hissed in Russian, I think. I documented this finding. I drew a picture of Russia and made a note with an Expo marker to remind me to tell the team when they got home. 'Mozzarella is fluent in Russian. Unsure of her citizenship status.'

I will give Mickey five minutes. I twirled my phone in circles on the table as I watched each minute pass on the microwave clock.

Fuck! Fuck! Fuck! Maybe I will try and focus on something else. Like the murder board.

I walked over to the board, but the pull to figure out why the hell Mickey was avoiding me was too strong.

"Call me, Mickey. Please, call me." My phone started to buzz. "Mickey!" I tried not to sound panicked and failed.

"Soda Pop, you okay?" Mickey sounded worried.

"Besides the fact it's taken you over an hour to respond to me. I almost came to your house, you asshole."

"It was two minutes and that wouldn't have helped. I'm already downtown working on the case. Soda Pop, we really need to talk about your obsession with these phone calls. Maybe it's time we talk about the accident."

Oh, now he wants to talk about the morning I kept him from saving our parent's and sister's lives. From getting in that car. From getting hit by that train. I decided to ignore his comment and got down to business. "I thought you were getting pulled from the case. Did they change their minds?"

"I was never getting pulled from the case. Sometimes when they are sending one of us undercover, they make it sound like that, and I'm going undercover. I can't share anything else, Millie, but I might not be around or be able to answer my phone, okay? I will always check every day and do my best to keep our Sunday dinner plans, but if something comes up with the case, you know it's my job, right?"

Why did I feel like he was in danger?

"Can you tell me where you are going? You know I won't tell anyone. I promise."

"You know I can't, Soda Pop. It will be fine. By the way, I heard things are well over at the warehouse. Keep it up, Millie. They might hire you full time. You could have a solid job with some benefits. Maybe we could get you on some good meds to help with your y'know... problems."

"Well, sounds like someone is calling me. Have a good day, bro."

Just as I hung up with Mickey, my phone rang again. Unknown caller.

"Hello?"

"Step outside," the strange voice requested.

Is this who I think it is?

"For what?" My stomach dropped.

"Ah come on, are you scared?"

"No, why would I be scared of you? You're just a cell phone warrior. Calling people with bottomless demands that make no sense."

"Well step outside then," the voice hummed.

"On my way." I decided to forgo grabbing my jacket and rushed down the staircase.

When I arrived at the lobby door I paused before I opened it. "What happens when I come outside? Are you going to take a shot at me?"

"Now why would I do that? I need you, and you need me. We're friends."

I pushed the door open and dropped onto the sidewalk. A blast of frigid air made me immediately regret not putting on my jacket. The street was bustling with pedestrians commuting to work and people walking their dogs. I looked around to see if I could find another person on their phone, but I didn't see anyone.

"Okay, I'm out here, now what?" My heart was pounding.

"Wow, blue really makes your eyes pop, Millie."

"Nice touch, psychopath. You can clearly see me, but I can't see you. You have ten seconds to tell me what the hell you want, or I'm going back inside."

"Name calling is not nice; my feelings are hurt. I would never do that to you. Walk toward Hans. Go to the far table and sit down."

"You're pretty sensitive for a murderer."

"You're a pretty big bully for a wanna be hero," the voice retorted in jest.

I ignored this last comment, hurried across the street, and found the table. I sat down with my back toward Hans's window. "So now what? You have five seconds before I leave."

"So pushy, fine. Reach under the table. You will find an envelope. Tell me what you see inside."

I reached under the table and felt an envelope taped to the bottom. I tore it off and ripped it open to find pictures of me, Cici, and Trae strolling down the street together. There were also pictures of Mickey in the assortment of photos with a note that said, "who will be next?"

I looked around angrily, grinding my teeth. "You son of bitch!" I growled. "If you touch any of my friends or family I swear to god, I will fucking find you and kill you myself. Do you hear me?"

"Give me what I want, Millie. You are out of time." The phone went dead.

CHAPTER 17

Trae and Cici arrived home from work later that afternoon. I tried to sleep most of the day but tossed and turned, unable to wrap my head around what was making me feel most anxious. Was it the phone call? Was it my brother's undercover situation? Was it just the investigation itself?

Trae could immediately tell I was stressed out and tried to ease my worries. "What's going on with you? You know I'm really enjoying Cici living here. They even cleaned the whole damn condo."

I raised my hand in the air. "What? Wait! Who cleaned the condo?"

Trae sounded more like he was confessing to the murders than complimenting Cici. "Ummm... yeah, Cici picked up, vacuumed, dusted, and cleaned out the fridge." Trae peeked fearfully out of the corner of his eye. He continued, trying to sound more upbeat this time. "Cici, did I see that you built a privacy fence at some point last night between your bed and the garden?"

Cici looked at Trae. "I don't care if they are bits and bolts; I don't want them to see me naked."

I stared at the fridge.

Cici shouldn't have done that. They should have never cleaned out the fridge.

I looked back at Trae, who suddenly realized the magnitude of what Cici did. He could tell I was about to lose my shit.

How could he let them do this? Why would he let this happen?

"I have an idea," I said urgently. "Why don't we all take a nap and reconvene in a bit? Then we can meet back here in the kitchen at 4 p.m.? Sound good?"

Everyone nodded in agreement and headed toward their respective bedrooms.

Panic was rising in my chest, followed by a thick growing lump in my throat.□I could feel it—the gripping pressure around my ribcage, squeezing tighter and tighter. I felt the air slowly being pulled from my lungs. I had the overwhelming urge to inspect what Cici had done to the fridge. Even though I knew her actions were meant to be helpful and kind, it didn't matter.

Beads of sweat gathered on my forehead, and my breaths shortened.

Everyone needs to fucking go to bed! Why won't they just hurry up and leave? What is taking them so fucking long?

Logically, I knew this was ridiculous. No one was going to die if the condiments weren't in the right spot. But last time I rearranged the condiments, someone did die. Trae's grandma died because I switched the mayo with the ketchup and an hour later, she was dead.

My God, what did Cici do? What did they do?

As soon as I heard their doors shut, I sprinted out of my room to the fridge.

"No, no, no, God Cici, what did you do? You moved everything! Where are the pickles?" With tears now pouring from my eyes, I emptied every last bottle, container, and wrapped item before placing them in a circle around me. "Where are the pickles?" I asked again as I checked the cupboards.

They probably put them in the cupboard because they don't need to be refrigerated.

I tore apart every cupboard.

Maybe they put them behind this stack of plates or behind the cleaning supplies?

I rummaged under the sink.

I was falling into a chaotic thought loop that was quickly spiraling out of control.

Grandma walking... Grandma tripping... Grandma falling...

My thoughts were becoming so revolting that my stomach started to turn as bile entered my throat.

Please don't throw up. Please, not on the kitchen floor. Grandma walking... Grandma tripping... Grandma falling... Hitting head... Blood... Grandma dead.

Trae peeked out of his room. "Millie? My God, it's okay. It's going to be okay." He hurried to my side, sat on the floor behind me, and wrapped his long legs around my body. Like my last panic attack and the time before that one, he pulled me into his chest as we swayed back and forth.

We sat in the middle of the kitchen, and Trae stroked my hair and matched my rocking motions, repeating words of comfort in his soft monotone voice. "Everything is going to be okay..."

There wasn't one item left in the drawers, cabinets, or the fridge. Everything was on the floor with every door wide open and every shelf and drawer bare.

I was crying so hard I could barely speak without choking on every inhale. "Trae, they threw away the pickles. Someone is going to die. I don't know who, but someone is going to die!"

He continued to stroke my hair. "I got you baby girl. I got you. No one is going to die. I won't let that happen. I will reverse this with a new jar of pickles, a better jar, a more powerful jar. Okay? I want you to go to bed, and I will clean this up. By the time you wake up, I will have everything back to normal, okay? I promise. Remember Millie, I got you; you got me. I put the forever in your best friend. BFFs!"

I pulled my weak body from the floor, leaving Trae sitting, probably wondering if I will ever be able to get these attacks under control. I gave him a scared look, which he returned with an encouraging smile as I made my way to my room.

Instead of going to bed, I stripped my clothes off, folded them with perfect creases, and placed them in my hamper. I would never fight with my clothes again because last time, my parents and sister died. "Nice and neat, so no one will die. Perfect creases," I whispered through my tears.

Okay. I can fold them the other way. Left to right and underneath so, you can't see the length as much. Yes, yes, that works!

I laid them back in the hamper. I clasped my bra and laid it centered on my jeans. Then I turned to go to the shower but wait...

Mom, Dad, Sister driving... Train brakes screeching... Train horn blaring... Bright light...

I was nauseous again...

Please don't throw up. Mom, Dad, Sister driving... Train brakes screeching... Train horn blaring... Bright light... Family scream-ing..."Millie, get dressed; the phone is ringing"... Train Smashing... Silence...

My heart started to pound harder as I hurried back to my hamper and tore everything out and started over. My clothes still weren't right.

Someone was going to die; I could just feel it. I couldn't get into the shower until I made sure my clothes were folded with perfect creases. My hands shook so hard that I could barely grip my jeans. A tear fell from the tip of my nose. I promised over and over that I wouldn't fight with my clothes anymore.

Prefect creases... prefect creases... prefect creases...

I'm not sure how long it took me to get everything folded, but I was finally able to shower. I scrubbed my face until I couldn't feel or see the tear stains anymore.

I think they are gone. It took an hour, but I think they are gone.

I looked at myself in the shower mirror.

Ugh, I can still see them.

Then I heard a knock on the door. "Baby girl, it's time to come out of there. It's okay."

I didn't respond. I turned off the water and wrapped myself in a towel.

Okay, I got this. Just go out there and be normal, act normal. You can do this; you do this all the time.

I wiped the fog from the bathroom mirror to find a woman who I barely recognized staring back at me.

I think I got them all. The tear stains are gone.

I exhaled as I examined my puffy, bright-red face. I dried off and dressed before going straight to the kitchen where I found Trae sitting at the counter with a platter of pancakes, a bowl of scrambled eggs, a plate piled high with toast, and a pitcher of orange juice.

"Wow, I sure could get used to living like this if we get breakfast for dinner every day." Cici snuck up behind me.

Trae started to move the breakfast items to the table as I walked past him to the fridge. I tugged open the door to see everything exactly as it should be, including a new jar of pickles. I sighed with relief, and I turned to see Trae with his fingers in the shape of a heart. I returned the gesture with a teary smile.

"You two are weird. Can we eat, please?"

The purple bot started to sharpen two knives against each other in front of Cici's plate, when the pink bot rolled over and pushed the purple bot aside.

"Pink. Save. Cici."

Trae turned the purple bot over and took the knives. "Weird, he normally just cuts the blueberry lemon loaf and goes back to the garden. I'm not sure why he got stuck like that."

Cici jumped in to provide their assessment. "Ah, because he wants to murder me. I swear if it was possible, I would add your bots to the suspect list."

After our meal, I tried to be the great pretender I always was and got right to business.

"Two things. First, Mozzarella isn't a normal cat. She hissed at me in a foreign language, and I'm pretty sure it was Russian. I don't think we can exclude that the Russians are involved, and until we can fully eliminate them as suspects." I pointed toward the whiteboard in the living room. "Secondly, I talked to Mickey. He is going undercover but won't give me any details. That means the police might have some leads though." I let out a big sigh, trying to release the nervousness in my body.

Cici was attempting to get Mozzarella to hiss in Russian by blowing in her face. "Maybe? Trae did say he saw Mickey surveilling the gaming building, so I'm not sure that is a great lead."

"Good to know. Okay then, let's take a look at what else we have." I nodded at the murder board.

Trae looked confused. "What Millie? It's a blank board."

"No Trae, it is actually our murder board." I flipped the board around to reveal pictures of suspects and all the evidence we've collected so far.

"Holy shit, Millie this is awesome! It's like you're telling us a whole damn story here." Cici admired my work as they wheeled over to the board." I mean it's okay. I've seen better."

Trae's eyes were wide as he ran his fingers along the pieces of string that ran from each picture of evidence and each photo of random individuals. "Millie, this is incredible. I have never seen anything like this before, not even on TV! It's like I'm looking inside the head of the killer."

"What do the different colors of string represent?" Cici ran their finger along the blue string.

"Good question. The blue string means the trail is cold. Orange means we are getting warmer. Red means we are hot. And green means it's go time, and we are executing a plan. And no one executes on green without alerting the rest of the team. Got it?" I looked at my friends to ensure we were all in agreement.

"You won't hear any argument from me," Trae confirmed.

"I can take care of myself. If I see something going down, I might just have to deal with it. It's not like we can wait for each other to get to wherever we are." Cici blew at the cat again and finally got Mozzarella to hiss. "No, I think it's German."

"I will print out a picture of Germany for the board. But Cici, I'm serious. If something goes down and Trae and I are not around to protect you, you need to call 911 immediately." I had never felt so concerned for another human in my life, except maybe for Mickey.

"Fine!" Cici replied heatedly.

I stepped in front of the board to start my presentation. "So, I went to Westlake Center yesterday. I didn't get much, but you are never going to believe who I saw chatting it up with Noble Pines. The one and only, Tim Lewis. I was able to pull together a few items of interest." I pointed to my bullet points.

- Noble and Tim were chumming it up on the street.

Maybe it's a coincidence or maybe there is a connection. Either way, they are both suspects on the board for now.

- The software engineer, Darrin Russel, was seen talking with Keepers of the Pines group members multiple times.

- He helps shuck corn for the unhoused dinners. He was one of the murder victims at Stone Water Games.

- The Keepers of the Pines members don't seem to know he is dead yet.

I paused for questions and then continued. "Okay, starting at the top right hand side of the board is murder scene number one." I nodded to a picture of Trae's office building. "Each victim's name is noted by their picture. There's nothing on here that you all don't know. However, there is now another crime scene: murder scene number two."

I stepped back to assess the room to find Cici and Trae listening intently. Although I was feeling exhausted by my earlier attack, I was grateful that they were really invested in my dialogue. I continued. "Earlier today, a Medical One helicopter was heading to a car accident when the all-female crew called in with engine trouble before going down in a crash. When the rescue crew arrived on scene, the helicopter didn't have any serious damage, but there was another bloody crime scene with no bodies. This picture is the exact make and model of the chopper that went down." I pinned the photo on the board.

"Who were they, Millie? Give them a name. These women deserve a goddamn name, Millie!" Trae yelled. "What are their fucking names?"

"Of course, Trae. Their names are Laurie Jordan, Casey White, and Monica Gordon. I didn't mean to suggest that they were just victims and not people."

Trae ignored my comment, walked over to the board, and took down the picture of the chopper. "This is a repeat of the office crime scene, Millie, just in a different location. There's a connection here, isn't there?"

I released a deep sigh and returned to my seat at the table. "Yeah, that's what the cops are saying. Especially because when they arrived at the location where the chopper was headed, there was no car accident at all. As if someone called it in to get the flight in the air, only to somehow make it crash."

We were quiet as we stared at the board. Then Mozzarella hissed. Again. "Jesus, that scared me." Cici wheeled over to her, but Mozzarella jumped into Trae's lap.

"I think she misses Beth." Trae kissed the top of her head.

"So, what are our next steps?" Cici took out their notebook, ready to take notes.

"I'm borrowing Mickey's fishing boat and heading to Blake Island in the morning," I announced proudly, shoving a piece of pancake into my mouth, only to miss and have a long string of syrup drizzle down my tan shirt. "Every fucking time."

"The hell you are!" Cici and Trae shouted in tandem.

CHAPTER 18

"H ere we go gang!"

"Whistle while you boat—peep, wee, peep, peep, peep, peep, peep."

"Millie, what the hell are you doing? For fuck's sake, you're blowing out my ear drums!" Cici snapped through the ear piece. I was excited to check out the Keepers of the Pines's secret hideout. I had no weapons, but I did have surveillance gear so my friends could keep an eye on me. I'm not a huge fan of this tech, but if it makes Trae feel better, then so be it.

Trae responded to Cici. "She's never been able to remember the words to songs, so she makes them fit into a whistle. It's a quirk. It's fine. Ignore it."

"Peep...peep...pee...weep...peep...peep...peep."

"Millie, seriously! Can you please focus?" Cici still sounded annoyed.

"Roger that, Captain Cici."

"Don't call me that."

"Aye aye, matey."

"Nope, don't call me that either."

"As much as I'm enjoying the two of you exploring each other's boundaries, Millie, you are going to be docking in less than one minute. Are you sure you're ready for this?" Trae's voice sounded concerned.

"Puuumppped!" I reduced the throttle until I could feel the boat rock slowly back and forth as I eased into my final approach. The bow slid up onto the pebbled shore, and I jerked to a stop. It was eerily quiet for almost eight o'clock in the morning.

I sat in the boat staring at the one bar on my cell phone. I knew I would only have this one chance to call Mickey before heading into the woods. Two minutes had passed before I watched the time to turn from 7:59 a.m. to 8 a.m. At the top of the hour, I went to my call log and selected my brother's name from my recent calls. He answered on the first ring.

"Still kicking," Mickey mumbled with a deep grunt that suggested he was stretching.

"Great! I will call you later." I tapped End on the call.

I killed the motor and stepped out of the old wooden fishing boat. Now, feeling nervous, I dragged the bow up a little further onto the rocky shoreline to secure it in place. Turning toward the woods, I surveyed my surroundings.

Being from the city, I instantly noticed the difference in the atmosphere on the island. With a deep inhale of the untainted air, the salty sea breeze passed across my tongue and filled my lungs. A smile crossed my lips as I tasted the sweetness of the pine and cedar trees lining the shores.

This is truly a precious little island. I can see why someone would want to live out here.

I turned and took one last tug on the bow to make sure the afternoon high tide wouldn't wash Mickey's boat away.

"I didn't expect to see you again, especially out here," said a sweet feminine voice.

Startled, I whipped around to meet the beautiful honey-colored eyes of the woman who I toppled into at Westlake Center. Juniper.

"I didn't think you would remember me. I'm Millie." I reintroduced myself as I walked toward her, extending my hand while trying not to trip on the slippery rocks.

"I remember you, Millie," she said, stepping back. "I'm Juniper in case you didn't remember my name." Ignoring my hand, Juniper returned to her path into the woods.

"I remember..." I whispered. I had never felt so curious, mesmerized, and slightly scared all at once. I decided to follow her. "Killing all comms," I murmured. "I don't want to risk it."

"No, Millie, don't do th—" Trae begged as I turned off my earpieces.

We walked in silence for almost twenty minutes as I followed Juniper. My eyes followed the curve of her neck leading to her beautifully sculpted thin shoulders. I felt a familiar tingle in my stomach that grew stronger as the sensation traveled between my legs. She became gorgeously thicker at her hips. Her honey-colored eyes would wrinkle as she turned and smiled ever so slightly at me. It was almost like she was glad I was still there, still following behind her, that I hadn't run away. This mission was going to take a lot of restraint because I could already feel my passion for this woman intensifying. I wondered...

Is she attracted to me too?

"We're almost home," Juniper said as she glided through the brush and trees like she was one with the forest, not a scratch or mark on her. You could tell she walked these woods daily. They knew her, and she knew them.

I wish I could say the same, but I was already covered in scratches. "What is home?"

"You'll see." She smiled and grabbed my hand. "Close your eyes."

"Why would I do that?" I was cautiously curious.

"Don't you trust me?"

"Hmmmm... okay... I'll close my eyes." Juniper guided me several more feet along the forest floor. When I stumbled, she steadied me.

She paused and I stopped beside her. "Okay, you can open your eyes." Juniper dropped my hand. We stood looking out across a large clearing in the center of a compound. There were at least twenty-five tents on either side of two dirt roads, each road shaped as a crescent moon on opposite sides of the center's clearing. Each tent entrance was marked by a small porch made of repurposed pallets and framed by two tiki torches, one on either side of the entryways. Some of the tents had wooden signs indicating establishments: hospital, bank, seamstress, general store. At the end of the village was an impressive red brick communal kitchen that encompassed a large fire pit with dozens of picnic tables to one side.

I was blown away. We watched the bustling community. I couldn't believe how all these people were working together, some washing clothes in a large wooden tub and others hanging the freshly washed items on a clothesline to dry. Just beyond the washing station, a woman was chopping wood while others stacked the logs into piles. I snapped a quick picture with my watch.

In the kitchen, a man was cooking something in the brick oven that smelled of hickory and maple, and it made my mouth water. Off in the distance, I could see what appeared to be several others working in the numerous garden beds. This was a self-sufficient community that worked in harmony and seemed to function seamlessly.

"Juniper, who is your new friend?" I heard a male voice call out, and I looked over to find him standing at the opening of the largest tent in the village.

Juniper grabbed my hand excitedly and gently tugged me in his direction. "Come meet Father Noble!" Maybe she sounded more nervous than excited. I wasn't quite sure. "Are you coming?" She squeezed my hand tighter, while dragging me forward.

"Father, this is Millie." Juniper placed her hand on my shoulder. I dropped Juniper's other hand to extend it to Noble, but he did not accept the gesture.

Well, well, well. If it isn't Noble Pines himself. The famous cult leader of the Keepers of the Pines.

As far as anyone knew, the group was fairly harmless, at least from all our research, but isn't that what they all say until they are connected to something much more sinister.

That's why I'm here. I'm on a fact-finding mission to make that connection to what they are really all about. To expose Noble Pines. If the police can't find the evidence to put this murderer in jail, I will.

Noble gave me a quick once-over and said in a suspicious tone, "Care to join us for breakfast, Millie?"

Accepting his offer in the same suspicious tone, I said, "I would love to, Mr. Pines." I tried to smile, but he was already walking away from us.

We sat at one of the picnic tables, and I felt Juniper place her hand on my thigh. She gave me a warm smile when I returned the gesture, placing my hand over hers.

"Juniper, would you like to give thanks before we eat?" The crowd hushed.

"I would be honored, Father." Everyone placed their palms firmly on their tables on either side of their plates and lowered their heads.

"From the rains to the roots, beneath the soils we grieve. We send our thanks to our fallen trees." Juniper's voice shook, and she paused before speeding through the remainder of the prayer. "Thank you for your abundance of love, warmth, security, and shelter. Blessings to the Pines."

"Blessings to the Pines," a chorus of voices chimed.

The clanking of forks against plates grew louder as people began to eat. I could tell Juniper was edgy because she hadn't touched any of her food when finally she couldn't take any longer and stood up. "Please quiet down. I have a final message."

A hush fell immediately among the crowd...

Wow, when Juniper speaks, people listen.

I was impressed.

"I must prepare you all because in a mere few days, the rise of the King Tides will occur when you are all slumbering under the Saltwater Moon. Our goddess—"

Noble slammed his hand down, vibrating the table, and we all jumped.

"Juniper, stop with this nonsense right now! The only gods we seek protection from are those who shelter us from the very storm you claim will destroy us. You will not give blessings to our trees and then turn your loyalties to another. You bring fear to our peaceful home, and I will not tolerate it. You will not speak another word of this Saltwater Moon, or our Goddess Gaia bringing war in this way. She holds us all in her loving embrace. Always. The hundred-year storm is a time to celebrate our growth under the Saltwater Moon. You will fall in line immediately."

Holy fuck shit! These people take their pine trees seriously. But what is this about the Saltwater Moon and the King Tide? And who the fuck is Goddess Gaia?

I let out a little uncomfortable giggle, only to see Juniper respond with a look of sadness at my reaction.

"My apologies, Father and family. Please everyone, eat your breakfast." Juniper sat back down.

I avoided eye contact with her and, instead, picked up my fork and played with my food before taking the first bite. "I didn't mean anything by it. I'm just not a religious person at all, and it just made me a little uncomfortable when Noble got angry."

Suddenly, a large crow flew in, landing in front of my plate and screaming in my face. I stood up frantically and tripped backward over the picnic bench, landing on the ground and on my ass as the crow repositioned itself on the bench and continued to caw. I tried to sit up only to have the large black bird pick up and drop a dead, slimy carcass onto my stomach, staining my shirt. "You've got to be kidding me. Every fucking time."

"Missy, stop that," Juniper exclaimed. "Millie is our friend. Don't be so moody." She stretched her arm out and the crow happily perched.

I laid there and watched this creepy-ass rendition of *Snow White* in disgust and shock, but I realized I needed to play it cool. "Cute bird." I rolled myself off the ground.

"This is my Corvus, and her name is Missy. She brought you a gift to welcome you." The people seated nearby started laughing because I think they all knew a dead slimy animal was no gift. "Anyway, we are not a religious group. No matter what you have read on the internet. Why did you come out here?"

I returned to my seat at the picnic table, giving Missy extra space. "You gave me that flyer the other day, and I was curious about what you all had going on out here, so I decided to come check out the island."

"Interesting, because the flyer I gave you was for a clothing and food drive with collection drop locations in the city. So, I'm going to ask you again. Why did you show up at Westlake and why are you here on the island today?"

"You said something to me; you said something about we are all going to di—"

Juniper cut me off. "Oh, so you want to learn more about our belief system and culture here at the compound? Maybe to learn more about how you can help the needy? I mean, we aren't really taking new members right now, and it's a super lengthy process. But if you really want to help, I think that is great."

We locked eyes, and I immediately knew that we were talking about the same thing. She needed help, but she couldn't just ask for it. Now, whether that had anything to do with the murders or not, I had no idea. But clearly there was something going on in these woods, and I was going to find out what the hell it was.

"Hi, I'm Douglas." A scrawny old guy with glasses and a gray ponytail plopped down across the table from us.

Again, I couldn't help but giggle. I recognized him as the cook. I'm seeing a pattern here with the tree names, everyone I met so far seemed to be named after a pine tree. I extended my hand for Douglas to shake, which he did not. "Hi, I'm Millie."

"Where are you from?" Douglas asked, staring at my bare-ly-touched plate of food.

"I live in Seattle and just came out for a hike when I ran into Juniper on the beach. This is quite the setup out here. Thanks for including me for breakfast; you're a great cook."

"You are welcome and thank you. I'm curious, Millie. When you're in Seattle, where you say you are from, do you see yourself as an extension of God, the government, or the Earth?"

"Great question, Douglas. I guess I see myself as an extension of myself. Like if I can't be me, then who am I really? If I say I am an extension of God, then I am just a servant to a claimed higher power that I am not sure exists. And if I say I am an extension of the government, then I am agreeing to a foundational structure that still believes in the patriarchy. And well, *fuck that shit*. And if I say I am an extension of the Earth, then I am not flesh and blood and so I'm no longer human? So, Douglas, please educate me. What do you believe?"

Douglas sat with my challenge for a moment. He opened his mouth to respond when Noble approached and placed his hand on Douglas's shoulder.

"Time to clean up and start prepping for lunch, Douglas. Our guest can't stay all day, I'm sure." Noble stood tall, staring at me the entire time.

Juniper interrupted. "Father, I was hoping to give Millie a tour of our village. Millie was telling me all about the food banks and resource centers she has access to back in the city. Weren't you, Millie?"

"I was in fact telling Juniper about all the food banks and resource centers that I have access to back in the city. I would also love a tour of your sweet little village. You have created a beautiful home here, Mr. Pines," I flashed a smile. I was determined to make this man trust me and let me into their little family, at least as a distant cousin.

"Thank you, Millie. I hope you enjoy the tour, and we look forward to your kind donations. We always appreciate those who are willing to help us and the larger communities we serve."

I smiled; he smiled. We both smiled, knowing neither one of us was willing to stop smiling at the other.

Juniper pulled my arm. "Come on, Millie. If we want to see the whole village before you have to head back, we better get going."

I turned to follow Juniper in the direction of the dusty road, heading toward the village tents. Our first stop was the general store. At initial glance, the inside of the store looked like the produce section of a standard grocery store. Tables at the sides of the tent were filled with fresh veggies and throughout the middle were aisles of shelves displaying jars of canned food items; Juniper said they were canned onsite. I took another picture with my watch.

"Are you all vegan?" I pretty much knew the answer to my own question as I picked up a jar of garlic.

"Of course we are. The Earth provides us with everything we need." Juniper took the jar from my hand and placed it back on the shelf.

"Do you want to see our hospital?"

"I do! Let's go." I followed her out of the tent.

We walked into the hospital where there was a limited number of medical supplies to one side of the room and a wooden table in the middle. That was it. I pointed my watch toward the medical shelf and took a photo.

"Is this where you come if you get sick?" I walked around the empty space, stopping to survey the small blood donation machine.

"Well, no. We don't technically go anywhere if we get sick or even if we get hurt for that matter. I mean, if it's really bad, Red will come see us and she will nurse us back to health in our home."

"Okay, I see what you did there. You called her Red.' That's another type of pine tree, so I have to ask, what is up with all the pine tree names?"

"During our naming ceremony when we join the community, we become one with the Earth. It is a ceremony that is beautifully synchronized to occur when all the planets align, and the moon is full. Father Noble strips us of our birth name and honors each of us with our Pine names."

"Can you tell me more about the Saltwater Moon and the King Tide? And who is Goddess Gaia?"

We walked out of the hospital and Juniper pointed to a bench. "Let's sit down while I tell you the story." We sat on the wooden bench, which appeared to be carved from a single tree trunk. "Goddess Gaia is our Mother Earth. The King Tides occur twice a year when the moon and sun align with the Earth, then a strong gravitational pull creates ocean tides that are very large, but some are more angry than others."

I leaned in closer and whispered. "So, Gaia is everything related to our Earth?"

"Yes, but there is so much more. You see, our Native, Celtic, and Old English ancestors nicknamed the phases of the moon that aligned to each month. You have likely heard the most common name like the Wolf Moon, which is□ January's full moon. This is when our ancestors would hear the wolves that howled in hunger during the coldest month of winter. You have also likely heard of June's Strawberry Moon when the strawberries first become ripe. You have possibly heard of the Corn Moon, which signifies when the Native Americans harvested their corn."

I was mesmerized by Juniper's storytelling. "Yeah, I have heard of those..."

"Well, there are even more moon phases in our belief system such as the Saltwater Moon. Our ancestors believed that once every hundred years, the armies of gods would fight on the ocean floors and cause the ocean's saltwater to reach the moon. When this happens, the moon fills with ocean water and swells until it is so saturated that the saltwater pours down, returning to the ocean like a raging waterfall with devastating results: flooding, major damage, destruction, and even death. Millie, this is the year we are expecting the hundred-year Saltwater Moon."

My mouth fell slightly ajar as I gasped. "Oh Juniper, that sounds really scary. How are you preparing?"

"Father Noble doesn't see the danger like some of the rest of us. He doesn't see the potential magnitude of devastation that may occur if we don't prepare for the Saltwater Moon. The protection of these trees will mean nothing. But, Father has spoken. He is not to be bothered with this, and I do not want to anger him. In the end, the only protection we need will come from the depths of our mother's womb. Gaia will protect us. I can say no more." Juniper concluded with tears streaming down her cheeks.

"Why are you crying?" I wrapped two of her fingers in my gentle grip.

"Father is preoccupied with so many other things lately, so he doesn't care about what our ancestors are clearly trying to tell us—to warn us about anyways. He sees the hundred-year storm as an opportunity for himself and our community to grow. He is not always a good person, Millie. He can be quite old fashioned in his ways, especially when it comes to me."

"What is he preoccupied with, Juniper? What do you mean by 'old fashioned' and why is it focused on you? What does he want from you?" I tried to sound as empathic as possible as I rubbed my thumb along the side of her hand.

"I just can't talk about this anymore right now, Millie. Maybe you should leave." Juniper slipped her fingers from mine and sauntered off, leaving me alone on the bench. I let out a long sigh as I looked around the forest and wondered how I would find my way back to the shore and Mickey's boat.

After traipsing in circles for over an hour, I made it back to the coast. I climbed into the boat and pulled the cord to start the motor while I remained deep in thought. All the events that happened on Blake Island today kept running through my mind. My team was going to be very interested to learn all this new information.

As I shifted the boat's transmission into reverse, I looked up and noticed Noble standing only ten feet away from edge of the trees with one finger pressed to his lips as if asking me to keep my silence.

I stepped out of the boat and yelled out to him. "Do you need something, Mr. Pines?" He offered no response and didn't move. "Can I help you with something, Mr. Pines?" Still no response, but now he lowered his finger from his lips. I took a couple of steps in his direction. "Mr. Pines, is there something you want to say to me?"

Before I could get any closer, Noble turned around and walked back into the woods. As I turned back, out of the corner of my eye, I noticed Juniper looking over her shoulder at me as she walked away beside him.

CHAPTER 19

"Don't you ever cut comms like that again, Millie. Not acceptable," Cici scolded as my body bounced off the boat seat with each rippling wave. I was racing to get Mickey's boat back to West Seattle before he noticed I had taken it.

"Aww, Cici! You love me. You really, *really* love me! I'm going to hug you so tight when I get home to show you how much I appreciate all this love bombing you are—"

"Touch me and die, Millie," Cici warned. "Seriously, I will literally sign on with this serial killer to make you their next victim. *That* is how much I *hate* hugs."

"I'm pulling into the dock now. Be home by 2 p.m. Over and out, matey."

"Shut up." Cici had had enough of me, and it wasn't even dark yet.

"Shutting up and out," I chirped as I turned off my comms.

Back at my condo, I was fiddling excitedly with my watch, download-ing all the pictures I'd taken.

"So, what do you think, Trae?" I wanted to share the pictures. I was dying to show him what I'd experienced.

"I think we should wait for Cici to get here before we discuss your *little adventure.*"

Cici burst through the door and announced proudly, "I got us all a gift!" They wheeled over with a large paper bag on their lap.

I jumped up from the couch with my arms wide with excitement. "No one ever buys me gifts!"

"Seriously, touch me and die." Cici raised their hand to my face, stopping me cold before I could hug them.

Clapping excitedly, Trae ran up beside me. "What is it? I love gifts too!"

"I got all four of us DNA test kits!" They spilled the contents of the bag onto the dining room table.

Trae and I looked at each other in confusion. "Why? What do we need those for?"

"Because we need to know Mozzarella's origin story, don't you think? That way we can rule out any foreign conspiracy theories."

I nodded slowly, contemplating their logic. "That actually makes sense." Without bothering with the directions, I grabbed one of the kits, ripped it open, and started to fill the little tube with spit. Then I sealed my specimen, filled out the form and prepped the package to ship back before setting up my account online on my phone.

Wham! Bam! Done.

"That was easy!"

"I'm done too. Who wants to help me swab my pretty little princess?" Trae cooed as he tickled Mozzarella's tummy. "We got you, sweetie. We are going to figure out where you came from and maybe someday, even get you citizenship."

"I'm not fucking doing it." I walked over to the couch and sat down.

Cici rolled their eyes at me. "Give me the damn cat. I will hold her, while you swab her. How hard can this be? She's like ten pounds."

And those were their famous last words. Cici and Trae's friendship would be tested, through a shared a common goal of identifying the family origin of a long hair white Russian, possibly German, hissing kitty named Mozzarella. Cici took the firm football hold approach. Their plan was to pry the cat's mouth open on the count of three, and Trae would gently glide in the swab and swipe, swipe, swipe.

It was a good plan. A solid plan, in fact. Until Cici grabbed the cat. As soon as they went in for the hold, Cici might as well have put their hand in a river full of piranhas because that sweet baby kitty went to town on their arm like bees on honey. Trae screamed at the first site of blood, while hopping from leg to leg, still attempting to poke the swab into Mozzarella's mouth only to continually stab Cici in the cheek.

Cici screamed. I screamed. Mozzarella la hissed... in French, I think, then grabbed the swab from Trae's hand, shook it in her mouth, and dropped it on Cici's lap.

"Nice. Mozzarella just took her own test. Why didn't you two just let her do it on her own in the first place?" I asked.

Trae and Cici looked at each other, then at me. "I want to run you over with my wheelchair, Millie. A lot."

Trae tossed Cici a towel for their arm and then sat next to me on the couch. "That was so unlike my princess. She just needs rest, I think. I will drop the test kits off in the mailbox on my way to work tomorrow morning. Now, we need to talk about the real topic at hand. What happened on the island today since you *conveniently* cut us out of the investigation?" Trae said in awry tone, giving me his best evil eye.

"Yeah what happened to not taking matters into our own hands, Millie?" Cici rolled their eyes.

"Okay, here are the highlights, folks." I got up from the couch and walked over to the dry erase board and started listing my bullet points.

- Juniper, woman in the cult, met at Westlake Center

  ○ Seems kind and has a pet crow named Missy

  ○ Claims there is a hundred-year storm coming that is going to cause major damage and death

- Noble Pines, leader of the Keepers of the Pines.

  ○ Called "Father"

  ○ Very skeptical of me being around, but going to win him over

  ○ Island inhabitants have built an entirely self-sufficient community

  ○ Similar to an old western town but tents instead of buildings

  ○ Claim to be non-religious, more humanitarians

"I don't know," I continued. "I really don't see any evidence linking them to our serial killer so far, just a strong gut feeling. Plus, before I left, Noble told me to keep quiet about what I saw on the island."

Cici and Trae exchanged a concerned look.

"Millie, I'm worried about you being on that island with your comms off." Cici sounded scared. "If this Noble guy really doesn't like you there, then we need to make sure we can get someone to the island to help you if shit goes sideways."

"I get it. I do. But at the same time, I needed to be extra cautious going out there for the first time. My primary focus is to build their trust. It won't happen again. I promise."

Trae gave me a distrustful look. "It better not." Trae continued with a wink. "Because my bot boys are not waterproof. At least not yet."

"Yet? It sounds like you have something interesting in the works, Trae. Do tell!" I begged.

"Nope, I can't give away all my secrets. Just know that the boys and I are working on something that will provide protection if you get into a bind out there. But I need a couple more weeks, Millie, so *please* keep yourself out of trouble until then." Trae walked to the white board, took the marker from my hand, and drew a heart with *M + T* and *BFF* in the middle.

"You two legit make me want to puke, you know that right?" Cici ignored Trae's giggles.

I swear he does this stuff to annoy Cici.

"Okay, my turn. This is what I found out at the office today." Trae started their run down of events while writing the bullet points to the side of mine.

- Tim Lewis

  - Was seen going to lunch with Darrin Russel by one of the engineers on the network team

  - Donates books and money to the Keepers of the Pines from the library funds

    ◦ Opens his library to the group every Tuesday morning one hour prior to public hours

- Liza and Tim may be having marital problems

    ◦ Were seen arguing in her office at work

    ◦ Speculation because the actual conversation wasn't heard

Cici threw down a newspaper. "Well, here is my latest headline."

Police have dubbed this ruthless serial killer "The Body Goblin," a spokesperson from the Seattle Police Department said at their daily media conference. They also shared new information that they are homing in on a few promising leads but did not say what evidence has led them to feel confident they are on the right track. When asked if the public should be worried about their immediate safety, Chief of Police Tonya Warren said, "It is always a good idea to be aware of your surroundings and to be diligent about your personal safety, but we do not have any information that leads us to believe the public is in any immediate danger."

The reassurance from the chief hasn't put the city at ease, however. The Seattle Times spoke with Paula Flores from Paula's Pounders, who told us that she has seen a recent spike in applications for her self-defense courses to the point she has added extra classes on Sundays to accommodate the overflow. With a city on edge, everyone is wondering, who will the body goblin take next?

"We are calling the killer The Body Goblin because of their self-indulgent tendencies to take the bodies, thus not allowing the families any closure," Cici explained to us.

"Dang, this is great, Cici. So witty! I have to work tonight so I'll see what evidence I can get from the helicopter murder scene. And just so you both know, I plan to head back out to the island in a couple of days. Trae, keep working on my security plan. Cici, keep being you. You are doing great!"

We exchanged looks, proud of the progress we had made thus far. Everyone turned around as I tried to go all hands in, so I wound up nodding to no one.

My phone buzzed in my pocket. I pulled it from my jeans, my brow furrowing at the unknown number. "Huh? Trae, Cici, I'm going to take this in my room." I hurried down the hall.

"Hello?" I cautiously greeted the stranger as I sat down on the edge of my bed.

"Hey," responded a soft voice that I recognized immediately.

I smiled. "Juniper, hey! I'm surprised you're calling me. I didn't recognize the phone number; I'll have to save it in my phone." I kicked off my shoes and laid back, resting my head on the pillow.

"Is it okay that I called you? I mean, you mentioned at Westlake I could call anytime when you gave me your number. I was... I mean... I just wanted to say it was nice that you came out to the island and that we were able to spend some time together. I'm sorry I rushed off the way I did. I'm really embarrassed I acted that way."

"Aww, please don't be embarrassed. It really wasn't a big deal, and I understand why you were upset. This storm sounds really scary and the fact that Noble hasn't taken the threat seriously must be frustrating." I hoped my supportive approach would open the door for an invitation back to the island so I wouldn't have to just show up again.

"You're really sweet, Millie. I feel like I'm connecting with someone for the first time in a while. It's been a long time since anyone, I mean a woman, has taken an interest in me. And it's like you are so easy to talk to. Umm... can I ask you a question?"

"Yeah, of course. Ask me anything." Something about this woman was different. I didn't normally feel my stomach doing backflips, at least not in this weird, good way. Not in a way that made me blush uncontrollably.

"What is your favorite color?" Her giggle was so infectious, I couldn't help but giggle too.

"That's your question? You want to know my favorite color? I expected something hard. Well, okay, it's not a fun answer, but my favorite color is blue, like light blue."

"Light blue? Alright, that answer is a little different than I expected. Why light blue?"

"Because that is the color of my favorite Care Bear. My sister wasn't around when I was growing up, so I carried around this Care Bear that was hers growing up. It was my absolute favorite toy, maybe because it smelled like her? I can't believe I'm sharing all of this with you." I got teary, even though I knew Juniper couldn't see me.

"Oh, Millie, that is so precious. I've seen those bears in toy stores; what was the name of the light blue Care Bear?" Juniper seemed genuinely excited, and it made my heart race.

"His name is Grumpy Bear. Now your turn. What's your favorite color?"

"Purple."

"I don't know why, but I expected you to say green. Why purple?" I twirled the string on my sweatshirt as I waited on her response.

"Well, kinda like you, it came from a childhood memory. When I was little, my parents and I were unhoused, living in a tent city. My mom and I would go for these long walks while my dad would cool down from his angry drugged-induced episodes. My mom loved flowers and gardening. She knew the names of every flower and would point them out to me and tell me all about them. My favorite flowers were the purple pansies. I would pick the pansies and when we got back to our tent, I put them in a red plastic drinking cup with water. I was convinced the purple flowers made our tent pretty and that they calmed my dad down."

I thought I heard her voice shake. "When my parents were arrested for selling drugs and sent to prison, I came to live with Noble, who cared for me like a father would. He knew I loved purple pansies and created an area for me on the island to plant my very own flower garden to honor my mother. That was back when he was nicer."

"Oh Juniper, what a sweet story. It sounds like we both lost our parents at a young age. I'm glad that Noble was there to take you in and give you so much, but I'm also sorry that he isn't as nice as he used to be. What do you think changed in him?"

Well, she opened the door, so of course I'm going to walk in.

"I don't know. Who cares! It's probably the stereotypical grumpy-old-man syndrome. Can I ask you another question?" I could feel Juniper's smile through the phone.

"Please."

"If you could be any animal, what would you be?" Juniper was laughing at her own question.

"No! I seriously hate this question. I always feel like I'm supposed to pick a lion to be tough or an elephant to be smart when really, I'm just a raccoon who's super sneaky and adorable. Now you, what animal would you be?" I was laughing just as hard now.

"Hmmm... I would be a Care Bear, a grumpy Care Bear because then you would want to cuddle with me," she softly hummed.

We both fell silent, and I felt a charge run through my body.

"Can I ask you a question, Juniper?"

"Sure," she replied quietly.

"When can I see you again?" I needed to change the subject to distract myself from the quickening pulse between my legs.

"Whenever you want, Millie. I really like you, and I think you like me too. God, I sound like a sixth grader! But honestly, I really do like you." Her voice sounded youthful, which I found enduring.

"I really like you too, Juniper. I will take that as an open invitation to swing by and see you any time."

Why am I smiling so loud right now? Stop it, Millie!

I realized that I needed to get off this call before I got myself into trouble.

"Yay! I'm excited to see you again. Maybe we can go for coffee, or there is this super cute vegan restaurant where I would love to take you. I'm totally up for anything that sounds fun to you too." The energy coming through the phone was electrifying.

"Any of those things sound great as long as I'm spending time with you. Let's start with coffee and we can figure it out from there. Unfortunately, I should probably get going, but I'm really glad you called me."

"Hmmm, well, thank you for answering, Millie. You have my number now too, so you can call me anytime." She sounded hopeful, like I would make that next move.

"I will call you. I promise. Talk with you soon!" I hung up and took a deep breath with a long exhale.

I have this girl exactly where I want her. Holy shit! Do I want her? Be professional, Millie Myles.

I rolled over and buried my face in my pillow with a long groan.

CHAPTER 20

Walking into what seemed like a very somber team of evidence specialists, I called out to Eddie who was two tables down from me.

"Eddie! What's new, my friend? Any updates on my workload that I should be aware of?"

"Yep." He wrote something on his pad of paper.

"Are you going to share it with me?" I walked over to his table.

"Nope." He continued to write.

"Is there something you want to talk about? Seems like you might be in your feelings a bit?"

"What are our rules here, Millie?" Eddie looked up from his paper finally and turned toward me.

"Ummm... we don't talk to the police about our cases, and we eat lunch together," I recited as I narrowed my eyes at him, hoping I was right.

"And..." He dangled the opportunity for me to continue, crossing his arms.

"Pretty sure you only gave me those two rules, Eddie." I also crossed my arms in defiance.

"For crying out loud, Millie. Rule number three. You share all you know with us. If you see something, say something. That isn't just for the airports, you know. We are a team here. So, why didn't you tell me you have been getting weird phone calls?"

"So, you talked to my brother, I take it? Why follow rule number three when you have a big brother who does it for you?"

"I suppose that's true. You can ignore rule number three. Your brother tells me everything about you." Eddie went back to writing.

Heading back to my table, I gazed at the overwhelming pile of evidence from the helicopter mess. One by one, I started to go through boxes. Some contained pieces of blood-stained medical supplies. One box had headphones bagged and tagged that I assumed the pilot wore. In the same box as the headphones, there were two stethoscopes and a bunch of ace bandages.

I wonder if they were alive when they crashed? I kind of hope not. I hope they passed out before the crash or at least were already dead from the impact. That way when this psychopath didn't get to see the fear in their eyes when he took their lives, he only got to take their bodies. Which I promise, we will find.

While I logged boxes, I found a large evidence inventory log with an access code to the impound lot at the end of my table where the chopper was being held.

No fucking way!

I had the opportunity to search the chopper myself.

I grabbed my gear and ran to the bay door that led to the impound lot. The chopper was sitting on the other side of a chain-link fence gate. The air was chilly, almost like I could feel the ghosts of that poor medical team.

I unlocked the fence and circled the outside of the large machine, trying to connect with the scene as my gloved fingers ran along the metal.

I wonder if this was how my parents and sister felt after their accident. Like their souls were trapped in the car, unable to get out.

Sometimes it felt weird thinking about people I didn't know. Every now and then, I would dream about calling my sister for advice. I wondered what it would feel like to call my mom for a recipe, Mickey said mom was the best cook. Or maybe talk to my dad about the basketball game. Mickey told me how much he loved basketball like me.

I started to get emotional even though I didn't have any memories of ever being around them. Was it actually their spirits that made me miss my family or the memories that Mickey created of them for me?

I pulled on a paper gown including booties, a face shield, and gloves. The smell of human rot coming from the helicopter was so intense that I had to grab Vicks VapoRub from my gear bag and put it under my nose to temper the horrid smell.

It was eerily still outside. There was no wind or any movement to suggest that I wasn't alone. But still, for some reason, I felt like someone was watching me. I lifted my flashlight and scanned the perimeter of the impound lot. The beam of light scanned the fence line and around the parking lot, but there was nothing of note.

Shrugging, I proceeded with my evidence investigation and climbed into the chopper. My plan was simple: look for anything that the evidence team might have missed or thought to be unimportant.

I started with the cockpit, sitting where the pilot would have, or at least should have, called in a mayday. I was trying to examine the area from their vantage point. I noticed the controls had been dusted for fingerprints. Seemed standard. There was nothing unusual.

The most important evidence from the helicopter would be on the black box, and I was sure the National Transportation Safety Board investigators were probably analyzing the data that very minute.

Since I will probably never get those results, maybe Cici can obtain it through their media connections.

I continued with my search, going through every compartment, corner, and crevice.

Nothing.

I moved on to the helicopter's cabin where the medical team would have been seated.

Wow, this area is full of medical equipment and gear.

I looked around imagining the crew strapped in their seats with their headgear on waiting to arrive at the scene of the car accident.

BANG!

I covered my head as if a bomb was dropped on top of the chopper.

My first reaction was to run when the loud noise hit the roof above me.

"What the fuck was that?" I jumped out of the chopper and pointed my flashlight in every direction. "Eddie, are you messing with me? I don't scare easily. I have a brother y'know."

I walked around the helicopter slowly.

Who was out there? Asshole, I thought, shaking my head as I climbed back into the chopper's cabin.

I sat in one of the jumper seats, admiring the technology. There were so many monitors; it looked like a small emergency room, plus a gurney and two flight seats for the medical crew members.

BANG! BANG! I covered my ears from the loud vibration and jolted from my seat again, hitting my head on the ceiling.

"Okay, that's it. I'm going to kick your ass, Eddie!" I yelled as I jumped to the ground. As I moved the flashlight toward the perimeter, I caught a glimpse of someone running outside of the fence away from me.

"Hey, you! What are you doing here? You're not supposed to be here; this is private property!" By the time I finished yelling, they were just a shadow in the night. "Fucking kids!" I hollered.

As I turned, I stumbled on a rock. I bent over and spotted a pile of rocks, and one had a note secured to it with a rubber band. I removed the note and read it out loud.

"You are out of time. Maybe next time you will take me more seriously. The Body Goblin."

"Is this a joke?" I swallowed hard and stumbled back toward the warehouse. My hands were shaking, and I kept dropping the lever as I tried to open the gate. Once inside, I started screaming.

"Eddie, he was here! Outside! Watching me go through the chopper, Eddie! He knows who I am! We have to call Mickey!" I screeched as I slid to a stop in front of Eddie's desk.

"Whoa, whoa, Millie. Slowdown, slow it way down now, Millie. Who was here? What are you talking about? Tell me from the beginning." Eddie attempted a calming voice.

I tried to take a couple deep breaths, but I just spewed out what happened rapid fire. "The Body Goblin. He was outside. I was looking for evidence in the chopper when *bang, bang, bang!*" I shoved the note into Eddie's chest, and I paused to catch my breath.

Eddie read the note and started laughing. "Millie, someone is just messing with you. No serial killer is stupid enough to show up at a fully-staffed evidence warehouse to taunt the very people trying to put their ass in jail. It's just not going to happen. Who knows, it's probably your brother. But you do know you can't tell him about this, right?

What happens here, stays here. Got it?" Eddie emphasized his point by poking me in the forehead before walking away.

Jerk.

Rubbing my forehead, I went back to my table but couldn't shake the uneasy feeling. I tried to return to evidence logging but I couldn't concentrate, so I was taking my time to avoid mistakes. I put the note in my pocket to show Trae and Cici when I got home. Maybe Eddie was right, but I wasn't convinced his theory about my brother was correct. I knew Mickey, and there was no way he would pull a stunt like this. He took his job too seriously. Plus, he was undercover, so he wasn't even around.

Thankfully, the next box was a good distraction. Inside was another piece of vintage paper with more lines drawn on it and a library book on architecture.

Could this be the killer's book? Or was one of the medical crew a student? Did Tim Lewis, our very own chief librarian, have something to do with this?

So many questions, but so few answers.

I stared at the piece of paper through the thick plastic bag, puzzled. I checked the first crime scene evidence box that contained the other piece of paper. I tried to fit them together like puzzle pieces, but they didn't line up. However, both pieces were obviously torn from a larger piece of the same something. They were definitely connected. I took pictures of the book cover and the vintage paper and flipped open the book to snap a picture of the checkout slip, making note of the date so we could trace it back to whoever checked it out last.

This was the second time Tim and his library had been brought to my attention in the last twenty-four hours. He was becoming a common thread, and I didn't trust coincidences anymore. Tim may not be an innocent man, and I was going to find out what his connection was to all this.

After I tagged and bagged the book, I sat down on my stool and contemplated the evidence so far. If Noble and Tim were working together, what was their connection to one another? What could their motives be?

I considered the victims. Why these people? Were they just innocents who were in the wrong place at the wrong time? I mean, the Stone Water Games offices were the perfect locations to plan a big kill: a small group of people working in an empty building overnight. Tim's wife owned the building, so Tim would know their hours. But the medical crew? What was the possible thread to Tim and Noble? How were the victims chosen? And what is there to gain from all of this?

"Myles, let me see that note again," Eddie yelled from his table.

I walked over and handed him the note.

"Just so you know, we alerted your brother, and he asked us to pull surveillance. I saw someone out there with you. Whoever it was, they watched you the entire time. They were wearing dark clothes, including a dark hoodie covering their head. I couldn't tell their gender, height, or weight from the angle of the camera, but they definitely held an object that was reflective, Millie. Maybe a knife or a gun? I don't think your brother would show up here with a weapon. I think this sick son-of-a-bitch is watching us and ready for a fight if need be. From now on, you don't go anywhere alone. None of us do, not even to the fucking can. Got it?"

"I can't pee by myself?" I looked at him confused and slightly concerned.

"Well technically yes, you can pee by yourself... but don't go outside by yourself. I've already notified leadership about what happened tonight, and they will probably have some questions for you. I'll hand over this note to them after processing it as evidence. Millie, this has never happened before in all my time doing this job. You Myles's. You fuckers have some dumbass luck, y'know that?" Eddie walked away shaking his head.

"You don't have to tell me..." I jumped when I felt the vibration of my phone in my pocket but was relieved to see it was a text message from Mickey.

> **Mickey:** It's going to be okay, Soda Pop. Love you.

CHAPTER 21

I stepped out of the warehouse into rain mixed with sleet and winds that whistled so loudly through the parking lot, I swore I could hear someone whisper *stop looking*. The whole morning vibe felt incredibly eerie.

I decided that I wanted to visit my brother instead of walking home. It was a little over a week from Thanksgiving, so surprising Mickey with a turkey sounded like a good idea. I called a Lyft and swung by the store, bought a turkey, and continued on across the West Seattle bridge to Mickey's house.

Being early, I didn't want to startle Mickey. I slowly opened the front door, scanning the living room, but I didn't see him sitting in his recliner drinking his morning coffee. I checked my watch to verify I wasn't too early, which I wasn't. I crept across the living room floor attempting to miss all the creaky spots on my way into the kitchen to put the turkey in the freezer.

"Mickey, where the fuck are you? You still in bed, bro?" I called out, heading toward his bedroom. As a joke, I threw open his door to startle him, only to be the one who was startled when I found him in bed with Officer Palmer. "Oh my God. Gross! You're naked kissing. I'm so sorry. What the fuck, Mickey?"

"Millie, shut the goddamn door." I shut the door. Then I opened it again to see them getting dressed. I slammed the door shut again.

I yelled through the door. "Mickey, are you sleeping with my boss?"

Mickey came out of his bedroom and grabbed my shoulders. "Don't look at her as your boss in my home. She's a wonderful woman, and I really like her, Soda Pop."

Officer Palmer slid out behind Mickey. "Nice to see you, Millie. Mickey, I think I'm going to head out. Call me later, okay?"

"Nice to see you as well, Office Palmer." I tried to be polite to my boss, then pivoted and kicked Mickey in the shin.

He released my shoulders, grabbing his leg. "What the hell is wrong with you?"

"You couldn't sleep with someone else's boss? Really? I bought a turkey for Thanksgiving. It's in the freezer. I have to go." I ran out of the house and walked up to the bus stop in the pouring sleety rain.

I clocked into work one minute late. I never thought I would be late to this job, but with what I witnessed at Mickey's house earlier this morning, I was reeling.

Even though I still felt overwhelmed, I knew I needed to call Mickey and apologize.

I can't believe I was so rude about Officer Palmer, but I have to work with her!

Mickey was probably trying to protect me by not telling me about their relationship. I needed a break from him, so I didn't go back there or call him. Last night was my only night off this week, and I just wanted to be alone and collect my thoughts and focus on the case.

I left a note on the kitchen island that I wasn't feeling well with strict instructions for Trae and Cici not to bother me. I locked myself in my room until it was time to get ready for work this afternoon.

I will call Mickey at lunch.

I arrived at my desk and Officer Palmer approached me quickly dressed in her civilian clothes. "Myles! My office! Now!" She turned and walked away, obviously expecting me to follow.

I hurried after her, shutting her office door behind me. I was determined to clear the air about what happened at Mickey's house yesterday. But before I could speak, she dropped a bomb on me. "Millie, we received some alarming news today." She took a deep breath, leveling her gaze at me. "Your brother is missing."

I fell back into the wall, my knees weak, and I felt Officer Palmer guiding me to the floor. "Millie, can you hear me? Millie, open your eyes. Millie? Eddie! I need some help!"

Her face was swimming in and out of focus until I felt a few drops of water on my lips. Then, the fuzziness started to clear.

"Millie, I need you to wake up and look at me. You passed out, but it'll be okay. Can you stand up and get in this chair?" I felt her arm under my armpit as I looked to my other side where Eddie was positioned similarly to help pull me off the ground.

I was able to walk a few steps to the chair with their support before collapsing into it. "What do you mean he's missing? We just saw him yesterday."

"He didn't show up to Stone Water Games," said Officer Palmer. "And being that he is undercover, an immediate alert went out for an Emergency Request for Contact and an officer was dispatched to Mickey's home. Upon arrival, the officer found obvious signs of a struggle. They also found children's toys and clothes strewn all over the living room. We aren't sure if Mickey was bringing up boxes from the basement or if someone was looking for something in the basement." Seeing the rising panic in my eyes, Officer Palmer went on in a calm voice. "Millie, we are doing everything we can to find your brother. I promise, we will find him."

Hearing her call him my brother stung deep knowing everything I found out yesterday. I wondered if this was the decision the Body Goblin mentioned in his letter.

Is my decision to drop this investigation and let the killer go or save my brother's life?

"I need to tell you both something and I don't think you are going to be very happy with me..."

I spent the next hour telling Eddie and Officer Palmer about the notes from the Body Goblin and my suspicions about Noble Pine and Tim Lewis. I told them everything I thought might help them find Mickey. And I was right. They weren't very happy with me at all.

Officer Palmer stepped into boss mode and made it very clear that my job was in jeopardy because we had been trying to solve the crime alongside the police. This would be my only and last warning, and she said if she caught me messing with a police investigation again, I would be arrested for obstruction and tampering with evidence.

Eddie told me to stay away from Noble and Tim but he also said he was disappointed in me, which stung the most.

I promised to limit my involvement in the case—just tagging and bagging evidence, and I swore that I would immediately report any contact from the Body Goblin.

When I stood to leave, Officer Palmer grabbed me in a hug. "I really am sorry Millie. We *are* going to find Mickey and the son of a bitch who did this. A lot has happened in the last few hours, so if you need to take the rest of the night off, we understand."

"No, I want to work. I need the distraction. There's nothing I can do out there anyway." I saluted Officer Palmer, holding back tears. "Ma'am."

Instead of going back to my desk, I went straight to the bathroom. Against all my morals, I punched the handicap button to the single-stall accessible bathroom that housed one toilet and one sink. I ran inside and pushed all my body weight against the hydraulic door. As soon as the door closed, I ran to the sink and turned on the water.

For a long time. Because I'm dirty.

I slid down the metal door frame. This was all my fault because I was so fucking pissed at Mickey that I decided not to call him this morning. I missed one fucking call and this is what happened. I fucking knew it. My stomach started to turn at the same time monstrous images began to strike into my brain, one after another, like a venomous snake attacking its prey.

The room spun as fast as my mind, and I fell into another chaotic thought loop that was quickly spiraling out of my control.

Mickey stabbed... Mickey shot...

My thoughts became more gruesome, and my stomach churned more, bile entering my throat.

Please don't throw up. Please, not at work. Mickey stabbed... Mickey shot... Mickey bludgeoned... Screaming... Blood... Mickey dead.

I stood up and paced the bathroom.

I killed Mickey. It finally happened.

I walked to the toilet, then back to the door.

I can't believe I killed him. I didn't mean to kill him. This wasn't supposed to happen like this. He is all I have. All I had?

I walked back to the sink then to the door, pausing to bang my forehead on it. I couldn't breathe well.

Why does my chest feel like I'm at the bottom of a collapsed pyramid?

...Mickey stabbed... Mickey shot... No... No...No... Please don't throw up. Please not at work. Mickey stabbed... Mickey shot... Mickey blunged... Screaming... Blood... Mickey dead.

I couldn't take it anymore. I needed to go home. I burst from the bathroom into Officer Palmer's arms. I was crying so hard that snot and tears garbled my words, and I started to hyperventilate. "Mickey is dead. I killed Mickey!" I fell to the floor, violently shaking as I curled up into the fetal position.

I let Officer Palmer hold me for a few minutes. This was the first time she'd witnessed one of my panic attacks.

"This was a bad one, Officer Palmer." I looked up at her, barely able to speak around my quivering jaw.

"I see that, honey. It looked really bad, but we are going to find him, I promise." Officer Palmer sounded scared as a tear rolled down her cheek.

CHAPTER 22

*W*hat the hell is a body goblin? I mean I get the concept per se, but I had to Google the image of a goblin to see what one looked like, and I was stunned. They are such ugly little green creatures. I don't see why the media thought I fit the mold, so then, I Googled the textbook definition, which claims goblins are mischievous and resemble dwarves? In other words, the media, and therefore the public, thinks I'm an ugly green dwarf who steals dead bodies to be mischievous. I swear, the creativity of these people is pathetic. I knew I should have been like The Zodiac Killer; I should have written at least one letter to the papers to give myself a proper name. Now I'm stuck with a hooked nose on a warty, green-faced dwarf that fucks with people. So disappointing.

But if it keeps them from seeing the real me, I will go along with it. Although for the record, I hate it.

Oh, friends, I have such wonderful news to share. I have a new pet. Surprise! It's a boy! His name is Mickey. Yes, Mickey. He is the brother of my other pet, Millie. She just couldn't keep her nose out of my business, *so now I'm in hers. I have her brother, and if she wants to see him again, she is going to have to back the fuck off and give me what I want.*

Let this be a lesson to all of you. We may be friends now, but if you double cross me or get too close to my mission, I will take what you love the most in a heartbeat.

I was excited when I arrived at Mickey's house to kidnap him. My girl showed up too. For a split second, I thought maybe I would take them both, but then, some lady went running from the house and shortly after Millie charged out the door like a freight train. That's my Millie, so much energy.

But now I'm stuck with just the brother. He is refusing to talk right now, but that will change soon. I will not let some mediocre detective who has never solved a murder on his own be the one to solve the Seattle Body Goblin case.

Ugh! Seriously, that is the most stupid name ever.

So, question for all of you, my friends. What does a meathead eat? What should I feed him? I threw a French bread loaf in his cell, which he nibbled on. I also put an Italian salad in there. He didn't seem very excited about it. Cheese pizza?

CHAPTER 23

Officer Palmer put me in a Lyft home, but instead I told the driver to go to Mickey's house. I asked him to stay as I stood across the street and watched the flurry of police activity wrap up and leave his house empty. Once the last cop car drove away, I ran over and ducked under the crime scene. I needed to understand what Mickey was doing before he was taken.

Why would he be going through all my childhood boxes? Did I hurt him so badly that he was planning to get rid of it all?

The door was locked with a piece of tape across the frame to officially seal it as a crime scene. I took out my pocketknife and slit the tape and unlocked the door. When I entered the house, memories with my entire family flashed before my eyes. I didn't know if they were real or stories that Mickey had shared. I saw boxes of Christmas decorations strewn across the floor, as my sister held me up to put the star on top of the tree.

I grabbed a box marked Myles and sat on the couch. "Mickey, where are you? I promise I will find you Mickey." Tears filled my eyes.

I took in the state of the room, trying to recreate what Mickey might have been up to before he was taken. Maybe he was getting Christmas decorations out to put the tree up next week after Thanksgiving dinner. I searched the room for other clues. I noticed boxes with my name on them, their contents dumped onto the floor. Toys, clothes, and some odds and ends from my school years were scattered everywhere.

I opened the box in my lap and pulled out a collection of trinkets and family heirlooms that probably belonged to my mother or grandmother. At the bottom of the box was a manilla envelope that read death certificates. I took a deep breath because I had actually never seen this information before.

I pulled the little strings and twisted it around until the flap popped open. I pulled the papers out one by one. Each death was recorded as a traumatic brain injury, multiple fractures, and internal injuries that were sustained due to an automobile accident. I shivered. When I flipped from the last page, there was a torn newspaper article with an unexpected headline.

"What the fuck? Mia, a young mother? I don't understand." Shock washed over me and I dropped the paper, stood, and ran to the front door, locking it behind me. I jumped into the Lyft. "Can you take me to the DeCafé in Pioneer Square?"

"Yep, great place. Although that German guy is kinda weird." He pulled away from the curb.

"Why would you say something like that? Hans is so nice. What did he do that you found so weird?"

"He talks funny and elbows me a lot, just weird." After a few minutes, the driver exited the bridge taking the First Avenue exit toward Pioneer Square.

I was still offended by the way he was talking about my friend. "Well, the way you drive is weird, and you also sound like a Southerner."

The Lyft driver pulled to a stop in front of the DeCafé's front door and agreed. "I grew up thirty minutes south from here. In Tacoma."

"Like I said, Southern." I got out of the car, shut the door, and headed up the street to my condo. I always had drivers drop me off at the coffee shop because I didn't like them to know where I lived.

I entered the condo and found Cici and Trae waiting for me with open arms. I lost my shit as I dropped my backpack and ran to them, bawling. I was so glad Trae had texted to let me know Officer Palmer reached out to check on me after my panic attack. She told him about Mickey, so I didn't have to explain myself. They held me and let me cry until I was completely dried up.

"You are a really good snuggler, Cici. Let me go grab some water so I can replenish my tear bank and cry in your arms some more."

"That was a one-time deal, my friend. We have been worried about you. It's been all over the news."

I sat down on the couch and opened my water, taking a long drink. "Yesterday, I dropped off a turkey for Thanksgiving. I left work pretty upset because I got a note from the Body Goblin, but when I got to Mickey's house, I found him in bed with my boss."

Trae's eyes widened and he gasped. "No! Queen sure didn't mention that when she called me to check in on you."

I nodded quickly and continued. "I had planned to call Mickey during my lunch hour overnight to apologize, but Officer Palmer pulled me into her office not long after my shift started to tell me Mickey was missing."

I hung my head, feeling the shame from earlier.

"I had to tell Officer Palmer and Eddie everything about the case—well, almost everything. I told them about the notes from the Body Goblin and that we've been spying on Noble and Tim. Officer Palmer didn't give me any details about what the police know, and she made it very clear that we need to back off. And Eddie was disappointed in me. It was awful!" I took a deep breath. "Then I had a complete panic attack in the work bathroom and Officer Palmer sent me home. But I went back to Mickey's instead. I had to see the crime scene, you know? Then, I found a weird newspaper article, and I think Mickey has been lying to me about my family!"

Trae looked concerned. "What do you think he was lying about?"

"I'm not sure. I need more time to think everything through."

"That was a lot of information," Cici mumbled. They wheeled their chair over to the couch and placed their hand on my leg. With unexpected sincerity and seriousness, they said, "I want you to know that we are going to find Mickey. We will help you; I will help you. And when we do, we will find this killer and we will find out the truth about your family. This all hits close to home for me. Where I couldn't help my own family, I will do anything to help yours."

My heart sank at Cici's words, realizing there was so much I still didn't know about them. I didn't want to pry, but at the same time, they opened a door that felt like an offer to walk in. "What happened to your family, Cici? You don't have to answer if you don't want to, but we are here for you too."

Cici didn't move away from me, and, to my surprise, they didn't take their hand from my leg either. I took the opportunity to slide my hand over theirs. Cici looked up at me with sad eyes.

"I haven't been in this wheelchair my entire life, you know. I'm sure you both thought I had because of my mad racing skills." We chuckled.

Cici went on. "As you know, I just moved from Oregon to Seattle in the last few months. Life in Portland was good, normal. I had a partner and a family who I loved and who loved me. It was Christmas Eve when my partner and I were headed to my parent's house for dinner. I'm pansexual, and my partner is..." Cici paused and took a deep breath, "was... a trans man. We were holding hands as we walked down the street when this group of cis men approached us. They started harassing us about being queer. I wanted to keep walking, but

Jay had to be tough and stand up for us. I begged him to leave it alone, but he wouldn't, and everything escalated quickly from there." They swallowed, eyes brimming with tears. "Long story short, I ended up in this wheelchair and Jay ended up in a casket. I couldn't stay in Portland after that because everything reminded me of him. I needed a new start to a new life somewhere that didn't hold those memories. And so, I ended up here...with the two of you."

It was our turn to engulf Cici in the biggest bear hug. This was the first time Trae and I had seen Cici be vulnerable. We let them cry until they finally felt safe again. I think we all needed to feel safe again. And if these friends were my new family, we would create a safe space together... we were the luckiest queers on this planet.

Trae and I hugged Cici even tighter.

"Okay, get off of me," Cici demanded, pushing us away. "I know this wheelchair is my new reality. The doctor said I would never fully heal from the spinal cord injury. I will never walk again, but I was lucky." Cici paused looking down at their lap. "Lucky was the worst word he could have used, especially when he went on to tell me Jay had been kicked in the head so many times that he wasn't recognizable, making an open casket viewing impossible. I would never see him again." Again, Cici stopped and started to sniffle.

I didn't care; I put an arm around Cici's shoulder. They looked at me but didn't ask me to stop. Cici blew out a huff of air and continued. "Lucky was the worst word he could have used to explain my situation when I heard Jay scream for his mom. Lucky was the worst word that he could have used when I woke up from my surgery to hear the doctor say that even life support wasn't enough to keep Jay alive. At what point was I supposed to feel lucky? My world was broken."

Cici looked at Trae, then over at me. There wasn't a dry eye in the room as Cici placed a hand on each of our legs. "The two of you are my new family," they said, echoing my thoughts from earlier. "This silly private investigation business keeps me going, gives me purpose again to save lives when I couldn't save Jay's. We can't back off now. Let's get this bastard!"

I didn't want to ask a lot of questions but I needed to know if those bastards were still out there. "Cici, did the police ever catch them?"

"Yes, they got involuntary manslaughter and a bunch of assault charges. We tried so hard to get murder two, but they all swear they didn't mean to kill him, or hurt me as bad as they did, only rough us up. They will all be back on the streets in five to ten years. But as convicted felons, who will have to explain what they did to two queer people at every job interview. It will never be enough. They stole my happiness. My heart. My forever and always. My Jay."

"Pink. Bot. Boy. Love. Cici. Tissue." Trae's little pink bot peeked out from the garden room and brought Cici one tissue to blow their nose.

"Thank you, pink." Cici tickled its belly.

Suddenly an alarm went off. "High. Temp. Alert. Pink. Bot. Over-heating. Alert. Alert." The pink bot immediately shut down and went into cooling mode.

I tugged my arm tighter around Cici's shoulder and gave my all in. "Yes! Let's get this bastard and bring Mickey home!"

"How about I buy us some coffees and pastries," Trae said. "I think I'm feeling brave enough to talk to Gloria again." He giggled nervously.

We all headed over to Hans's. We were greeted by Gloria as soon as we walked through the door. It was very quiet in the café; in fact, we were the only patrons in the entire place.

"Well, hello there, my sweet tooth just got sweeter." Gloria licked her lips, looking Trae up and down.

"What the fuck," Cici muttered.

"Told ya," I murmured back.

"Trae, you go up there and talk to her while you order our food and drinks. Cici and I will grab a table in the back to give you some privacy."

"No. No. No..." Trae begged us not to go out of earshot, only to turn around and find Gloria in his face.

"What can I get you and your friend sugar lips?"

"Um... two mochas, one root beer, and three blueberry muffins." He tapped his fingers on the counter. "So, Gloria, I was hoping to ask you about Beth."

"What about her?"

"I hadn't seen much of her the last couple of weeks before she died. How was she doing? Was anything going on?"

"Trae, I will be honest, in the last six months, she really changed. When Beth would have friends over, she made me leave the apartment. She had never done that before. She was suddenly so uptight. She acted anxious and was really short with me." She placed a hand on her hip. "That's why I planned on moving out."

"How strange," Trae replied as Gloria handed him his order. Trae brought over our drinks and muffins and sat down.

"Did you hear that? Sounds like Beth was acting differently for a while. I have no idea what to do next."

My muffin looked weird. I poked at it with my fork suspiciously. The inside of the pastry looked more appetizing than the outside. I would give the muffin lady that, but she certainly didn't butter it from edge to edge.

We enjoyed our treats, lost in our own thoughts about our next steps when, to our surprise, tiny bursts of pops, snaps, and crackles erupted in our mouths.

Nice touch, Gloria. Pop rocks.

Mickey would have loved these. I chuckled to myself as I took a drink of my root beer, which made the popping even more intense. Oh, and of course the foaming liquid slipped through the invisible hole in my lip and landed on my green button-down shirt.

"Every fucking time." I dabbed my shirt with the most non-ab-sorbent napkin ever.

"Trae, go back and see what else she knows. We don't have a minute to lose. Mickey is out there somewhere I can't let him die."

"Okay, Millie. I'll try again." Trae went back to the counter.

"So, Gloria, give me more details about Beth acting differently. What else changed?"

Gloria leaned back on a stool and nodded. "I was so mad at Beth the way she treated me, Trae. But I do miss her. She had changed so much, and I don't know why. She used to love her rocks and gems, but then out of the blue, she became infatuated with these maps. I didn't want the police to take them because they seemed to mean so much to her, so I put them in my car. Those maps had become her prize possessions." Gloria gave Trae a look. "You were one of her best friends, Trae. Do you want them? I bet Beth would want you to have them."

"Maps!" Cici and I sang in unison.

CHAPTER 24

On our journey back to the condo from the DeCafé, I pulled up a voicemail from Officer Palmer and held my phone up to play it aloud so we could all listen "It's my boss, and it's not good news."

"Millie, I don't know where you are right now, but I need you to stay home, you hear me? Nothing but work and home." Her voice was panicked. "There was another murder. Jesus, Millie, I mean murders, multiple; there was another set of murders. This time it was some berry farmers out in Duvall—an elderly man, his wife, and their adult son who was living with them."

We collectively said, "What the fuck?"

Officer Palmer's voice continued. "Neighbors alerted the fire department to a burning barn and when the first responders arrived, same shit. They found the house with blood all over the place, a slaughterhouse. We think the son tried to leave a clue, wrote a message on some junk mail, but nothing confirmed yet. I will try and call you later. Stay home, Millie. You're not a Ghostbuster! Let the police do their jobs. Your brother would want me to tell you that."

I tapped End on the voicemail at the same time Cici said, "I'm going to puke; move out of my way. NOW!"

Trae moved to the side so Cici could get sick in the grass. When finished they tilted their head back against the seat of their wheelchair and let the fresh air calm them before we started moving again.□

"Are you okay, Cici? Do you want some water?" I offered.

"Yeah, water would be nice," Cici replied as they collected their thoughts. "First Mickey is kidnapped, now another murder. I just don't get it. How can someone target little old people? I bet the son surprised the killer, then tried to save his parents and ended up dead too. We need to find this bastard and when we do, I swear to fucking—"

Cici paused to gather their composure before continuing. "I'm going to beat them within an inch of their life! Just so they know how it feels. Only I won't let them die; I won't let them off that easily. I hope they feel every bit of pain I inflict on them."

Cici sat quietly for a moment before pivoting from anger to curiosity. "What's a Ghostbuster? Why did your Officer Palmer say that?" Cici's eyes were wet, trying to control their emotions.

Recognizing the subject change might ease Cici's anxiety, I answered their question. "The Ghostbusters were a bunch of old professors, who used vacuum cleaners to suck up ghosts and marshmallows."

"Is that where you got your idea for your spider safe-slayer business model?" Cici took a long pull of their water.

"Sort of, I mean the ghost thing never really worked out, but spiders are everywhere and so are vacuums. I'm still open to taking on ghost cases though." I gave Cici a soft smile.

We walked in silence the rest of the way home. Every life lost was hard, but finding out someone was deranged enough to take the life of the elderly, made it harder. We were dealing with one of the sickest people to ever walk this Earth. We had to stop this madness.

Even Mozzarella could detect the somber mood when we entered the condo carrying a box of Beth's maps. The cat didn't even hiss or take a swipe at me as I passed her kitty condo. Instead, she hopped down and ran over to Trae, doing figure eights through his legs until he picked her up and went to the couch to sit down and snuggle.

"Millie, I really don't know what we are going to do next. We have a hodge-podge of evidence and no real theories, so what are we doing here? I'm starting to think that we should just let the police do their jobs. I'm tired." Trae pulled Mozzarella up to his jawline to rub her head against his stubbly chin, which she seemed to love by her loud purr.

"Ummm... guys," Cici interrupted.

"Trae, we are not giving up. Mickey is missing. I will not stop until we find my brother."

"Millie, Trae—" Cici interrupted again.

"And I do have a plan, Trae. I'm going back to the island right after work. You just need to trust me on this one," I implored.

"GUYS!" Cici snapped at us.

"WHAT?" Trae and I snapped back.□□

Cici held up a vintage paper map that had two very distinctive missing pieces from it. Two pieces that appeared to be the pieces of evidence that sat at the warehouse from two very different crime scenes.

"Holy hole in the map, Batman, I think you solved the fucking puzzle, Cici!" I ran to the murder board and grabbed the pictures of vintage paper.

"What the hell was Beth into?" Trae dropped Mozzarella onto the couch before walking over to the table. He took the map out of Cici's hands. "This can't be real. Do you think Beth was killed for something she was involved with? Something she knew?"

"That is a real possibility." I slid the two photographs out from under the knife-shaped magnets. "Lay the map flat on the table so we can see if these two pieces fit."

Trae brought the map over to the table and did as I asked. I slipped each picture under the map and maneuvered the photos until the holes were filled, arranging the pieces where they lined up the best. And sure as shit, there was no question that the scraps of paper found at the crime scenes were the missing parts to this map. The pieces that completed the map showed a drawing of what appeared to be some sort of floor plans of a neighborhood and a city. But it could be literally anywhere. There were no street signs or shop names. We couldn't even tell what city or town we were looking at. The pine trees on the edge of the town were throwing me off.

Could this where Mickey is being held?

But believe it or not, even though they were a perfect fit, they gave zero new information about the case or what any of it meant.

"Fuck!"

Cici rolled their wheelchair into the kitchen. They opened the cabinet and reached for the chips. "The map looks familiar. I know I have seen at least parts of it before. I think I can figure out what property or land it covers. Give me some time with it. It's bugging me though. The front part looks so familiar, like a hobbit door of sorts, but definitely not a hobbit door at the same time. These cage-like bars are throwing me off." Suddenly Cici's voice was reverberating from inside the fridge, which made my muscles tighten.

They better not be thinking about another stress clean.

Cici turned around with a jar of salsa and my heart rate dropped. Trae was oblivious to anything going on around him but that damn cat, who followed him to the table. Even his bot boys were starting to notice that Mozzarella was getting more attention. I swear I overheard them plotting a strike around the herb garden the other day.

"I have a few things to take care of before work tomorrow. I will send pictures of whatever evidence I find. Cici, sounds like you are all over these maps." I pointed at Trae. "I have an investigative research job for you. I want to know what every single victim was doing on the last day they were alive. Do you think you can pull yourself away from your cat long enough to help us out? Also, we need you to keep in touch with Gloria in case she has more info about Beth. I'll head back to Blake Island soon. I want you to know that my plan is to spend the night out there, so don't freak out when you don't find me home in the morning."

I handed out those instructions like a boss, and to my surprise, everyone agreed.

Maybe I'm meant to run a PI business after all?

I walked into the coffee shop the next day for my date with Juniper and looked for a table. I had already convinced myself of all the reasons why it was okay to keep my date a secret. I had a plan, but I didn't want my friends to know that Juniper and I were meeting. They would accuse me of mixing business with pleasure, which obviously I wasn't because I'm a strong, smart, talented, and responsible almost private investigator.

I sat down at a table for two. I was fully capable of having a cup of coffee with a beautiful, funny, sweet, kind, and giving woman without sleeping with her. In fact, I barely even noticed the dimple on her right cheek that fell a quarter of an inch deeper than the one on her left cheek. I was completely oblivious to how she threw her head back with a full belly laugh when I made Dad jokes. Plus, who even cares when our breaths catch at the exact same time whenever we accidentally brush against each other? Maybe I have a bit of asthma or something.

"Hey, you!" I looked up to see Juniper walking toward the table with a blanket in hand. "Am I interrupting your deepest, darkest thoughts? Please, do share them with me." She dropped down in the seat across from me with the sweetest smile.

"I was actually thinking about you. What's the blanket for?" I returned her smile, blushing.

"Really? I've been thinking about you too, and it's a surprise." Juniper reached across the table and interlaced our fingers. "I don't really feel like coffee; let's get out of here." She raised her eyebrows flirtatiously.

"Where do you want to go? Unfortunately, I do have to work tonight." I gave her my best sad face.

"Seriously Millie, if I told you where we were going for our first date, it wouldn't be much of a surprise now would it? I promise not to make you late for work." Juniper scooted back from the table and waited for me to follow.

"Alright, let's do it then." I stood, pushed my chair in, and hurried after her.

Once outside, we started toward Pike Place Market. We continued down to the waterfront, and I couldn't help feeling deeply curious.

People liked to say it rained a lot in Seattle, but in reality, the city had a lot of gorgeous, sunny days, and today definitely did not disappoint. Juniper slipped her hand into mine, which gave me a warm, calm feeling. It had been a really long time since I had held a woman's hand.

This waterfront had so much culture, from music to vendors selling artwork, clothing, or knick knacks. As we meandered through the displays and dodged the crowds of people, a cool breeze drifted through, and we decided to grab some hot chocolates and a churro.

"Come on! I want to show you something." Juniper trotted off to the end of the pier where a large crowd had gathered. "I know a secret hiding spot that I want to show you." She pointed to the Seattle Aquarium, then skipped off with her cocoa in one hand and our churro in the other.

I couldn't help but laugh at Juniper's excitement. The feeling was contagious, and I picked up my pace, jogging to catch up.

Before we reached the back side of the aquarium, a fence stopped us. Juniper handed me her drink and pulled back a section of the fence. "Come on. Careful not to snag your shirt," she warned as we climbed through and walked along the pier to the back of the building, where we found ourselves alone on a large empty concrete platform with two concrete blocks, a few blue barrels, and some large fishing nets.

We hopped onto one of the concrete blocks, and Juniper snuggled into me and spread the blanket over our legs before she unwrapped our churro. "You have the first bite."

"Thank you. This is a nice spot. How did you find it?"

"When I was little and I would get mad at Noble or just didn't want to work at Westlake, I would run away and hide back here."

And I'm in...

I lightly interrogated Juniper. "Noble doesn't seem like he likes me much. What's his deal anyway?"

"He's just really protective of me is all. If it was up to him, I would be married to one of the other followers with five kids by now. Which obviously isn't ever going to happen." She scuffed her feet against the rock.

"So, he just hangs out at Westlake and the Island all day? Sounds like a pretty boring life."

"Oh no, in the last six months, he started going on these pilgrimages with Tim. Sometimes they are gone for a whole week."

"What do they do on these pilgrimages?"

This aligns to when Beth started acting weird.

"Honestly, I don't know. He doesn't speak of them much. He says they are to eliminate the evils of the world and return what is good. That's all I know. But then again he always says dumb stuff like that."

"So why does he have such a problem with me? I'm always nice to him. He acts so suspicious of me, like I'm coming around to cause trouble."

"Are you?" Juniper smiled.

"Of course not. I like you."

"Well, don't worry about him then." She jumped to the ground and pointed to the water. "Look! Millie, Look! There they are!"

I jumped down, trying to see what she was pointing at. "Who? What are we looking at?" I searched the bay when the water came to life.

"Your surprise, Millie!"

I stood there in amazement while a mother whale and her calf, along with two other adult orcas, passed by us. They were oblivious to the world around them, breaching before diving back under the water. The pod made life look so simple, as if swimming, eating, playing, and loving each other was as complicated as life would ever be.

Juniper stepped in front of me and wrapped her arms around my waist, pulling me close. "I don't think there is anything more romantic than sipping a cup of hot cocoa, sharing a churro, and watching a family of orcas playing in the wild. I can't think of anyone else I would want to experience this magical moment with other than you, Millie."

I can't do this. I want to do this. NO! I cannot do this. Naughty. Naughty. Millie.

"So, how did you know that there would be whales out here today? You must be magic to make this date so special." I tapped her playfully on the nose.

Did I just seriously tap her on the nose? What the actual fuck, Millie?

Juniper giggled at my awkward tap but answered my question anyway. "People have been talking about the mother and her calf all day at work. Even some of the unhoused who stopped by Westlake today for a meal knew the orcas were swimming through today. The pod has been swimming south for hours, and I was hoping we would get here in time to see them. And luckily we did." Juniper released a long sigh as she sucked in her lip. "Millie, will you kiss me?"

Undercover private investigators kiss people for work all the time, every second of the day, in fact.

"Ummm... sure. I mean, yeah. Yes." She wrapped the blanket around us both. I leaned in as her eyes closed slowly. I took my time, teasing her as I brushed our lips together before pressing my mouth firmly onto hers.

The urge to take her right there was strong, but I knew I needed to control myself. I moaned softly as her hand slid over the side of my breast, searching for my nipple with gentle circles against my shirt. The more tightly she cupped my breast, the harder my nipple grew.

My heart was pounding against her hand as she slid my nipple between her finger and thumb. I groaned deeply, throwing my head back as Juniper ran her tongue along my neck.

I started to slide my hand under Juniper's shirt when an unhoused man came around the corner, interrupting us. "You got a dollar? Some change? Something to eat maybe?"

We pulled apart quickly and silently agreed with a look that this was an intervention neither of us wanted but probably needed.

I stepped away from Juniper and gave the man *a* dollar.

"I should probably get to work."

"I'll walk you back to the coffee shop." Juniper fell in step beside me and we retraced our steps back.

"Hey, would you mind if I came out to the island tomorrow morning when I get off work? I could stay for dinner and then we could watch the meteorite shower that's supposed to come through."

"I would really like that, Millie." A fearful look crossed her face. "Some of us are preparing for the hundred-year storm of the Saltwater Moon. It's getting closer, and we're running out of time. If we're not ready, people will die." She glanced around. "I should warn you that Noble is holding a gathering for his followers to discuss preparations as well, but just in a different way. Like I've said before, we see this event very differently. I'm scared, Millie." Juniper crossed her arms and gazed into the setting sun.

"I know, Juniper. I want to help." I wrapped my arm around her waist at the same time her head fell on my shoulder. We continued our walk back to the coffee shop in silence.

CHAPTER 25

Did you all read about my last murder? It was so beautiful, wasn't it? You can't tell me you didn't enjoy it. I mean, you have stuck around this long already so something keeps you coming back for more.

Although I will say, even adult children these days are a little more... how do I say this without sounding judgmental... ummm... sensitive? Crying about his parents. How much he was going to miss them. Aren't we all going to miss someone when they die? That's life, or death, or however you want to look at it. So, I took him too.

Be strong, sir. The other side holds so much beauty and freedom. I will tell you what I told this gentleman right before I sprayed his blood across the basement walls. I said, "sad man, do not cry. Yes, I will take your body from this world but in return, I'm giving you back the soul that this world took from you." They did struggle, both physically and emotionally, but it was a beautiful moment for us all. Once it was all done, I think we all felt so much better.

Why does this warm my heart so much, you ask? Because this is an art, and I am the artist, the creator, the builder. I am his fucking savior. It just took him a few minutes to realize this, that's all.

Ugh! I have so many balls in the air. I almost forgot to give you an update on my pets. Millie is the biggest pain. I wish she was more like her brother. He sleeps a lot, is quiet, and doesn't eat much, but then again, we keep him at peace. Millie was never a part of my original plan... but she is now. She doesn't know it yet, but she won't live to see the end of this story. I will be her savior too.

CHAPTER 26

When I arrived at work, I found Eddie and Officer Palmer standing at my table.

"Millie, we are assigning you a partner to work with because this case is getting too big for one person," Officer Palmer said. "Plus, after what happened with the rock and the notes, and your brother going missing, we just can't risk you walking around here by yourself."

Shit! This will make it ten times harder to gather my own evidence and share it with the team.

"Will I still be the lead person? I'm very efficient and have been keeping up on my own. After all, I have created my own method of bagging and tagging here. I don't need someone coming in and messing up my groove." I splayed my arms across my desk.

Officer Palmer thought about this for a second. "I have been very impressed with your work and so has Eddie. I tell you what, I was going to have Bernice back you up, but I think I will instead assign Phillip to assist you.

"Phil? Ummm... he literally just started yesterday and is still in high school." He would definitely be more in the way than helpful.

"Phillip is not still in high school; he's a college student who came to us as an intern studying criminal justice. But you are correct that he did only start yesterday. Since Phillip will be here for the rest of the school semester, teach him everything you know. And Myles, I rely on this program for additional state grants, so don't fuck it up." Officer Palmer pointed her finger at my chest.

"No sir... I mean, no ma'am. I won't fuck it up. What time does he get here?" I looked around for Phil.

"He should actually be here already," Eddie responded, perplexed as he looked around. "For the love of... What the hell is that kid doing?" Eddie yelled across the warehouse at Phil who had his arms full of snacks and energy drinks. "Put that shit back in the kitchen and get your ass over here, Phillip."

Phil did as he was told and skipped over to us. "Is Phil actually skipping toward us?"□

They both responded together. "Uh, yeah..."

Neither of my superior officers could get away fast enough as Phil approached.

"Hello Officer Millie. I'm Phillip but you can call me Phil." He gave an enthusiastic hand wave.

"Hi, Phil. I'm not an officer technically, just a property and evidence control specialist. Basically, we are just here to bag and tag the evidence, Phil. Nothing more, nothing less. Got it? Just follow my instructions and you will be home by breakfast."

"Ummm... I typically eat breakfast after my shadow work, so maybe a better way to say it is, "I will be home in time for my shadow work."

I tossed around the idea that Phil was seeing ghosts.

What the hell is shadow work?

But before I could ask questions, Phil pulled a small, stained bag from his pocket and was setting crystals out on the table.

If I take the time to get to know him, I might actually understand what the fuck he's talking about.

I decided to bite. "Okay, Phil, consider me curious. What is shadow work? And why are you placing these crystals all over our work area?"

"It's simple, really. The shadow is the part of me that I ignore or may be repressed by trauma. I work to understand and uncover the shadow and once I do, I give it a proper name, confront it, and work with it. Only then can I truly start the healing process."

"Seriously, Phil, how much trauma do you have that you need to do this every morning before breakfast?"

Pointing his crystal toward the boxes of evidence, Phil paused and tilted his head at me. "Everyone has some trauma, Millie. You could probably benefit from a little shadow work yourself."

I broke eye contact and picked up the blue crystal. "What does this one do?"

Plucking the crystal from my fingers, Phil spent the next twenty minutes educating me. Each crystal was to protect us, give us wisdom, or provide clarity.

After that little waste of time, I decided to give Phil a job that would keep him busy for several hours, so I had freedom to gather the evidence I needed. "As I understand it, the theory is that Mr. Sheldon Sr. was killed in the living room while sorting through his coin collection. There must be at least a thousand individual coins here. Since we have no idea if any of the coins have significant value or meaning, you can create a new evidence sheet and log each item. Then, go ahead and put the items you log into a box, and write the box number at the top of your log sheet. Got it?"

Nodding his head, Phil turned to me with a sad look. "Do you have nightmares?"

"Not yet, Phil. I haven't had any nightmares yet. And if you stay focused on logging this evidence, then we will all have the same sweet dreams after we hear the jury come back with a guilty verdict."

I left Phil at the table covered in crystals to bag and tag each coin. "Phil, keep your eyes open for anything out of the ordinary, something that doesn't look like it should be here. Okay?"

"Got it. Because all these bloody coins are normal," Phil sarcastically replied.

As I worked through the new evidence, none of it seemed to match or make sense, which was concerning. Each box was filled with your average household items: TV remotes, pillows, kitchen utensils, books, and trinkets. The junk mail looked like one of the Seattle Underground Tour brochures I got from Hans. It said, 'ten ct BL, ten ct BU and twenty CH,' then 'help downstairs.' This must be the clue Officer Palmer was telling me about, so I decided to snap a picture and send it to my friends.

Then I found it. The clue of all clues. "Jackpot," I exclaimed softly under my breath as I untied the manila envelope: Victim: "Jason Sheldon, age 47, cell phone. Code - 1111," I flipped over the envelope, shaking my head in disbelief.

Jason Sheldon, the son of the berry farmers. I can't believe this guy used all ones as a code. That had to be the easiest code crack ever.

I chuckled as I began to untie the envelope string. I slid the phone out into my gloved hand and powered it on. I started with the victim's text messages, finding most were to his friends. He was also texting with a woman, but it was hard to tell the nature of their relationship. Nothing seemed romantic and most of the recent text messages were somber, almost like he knew something was coming. In fact, his last text literally said,

Jason: Something is coming, I can feel it.

I didn't find anything else of note from his phone, but I snapped pictures of the text messages as well as the cryptic note.

"What are you doing?" I jumped.

"Documenting, Phil. I'm documenting. How is bagging those coins going?"

"I'm done," Phil pointed to the table that was, in fact, cleared of coins. "What's next? Should I help you finish your table? You seem to be struggling." He scanned my half-empty boxes and bags.

"I have a method." I stood a little taller.

"Do you? Because your method," he said using air quotes," looks like the leftovers of a garage sale at four o'clock in the afternoon."□

I looked over my table, then back at Phil. "It's called organized chaos. In other words, every item has a place and purpose."

Phil placed his hands on my arms. "Like your life, Millie? Name your shadow, Millie. Give her a name. Free yourself from your trauma."

"Lunch time," Eddie yelled.

Giving my arms one last squeeze, Phil said," think about it," before he turned and skipped to the lunchroom.

Chapter 27

Juniper thought I was coming to Blake Island to help prepare for the hundred-year storm, but in reality, I had a mission to get inside of Noble's tent and uncover all his secrets.

I agreed to take pictures with my watch and keep my earpieces on unless I felt like there was danger in doing so. Trae and I pinky swore while Cici observed with their standard eye roll.

Mickey's boat glided onto the beach. I hopped out into the water and dragged the bow onto the rocky shore just enough to make sure she wasn't going to float away during high tide. Being out in the middle of the ocean dropped the temperature at least ten degrees, so I was glad I brought extra clothes, and I pulled up my sweatshirt hood to keep my neck and ears warm.

I stood next to the boat, staring at the one bar on my cell phone. Once again, I would only have one chance to call Mickey before heading into the woods. Two minutes passed and the time ticked from 7:59

a.m. to 8 a.m. At the top of the hour, I went to my call log and selected my brother's name from my recent calls.

It went straight to voicemail. "Mickey, if you get this, I want you to know I'm doing everything I can to find you. I will never stop looking for you. I love you, Mickey." I tapped End on the call.

I grabbed my backpack and hit the trail. Now that I wasn't distracted by a beautiful woman, I noticed there was a definite path to the camp.

The peaceful walk through the woods kept me focused on why I was here. I needed to get into Noble's tent, and I would find out where they had taken my brother and why Noble was killing all these people.

Even though ugly thoughts of the case were running through my mind, I appreciated the abundance of gifts that mother nature gave us with each step I took.

A small yellow banana slug slithered through the dirt. "Aww! Hey little guy, you should probably move off this path!" I grabbed a stick to transport it into the damp brush.

I stopped and spun in circles slowly. I swung my arms around as the cold breeze stirred up the sweet scents of cedar and florals. I admired the glimmering sunlight shining through the treetops, warming my skin. For the first time in my life, I felt like part of something much greater than myself.

Missy the crow startled me with a loud squawk.

I looked up at her. "Nothing like stealing my moment, stalker!" I flipped her off and kept moving.

Stopping short of the village, I crouched behind the grocery store. I listened for chatter before announcing my arrival. "Did you hear Noble has a big announcement this evening after dinner?" said a woman's voice.

"I did! I wonder if it's what we've been waiting for," replied another woman. They giggled with excitement. Their voices grew quieter as they moved away from me.

Oh, how curious! I had to find out what the announcement was.

I stood and tip-toed around the corner. With my backpack in hand, I made my way down the dirt road to the center of town. I searched for Juniper but didn't see her anywhere. I hoped she remembered that I was coming out today. Douglas, the cook from my last visit to the island, was sweating behind the massive grill.

I spotted Douglas moving vegetables around the grill with a large spatula. "Hey, have you seen Juniper around?"

He didn't even look up at me. "Not here, in the city with Noble," he mumbled. Douglas leaned back to avoid the smoke and ash drifting through the air.

"Is there somewhere I can wait for her?" I waved the smoke from my eyes.

He pointed to a large fire pit surrounded by wooden benches. It looked like a communal space for gathering.

Could my luck get any better?

Now that I knew Juniper and Noble were in the city, I had my chance to check out Noble's quarters.

I strolled through town, hoping I looked innocent. Since I had only visited once, I was getting curious looks from the locals, but no one approached me. When I arrived at Noble's tent, I waited until the coast was clear before I made my move, untying the bottom canvas entrance strings to crawl inside.

When I slid into his tent, I was surprised to see his modest setup. On one side, a pad on the floor with a blanket and a meditation station with a rug graced the other side. The station was decorated with candles, a statue of Gaia, incense in a pottery bowl, and an hourglass.

Then, I heard a voice outside. "I saw the woman over in this area, but maybe she left already."

"Let's go down to the shore and see if her boat is still here. If not, we should send out a search party. Noble won't like her snooping around. You know what happened when Juniper's last friend did that." He sounded frightened.

"I do, and I don't have the stomach for it again. Let's go."

I snapped a few pictures with my watch and was headed back to the entrance when I noticed a large sword laying alongside the pad.

"What the fuck is that?" I snapped another picture before I crawled out and quickly tied the canvas strings shut.

I moseyed back to the communal area and dropped my backpack on a bench, deciding it was a good time to check in with Trae and Cici.

I made sure no one was too close. Then, I whispered into my comms, trying not to look suspicious. "No one is really around today. The cook said they are all out at Westlake still. I snuck into Noble's tent. Not much in there. I will send over the pictures. I will check back in later."

Trae's voice crackled in my ear. "Maybe just lay low until Juniper comes back. The last thing you need is for Noble to catch you snooping around more than you already have. Be safe, Millie. For the record, I hate that you are spending the night out there. I really think you should just come back home, I mean you got in his tent. That is why you went there in the first place." He sounded apprehensive.

"It'll be fine, Trae. Pretend I'm going on a camping trip. On my way in, I saw a hotel tent that seemed to have a free bed, so I'll sleep there tonight. I promise not to poke around too much more. Plus, it sounds like there is going to be a big announcement tonight. I'll blend into the crowd. Remember, we have to get justice for Beth and to bring

Mickey home." Despite my efforts to reassure him, I knew if the tables were turned, I would feel the exact same way.

Cici piped up. "You two are going to have to really toughen up if you want to have a PI business that handles more than lost fucking puppies, you big fucking pussies."

"Cici, were you held much as a child? Because maybe you need to name that shadow, just saying," I snarked.

"What the hell are you talking about? Never mind, I don't even want to know." Cici went silent.

Using my backpack as a pillow, I laid down on the bench and stared up at the bright blue sky through the pockets of leaves in the trees. My eyes grew heavy as a soft wind blew across my forehead and cooled the sweat that had gathered on my trek into camp. The finch songs soothed me into a light slumber.

I had no idea how long I was asleep when I woke up to Juniper and Noble arguing.

Maybe if I pretend to be asleep, I might hear something.

"Father, I like her. She's funny, and nice, and I want her to stay. Why do you always get so mad when I bring friends over to visit?"

"Juniper, I told you I don't trust her, and I don't want her out here. She seems like she is fishing for something, and I just don't like it."

"It's not like we have anything to hide, right? Father! Right? Where are you going and why did you look at me like that? Father? Come back here! Why did you look at me that way? Don't walk away. Father..."

"Juniper, if you don't stop her from coming out here, I will. And trust me, you won't like how I do it," Noble threatened.

Noble's voice trailed off as his footsteps retreated. I wasn't sure if I should get up or continue to lay here, but the decision was made for me.

"Millie, it's time to wake up. A lite lunch will be ready soon, then we have some work to do before the ceremony tonight." Juniper's fingers tousled my hair.

I sat up and stretched my arms into the air. "What time is it?" I asked, rubbing the sleep from my tired eyes.

"Just before noon," she answered, scanning my body with a thirsty grin as I slowly dropped my arms.

"I'm never getting back to sleep tonight; I feel like I slept all day! It's so peaceful out here; how do you get anything done?"

Juniper shrugged. "I see you packed a bag. I thought you were just coming for the evening. Is your plan to stay out here tonight? If you are, I don't think sleep will be in my plans," Juniper teased as she lowered her eyes and sucked in her bottom lip.

I knew painfully well that that was never going to happen. Trying my best to ignore this rapidly rising chemistry between us, I changed the subject. "What are our plans after dinner? What does a typical evening out here look like?"

"You'll see, but first we need to prepare for the hundred-year storm that's coming in a few days...." Juniper held out her hand, which I took.

We spent the rest of the afternoon filling sandbags and stacking them three levels high on the water side of town. There wasn't anything we could do with the number of trees that surround their tiny community, so instead everyone focused on the flooding. They believed as long as their property wasn't washed away, they could rebuild.

It was close to dinner time, and Juniper took me to the showers so we could clean up. The space had a line of four curtains, each with their own shower heads. Nearby were large pumps with a pedal on the inside of each one.

Juniper smiled and pointed toward the showers. "Take your pick. We have all-natural soaps and shampoos. You just press your foot on the pedal and water will spray out of the shower head when you need it."

"A shower sounds so good right now." I hurried over and closed the curtain and began to undress, tossing my clothes on the ground near my backpack just outside.

"Millie, I should probably warn you—"

"SHIVER ME NIPPLES this water is ice cold!" I screamed.

"The water isn't heated..." Juniper giggled. "It's November and only forty-two degrees outside."

⚔ ⚔ ⚔

We arrived at dinner to find a table set for what looked like an important visitor, like the mayor was coming or something. "This looks very different from breakfast the other morning. What's the special occasion?" I took my seat next to Juniper.

"Oh, Tim Lewis will be staying at the hotel tonight after he gives a speech at the bonfire. Father plans to give him a tour of the Island."

My water glass stopped short of my lips, at the same time my mind started to race. "I thought I might stay at the hotel tonight?"

"You don't want to stay at the hotel. It's the worst tent in town. It has a lumpy bed, and only two candles. No one ever stays there, so we don't keep it up. It smells like mildew. So, I guess you will have to stay at my place instead." Juniper took a bite of a portobello mushroom bruschetta as she stared ahead with a mischievous smile.

I gulped my water down in one swallow and then refilled my glass again.

I think I'm going to need to be fully hydrated to fight off this woman tonight.

A platter of grilled teriyaki tofu kabobs with pineapple, peppers, and onions were passed to me. I added some to my plate, which was already filled with buffalo corn-on-the-cob and creamy chopped dill pickle salad.

I watched Tim and Noble walk in late like two kings and take their thrones facing the rest of us. Their placement made it easy to keep my eye on them throughout the rest of our meal. You'd think these two men had been friends for years by the way they laughed and enjoyed each other's company. They acted like old fraternity brothers. Juniper shared that Tim had only been coming around since the pandemic began in 2020. But I wondered if they had a much longer history than Juniper knew.

After dinner, at least a hundred people gathered at the center of town to listen to Noble's teachings, as Juniper called them.

"There are a lot more people here than there were at dinner," I noted. Several people looked like they hadn't showered or shaved in a while.

"Those men are true woods men. We refer to them as the elders of the woods, our protectors. They don't sleep in shelters or eat from our gardens." Juniper pointed to a man with a gray T-shirt that I assumed was once white. "That's Elder Limber. He is ninety-two with no signs of slowing down anytime soon. Fair warning, you might not want to get too close to those guys if you want to keep your dinner. They haven't showered in decades." Juniper waved her hand in front of her nose.

Behind Noble and Tim, a large fire crackled and burned so high that we could feel the warmth even though we were at least ten feet away.

Noble rapped on a bongo drum to get everyone's attention. "Thank you all for being here, together, as a family. I, your father, have a message from our Goddess Gaia. I have spent many months, days, and hours meditating, asking our Mother Earth to tell us her wishes and to guide us through her spirit. She has come to me through the light we seek and has asked me to honor the Saltwater Moon with the greatest and largest naming ceremony yet. I will be naming one-hundred new followers on Tuesday evening, and I want you all there to bear witness to this massive event."

Cheers roared through the crowd as Millie grabbed my hand and squeezed. I looked over at her to find her eyes wider than I had ever seen them.

I turned my attention back to Noble. "I brought Tim here tonight to share in this moment because you all know that we've been on many pilgrimages over the past few months, hand selecting new followers, although some of these sad souls unfortunately just didn't make the *cut*." Noble and Tim turned to each other and began to laugh uncontrollably.

Noble continued. "Thank you for being here, Tim. It is always an honor to share our home with friends, with those who hold the same values as we do, our values of love and caring for the less fortunate. Welcome, Tim. All, Tim would like to say a few words this evening."

Contemplating the crowd while he paced, Tim looked as though he was about to give a TED Talk.

Obviously not his first rodeo.

"Thank you for the warm welcome, Noble. And thank you all for inviting me into your sacred space. Before I arrived today, I debated whether I should tell you all about my history. I grew up impoverished myself and that's why I was attracted to the Keepers of the Pines and your mission. At first, I thought no one would want to hear a sob story, but then I realized that to gain your trust, it's important that you all know where I came from and why I'm here now. I promise to keep it short."

I looked around the crowd to get a feel for everyone's reactions. The audience sat with their legs crossed, hands in their laps, and they listened intently.

If this wasn't a cult, I don't know what the hell is.

Tim went on with his speech about how he came from poverty. At one point Noble embraced Tim while he wept. Tim explained that his only escape was his love of books. He went on and on. I was getting tired, and right before I was about to fall asleep, I noticed Tim was limping.

What happened to his leg? Maybe a fight with a victim trying to save themselves?

Just as Tim turned toward me, I snapped a picture with my watch. I noticed a red shimmery object slide from his unbuttoned shirt.

Is he wearing a blood drop as a necklace? This man is walking evidence. I need to figure out how to tag and bag him.

Tim walked past me. "From that day forward... the library saved my life." Tim stopped. "As the chief librarian of the Seattle Public Library system, I'm now giving back what was given to me. In addition to my ongoing donations of time and books, I will be making a personal monthly donation of one thousand dollars, indefinitely, to Keepers of the Pines." Tim pulled Noble into a brotherly hug.

This trip to the island has made one thing clear: Noble and Tim are involved in these murders. Mickey told me they had Noble on their radar. Now I could see why.

I applauded with the crowd as I leaned over and whispered into Juniper's ear. "What will the money be used for?"

"Seed, materials, gas for the boats, maintenance for this place. Typical upkeep expenses so we can stay in business. This is just the beginning Millie," she whispered back.

"Everyone, please make your way back to the dining area for drinks, dessert, and dancing to celebrate this joyous occasion and to say thank you to our good friend, Tim."

Juniper seemed to have no interest in the evening events. "I can't listen to any more of this. More followers, and Noble doesn't care that the hundred-year storm will be so powerful it will kill us all. He just wants to bring more people to this island. I think I just want to go home."

"Me too. We can skip the dessert." I smiled at Juniper.

I think I gathered all the evidence I came here for...

CHAPTER 28

I tried to keep my cool while we walked back to Juniper's tent.

Just keep your distance, Millie. Okay, no big deal, so our hands just touched. In all fairness, I wasn't a science major. I'm not an expert on how the laws of motion work, but there's probably one involving the magnetic forces pulling two women's hands together... I can't do this...

She interlocked her fingers with mine. I had no idea how I was going to avoid this overwhelming sexual pull between us. And honestly, I wasn't sure if I even wanted to.

When we arrived at her tent, the first thing I noticed was a beautiful mosaic bird bath in the shape of a daisy just outside the entrance. "This is so pretty. Did you make it?"

"I did, actually. I put pieces of food and peanuts in there for Missy, and she leaves me all sorts of pretty trinkets like coins, buttons, and even jewelry."

"Oh, that's nice of Missy." I smiled as I stepped onto the pallet that served as her front porch. I studied an unlit torch. "Do you want me to light this for you?" I dug into my pocket for the small box of matches I nabbed off the counter at Hans's coffee shop.

"I love that you want to take care of me. Shoes off before you come in," Juniper requested before leaving me outside to light the torch. But this favor for Juniper wasn't just out of the kindness of my heart. It was also a ploy so I could catch my breath and ask the universe to throw me a bone.

I bowed my head. "Okay, almighty pines, conifer, or whoever the hell you woodchuck, mother fuckin, leaf-loving, branchy son of sapling hole you are. You better get me through this damn night without selling my soul to some saltwater moon god, got it?" I opened the matchbox.

I slid the first match out of the box and pulled the sulfur along the sandpaper, igniting a small flame. I stood on my tiptoes to reach the torch wick, but the wind blew out the match.

"Shit." I took out another match and struck it again, but this time, the match snapped in half. "You've gotta be kidding me!" I exclaimed and opened the matchbox to find there was only one left. This time, I used less force and then carefully raised the match towards the wick, protecting the flame and moving very slowly.

"Ouch!" I jerked back and instinctively shook the match, which immediately extinguished. "Fuck! I burnt my finger." I sat on the edge of the pallet in defeat. "All those years in Girl Scouts, and I still don't know how to use fire."

"Millie? Who are you talking to out there?"

I stood up quickly and stepped inside. "I was just talking to myself. I couldn't get the torch lit. I think it's..." I raised my eyes, and my jaw dropped. Juniper was lying on the bed in nothing but a sheet.

I should really be trying to get out of this situation.

My breaths quickened as she slid the sheet off one of her breasts and started to lightly circle the tip of her nipple with her finger. My body tingled as my eyes searched every inch of her body, which was outlined perfectly by the glow of more than a dozen candles.

Every inch of her beautiful, voluptuous body waited for me as her hips gently moved back and forth begging me to climb on top of her.

"Ummm... what are you doing under those covers?" I sucked in my bottom lip as her hand caressed between her legs. "I could lend you a hand..." The throbbing between my own legs was getting stronger. The light humming of her moans grew louder the more she pleasured herself under the sheet.

"Well, what are you waiting for?" Juniper smirked as she scooted to the bottom of the bed and grabbed the front of my jeans, pulling me toward her.

Wasting no time, Juniper unbuttoned my pants, and then she slowly lowered my zipper. Her gaze met mine, making sure we were on the same page where this was going.

I smiled while I removed a strand of hair that had fallen across her lips. She gave me a playful smile in return before she pulled my finger into her mouth and started to slowly suck, never unlocking her eyes from mine. I felt Juniper's hand slide up my shirt, her mouth let go of my finger as she moved down to kiss my skin with fervor. A strong pulsating sensation grew in my chest and my core with every touch of the tip of her tongue.

But as soon as she started to slide my jeans down my hips, I began to have second thoughts. I placed my hands on her shoulders, halting her movements, walked over to a small couch and sat down.

I needed a minute. I wasn't sure if I could do this. I was an almost professional private investigator, after all. I tried to measure my logical thoughts against my physical desires, but the heat rushing down the center of my body was winning against my logical side. I knew damn well this was exactly where I wanted to be.

Juniper didn't hesitate to follow me, rightfully confused. "Don't you want me, Millie?"

"I do, Juniper." I held out my hand to draw her closer.

She spread her legs and straddled my lap. I gasped when I felt her wetness as she lowered her body onto my fingers. I parted her with my thumb to find her hard clit waiting for me. Juniper started to grind her body against my hand while my thumb rolled over her flesh. She quickened the thrust of her hips against me as my fingers found the perfect rhythm deep inside her.

Our eyes locked and Juniper slowed, still gently rocking her body. "I love the way you feel inside of me. I don't want to come yet, but I don't think I can wait."

"You don't have to." I smiled deviously and ran my tongue along the center of her chest, and across her soft skin to take her breast in my mouth. With a long suck and pull of my teeth, I twirled and teased her erect nipple. Juniper started to ride my hand faster and harder. Her breaths quickened followed by a pleasurable groan with every nibble I took. I slid my fingers out of her to give her some reprieve, but she stopped me.

"No, please don't. Stay inside of me. Fuck me, Millie. I'm going to… ahhhh…"

I didn't hesitate. I pushed back inside her as I flexed my fingers against her wall. Her body clenched around my fingers, and her silkiness lubricated my hand as she orgasmed. "Ahhhh. Harder… ah-hhh—" Juniper panted heavily as she grinded harder and faster until her head dropped to my shoulder.

I kissed Juniper's chest. Then brought her lips to meet mine. I was so hungry for her. I opened her mouth with the tip of my tongue, and she softly bit my lip before sliding her tongue into my mouth. Our lips pressed together so feverishly that I swear we forgot to breathe. I was getting wetter by the second.

She pulled away from me and stood, taking me with her. "Let's get these clothes off you, shall we?" I didn't argue.

Juniper took her time undressing me. This time, I didn't stop her from removing my jeans and underwear. Then, she pulled my shirt over my head, gliding her hand around my chest to unsnap my bra. When she slid my bra straps from my shoulders to expose my breasts, she let out a soft moan.

"You are so beautiful, Millie." Juniper licked one of my nipples, which sent a shock wave through my body.

When I was completely naked, Juniper gently pushed me back to sit on the couch. I felt like I was overheating when her thumbs gently pushed on the insides of my knees, parting my legs. She slid each hand up the inside of my thighs.

"Is this okay?" Her eyes met mine.

"Oh my God, yes. Please touch me," I begged as I dropped my head against the couch cushion.

Juniper settled her torso into my core. I tried to reach out to touch her cheek, but she pushed my hand aside. "No touching. It's your turn." Juniper pressed her naked body into my center.

She took her time kissing along my neck, stopping at my nipples to suck one while she played with the other. My body tensed with pleasure, my nipples hardening in response to her touch. Juniper moved to my stomach, then the tip of her tongue skimmed my skin, before reaching the inside of my thighs.

She paused, "Can I taste you, Millie?"

Professional private investigator... in training.

"Yes... please... yes!" Juniper started to kiss the inside of my right thigh. I was already going crazy when her lips traveled up to my center. I was *so* wet... I tipped my head back and pulled a pillow over my face as soon as her hot breath and the flick of her tongue stimulated my sensitive clit. A mini orgasm jolted my core. "Juniper, what are you doing to me?"

"Mmmm... I'm just getting started, baby." She wasted no time sliding her tongue inside me, from my center to my clit, which she took into her mouth.

It felt like we had done this a thousand times as my hips moved in perfect rhythm with her tongue. The way she sucked and played with me, made me want to scream. I loved the way she fucked me, and I didn't want it to end, but I couldn't hold on. I came hard, my vision darkening at the edges, as if I might pass out.

I lowered my gaze to find this breathtaking woman resting her chin on my stomach, smiling back up at me.

Juniper rose from the floor and walked over to the bed. "Come to bed with me?" She lifted the sheet. "Come on?" She gave me a devilish grin as she waited for me to make the next move.

"You are so beautiful." I was completely mesmerized by the way she returned my stare. If I was reading her right, I was in for an unforgettable night. "What am I getting myself into?" I moved toward the bed.

"Lay down," she directed as she ran her finger over my hard nipple.

I didn't argue. I laid down, giving her my full trust.

What was I thinking?

Juniper opened the drawer of a small dresser next to the bed and pulled out two pieces of silk fabric. "Do you trust me, Millie?"

I watched her, following the shiny blue fabric with curious eyes as she ran the cool silkiness ever so lightly along my skin. With every pass across my center, my hips rose, craving touch, "Do you trust me?" She asked again.

It was like I was in a trance. "Yes."

Never letting the silk fabric leave my body, Juniper flowed it down my right arm and took my hand. She tied it loosely to the bed frame. "If at any point you want to get out, just pull. The fabric will come undone. We should also pick a safe word."

"Hmmm... Juniper?" I tried not to giggle. I'd never picked a safe word before.

"Oh baby, you're going to scream my name all night long. You need to pick something else."

"Ummm... how about bear?"

"Bear?" She looked confused.

"I don't know. We are in the woods." I smiled sheepishly.

"Okay, but if everyone in the village starts running into my tent, you might have a lot of explaining to do," she warned with a shake of her head and a smirk.

"No one is that close to your tent," I pointed out.

She moved to my left side and tied my other wrist in the same manner. I felt safe and so fucking hot. Juniper climbed onto the bed, kissing every inch of my body until she reached my lips. "Do you want to taste me?" Her breaths quickened as her thigh pressed against my hard clit.

"Yes, so bad..." I could barely catch my breath as our mouths pressed together, and Juniper started to grind against my center.

Resting her forehead to mine, she pushed hard against me, I was getting more aroused the more her body slid against mine. "Tell me how much you want to fuck me, Millie."

"I want to fuck you so hard. Come up here and let me taste you."

Juniper brought her body up to my chin and placed her knees on either side of my head. She lowered herself onto my tongue where I took her into mouth.

I tore my wrists from the restraints and grabbed her ass as I twirled my tongue around her clit, flicking her throbbing flesh, and sucking her while she begged me for more.

"Don't stop, Millie, faster, harder, don't stop." I knew I hit her perfect rhythm when she began to thrust harder against my mouth and let out a long moan of pleasure. As the orgasm hit her, I could taste the evidence of her excitement that coated my lips.

Juniper collapsed by my side, pulling the sheet over us. We turned toward each other and smiled, exhausted.

"Oh my, Millie. I have never... felt... so connected to someone... and such an out of body feeling before. I can barely speak." Juniper's smile fell. "I mean, that felt so... amazing."

Closing her eyes, she softly traced small circles along my chest. I shivered, goosebumps rising on my skin.

"You are staying the night, right? Sometimes people leave. I want you to hold me. I want to fall asleep in your arms. I don't want you to leave in the middle of the night. Will you stay with me until the sun rises?"

For some reason, I felt like Juniper was scared to be alone. I brushed strands of hair behind her ear. "I'll be here when you wake up. I promise."

I woke to the songs of the sparrows and finches.

I sighed contentedly, but guilt clogged my throat at the same time. I had sex with someone I cared about, but I was also using her as an informant. My feelings felt real, and that scared me.

I slid out from under Juniper's head and got dressed. I peeked out the window. The sun shone brightly, and the smells of the morning dew flowers filled the damp air. I took a deep breath. I felt better than I had in a long time.

Was that a good thing, though? *How much of my heart am I putting on the line when it comes to Juniper? She'll be devastated when she finds out that I'm the reason Father Noble goes to jail.*

Then I had a ridiculous thought, and I chuckled.

But maybe she will want to come live with me and start a new life. What the hell am I thinking? I'm so close to being a professional private investigator.

"Good morning, beautiful." Juniper's melodious voice startled me, and I turned around to see her putting on a green fleece robe. "Would you like some coffee? I could make us some."

"I must have been in a completely meditative state over here because I didn't hear you wake up. Yes, thank you, coffee sounds really good. I was just going to step outside to listen to the birds. Would you like to join me?" I opened the tent doors to see Missy had left Juniper a gift. "Aww, your crow left you an earring."

I went to put on my shoes and found that Missy had left me a gift as well, a burnt piece of coal.

I really don't care for Missy. We are obviously fighting for the same woman's attention here.

I watched Juniper making us coffee through the open doorway. "I have to get back to the city, but I promise I will come back out and see you soon, okay?" I tried to sound reassuring. I didn't want her to think she was just a one-night stand, because she wasn't. But by the look on her face, I wasn't very convincing.

"Well, I hope I get to at least see you before the King Tides," she said dismissively as she handed me my coffee and went back inside.

I followed her. "I'm not trying to downplay the seriousness of the coming storm, but I mean, we have King Tides twice a year, and, for the most part, they are pretty harmless as long as people stay out of the water." I sat down next to her on the bed, placing my coffee on the nightstand.

"You just don't get it. It's a prophecy, Millie. It's happening and whether you believe it or not. There's a good chance that a lot of people will die. I just hope that we get to see each other again before that happens. That's all I was trying to say." Juniper laid her head on my shoulder and continued. "Because I'm going to miss you..." She sounded sad.

I kissed the top of her head before lifting her chin and looking deep into her honey eyes. "I'm not going anywhere, Juniper." I brought my lips to hers and parted them with my tongue as I untied her robe.

I watched her pupils dilate. "My God, Juniper, you make my heart stand still when you look at me like that." I spread apart the opening of her fleece robe, exposing her breasts. I groaned softly

Guess I'm not going back into the city anytime soon.

CHAPTER 29

I prepared myself for a lecture on my way home because of how late I was. Plus, I turned my comms off again, and everyone knew Cici would be upset. The front door flew open before the key was even in the lock and I was assaulted with dirty looks and ridiculous comments.

"Welcome home, so glad you're not dead. How was your slumber party with the stick people?"

Trae didn't hesitate to join in on Cici's condescending comments. "Yeah, how?"

Cici rolled their eyes. "Whatever, let's just get back to work." They wheeled over to the couch. "Millie, did anything come out of last night? Or did we waste our time and emotions worrying about you? Are we ready to leave that little cult alone and move in another direction?"

I didn't hear Cici's question because I was distracted by images of Juniper's soft skin and curvy hips pressing against my body. "Huh? What did you ask me?"

Cici gave an annoyed huff. "I asked if we are ready to stop going out to the island? Are we wasting our time? What the hell is wrong with you, Millie?"

"Absolutely not! Tim Lewis was out there last night." I walked over to the murder board and placed Noble and Tim's pictures next to each other. "Noble all but admitted that he and Tim have been recruiting new followers for a massive naming ceremony under the Saltwater Moon." I did air quotes. "But some of the recruits didn't make the cut. Sounds pretty ominous if you ask me. Also, I helped Juniper prepare for the hundred-year storm. They are *convinced* that it will cause major flooding, severe wind damage, and many deaths. All from the *Hundred-Year Saltwater Moon*."

Now, invested in the conversation, Trae put down his phone. "So, what happens during this Saltwater Moon?"

I lowered my voice, setting the mood and told Trae and Cici the same story that Juniper told me. Trae leaned in when I described the gods fighting on the ocean floor, and he hugged Mozzarella tightly when I got to the part about a King Tide so large that all the ocean's saltwater ended up on the moon.

"Then what happened?" Trae buried his face in the cat's fur.

I stood up and splayed my arms across the room as I explained that the moon was unable to sustain the saturation from the ocean water, so it turned to rainwater pouring back to the earth like a raging waterfall and everyone died.

"Yep, this is *the year* of the Hundred Year Saltwater Moon." I sat back down on the couch.

Trae swallowed hard. "Millie, when is this storm going to happen?"

"Two days, with the next full moon." I held up two fingers for emphasis.

We all jumped when my phone rang. I grabbed it off the coffee table when I saw Juniper's face on the screen but fumbled while trying to slide the bar. "Hey you, what's going on?" I was as peppy as I could be considering we were all just talking about her.

"I'm calling to ask if you wanted to go to a movie with me?" She giggled softly. "I feel like we left things on a somber note, and I don't want you to think I'm no fun," she whispered.

My smile couldn't have grown any bigger. Trae and Cici eyed me suspiciously. "I certainly don't think that. I would lov—"

Whoosh!

BANG!

Something heavy thudded to the floor of the garden room. We all jolted and screamed following the loud crash.

One of the bots set off an alarm "Intruder. Intruder. Intruder. Yellow. Bot. Boy. Scared."

"What the hell was that?" I shouted. "Trae, it came from your garden." Trae and I ran to the closed garden room door.□

"I will have to call you back," I told Juniper and hung up.

"Millie, you open the door," Cici instructed.

"No! Cici, *you* open the door." I positioned their wheelchair in front of me.

"Really? You two assholes are going to have the person in the wheelchair open the door to find a murderer waiting to kill us all?" Cici scoffed with their arms splayed out in disgust.

Trae and I contemplated this for a moment before I pulled Cici back from the door.

"Ugh, fine, I'll do it." I cracked the door just enough to peek inside when Cici knocked it open so hard it slammed on the inside of the wall.

We rushed into the room to find all the bot boys hiding in the corn field with their little robot arms covering their beady red eyes. They were obviously shaken up. On the floor next to the garden was a busted-up pot with soil and a few garlic plants scattered across the floor.

"Was that the pot you had sitting on the windowsill?" I looked back at Trae while I kneeled to inspect the mess. That's when I noticed a brick with something taped to it.

Before I could piece together what had happened, Trae gasped, "My babies! Look what they did to my babies! Wait until I get my hands on that son of a bitch. I'm going to tear him to pieces—" He fell to the ground and started to scoop the soil back into the pot.

I grabbed Trae by the shoulders. "Trae, pull yourself together, man. It's one garlic plant! Okay, four, but it's just garlic. What we should be more concerned about is the fact that *someone threw a brick through our window*! Thank God the window was open."

We circled the brick. "Should we read the note or bag it and take it to the warehouse to check for fingerprints?"

"I mean, it's not addressed to the warehouse," Cici said.

"And it wasn't thrown through the warehouse window."□ Trae also had a valid point.

I picked up the brick and tore off the slip of paper. "All good points. Plus, it's my letter and I shall read it."

Millie,

You have something I want, and now I have something you want. One day every murderer will eventually come face to face with their captor, but you and I will be different. We will look each other in the eye, and you will be forced to make a decision that will change the course of your life... or death.

The Body Goblin

(I hate that name, by the way; it's dumb).

Cici ripped the note from my hand. "What the hell does that mean?"

I sat down on the end of the futon in a daze. "I fucking hate riddles. This is a riddle, right? When it doesn't make sense?"

Trae snatched the note from Cici. "Nah, it's not a riddle, but I do think it's proof of life. It sounds like they are saying they have Mickey. I read this as you will have to either give them what they want, or Mickey will die. But what do they want?"

"You really think so?" I popped up and started to pace around the room nervously. "So, you think this means Mickey is alive? Do you think I will have to fight the Goblin? Because I fucking will."

As I spoke these words aloud, I stopped pacing and slid into my jujutsu position to execute my best in air chop, chop, undercut, swipe, high kick move, only to land flat on my ass on the floor.

Ignoring my fall, Trae looked over the note more closely. "We have to show this note to Officer Palmer. We can't keep this to ourselves. This is not something to take lightly. It might be a good idea to get someone to watch the condo in case this creep comes back."

"I don't disagree, but before we do that, let's try and see if we can figure out what they want from me. Maybe they are taunting me, and this is just another layer in their sick game. If we call the police now, then we risk this person not coming anymore, and we lose our angle. And yes, I know how insane I sound. But if the killer's goal was to get my attention, then let's see what they think I have."

Cici took a deep breath. "I can't believe I'm actually entertaining this. What were you thinking?"

I grabbed the pad of paper and pen from the potting station, which set off the red bot's alarm.

"Alert. Thief. Thief. Alert. Thief. Cici is a thief. Alert."□

Cici threw their hands in the air. "Go to hell you little Coke-can wannabe."

"No. Touch. Cici. My. Love. Human." The pink bot knocked over the red bot, before Trae could break them up.

Trae and I looked at Cici with concern.

"Pink. Bot and I are growing closer, so what?" Cici shrugged.

I shook my head and started to draft my response to the killer's note.

To The Body Goblin,

(I like the name. It seems appropriate.)

If anything happens to my brother, I will hunt you down. What do you want from me? I have nothing to give you.

Millie

I taped the note to the brick and tossed it back out the window before either of my friends could stop me, and it landed with a loud crack on the sidewalk.

We watched the brick for what seemed like forever, hoping to catch sight of the killer retrieving my note. Trae was the first to call it quits.

"Can we find something more productive to do? I can't sit here and stare at a brick all night. Cici, do you want a ride to the paper in the morning?" Trae offered.

Cici turned their wheelchair around and headed toward the door. "No, I'm taking the day off to go pull some maps from the library's collection and see if I can compare any of them to Beth's map. I want to find that hobbit, cage-looking doorway. So, if you all wouldn't mind giving me and the bot boys some peace and quiet, I would like to get some rest." They held the door open for me and Trae to leave. "Night, all."

We left the room, and I walked up to the murder board, pining the note. When I looked back at the garden, Cici had already shut the door. "Trae, who do you think is doing this?" I pulled Noble's picture from the board.

Trae pulled down Tim's picture and set it alongside Noble's on the table. After a few moments studying the pictures, I looked at Trae. "I have an idea. I want to talk through what we know but not from the perspective of our evidence and suspects. Instead, let's talk through what evidence is *not* up here and *who* might be missing."

Trae grabbed a knife magnet and pinned the picture of Tim back up. "Love it! Where are the gaps or holes?"

"Of course it's a good idea! I'm a private investigator. Almost. Maybe someday."

We sat on the couch and looked at the board again, taking in the evidence broken down by the crime scene.

Crime Scene One: Stone Water Games

Victims: Stacia Petersen, Stan Smith, Darrin Russel, and Beth Weber

Evidence:

1. broken pieces of pottery

2. candle wick

3. broken pieces of colored glass

4. pine needle

5. rope

6. piece of a map

7. blood samples

8. discarded clothes

9. dirt samples

10. Flyers

Crime Scene Two: Helicopter Crash

Victims: Laurie Jordan, Casey White, and Monica Gordon

Evidence:

1. piece of a map

2. library book on architecture

Crime Scene Three: Sheldon Family Home

Victims: The Sheldon Family – June (mother), Troy (father), and Jason (son)

1. Text message: Something is coming, I can feel it.

2. Note written on a piece of junk mail: "Help downstairs"

Suspects:

1. Tim Lewis

2. Noble Pines

3. Gloria, The Cake Baker

4. Unknown

We collectively took a deep breath and at the exact same time uttered, "Well, what's next? Jinx!" We quickly pointed at each other, giggling.

Confidently slapping my hands on my knees, I stood and glanced at the board. "Well, obviously, we can take Gloria off the list. I really can't imagine she killed anyone. Because seriously, she could barely flirt with you without needing to catch her breath. How could she possibly kill a bunch of people and get rid of their bodies?" I took her picture and tossed it aside.

Trae stood and joined me. "Yeah, I agree that Gloria isn't a suspect. But I do want to chat with her a little more because I feel like she knows Beth better than anyone. I'm going to a party she's catering tomorrow and plan to dig in more on Beth's comings and goings the last few days she was alive."

"That's great Trae. Anything else of interest?"

"I'm putting together a report on the victim's last days. I just have the helicopter crew left."

"Maybe I will just vacation out on the island and let you take over this mess." I ribbed Trae a bit as I removed the blue string between Tim and Noble and replaced it with an orange string to signal that the lead was getting warmer. "I still have this feeling there is someone we're missing, don't you?"

After a bit more contemplation, Trae yawned. "Maybe we should call it a night." I paused and took a deep breath. "Trae?"

"Yeah, baby girl?"

"We're going to find Mickey, right?"

"Like I would give up Detective Hottie," Trae scoffed.

"That's disgusting, Trae. He's my brother."

Trae smiled supportively. "We'll find him. I promise."

Trae stood up, then gathered Mozzarella from her perch and went toward the hall. He stopped short of his bedroom door and turned. "I have a feeling the Body Goblin is going to keep talking to you. I just really hope no one else gets hurt in the process. I mean, me and you, Millie. We can run or fight. But Cici? How can Cici defend themselves if we're not around?" He nodded toward the murder board. "Think about that, okay?"

Dropping onto the couch, I laid my head back and stared at the ceiling fan rotating slowly above me. With each wobbly turn, I always expected it to have fallen on my face, but it never had. The fan blades resembled my life right now, moving slowly, getting shakier with every turn, and getting more fucking out of control. But they don't fall. Like me.

A thought popped in my head: *It's only 9 p.m. and the DeCafé doesn't close until ten. Maybe I will go see if Hans has heard anything else from his patrons.*

I stood, grabbed my jacket from the coat rack, and headed out the door and to the stairwell.

I will stick to the main streets. There's plenty of foot traffic at this hour, so the Body Goblin would be an idiot to confront me now

I took note of the brick with my note taped to it on the ground as I exited the building.

If the note is still there when I get back, I will take it upstairs. No need to scare the public.

The familiar bells rang as I pushed through the DeCafé's heavy wooden door, and I felt a warm comfort that I didn't expect but immediately embraced. It was nice to be someplace safe after the weird night we had at the condo.

"Hi ya, Hans, how's it going?" I walked up to the counter to scan the menu.

"Millie, *wie geht es dir*?" Hans greeted me as he wiped the counter before tossing the rag onto his shoulder.

I placed a five-dollar bill on the counter, and I attempted a guess at what he had said. "Well, if you asked me how I'm doing, I'm average, not good and not bad. I need to get some sleep tonight, so just water for me."

Hans poured fresh coffee grounds into the machine and selected Start. I could hear the water start to boil, and I shook my head because I knew what he was going to say.

"Millie, Millie, Millie," Hans tisked. "No one drinks only water in my café. I will make a fresh pot of decaf, and we can sit and talk about you being an average *Frau*."

Turning around to scan my seat selection, I noticed the stark difference between the morning and the evening. With no customers around, the space smelled like coffee mixed with cleaning supplies. Without the bright morning sunlight, it was dimly lit and intimate, and I could hear *everything*. The scrap of a chair, the opening of a fridge, the turn of a door handle. I could hear every word Hans said.

Moments later, Hans placed my coffee with teddy bear latte art and a cookie in front of me. "Ja, more customers dying. I cry every time I see them in the newspaper." He walked away grumbling.

I used the cookie to stir the teddy bear into a perfect swirl. I was lost in thought, when a thought hit me. "Wait, come back here! Did you just say that these people from the other murders were also customers of yours?"

"Ja, some, ja, ja. Besides all the computer people across the street, there was Laurie Jordan, Lamar's little sister from Stone Water Games. Lamar and Laurie would come drink my new monthly blends together. Oh, and the berry farmers. I used to get all my berries from the Sheldons for my baked goodies that Gloria makes. But now I lost my friends and my berries, Millie." Hans threw his hands in the air in frustration.

Leaving my coffee with Hans, I stood up and offered him my elbow in farewell. "I have to go, Hans. This has been a very informative conversation."

"I can make coffee to go, just give me seconds, Millie!" I could hear my coffee cup clanging against the saucer as Hans ran it back behind the counter, but I didn't turn around.□

"Sorry no time, *Tschüss*!" I pulled the door open and tripped over Else's feet, falling to my knees.

"Ahhhhhh, murderer, Roy, murderer! They are coming to get me! Roy. Help!" Roy jumped onto my back and threw a croissant basket over my head.

"Stop, I'm not the murderer! It's me, Millie. Remember? I bought you hot cocoas and croissant sandwiches the other day?" The heaviness eased from my back and the streetlights reappeared as the basket was removed. I rolled to a sitting position and brushed off my knees as I collected myself. "Thank you. I didn't mean to trip over you, Else. I wasn't expecting you there since you weren't here when I came in earlier."

Else focused on smoothing out her blanket, ignoring my apology.

"Well, you be careful, Millie. There is some weird stuff going on around here lately. People come out of the Stone Water Games building, but we never see people enter. They just drift away like ghosts into the night."

I acknowledged Roy's warning with a slight nod and smile that seemed appropriate for the drunk unhoused couple who were now seeing ghosts. "I promise to be careful," I added as I spun around to hurry back to the condo.

I shuffled to a stop in front of my building, remembering that I needed to grab the brick. I kicked it over with my foot, expecting to see my note, but a new note was in its place. A chill went down my spine. The Body Goblin had responded while I was at Hans's café: *You know what I want, Millie, and if I don't get it in three days, I will take your body too.*

CHAPTER 30

C ici and I must have been woken from the same aromas wafting into our bedrooms because we opened our doors at the exact same time. I smelled the coffee first, but it was the sweet scent of honey butter batter with a hint of vanilla that got me out of bed. One of Trae's culinary passions was using fresh ingredients. Today he had used vanilla beans from the plant I bought him for his famous Belgian waffles. He served them with a side of blueberry syrup, also made from his own garden, along with freshly squeezed orange juice.

"Trae, you should quit coding and open a breakfast restaurant. You are an amazing cook! Oh, and hire Gloria as your baker because you two would make an awesome team," Cici jested.

Raising an eyebrow, Trae slapped a waffle on Cici's plate. "No, thank you. I don't think she could follow the no sexual harassment rule."

Watching as they teased each other, I figured this was my chance to make light of a serious situation and break the news from last night.

I threw the Body Goblin's note onto the middle of the table. Cici reached for it and read the note aloud.

"You know what I want, Millie and if I don't get it in three days, I will take your body too."

Cici's look morphed from confusion to fear as they handed the note to Trae. "Millie, I'm worried. These threats continue to escalate."

Trae looked over the note with his finger pressed to his lips. "You know, I'm not so sure this is a threat as much as he is trying to scare you. I mean, if this nut job really wanted you dead, he would have killed you by now. He's had an opportunity. We just need to figure out why and what he wants from you, Millie." Trae tossed the note back on the table with a sigh and sat down next to me. "I can't believe I'm saying this as if we aren't living people who could die. Do all detectives dissociate like this?"

I picked up the creased paper and contemplated the message. "Such nice handwriting for a killer. Should I write back? Holy shit, I think I just did the same thing, Trae. The whole dissociating thing." I folded the note and put it in my pocket.

"Pass me the syrup, will you, pink bot? "Cici asked. "And no, you should not write him back. Do not entertain this weird-ass game any longer. You know what I could use? I could use a hot cup of coffee. And yes, we are all very fucked up in the head right now." They reached for the pitcher of syrup that the pink bot pushed over from the opposite side of the table.

Returning to my delicious breakfast, I cut a bite of waffle, which made it halfway to my mouth before a glop of blueberry syrup dripped onto my gray shirt. "Every fucking time..."

I placed my fork back on my plate and stood to walk into the kitchen to clean myself up. As I turned on the water and wiped at my shirt, it hit me that I almost forgot to tell my friends that Lamar and

Laurie Jordan, the Sheldons, and the network team all have connections to Hans's DeCafé.

I scrubbed the blueberries off my shirt with the sponge. "I can't believe I forgot to tell you both about my discovery last night at the coffee shop." I tossed the sponge back in the sink. I grabbed a towel to dry my hands before I continued. "While at DeCafé after you both went to bed, I went to see if Hans had heard any neighborhood gossip that could be useful. I got something even better! I learned that at least one person from each crime scene has a connection to Hans's establishment."

Trae grabbed Mozzarella from her perch, and she meowed at him in Spanish. "Do you think Hans is a suspect?"

"Of course not, but it turns out that Laurie Jordan is the little sister of Lamar, Beth's old boss at Stone Water Games. Apparently, Lamar and Laurie used to meet at the DeCafé for Hans's monthly blends taste testing. The Sheldons were berry farmers who sold their berries to Hans. And the networking team frequented the DeCafé because it was so close to the new office building. I think it is very likely that they all interacted, even if it was just in passing. Trae, did you ever finish your research on what the victims were doing on their last days?"

"Yes, we did, didn't we princess?" Trae cooed at Mozzarella, kissing her on the head and setting her back on her perch. "I was able to use a facial recognition program I built where I uploaded pictures of each victim into the system, then the software runs through every public street camera in the city." He frowned. "Here is where I went against all my morals. If they went into certain shops, restaurants, or buildings, I hacked those cameras as well, as long as they were online. Being that Stone Water Games hasn't been online, I obviously couldn't get any data from the night of the murders. But this is as close to real as it gets."

Cici pushed away from the table, grabbed their plate, and headed to the kitchen. "I'll get the bag of popcorn from the pantry."

I jumped up and scurried to the linen closet. "I'll get the couch blankets."

Trae retrieved his laptop and cast his screen onto the TV as we all settled into our favorite spots to watch the last day in the life of each murder victim. Poised to press play, Trae looked uncomfortable. "Are we weird? Like we are acting like this is a regular movie day?"

Cici tossed a few popped kernels into their mouth. "Huh? Why would you say that? Let's start with the old guy. I feel like he is going to be funny for some reason."

We both looked at Cici with deep concern.

"What? Go on. Push play." Cici made a remote-control clicker motion at the TV.

Trae shook his head, but did what he was told and narrated this first surveillance video of Darrin Russel.

I wasn't surprised that he had been successful in gathering all this information. I imagined all the victim's coworkers, friends, and family sharing openly with Trae to pull together the details of their loved one's last days alive. I mean it's Trae. Everybody trusts Trae.

Trae began his narration. "We don't know a lot about Darrin's morning except what we learned from talking to his daughter in Texas. She stated that her dad sounded somber on the phone even though he didn't say anything unusual. As you can see from this gas station footage, he filled up his truck, then drove through the Starbucks line to get what looks like a coffee before we see him pulling into the office parking garage."

At this point, Trae hit pause before continuing with the next movie short. "I will say that Stacia and Stan from the networking crew were similarly uneventful. It seems that people who work third shift tend to sleep until they have to go to work, like it was their morning routine. Do you want to watch their surveillance videos anyways?"

Cici and I looked at each other and shrugged. "No, if there wasn't anything that clearly indicated something coming or unexpected, then we can skip them. Who should we watch next?"

Trae closed his eyes and took a deep breath, "I'm not going to lie. Beth was so damn hard for a couple of reasons. The main reason I found researching her last day so difficult was because as I followed her movements throughout the morning, I realized I knew a lot less about her than I thought." Trae clicked play.

The clips of Beth's surveillance videos popped on the screen and, like Darrin, she was going through a Starbucks drive thru. Trae pointed to the screen. "You can see here that Beth is clearly on her cell phone in her car while she's ordering her drink, and when she hung up, she pulled over in the parking lot and you can see she is crying. Her next stop was Hans's Decafé where she met with an unknown person, shown with no face since their back was to us."

"Pause the video, Trae." I instructed. "So can we tell anything about the person? Height? Weight? Sex? Any information?"

"Nope, nothing at all. From the camera angle outside you can only see this sliver of their jacket. I was able to obtain some information from a text message that Beth's sister sent that morning. The message from Beth confirmed she couldn't talk and would call her sister later that night because she was late to meet someone at Hans's place. Like I said, the angle from the street cameras gave me nothing to work with. Keep watching."

Before resuming the video, Trae warned, "This next part is a bit fuzzy. I talked to several people at the café, but no one saw Beth there that day, except for Hans who said he saw her outside, but she never came in to get coffee. He also said he thought she looked upset through the window, but he didn't intervene. He claimed the other person was outside of his direct line of sight."

Trae clicked play again and we saw Beth walk away. "I was able to follow her through the city traffic camera's until she stopped at a hardware store where she purchased rope. Then I followed her home, where based on the fact that we found Mozzarella at the crime scene, she loaded her up and headed to work."

Cici placed their hand on Trae's shoulder. "Was it the same type of rope found at the crime scene? Do you believe Beth was involved somehow?"

Trae didn't try to maintain his composure. He allowed every devastating emotion to cross his face. I sat down next to him and took his hand. "It's okay to cry."

Trae looked at me with conflicted eyes. "Are you fucking kidding me, Millie? All I ever do is cry."

I squeezed his hand. "You're right. I should have said again; it's okay to cry again, Trae."

He started laughing through his tears. "I guess that's fair." He put his head on my shoulder.

"I feel horrible too, buddy," Cici said. "I mean, why was Beth bringing rope to work, unless you plan to do something sinister with it? This does make her look suspicious. Trae, I'm so sorry."

"Well, when you put it like that, Cici!" Trae ran to his bedroom and slammed the door.

I walked into the kitchen to grab a bottle of water, as I admonished Cici's lack of tact. "Gosh Cici, nothing like giving the poor man a visual. Let's take a break and give him a few minutes to collect himself. I can't imagine what it was like to find out that a person you care about might have actually been a part of something so horrible."

Trae stomped back out of his bedroom, obviously more irritable. "Okay, who do you want to see next? Nurses? Farmers? They are all boring as hell, leading completely boring fucking lives. Just like us. They get up in the morning, eat breakfast, go to work, have hanky panky with Jeremy—"

I raised my hand..."Whoa, whoa, whoa, just so everyone is completely clear here, I never," I inserted air quotes, "had hanky panky with Jeremy."

Trae dropped onto the couch and placed his feet on the coffee table. "Ugh! My point is that these are normal everyday people with normal everyday lives. If they were involved with something, they certainly didn't show it in their daily activities. Something much more sinister *is* going on here. Something bigger than we could ever imagine. And if it doesn't end soon, I'm scared that something massive and terrible will happen."

I felt a sudden, sharp twinge in my stomach because I knew Trae was right; something *was* about to happen. I don't know how or why I knew. Was I letting Juniper's talk of the hundred-year storm get to me? Or Noble's mass naming ceremony? Was I on edge because the Body Goblin was threatening to take my body? Or was I losing control of this investigation and just had no idea how to take it back before my brother ended up like all these other victims? We were running out of time.

I swallowed and looked at my friends. "I have an idea. It's bold, but why not? I say, let's orchestrate a meetup between Noble and Tim so they show up to the same place at the same time. Once they are there, we can get them talking and maybe they will say something that confirms their involvement or that they aren't involved at all. Then we have what we need to finally rule them out as suspects or have them arrested."

Cici pointed at Trae. "One, get your feet off the coffee table, Trae. Two, that is a horrible idea, Millie, because how would we ever get them to the same place? Third, we would have to blow our covers and honestly, what if they turned on us and we got hurt? Trae would cry."

"They aren't wrong. I would probably cry." Trae placed his head into his hands.

I pushed through the bridge of Trae's legs, and headed toward my bedroom, before I paused. "I need you both to trust me on this one."

I shut my bedroom door, but before I even sat down, there was a knock. "Millie, can I come in?" Trae asked and answered his own question by opening the door and entering my room. "I made you something that I would like you to wear because I'm pretty sure you are planning to do something stupid." Trae paused to gauge if he was right. When I didn't answer, he smirked. "That's what I thought." Then he handed me a pair of glasses.

I accepted them curiously. "You want me to wear a pair of glasses?" I slipped them on. Suddenly, I could see a digital map of my room, showing the walkways around the bed and other furniture. "Wow, Trae, these are so cool! But what am I really looking at here?"

"These glasses are GPS-enabled. So, let's say you are walking down the street, and someone starts following you and you need to get away fast, an escape route. To activate the glasses, tap once on the right to highlight the fastest way out of your current situation to reach a main street or populated area. Or tap the left once for thermal imaging that will locate heat signatures, and tap twice to activate night vision."

Trae sat down on my bed and spent the next couple hours sharing the intricate details about the glasses. It was good to know that if I swam to the bottom of the ocean or dropped them from the top of the Space Needle, they wouldn't break.

I tested the glasses by tapping once on the right, and sure enough, the route to my bedroom door was highlighted. Looking beyond, I saw the path to the condo door and interestingly enough, all the way to the stairs and outside to the main road in front of our building. "It wants me to take the stairs and not the elevator. Why is that?"

"Because an elevator comes with risk. For example, in an earthquake or a fire, you're always told to take the stairs, and this is the same concept. There is less risk of being caught or getting stuck when you take the stairs." Trae pulled the glasses off my face and made some quick adjustments.

At that moment, Trae looked less like a boy and more like a man, and I could tell that Trae took his work very seriously, which meant he took my safety seriously. Did that mean we were starting to grow up a little?

I slammed into Trae with a big hug.

"Whoa, baby girl! Are you okay?"

Not letting go, I gushed, "Thank you for always taking care of me, Trae. You put the forever in my best friend. I don't know what I would do without you."

Trae pulled away and cupped my face in his hands. "You would be in prison, or still living with your brother, but probably in prison." Giving me one last squeeze before returning the glasses to the bridge of my nose, Trae admired his work. "Perfect! Now just don't lose these because they are one of a kind. The glasses will only turn off when you take them off and will only turn on when you put them on. They have communication capabilities as well, so you no longer need to ditch comms. As soon as the glasses are activated, Cici and I will get an alert to our phones and can access the visual and audio feeds to see what you see and hear what you hear. We are a team."

With a large, toothy grin, I said, "Trae, what is our team name?"

"How about, cute spy guy?"

"How about rainbow spy solutions? Cici will love it I bet."

Trae gave me a wink. "I think we might be onto something."

CHAPTER 31

Backpack, check. Sack lunch, check. GPS glasses, check. Alright, I was off to see what these two alleged murderers were up to today. I was going to observe the Keepers of the Pines do their charity work in Westlake Center from a small coffee shop across the street.

Based on what I found out about Tim's routine, he should be dropping off books to Noble this morning. I knew my position had to be far away, and I was worried I wouldn't be able to hear their verbal exchange. When I told Trae this, he gave me this nifty long-distance sound receiver that used laser technology so I could hear them from up to two hundred feet away. The cool thing about this little gadget was it only picked up people's voices. I just popped the receivers in like a pair of earbuds.

My plan would only become tricky if they left Westlake, and I'd have to follow them. I don't drive often so I joined a car-sharing service for those Smart cars that are randomly parked throughout the city. This seemed like the best idea for the day because I could pick up and drop off a car as needed. The whole idea of driving made me a bit nauseous. I considered calling Lorraine to see if she would come get me to follow them around, but I could already hear her in my head saying, "Millie, get a real job."

I was only on my third latte when Tim pulled up in his van and started unloading boxes of books. As soon as I saw him, I hopped off my stool and walked outside where my voice sound receiver would pick up their voices. I found a seat at an empty table, put on my headphones, and pulled out the listening device, hiding it under the table. As I pushed the red button and pointed the device in Tim's direction, Noble arrived to greet him.

"Hot dogs! Get ya hot dogs! One-ninety-nine for a regular, two-ninety-nine for a footlong!" Startled by the loud booming voice, I pulled the headphones off and sat back as I contemplated getting a double relish doggie-dog from the hot dog vendor who was now parked directly in between me and my targets.

Focus, dammit!

I handed my sack lunch to an unhoused person, grabbed all my other stuff, and ran across the street to find a seat. Not waiting to get fully resituated in fear of missing something important, I pointed the laser-enhanced microphone toward the men again and took a seat at a chess table with a couple of older gentlemen.

"Why won't you just admit it? You don't love me anymore; you still love her. Admit that you would rather be in her bed than mine. You said you loved me; you said you wanted to be with me forever. But those were just words, weren't they? Words. Words. Words. You asshole; I hate you!"

What the fuck?

I looked to either side of the men I was surveilling to see two people standing to the right of Tim and Noble, engaged in what appeared to be a lover's quarrel.

Frustrated, I stood up again, gathered all my stuff, and made my way around the hot dog vendor.

"Come on universe! Mickey's life is at stake!" Someone out there must have been listening because suddenly Noble's voice came over my receiver.

"Oh, trust me Tim, we will know everything we need to know by then. Let's plan on bringing him out to the Island on the night of the hundred-year storm. It will be the ultimate sacrifice."

"Are you sure about this, Noble?" Tim asked. "What if something goes wrong?"

"You just leave everything up to me. I haven't messed up anything yet, have I?"

"And it better stay that way, Noble. I won't have my reputation ruined because of you."

"You no longer have a choice, Tim. You are in too deep."

My God, are they talking about Mickey? I have to go back to the island tomorrow. I need to save my brother.

They walked away, and I started to follow when I saw Juniper standing about ten feet in front of me. I had managed to avoid her all day so I could just focus on Noble, but my luck just ran out. I was just about to slide behind the vendor's cart when her gaze shifted toward me. I had no other choice but to engage.

"Juniper!" I stuffed all my spy stuff into my pockets.

With a bounce in her step, she made her way over. "Millie! What a nice surprise to see you here. What did I do to deserve this unexpected visit?" Juniper sounded so flirty, and I needed to come up with an excuse fast for why I showed up unannounced.

Think quick, think, think...

"I missed waking up with you this morning so I thought I would come to see you."

Juniper wrapped her arms around my waist and brought her mouth to my ear to nibble softly on my earlobe. "Tell me, what did you miss?" She whispered softly as she lightly ran her thumb over my covered nipple, which immediately hardened.

"Ummm, we are in the middle of the sidewalk, Juniper. I'm not sure what I can do with all this right now."

Juniper grabbed my hand and dragged across the street to a little clothing boutique. As we entered the shop, a woman behind the counter looked up and smiled at us.

"What are we doing here?" I turned to catch Juniper raising a not-so-flattering blouse to her chest. Or maybe it was flattering? I swear she could turn anything beautiful just by touching it. "Seriously, I don't need anything, do you?" Before I could protest further, she had two more items in her hands and was making her way to the back of the store. Looking over her shoulder, Juniper beckoned me into a dressing room with her alluring eyes.

Quickly shutting and locking the door, she dropped the clothes. "I like mirrors. I want to watch myself while I make you come," she whispered as she gently bit my earlobe. My entire body tensed when she found just the right spot to rub on the outside of my jeans.

I leaned my head back against the wall as Juniper ran her tongue the length of my throat and across my lips, before taking my mouth in a deep, passionate kiss. "Mmmmm... what if she hears us? Ahhhh... I love the way you taste."

"Well, I guess you're going to have to be quiet then..." The tip of her tongue slid back into my mouth to silence my words but not the pace of my breath as she unbuttoned my jeans and slid her hand into my underwear.

Juniper inserted her fingers inside of me slowly and I let out a long gasp. As if knowing I was close to climax already, she stopped. "I don't want you to come yet. I have something better for you."

Lowering her eyes while she sucked in her bottom lip, I knew exactly what she had in mind when she pulled my jeans and underwear off and tossed them to the side. I let her take the lead as she propped one of my legs up on the bench. My entire body quivered when she ran her fingers along the inside of my thighs to create space to fit between my legs. Juniper smiled and dropped to her knees.

"Tell me what you want, Millie." I felt a light flick of her tongue on my already tingling clit.

"I... ahhh... want... ahhh..." I was having a hard time forming my words.

"That's not good enough. What do you want me to do, Millie?" She ran her tongue from my wet center to my throbbing flesh, teasing me, sucking me, and flicking my clit again. "Millie, tell me what you want." My head bounced back against the wall as her fingers pushed inside of me, sliding them back out, then back in and holding them deep.

I want to come... no, not yet... fuuuck... this feels so amazing... god Juniper don't stop... don't ever stop fucking me...

"What do you want, Millie? Tell me what you want."

"Stay inside me... don't stop... fuck me, Juniper." She quickened her tongue in perfect rhythm, the motion of her fingers working deeper inside me. I could feel the pressure building and my clit swelled as my hips continued to grind against her hand and mouth. I grabbed her free hand and bit into her flesh to stifle my cry as I lost all control and erupted in an orgasm.

I melted onto the bench as my legs gave way. "You are fucking amazing. Come up here and kiss me." I pulled her up and kissed her nose, then her cheek, and finally tasted the wetness I left on her lips. "Mmmm... let me return the favor."

"Please..." Juniper whispered. She stood, so I could help her slide off her yoga pants and underwear. Goosebumps rose on her arms as I ran my fingers down the sides of her legs. She unbuttoned her shirt and slid it off her shoulders, and I stood, teasing her lips with mine until we were locked in a deep passionate kiss. I reached around to unclasp her bra.

"You said you like to watch, huh?" I questioned in a breathy voice.

"Mmmm... I do."

I lifted Juniper's hand high into the air and twirled her around to face the mirror. One by one I planted her hands on either side of the mirror so she could watch me while I fucked her from behind. "Ahhhh... I want to feel your tits on me, Millie."

I tore my shirt and bra off and pressed my body against hers, I carefully pulled her hair back to kiss the side of her neck while I traced my nipples along her silky back. When I reached my hand around her waist and found her throbbing, wet, round flesh, she pressed her thick ass into my clit. "Ahhh... Juniper, you are so fucking hot." I buried my mouth into her neck again.

My finger teased her opening, enjoying her wetness until I found my way back to her round flesh where I began to massage her slowly. "Do you like watching me fuck you?"

"Yes..." Juniper's breath caught, when I accelerated the tips of my fingers on her throbbing center. I could tell she was getting closer to coming when she started to grind her ass harder and faster against my swollen clit.

"Faster Millie... faster... harder..."

I did as she asked until we exploded with pleasure.

Our bodies collapsed against the wall, where we stood holding each other for a moment in silence. I laid against her back, exhausted.

"I think I found a new appreciation for clothes shopping." I turned Juniper around and buried my face in her chest. She kissed my forehead, before she leaned over to grab her clothes from the floor to get dressed.

She kissed me again. "I'm happy to be your personal shopper anytime, Millie Myles."

I stood and pulled my jeans over my hips and buttoned them. We did a quick check in the mirror before exiting the dressing room.

"Hey, so now what? Are you going back to work?" I questioned.

Juniper smirked at me out of the corner of her eye as we left the store and made our way back across the street. "Yeah, I should probably get back to work. I don't think you'll be missing me anymore." She winked at me. "How about you? What are you going to do now?"

We returned to the park where I noticed that Noble and Tim were gone. "Welp, I don't know, actually. I saw Tim here earlier and was thinking about talking to him about doing some volunteer work at the library. I was super impressed by his story the other night, and I want to help."

Juniper looked around. "Yeah, he was here earlier with Noble, but they likely went to lunch at that cute little DeCafé place in Pioneer Square before they head back to the library to have their planning meeting. I suppose you could always catch up with them there if you want. More importantly, when will I see you again?"

I tried not to react to the connection Juniper just made unknowingly, so I embraced her. "I'm not sure, but I promise it will be soon." I kissed her on the forehead.

"I'm serious about going to a movie, Millie. I want a real date with you. Promise me you will take me on a real date?" Juniper met my eyes with a serious expression.

"I promise. Any movie you want to see, and I will buy you all the vegan popcorn and candy you can eat." I gave her a quick peck on the lips before jogging down the street to find my car. I got about halfway down the street when I turned around to see Juniper was still watching me.

I have her exactly where I want her. In my heart... ugh!

CHAPTER 32

There had to be at least a dozen people pointing and laughing at something near where I had left the Smart car. As I drew closer to the crowd, I overheard a person snickering. "You have got to be kidding me! And in the middle of the goddamn day!"

I realized that I would have to go through the crowd, not just around it, to get back to my parking spot. I hesitated, then pushed to the front of the crowd to get a better look at the cause of the commotion.

A tow truck driver was writing something on a notepad. "Is this your car?" He gestured with a smirk on his face.

I looked over to find the Smart car where I had left it but not in the position I had left it in. "Uhhh, sort of? It's one of those car share rentals that you pick up in one location and leave it in another. I have it, well, I had reserved it for the day." I shook my head as I assessed the tipped Smart car. The windows were busted-out. They must have shattered when the hooligans pushed it over on its side. "Did anyone see who tipped it over?"

Was someone trying to get me off their trial? Was I getting close?

It was like I rang a bell, and the city watch showed up in the form of Else and Roy. "Maybe we did or maybe we didn't." Else waved her croissant basket back and forth.

I was getting a little tired of their trading food for information games. "You know, Else, if you saw who did it, you should say something. That is what my boss tells me. Not everything is leverage for money or food; sometimes, it's just about doing the right thing."

Else's shoulders shrunk as her eyes filled with tears. "But Millie, this is our job. We get up every morning like everyone else does. We get dressed, put on our shoes, and then we go to work. Our job is to watch over this city for the news people, the police, and well..." Else paused, giving me a knowing look and casually pointing at me before continuing. "Sometimes even for the professional ice rink hand-holders like you that come around asking questions."

I snapped my head around quickly. "Who told you about that? How do you know my work history?"

"Roy and I have owned an information-sharing business here for many years; we've seen you around. I'm just saying we all need to put food on the table. We aren't asking for handouts. We offer services in return for getting paid our going rate. We are trying to make a living just like everyone else. And we aren't hurting anyone doing it, either."

Rubbing the back of my neck, I decided I couldn't argue with Else's logic and pulled out a ten-dollar bill. I dropped the money into her basket. "You argue a mighty good case, Else. Did you see who tipped over my Smart car?"

Else snagged the ten dollars out of the basket and handed it to Roy. "We did not." They turned and continued down the street.

Frustrated, I left the car and hiked up the hill to the library. It would be a bit of a walk, but at least it was on my way home. I needed the time to sort out what the hell just happened with Juniper. Again. It was like she had some kind of spell over me.

I can't keep doing this with her. Sleeping with her is clouding my judgment and distracting me from finding my Mickey and solving this murder case. And I can't believe I let Tim and Noble get away!

If I didn't find them at the library when I got there, I was a failure. My mind wandered back to Juniper.

God, I love the way she smiles at me. How can her smile alone put me in such a trance that I literally lose my ability to speak?

I turned down Fourth Avenue. I had a straight shot to the library from here.

It's not like I love Juniper; I barely know her. I don't know if she has any siblings. She never mentioned any. All I know are bits and pieces that make up a fraction of a whole person. So how can I possibly consider if I'm falling in love with her? I'm not, it's just lust. It's just a part of the job, to get close, right? This is just a sacrifice I'm making, a very hot, lusty sacrifice.

I knew that the day would indeed come when I would have to sit down next to Juniper, take her hand ever-so-gently, and tell her that sometimes we have to break hearts to save hearts. Then, I will softly kiss her on the cheek and wipe away her tears before walking away to my next case.

I'm a Myles; I am Millie Myles, Private Investigator. Well, almost. Maybe someday.

I reached my destination faster than anticipated, which was good because I already lost a lot of time today. I nabbed an empty table and kept my eyes peeled for the two men while I unzipped my backpack.

"Shhhhh!" An elderly lady hushed me.

Geesh! Was my zipper really that disruptive?

I took out my GPS glasses and magnet stickers, placing one sticker behind each ear as I apologized. "Sorry, just getting some stuff out of my bag." The woman gave me a dirty look.

I slipped my glasses on and zipped my bag shut before heading towards the escalators to find Tim's office.

The hairs on the back of my neck stood up. I had a creepy feeling that I was being watched. I looked around, hoping that Noble and Tim hadn't spotted me when I noticed the little old lady peeking through a bookshelf at me. I wandered a few aisles over and decided that if this woman trailed me into the section on nursing homes, she was definitely following me.

Grabbing the first title I found, *The Guide to Seattle-Area Nursing Homes,* I looked out of the corner of my eye as she made her way around to the opposite side of the bookshelves.

I'm not being paranoid! She is following me. What does she want?

I put the book back and grabbed another random title off the shelf before approaching her. "Excuse me miss. I was wondering if you ever read this book before? I'm looking for something to cheer up my grandmother."

The woman took the book from my hand. Her head tilted as her eyes grew fearfully wide. She read the title of the book out loud: "Advice for Future Corpses (And Those Who Love Them) by Sallie Tisdale."

I ripped the book out of her hand defensively. "She's one hundred and three. She's ready." I put the book back on the shelf and changed the subject. "So, do you come here often?" I softened my tone.

"Look, young lady, I don't know what you're after, or why you are here, but I'm certainly no hussy and as the ground floor volunteer manager, I'm here to ensure all the rules of this library are adhered to. No food, no drink, and certainly no soliciting. You got that?"

"Oh no, you don't... you think... I'm not..." I tried to explain but the floor monitor wasn't having any of my excuses. She just wanted me to move along or leave the building.

"Just get, get, get, get... off my floor! And if I see you again, I will have security drag you out of here so fast that your—"

Trae's voice piped in my ear. "Millie now would be a good time to just walk away and quit fighting with the little old lady. Everyone knows how big and strong you are and that you could take her."

I took Trae's advice and walked away. "Fine. I could totally take her." I mumbled into my comms.

Cici chimed in. "Millie, I'm up in the map section. I would have told you sooner, but I was enjoying your little verbal scuffle with the matriarch floor warden too much to interrupt. Get up here. I think our case is about to change course. Trae, stay on the line. You're going to want to hear this."

I sprinted up the stairs to the map section, happy to have a destination. "I'm going to go past Tim's office then I'll be on my way!"

Tim's office door was shut, so I knocked and ran behind a bookshelf. I peeked around the corner when Tim opened the door, and I could see Noble sitting in a visitor's chair looking over his shoulder. Instead of closing the door, Noble stood up. He had a long tube in his hand, similar to the map tubes we already had in our possession. He shook Tim's hand and left, but not before doing a thorough recon of the area. I quickly blended deeper into the bookshelf to keep from being seen.

I tiptoed away and found Cici at a table with a few Seattle maps spread out in front of them.

"Grab a chair." Cici pointed across the table.

I pulled up a chair, and studied the spread of maps, which included one of North Seattle today. I can't say that I understood its importance, but Cici must have a reason to believe it contributed to the investigation.

"I just saw Noble leave with a tube that looked a lot like one of these map tubes. I think we are getting closer to him. So, what is your big revelation?"

The look on Cici's face said it all. They were about to deliver news that I knew I didn't want to hear. "I received an update on the official investigation from work. Tim and Liza Lewis have been cleared; they are no longer on the suspect list. Yes, the murders happened at their building but neither of them was in the state when the murders took place."

Setting the North Seattle map down, I considered this information. "Just because he wasn't there when it happened, doesn't mean Tim wasn't involved. We all know that these murders have more than one perpetrator because there are too many bodies. That was why we thought he was partnered with Noble, right?"

Cici continued to look at me with disappointed eyes. "Yeah, about that. We also have confirmation of Noble's alibi's during each murder. He was giving a speech every time so there is no way Noble was involved either. So unless they have minions doing all their dirty work, which I guess is possible, I think we might be back to ground zero."

"Maybe not totally from ground zero," Trae said into the comms. "I have a little surprise for you both when you get home."

Cici and I smiled at each other as they looked at their watch. "We can be home in an hour. I got what I need for my map research, anyway." Cici rolled the maps and started to pack their bag. "Let's hit the road."

Trae was holding Mozzarella and a piece of mail when we came through the door.

"She is full-blooded American," Trae handed me Mozzarella's DNA results. "She is a pure-bred Maine Coon, a breed originating in the United States. Mozzarella is officially meowing in perfect English, although we are probably hearing a little Jersey accent or something. I also have your DNA results for you CiCi." Trae presented their result letter.

Cici took the letter and ripped it open. "No surprises here. I already knew I was mostly Jewish. It says here that we can log in to find relatives. Let's do that." She tossed the paper aside.

"I had mine sent to Mickey's house." Like Cici, I already knew I was full blooded Italian through and through, but I was happy for Mozzarella. It had to be hard not knowing your origin story. I suddenly felt sad when I realized this week was Thanksgiving. Mickey always made us a turkey, but also included a traditional dinner of spaghetti and meatballs, garlic bread, and a salad. I missed my brother so much.

Hang on Mickey... I'm getting close.

CHAPTER 33

*Y*ou're back. That's great, it's only natural to return with more questions. It's important that you get your information directly from the source and not the media because they lie.

So, you want to know how I got my start? Good question. I wanted to keep a low profile but then it became clear what I needed to do. Murder. People needed to die to be saved.

When I first started this journey, no one noticed the people who were dying. That was intentional so I could practice all my different techniques. Then one day, while minding my own business, this woman bumped into me at a coffee shop. We started chatting about this and that. It was a lovely conversation. I listened to her hopes and dreams while I lied about my own. It became apparent that everything I worked so hard to keep a secret could not stay hidden any longer. If there was ever a chance to save these poor souls, they would, in fact, need to die.

I decided right then and there that she would be my first public murder victim. I listened to her talk about her job as a hairdresser and *how much she hated all the chemicals they made her use in the salon. She despised how she was contributing to killing the Earth. She wanted a different world. A better world. And I knew I could give that to her. She would just need to die first.*

Whoa... I just got chills when I said that out loud. I seriously love my work. When you take my ambition multiplied by my desire to take their lives, it equals art. This is what makes me the artist, the creator, the builder, ahhh yes... and I am their savior.

Oh my gosh. Me, me, me. I'm so selfish sometimes! You probably want an update on my little pet, Millie. Everyone always does. She has been very naughty, sticking her nose where it doesn't belong and asking a lot of questions. I have eyes everywhere, and she is getting close—too close. I don't want to hurt her because that serves me no purpose. But I will do what I need to do to protect what is mine.

It's all coming to an end anyway, my friends. Right on time and just as I planned. I may rise again, in my own way and in my own time. All the good ones do.

CHAPTER 34

"Myles, where the hell have you been?" Eddie interrupted my thoughts. "Phil has been wandering around the kitchen with the same bag of Funyuns for the last twenty minutes." Eddie pointed to the back of the warehouse.

"Sorry I'm late. Traffic was horrible today. I will go get Phil, and we'll get started." Phil was exactly where Eddie said he would be, pacing while he munched on his snack.

"Hey buddy, it's me, Millie. Chips look yummy. You doing okay?" He stopped but didn't turn around. "Phil, is there something you want to talk about? You're acting a bit odd. Is your shadow work getting you down this morning? Tell me your shadow's name and I'll kick his ass for you."

Phil looked back at me as he swallowed hard. "It's not me. It's what I found," His voice shook. "A lot more people are going to die if this murder doesn't get solved soon. I can't handle discovering all these clues; I'm just a college student! I can't be responsible for more people dying, Millie. I only have six pages left in my shadow book, and that's not enough pages!" I could see small beads of sweat forming on his forehead.

"Hey there, it's going to be okay, alright? Let's calm down, and I will buy you another book. Even though we just bag and tag, if we find something we should report it, so I will take the lead on that. Now, you said you found something that makes you believe there is going to be another murder? What did you find? Will you show me?" I took his Funyuns, threw them in the trash, and put my arm around his shoulders, leading him out of the kitchen.

When we reached our station, I noticed it was very organized, which was not how I liked it at all. "Phil, why does everything look so damn nice? You know I prefer a chaotic workspace."

Impatiently, Phil dumped a box of evidence bags on the table and roughly shuffled the neat stacks of papers around, knocking some onto the floor. "Better?"

"A bit better, yes. Now show me what you found."

Phil reached inside an evidence box and pulled out candles, broken glass pieces, which he had reconstructed into an hourglass, a statue of Gaia the goddess's head glued on backward, and a hand-made pottery bowl.

I picked up the bowl, turning it in my hand. "What am I looking at here, Phil? I bagged and tagged similar stuff before, and it's just household junk." I placed the bowl on the worktable and picked up the statue, noticing the connection to the island cult right away—especially, from inside Noble's tent. "What the fu—"

Phil interjected. "These are items from someone's seance or altar. When considering each piece separately, you're right, they look like someone's household junk, as you call it. But together, they are definitely someone's alter. The candles provide light for the dead to connect with the living. The statue represents who they seek guidance from. In this case the Goddess Gaia, who represents the Earth. The bowl smells as if it held incense, which was likely used to purify the space. And the hourglass could signify several things, such as approaching change, the flow of energy, or that time is running out."

My eyes widened as I realized that all these items were also found at Stone Water Games, the Sheldon's, and in Noble's tent. "Holy shit, Phil. You just found a major clue that connects the victims to Keepers of the Pines. I think Noble is still a suspect, and what you found here might just confirm that he is the murderer. He might have an alibi, but that doesn't mean he didn't get his followers to do his dirty work."

That son of a bitch!

I shook my head as I thought about all the bullshit Noble spewed during his speech the other night. Everything was coming together. I was going to bring that Noble Pines to justice and bring my brother home safe.

🔪🔪🔪

I walked in the door and immediately felt the energy shift in the room. We were done gathering evidence. It was time to capture a murderer. We were so close, whether my friends knew it or not. It all came down to tonight. I was rescuing Mickey.

Cici left Trae standing at the murder board and wheeled to the table where their maps were laid out when I entered. "I think I found a clue. It might be something, or it might be nothing. See this door on the map? I found the drawing odd and unique, so I researched the patterns and discovered it's a bank vault. My next step is to find the bank that houses the matching vault door. Once we know the bank, Trae can download the account info to cross reference to all the victims and suspects to see if we get any connections."

"Well, based on some critical findings from a few of the items we processed at the warehouse tonight, Tim and Noble are definitely still suspects."

Cici seemed thrilled with this new information. "Well then, if Noble or Tim has ties to the bank with these vaults, then I think we have enough to go to the police."

Trae frowned at Cici. "While that is a great find, Cici, there is no way I'm hacking into anything. Nope. Not going to jail. Plus, vaults like the one in your picture don't exist anymore, they probably don't have traceable serial numbers to connect owners to the vault. Most likely they bought it at an auction. Then to break... well that is a whole other story. It takes a special skill set to get into those. Like with a stethoscope and dynamite, I think. I only do digital systems. Where the money isn't physical. Where did you find this?"

Cici rummaged through their notes. "Oh, here it is. It was in the mid-1880 map archives, and I figured one of the banks had a historical vault on display or something." They handed Trae the info.

"Hmmm... still no."

I pleaded. "Come on, Trae. Mickey is missing, Beth is dead. This is our chance to save others."

"If I get caught, I could go to prison." Trae handed me the archive.

"Could you make it look like you are hacking the system from Tim Lewis' computer at the library?"

A smile crept across Trae's lips. "I could."

"Yeah, you could." We gave each other a high five.

"Okay, I will hack the system just this once. Only because people we love have been hurt and this asshole needs to be caught before anyone else dies. I have a program I think I can reuse for this." Trae grabbed his laptop from the coffee table and started typing.

Trae sat back, admiring his work with a cocky smile. "I have some backend code that I used to search for competitors within a fifty-mile radius who purchased Stone Water Games software. So, I just made a few quick code changes and I can hack into the local banking servers within the same radius. I added a parameter that also searches for antique bank vault doors. Then, I can cross reference that data with all the victim's names, including Tim and Noble." He did some furious typing. Honestly, I was impressed how fast he was geeking out. But then, Trae's expression fell. "Sorry, but nothing came back with these parameters." Trae shrugged.

"Thanks for trying, Trae." I studied Cici's notes for any detail that might explain the connection. "This is interesting. Tim is really into old shit. Maybe he has a vault in his home to secure his personal items." I looked up at my friends. "Another development I came across last night is that there may have been a séance happening at the crime scenes. My intern Phil noticed that both crime scenes have altars that honor Goddess Gaia."

Trae giggled. "Who is Goddess Gaia? She sounds woo woo."

"She is the Earth goddess, and, I believe, our connection to the Keepers of the Pines. I'm telling you, everything keeps pointing back to Noble and Tim. And get this: there was a broken hourglass at the last crime scene. Phil thought it could represent time running out. If that's true, Mickey might not have much time either. I believe they took Mickey for his connection to me for some reason. We have got to figure this out! I can't lose my brother. I can't lose Mickey. I just want my family back and for no one else to die."

Cici piped up. "What we need to do is give all this evidence to the police. I think we have all the proof we need for them to at least bring Noble in to talk to him."

"No, I need to find Mickey first. Yesterday at Westlake, I overheard that Noble and Tim plan to bring someone to the island tonight, and I really think it might be Mickey. I'm going to bring my brother home. After he is safe, I promise we will take everything we have to the cops, plus we will have Mickey as a witness to back us up."

We migrated to the murder board, including the yellow bot boy, who announced, "Yellow. Bot. Boy. Ready. To. Go."

Trae picked him up. "Not yet, little man." He looked back at us proudly. "I trained him to do that; isn't it so cute?" After placing the bot on the kitchen counter, Trae returned to the murder board.

No more fucking around. This ends now.

"Trae, get all your bot boys ready. The green string is activating now." I pulled the green string from Noble to Tim. "I will visit Blake Island one last time to locate my brother, and we need to close this investigation. Cici, I think you are spot on with that bank vault. Follow that lead to wherever it goes. Trae, are the bot boys ready? All electronics checked and working?"

Trae drew two check marks in the air. "Check and check, baby girl."

I threw my GPS glasses in my backpack. "I promise to stay connected and streaming so you can see and hear everything."

Trae looked worried. "Maybe you shouldn't go. The weather forecast looks pretty rough. The wind has already picked up and Mickey's boat isn't meant to be out on stormy waters. The storm expected tonight is supposed to be really nasty. That's all they have been talking about on the news today."

"I promise it'll be fine, and I will be careful." I tried to sound encouraging as I packed the remaining items into my bag. I turned and gave Trae a quick hug.

The windows rattled from the blowing wind, which drew my attention outside. Peering down at the street below, I watched as people hung onto their hats and debris blew around their feet. I pulled out my phone and checked the Weather app. The temperature had dropped at least fourteen degrees in the last hour.

"The Saltwater Moon," I whispered to myself as I pulled on my jacket and headed toward the door. This was going to be an interesting night. I could feel it in my bones.

I don't know who you are, Gaia, but if you are part of the universe that I'm always talking to, please keep me safe out there tonight.

I figured it couldn't hurt to throw out a little good karma.

I looked back at my friends and realized that something felt different this time. This moment didn't feel like a 'see ya later.' Tonight had the potential to be goodbye. Tears filled my eyes, but I refused to let them fall. I twisted the door handle and without looking back I whispered, "I love you," and walked out the door.

"Something seems off here. Holy shit, Millie! Wait—" Cici yelled.

I ignored them. Nothing was stopping me. I ran down the stairs and out into the street where the wind almost knocked me over.

Tonight, you answer to me Noble Pines.

CHAPTER 35

The boat dock was completely empty except for one sailor who had just come in. "You're not planning on going out there are you? The National Weather Service just issued a gale warning forty-five minutes ago. You should really think twice before getting in that boat." She was struggling to tie her own vessel to the pier.

"I'll go slow!" I yelled back as I worked to untie the first knot that secured the cover to Mickey's boat. The cover ripped right out my hands and flipped into the water. The wind was no joke today. I jumped into the boat and dragged the drenched cover back over the side, struggling to manage the extra water-weight.

I hope this isn't what the rest of my trip to Blake Island is going to look like, I thought to myself as I looked out at the angry white caps rising to clash with one another before rejoining the ocean waters.

The first hour of my crossing was extremely violent: the winds and waters were brutal, and if it weren't for my compass, I would have been completely lost. I did my best to steer the boat, but the waves volleyed me around like a game of badminton. My stomach contents turned to acid in my throat, and when I couldn't handle it any longer, I retched over the side into the ocean.

Just when I wasn't sure if I was going to come out of the next hour alive, the clouds burst open and torrential rains started to fill the boat. "One. Two. Three. Four. Five. Six. Seven." I recited my numbers so Mickey wouldn't die. I screamed for help as if someone was going to hear me and pluck me from this floating chunk of wood.

My heart pounded in my ears as terrifying images burst into my thoughts, one after another like lightning strikes across the stormy sky. I sunk into a full chaotic thought loop that was spiraling completely out of my control.

Stop it, Millie! Stop it! Stop it!

I started to rock back and forth.

Mickey beaten... Mickey stabbed... Mickey shot...

Was Mickey already dead? Will I get there in time?

Mickey beaten... Mickey stabbed... Mickey shot... Mickey bludgeoned... Screaming... Blood... Mickey dead.

I felt light headed and my skin started to tingle. "One. Two. Three. Four. Five. Six. Seven."

I focused on my breaths. I had to stay alive. I had to save Mickey. I grabbed a discarded cup and scooped water out of the boat. With each sway and tilt, I stumbled from one side to the back and then to the other side. Balance was no longer a concept.

Then, as rapidly as the storm began, the winds calmed, the rain lightened to a drizzle, and I could see Blake Island. I crawled to the bow of the boat, my clothes soaking wet, my body shaking uncontrollably with relief.

As soon as I was close to shore, I jumped onto the rocky terrain. I pulled the bow onto the shore as far as I could. The bottom of the skiff must've hit a rock because it was taking on water, so it was much heavier than normal so I couldn't drag it much farther than the Juniper tree rooted at the water's edge. Once Mickey's broken boat was semi secured, I rolled onto my backside, exhausted.

I'm not sure who to thank for keeping me alive on that trip but thank youuu!

After collecting my nerves and my energy with a few deep breaths, I pushed my drenched, muddy body up to standing.

What is going on with this storm? I have never seen anything like this in my life!

I watched the clouds racing rapidly across the sky, and I caught a fleeting glimpse of the moon as she appeared to be desperately searching for her place in the night's sky. But when the clouds finally parted, I gazed up at the largest, brightest moon I had ever seen in my life.

Did I just experience what Juniper had been telling me all along? Have I just survived the hundred-year storm? Was all this what Juniper was so worried about? Most importantly... was it over? Much like the battle Juniper had spoken of, I was too ready to fight, but my battle would be against the one she calls father.

"So, this is a Saltwater Moon," I whispered in awe while I watched the rise and fall of the King Tides as they crashed into the shores. The smell of seaweed and salt filled my nostrils. The tides were powerful; they were angry, yet incredibly beautiful.

I have to get to camp and figure out what all this means and how all of this connects to the murders. And I need to help Juniper and Mickey before Noble kills them too.

"I'm coming for you, Mickey! Hang on brother, hang on!" I called out to whoever could give me the strength to find the only family I had left.

I realized I'd left my backpack in the boat, which would be difficult to retrieve with the storm growing angrier by the minute. Sand and water pelted my skin as I scrambled back to Mickey's boat and searched until I located the waterlogged backpack in a puddle under one of the seats. I fished out my techie glasses and put them on.

"Testing. Testing. One, two, three." There was a long stretch of static, and then I heard Cici. At least I think it was Cici.

"Mil—" *bzzz.* "it's not—" *bzzz.* "writ—" *buzz.* "broc—" *bzzz.* "come—" *bzzz.* "map—" *bzzz.*

There seemed to be no reception out here in the storm. I shoved the glasses back into their waterproof case and put them in my pocket. Then I tossed my backpack back into the boat.

I searched the trail ahead, watching the trees sway ominously. The weather was not going to be my friend tonight.

I had at least a twenty-minute walk to camp, probably longer by the looks of the fallen trees and debris strewn across my path. I climbed over the first cluster of branches and started the trek. The storm did seem to quiet the further I walked into the woods. I took a moment to inhale the sweet scents of cedar and pine, finding comfort and safety of the timbers. Mickey used to make me feel safe and sheltered when it would storm at night. He held me when thunder rumbled through the house.

The winds whispered, guiding me along while the treetops danced like skeletons. The forest floor was damp and tender, and it provided me that same feeling of comfort that Mickey used to give.

I feel at home, but I shouldn't feel this way. Home is in the city, with Mickey and my friends. Not with the Keepers of the Pines. Not with these trees. Not with Juniper.

The tapping of rain against the leaves was eerie at first but became soothing as I hiked deeper into the forest. Then, I felt an odd vibration in the air.

Creeeak...

"What the fuck is that?"

Craaack...

BAM!

I was launched into the air, my arms windmilling as I slammed into the side of a tree stump before dropping back to the ground. I rolled to a stop in a thorny bush.

"Ow." I sat up, holding my right side. When I looked around, I realized a large pine tree had fallen only five feet away from where I was sitting.

"Holy shit, thanks Gaia," I pushed to my feet gingerly. A sharp pain lanced through my ribcage as I exhaled. "Fuck. Okay. This seems like a change of heart, Gaia. I think I have a broken rib. Wait, what the hell am I saying? I think this cult is getting to me."

I probably appeared drunk when I stumbled into camp.

One of Noble's followers ran to help me. "Are you alright? What the hell are you doing out here? Don't you know it's the Hundred Year Saltwater Moon? Are you trying to get yourself killed? You aren't supposed to be here."

Juniper's voice sounded behind me. "Yes, she is. She is exactly where she is supposed to be. I wondered if you would show up, Millie. Come with me, and I will get you some dry clothes." I turned and she held out her arms.

I fell to my knees in relief. I don't know what came over me as I sobbed, overwhelmed by my journey.

I'm finally here. I made it.

More people rushed to my aid, but Juniper stopped them. "Everyone, leave Millie and I alone, please." Juniper knelt and gently wrapped me in her warm embrace. "You're safe now," she said softly. "Everything is going to be okay. Nothing can hurt you. This storm is going to last several more hours, so let's get you out of those wet clothes before you catch a cold." Juniper ran her fingers through my hair. "Are you hungry? I have some hot soup in my tent."

She supported my body as I got to my feet. My legs began to shake, but I couldn't give in to the panic.

I can't let myself freak the fuck out right now. Maybe Juniper will help me save Mickey and get us out of here.

"I think I just want to go back home; I don't want to be out here anymore. Can we call the coast guard to come get us or something?"

If I could get the coast guard here, then they could help find Mickey.

Juniper didn't respond. She led me down the muddy trail, affectionately rubbing my back.

Destruction was evident all around us. Some tents were shredded, and Douglas's brick oven was a pile of rubble. Picnic tables were overturned, the wood splintered.

At Juniper's tent, the pallet that once served as her porch was gone, replaced by a deep pool of muddy water.

"Come this way. I have a second entrance on the other side."

Juniper was so calm. I was sure she had been through dozens of storms in these woods, but this had to be the most dangerous, right? I stood close behind her while she unzipped a plastic flap and stepped inside. I followed and shivered. The inside of the tent was cold, but at least it was dry.

Juniper lit a lantern, and I was temporarily mesmerized by the way the light danced along her irresistible curves.

"My God, you're beautiful." As horrible as I felt, this amazing woman stood before me like a Greek goddess able to take away all my fears, my OCD, and my anxiety. As if with one touch, I would never feel pain again. In it's place was pure bliss. She was magic.

Juniper is my unicorn.

Needing to relieve pressure from my ribcage, I hobbled to the bed and sat down breathing deeply.

Juniper rummaged through her dresser. "Here are some clothes you can wear. Nothing fancy, just a sweatshirt and sweatpants, but they're dry." She tossed the clothes next to me.

I looked around the space, taking in all the small details I hadn't noticed the first night I visited; the table was covered in art supplies and the small bookcases were stuffed with titles ranging from gardening to urban development. Juniper was obviously very intelligent.

Am I falling in love with her?

Struck by a sudden shiver, I stripped off my wet clothes and pulled on the dry ones, remembering to switch my GPS glasses from my jeans to the sweatpants. My anxiety lessened as soon as warm dry clothing touched my bare skin. Ever since I was little, I couldn't handle the feel of wet clothes, not even after swimming.

Juniper was staring. "Why are you looking at me like that?" She was so adorable when she blushed. She poured something from a kettle into a bowl and handed it to me. "This is a special soup that I always make when it's stormy. It's a little bitter, but I promise it will warm you from the inside out. It's mostly a broth, but I think you'll like it." She grabbed my wet clothes from the floor and hung them on a hook. Then started to pack a few items into a bag, which I hoped meant she had a plan to get us out of here.

I let the steam cover my entire face before blowing on the first spoonful of broth. I sipped it slowly so I wouldn't burn my tongue.

My lord, that is fucking disgusting. How could she possibly eat this shit and like it? It tasted like dirt and grass.

I set the bowl on her nightstand. "Wow, that is *really* hot. I think I will let it cool a bit first. Come sit by me." I patted the bed. "I want to snuggle."

Juniper zipped up her bag before turning back to me. She seemed distracted and a bit anxious when she finally responded. "Millie, we can't snuggle. Don't you get it? Tonight is a very special night. The gods have risen for the first time in one hundred years to fight under the Saltwater Moon. We can't just sit here and wait for the end to come; we have to create our own ending."

Now I was getting concerned that she really believed this story was coming to life. "What are you talking about? Honestly, you are being silly with this Saltwater Moon and god's war stuff. I know you talked about this before. But, could you walk me through it?"

Juniper's entire demeanor changed as she threw her bag over her shoulder. With the biggest smile that I had ever seen cross her lips, she said, "Walk you through it? How about I walk you *to* it?"

CHAPTER 36

I attempted to keep my balance as we tramped through the under-growth, maneuvering over fallen trees and debris. With each step I winced in pain and clutched my side tighter to apply pressure around my rib cage.

"Where are we going, Juniper? The storm is getting worse! Will you please slow the fuck down? I can't keep up at this pace. My ribs are killing me!" She didn't respond.

She must not have heard me over the rain and wind. Or maybe, she just didn't care. It broke my heart that this storm, this stupid legend was more important than me.

"Juniper! Juniper! STOP! I'm done! I won't go any further until you tell me what the fuck is going on. I'm just going to sit my ass down right here," I shouted as I fell back onto a crippled tree trunk. "One. Two. Three. Four. Five. Six. Seven." I recited my numbers so Mick-ey—*Mickey bleeding... Mickey shot...*—wouldn't die.

Juniper turned around and knelt in front of me. "We don't have time for this, Millie. What do you want to hear?" She was trying to sound calm, but I could hear the tremble in her voice. She was frustrated with me.

"I want to know where the fuck we are going and what we are going to do when we get there. I'm in pain, Juniper." My voice trailed off, and I started to cry. "One. Two. Three. Four. Five. Six. Seven. One. Two. Three. Four. Five. Six. Seven."

...Mickey stabbed... Mickey dead...

I wrapped my arms around my ribs.

Juniper wiped the tears from my cheeks and spoke in a softer tone. "Shhh... Millie, I need you to be stronger than this. We both need to be strong right now." She turned away but at least waited for me to rise.

"I can't be strong. I'm scared." My voice shook.

"Millie, when you're scared or hurt, tell it to the trees. They'll take on the rest."

"What? What does that mean?"

"It means the trees will hear your words and absorb your pain. They take your words and whisper them through their roots and down into the Earth. Millie, tell it to the trees."

I dragged myself to my feet and followed her feebly the rest of the way to the pebbled shore where there had to be at least a hundred people dancing, swaying, and singing. Noble evangelized to his followers through the music. This was the first time I really saw and understood the influence Noble had over these people. When Noble spoke, they leaned in. When Noble danced, they screamed and cried like he was a god himself. I glanced at Juniper. Her eyes were bright as she gazed at Noble, and I realized that she was no different.

I searched for any signs of my brother but didn't see him. Juniper pulled me behind the large Juniper tree and turned toward me.

"Do you love me, Millie? If I asked you to spend eternity with me, would you?" She took my hands in hers and fell to her knees.

"Juniper, will you please stand up? What are you saying? Can't you see all of this is crazy talk? Look at the way everyone around us is acting. It's like they're all on drugs or something. They're treating Noble like he's some kind of god who is going to save them. But save them from what? From whom? From this storm? From some made-up moon god? From themselves?" Her gaze dropped.

I pulled her in closer so she could hear me better over all the chaos. "Look, I'm sorry I said that, just come back to the city with me, Juniper. We can start a life together, help people, together. You and me, Juniper. We can stand against everything bad in this world. Please say you will come back with me."

Leaning back, she stared up at me with a look of sorrow. She wasn't going to say yes. She was going to say goodbye. "No, no, you are not going to do this to me. Please say yes... just say you'll come back with me. Damn it, Juniper!" I dropped to my knees and lifted her chin, holding her gaze. My hands and voice shook, full of fear. "Say yes to me right fucking now, Juniper!"

We rose from the ground and walked a few steps from the Juniper tree, but before I could say another word, a man took her hand.

"Don't you fucking touch her!" I yelled as I pushed him away. He stumbled back, and I recognized him, "Lamar? Lamar from work? What are you doing out here?" He looked shocked to see me and took off running back to the group.

I took Juniper's hand and gently pulled her in the opposite direction. "We are leaving. We are going to find shelter until this storm passes and then we will find a way to call for help so we can get back to Seattle. Juniper, I need you to trust me. We are not safe here. Something bad is going to happen, and we need to leave."

Juniper ripped her hand away. "No! I'm not going back to Seattle. Father Noble will baptize his new followers under the Saltwater Moon tonight, and it will make him even more powerful. Don't you get it? The cycle will continue. They will all keep going to the city, keep trying to help the poor who will continue to be poor, and keep following their conservative beliefs. The cycle will continue. These people will keep spreading his message, and keep recruiting more followers. They'll marry and reproduce and create more babies to follow him." Her eyes widened crazily. "Food is the cover; it's the hook to bring a select few in. But the majority will never have shelter or education and will never have a family to love them. I know I've acted like Father Noble has been a good man, but Millie he's not. He is a really bad person." Juniper paused to look back at Noble, who was now chanting in an unfamiliar language.

Her eyes locked with mine, full of sincerity and something like desperation. "Noble will recruit them as followers and use them as he sees fit to run his farms, build his homes, and cook his food. Until one day, he amasses the empire he has always dreamed of. The poor will always be poor, but he will become richer. I can't live like this anymore, Millie. It's different for some of us. This opportunity will never come again in our lifetime. This is our last chance and the only way for us to be free of him. He is a murderer, Millie. We need to act now."

"We will find another way, Juniper. We can call the police, but we don't have time to argue about this." I tugged her arm.

We have to find Mickey and get the fuck out of here.

"I'm not going with you, Millie," she said, pushing me away. "I can't continue to watch this vicious cycle. What if I told you that there truly is something better on the other side of this? The other side of this life? Where you are free of all your worries and pain. Where you will always feel loved. Sounds like heaven, right? If there was such a place, maybe it's within your reach. Maybe you just need to follow me to find it. Does that sound so bad or scary? What if I promised it won't hurt; would you do it then? Trust me. I can give you everything you've ever wanted. I will give you me, and we will become goddesses on the ocean floor, forever as one with Gaia."

I saw a flash of movement out of the corner of my eye, and I heard Noble's voice booming over the storm. Then, he pulled a large sword from a sheath as he asked his followers to kneel.

Juniper grabbed my chin and jerked my attention back to her. Our faces were millimeters apart. "Are you listening to me, Millie? I said I can give you me, for eternity."

"Juniper, this sounds crazy, and I have no idea what they're talking about. There is no such place." It was at that moment that I knew I'd lost her forever. Juniper pursed her lips and stared as if she were in a trance.

I touched her cheek gently. I wasn't sure if I was drying tears or rain. I searched for reason in Juniper's glassy eyes, but I only saw my reflection looking back.

Did I get it all wrong? I let Juniper down and now she was lost to me.

She pushed my hands away and took off running for the shore. She didn't even stop when her feet slammed into the freezing water.

"Juniper, NOOO!" I chased after her, wading into the same salty ocean that fed the moon. I was the only person trying to save her. "Somebody, help me!" I screamed. "JUNIPER! Baby, please come back up!" I dove under the water as deep as I could go before I resurfaced. "JUNIPER!" I dove back under again and swam in circles as I searched for her. I surfaced, gasped for more air, and dove again, going deeper until I couldn't stand the pressure building in my head. I jetted back up and sucked in a mouthful of air before I dove again.

The icy water began to weaken my muscles, severe cramps making it impossible to keep my head above water.

"JUNIPER..." I coughed, choking on bitter saltwater.

I think I'm drowning...

"JUN..." I couldn't catch my breath. I wasn't strong enough to reach the surface again.

It's so dark down here. I can't feel my body. I can't swim. I will float. Jun... i...per...

CHAPTER 37

The sterile smell of cleaning solution mixed with fresh linens made me realize that I was in some sort of hospital room before I even opened my eyes. I laid there as someone messed with what felt like an IV in my arm. Regardless of all the medical supplies surrounding me, I knew I was definitely not in a normal hospital environment.

"She's still out cold and it could be another hour before the serum completely wears off," said a woman's voice. "The brother is already awake, but I gave him another shot of the good stuff. He's eaten two pieces of cake and is watching old cartoons. I expect him to be flying high as a kite for hours, happy as a clam. He's only asked about his sister once." The woman laughed.

Mickey is alive! Oh, thank God, Mickey is alive. Wait. What a dick! Mickey was totally selling me out for Bugs Bunny and chocolate cake!

My feelings were hurt.

"I will check back on her again in a half hour." I could hear the rings of the curtain close, and a light flick off when she left the room. I heard rubber-soled footsteps walking away, and I cracked one eye open.

"Ow... ow!" My body felt like I was thrown off a mountain. A sharp, stabbing pain zapped through my skull every time I blinked. Tears collected in the corners of my eyes, softening the muddy crustiness.

I had no idea where I was, how long I'd been here, or how I had even gotten wherever this was. My mouth was dry as I ran my tongue along my swollen, split lip, tasting a mix of dirt and the heavy metallic flavor of blood. The room was blurry except for a glow that wrapped around the curtain across the room.

I was dizzy, and the harder I tried to focus, the more everything spun. Seconds later, I doubled over and retched onto the floor.

Dropping my head back on the pillow, I rubbed the back of my sore neck where I felt dried mud and blood clumped along my hairline.

Christ, what the hell happened to me? I must have taken a blow to the back of my head.

"What the fuck is going on?" I muttered into the near darkness.

When I could finally stand, I ripped the IV from my arm, and the effects of whatever drug they had given me hit me hard. I grabbed hold of the bed to steady myself so I didn't fall.

"Juniper"... I whispered. My heart was broken. I had tried. I had tried to save her. I wasn't going to let that bastard take Mickey from me too.

I carefully pulled on my sweatpants and socks and then slipped my feet into my shoes and nabbed my glasses, which were left on a bedside tray. I pulled off the hospital gown, but thankfully, I was still wearing my dirt-stained sweatshirt. I inched closer to the curtain and peered through the little opening to check that the coast was clear before I stepped into the hallway.

It wasn't hard to find Mickey. I just followed the sound of his belly laughs. He was at the end of the hallway sitting on a leather couch under a Mickey Mouse blanket shoving a spoon full of chocolate pudding into his mouth. He looked like a child with food all over his face. Mickey threw his head back with another loud laugh.

What the hell did they do to him?

He spotted me, and I could tell he knew I was disappointed by the way his demeanor changed from five-year-old man-baby to teenage Mickey in trouble with Mom.

I leaned forward with my fist on my hip and mouthed, "Get over here, now!" I raised my eyebrows and pointed my finger sternly at the ground.

Mickey mimicked my expression and pointed his finger first to his chest, then to the Mickey Mouse on his blanket, and then pointed to himself again, grinning widely, which I interpreted to mean he was excited that he and Mickey Mouse shared the same name.

I tried not to smile at the fact that Mickey, who was typically the tough guy, was now reduced to a little kid watching Saturday morning cartoons. Although somewhat adorable, I had to keep him on track to get us out of here fast, so when Mickey didn't move to stand up, I firmly mouthed, "seriously, get over here right now!"

This time, Mickey looked at me with sad eyes as he tore off the blanket, put down his spoon, did a quick recon scan, and tiptoed over to me.

"Are you mad, Soda Po—"

"Shhh! No, Mickey. I'm trying to get us out of here alive. I think we should just stay focused on getting home, okay?" I took his arm and scanned for an exit.

"Fine. But just so you know, this place is awesome, Millie! They have everything a boy—"

"Mickey, shhh," I repeated. "I don't know what drug they pumped into you, but you are clearly very high right now. So, the less you say, the better."

"You're right, little sister. The fact that you know I'm high on something tells me it isn't a good time to tell you that I can see dead people, or that my ring finger is longer than my index finger which means I'm a lesbian. See?" Mickey held up his hand.

I slapped his hand out of my face. "My God, Mickey, you are seriously losing your shit right now." I looked around to make sure no one was coming. "We have to get out of here before someone notices and we get hurt. So, stay close and keep your feet moving."

I put on my GPS glasses, which quickly identified our escape route.

"Millie! It's Trae and Cici, we are so glad to hear your voice. We've been so worried about you! I'm gathering your coordinates now." Trae paused. "Holy shit, this doesn't make sense. I have you in the Stone Water Games building, well sort off, something is off." I could hear Trae feverishly typing on his computer.

Before I could I say anything in response, I heard voices coming down the hallway. Any second now, the nurses would discover I wasn't sleeping in that triage room, which meant they would check on Mickey and find him gone too. "I can't talk, Trae," I whispered. "We have to go; they are coming for us."

"Millie, about Noble—"

I shut down my comms and jerked Mickey's arm. "Let's go!"

We sprinted down a hallway that very much resembled a normal hospital hallway, until we turned the corner. We found ourselves in an abandoned tunnel, dimly lit by hanging lanterns along each side of the long corridor. I turned off the night vision on my glasses. Looking up, I saw the ceiling propped up with large wood pylons, like the ones down at the pier. Along the long path were brick buildings, doorways, and store front windows.

We slid to a stop creating puffs of dust at our feet. "Sweet sewer rats of Seattle, Mickey. We are in the Seattle Underground. Trae and I took this tour the other day. I need to check out our navigation." I tapped on the glasses and looked closely at the map, which was now recommending a route that led us deeper into the city—probably because the exit doors above us were locked outside of tour hours.

"Millie," Mickey snuck up behind me as I fiddled with my glasses.

"Yeah, what's up?" I tapped the right side of the frames.

"How do you know if you are in love?" Mickey sounded like he was crying.

"What? Love? Mickey, do you think you are in love with Officer Palmer?" I paused as I looked over at him. But I couldn't give this topic my full attention. If I didn't get us out of here, Mickey would never get the chance to tell her.

"I don't know. I mean, I like her, but she *is* a bit bossy. She loves all the same stuff I love; she loves you. After all, we have been dating for six years."

My mouth dropped open. "Six years, Mickey? Holy shit! How have you hidden this from me for six years?" I was completely flabbergasted. "Okay, well I'm probably the worst person to ask about love. But I don't think it's about whether you can live *with* her, I think you need to ask yourself if you can live *without* her. Mickey, can you see your life without Officer Palmer?"

"No, Soda Pop. I don't think I can." Mickey looked down at his lesbian hands, turning them over to inspect the length of his fingers again.

"Then you have your answer and also know what you need to do next. Tell her you love her. I mean for fuck's sake, it's been six years." I gave him a jealous smile.

"Okay, back to getting us out of here. I say we trust the path the glasses gave us because Trae programmed them, and I trust Trae."

"I have a magic Mickey plan that can get us out of here." Mickey pointed to his head.

"Okay Mickey, I'm all ears. Whatcha got?"

"We gather all the dirt down here, break a pipe, put the dirt in the pipe, rub two pieces of wood together to start a fire, that will light my pipe bomb and KABAM!" Mickey yelled.

I quickly covered his mouth. "Mickey shut the fu—"

"My name isn't Mickey. It's MacGyver."

"Your name is not MacGyver. It's Mickey."

"I could be MacGyver."

"But you're not." I assured him.

"Okay, Mickey—"

"MacGyver," he whispered back.

"Alright. I tell you what, *MacGyver*. If my idea doesn't work, we will use your bomb. Deal?"

Mickey nodded happily as he nudged me to move further down the tunnel into the unknown.

CHAPTER 38

Mickey jumped at every little noise, as if something sinister lurked around every corner. I didn't blame him for being scared. He was drugged, so he likely didn't have a lot of control over his emotions. I even felt like the stillness in the air was spooky.

We took our time making our way to the end of the tunnel. So far it seemed as if we were completely alone. Suddenly, my GPS glasses lit up with a new path for us to follow.

"Mickey, in fifty feet we are going to take a right. Do you hear that? It sounds like water?" I could feel his arm trembling against my back.

"Yeah, I hear that. I'm thirsty. Do you want me to go first?" he asked, unconvincingly.

"Yeah, I think so." I smiled sheepishly.

"Really? You do?" Mickey sounded like he wanted to cry.

"Of course not! Just stay close and don't make any noises. We have to be really, really quiet."

But just as I said that, Mickey screamed. "Aggghhh, help me!!!" I turned as he started dancing. "Rat! Rat! Rat!"

I slapped my hand over his mouth. "My God, Mickey! Are you trying to get us fucking killed?! What the hell?"

We held our breath, and I kept my hand over Mickey's mouth while we waited in the silence.

I exhaled slowly. "Alright, you have *got* to keep it together." I had never seen such terror in Mickey's eyes. I clasped his hands in mine. "Look, I will make you a promise. I promise you, Mickey, that I will have us home in time for Thanksgiving dinner. You, me, and Officer Palmer. Okay? I just need you to keep quiet. No more screaming, okay? You and me, home in time to fill our bread bellies with Mama's spaghetti and meatballs. Your bread and two frothy glasses of Strawberry Quik on Thursday with Officer Palmer. Or should I start calling her Nancy now?"

Mickey still looked terrified, but he nodded his head. "Yeah, okay Millie. No more screaming. And you can call her Nancy. I think I'm just tired, and hungry. I haven't eaten much or slept in days." For a second, I thought he was having a lucid moment until he suddenly started to smile and pointed to the ground.

I looked down at my feet to see the perfectly shaped mountain top on which we stood.

It looked like we were standing on a model of Mt. Tahoma, or Mt. Rainier as out-of-towners called it.

I pointed to the waterfall pouring gracefully off the side of the mountain. "I knew I could hear water rushing." I kicked around the fake snow with my foot, wondering what the hell was going on down here.

"Millie?" Mickey crept up beside the fake rock where I was hiding.

"Yeah, Mickey?"

"It's like a dream come true, sis."

"What do you mean?"

"This is what I always imagined Fraggle Rock would look like. I want to live here, Soda Pop!" Then with a burst of excitement, Mickey attempted to slide down the side of the mountain.

"No Mickey, it's not Fraggle Rock. You're hallucinating!" I reached for his collar, but it tore away from his T-shirt as I tried to hold him back from sliding further down the fake snowy path. He slid hard into another fake rock and stopped, and I stumbled after him.

"I agree, it is beautiful Mickey, but we can't just go down there. Remember, Noble wants us dead. Why else would he bring us here?" We gazed down at the small, almost complete, and fully-functioning underground city. People were gardening, walking their dogs, and visiting with each other outside a small bookstore. It was like a wonderland.

Good thing we were at least thirty feet in the air and they couldn't see us behind this fake rock.

In the center of town stood a statue of Gaia positioned in the middle of an impressive fountain. The goddess stood tall, her arms stretched high above her head, her hands pressed together in prayer, and her long, flowing hair fell peacefully down her back. Water sprouted from the tips of her fingers. We were completely mesmerized.

I turned my gaze to the rest of the township. There was a bookstore called A Real Page Turner shaped like a book with tables and chairs clustered in the center of the open pages; a tea shop called The Leaf; and two restaurants: a breakfast place called Flapjacks and a diner called The Green Bean Grill. There was a hospital in a large house-shaped building, and at the far end of the city, there was what looked like a storage facility and a pharmacy. It wasn't lost on me that there were no police stations or churches.

Hovering above the city were multiple large-screen TVs welded together to create a cohesive image of the sky, which was currently simulating daytime.

Two blocks of tiny houses were positioned on one side of the town square, each five-house block representing a different neighborhood. The homes were individually painted in various bright colors. They all had front porches with cute little swings, old-fashioned lamp-posts, and mailboxes.

A common sidewalk meandered through the city, leading through the merchants to the town center. Not a car in sight.

Thriving trees and shrubs lined the pathways, and each home featured bountiful gardens, overflowing with fruits and vegetables.

Oddly, they had planted a small forest, still in its infancy, of entirely Noble pines as a backdrop, opposite the waterfall. The trees smelled sweet, and if I closed my eyes, I swore I was back on Blake Island.

We froze at the sound of raised voices. "Find them! If they get out of here, we will lose *everything!*"

"That's our cue! Follow me, Mickey!" We ran down the mountain and into the city. We hopped a fenced backyard and hid behind a shed as I tried to figure out our next move.

Suddenly, I smelled something skunky and looked over my shoulder to find Mickey taking a long drag off a joint. "What the actual fuck are you doing, Mickey?" I ripped the joint out of his hand and threw it to the ground where I quickly snuffed it out with my shoe. "Where did you get that?"

"Your room back home. I found it when I was cleaning or something. I had it hidden in my sock. You're naughty, Millie." Mickey giggled, poking me in the ribs.

I tried to ignore him, but each poke made me squirm a little more in pain until I finally broke. "Mickey, stop it!"

"You're a meanie, Soda Pop. Like, a big one."

"Mickey, I really need you to act like a grown man right now, okay?"

"MacGyver," he whispered.

I tried to refocus. It was weird to be underground in a small city that looked and smelled so real. I peered up at the fake sky and could tell that night was coming, which would be great cover for an escape.

"Millie! Oh no! Millie! A piece of my elbow bone is missing, and I think I left it at the top of the mountain. We have to go back and get it!" Mickey was swinging his arm back and forth like a robot.

"What? You have got to be kidding me. No, nothing is missing. All your bones are right where they are supposed to be, I promise." I peeked around the corner to see if we had a clear path to the wooded area, which I assumed would lead us back to the fork where we should have turned right.

"Then why is my arm so loose and squeaky?" Mickey was still swinging his arm.

"Oh wow, look here. I have an extra elbow bone in my pocket that you can borrow." I shoved a fake bone into his elbow.

Mickey started to sniffle. "I can't believe you just gave me your extra elbow bone. No one has ever been this nice to me before." He wiped his nose on his sleeve.

I smiled at him. "Not a problem, Mickey. But now we need to figure out how we are going to get from here to those woods over there. Here is what I'm thinking…" I took a nearby stick and started to draw a map in the dirt.

Mickey clapped his hands together. "I love to draw!"

I stared at him and shook my head. "We are going to shed hop through these three backyards until we get to the pharmacy on the west side of town." I bit my lip and stared at him intently while I thought of our next move. "Now this is where it's going to get tricky, and I need you to really focus, Mickey. Do you think you can do that?" He stared straight ahead, motionless. "Mickey, are you listening to me?"

"I'm focusing." Mickey didn't blink.

"I swear, when I get a hold of the fucking people who drugged you, I'm going to inject every one of their siblings with this same drug and then lock them all in an empty room for eight hours so they can experience every bit of this mini nightmare."

I returned to my drawing and dragged the stick through the soil to represent the path from the pharmacy to the storage building. "From the pharmacy, we have two options. First option: if the people chasing us go to the woods, we hide out in the storage building until the coast is clear. Second option: if they enter the storage building, we run into the woods, which is exactly where we want to go anyway, so let's hope for option two." I made a big circle around the woods to emphasize our objective. "You can quit focusing now, Mickey."

Mickey exhaled. "Can I draw while we wait?" He reached for the stick.

"Sure, buddy."

We waited behind the shed until the sun was fully set and then set off toward the woods. Shed hopping was easy because the fences were only two feet high between each house. The most problematic part was Mickey's quiet "wee, wee, wee, weeeeee" like that Geico pig every time he hopped over a fence.

When we reached the last house, sure enough, our luck ran out. Half a dozen people were spread out, searching for us along the edge of the forest.

I turned to Mickey, who was rubbing his head as if waking up from a dream. "We are stuck with option one, Mickey. We need to sneak to the storage building and hide there for a bit. How are you doing? Remember what I promised you? I'm going to have us home for Thanksgiving dinner, Mickey."

He was still rubbing his head. "Yeah, I hope so, because I could use some aspirin and a nap right now."

"Me too, buddy. Me too." I blew out a long exhale.

We jogged low and tender-footed along the grass for about thirty yards from the pharmacy to the storage building door, which was luckily unlocked. I cracked the door open just enough to peer inside. It was dark, so I had to make a call.

"Let's go. I think no one's in here." We opened the door fully and tip-toed inside. There was just enough light from the outside I could make out outer walls, a roof, a dirt floor, and a few dangling light bulbs, but we had nowhere to hide.

Then, we heard the pounding of boots against the dirt floor, and I knew we were caught. I tensed, prepared to defend Mickey.

A large group closed in around us. "Millie?" someone said softly from the crowd. I remained silent, even when the lightbulb above my head popped on. I stepped in front of my brother protectively.

I couldn't identify anyone beyond the swinging light, but one upside to having OCD was masking my reactions. Inside, I wanted to freak out, but I stood strong and fearless even though I could feel Mickey shaking against my back.

"What do you want from us? Why are we here?" I reached behind me to grab Mickey's hand. If we were going to die, I was going to be holding his hand.

"You know exactly why you're here. You just couldn't stay away, and you didn't give us what we asked for, Millie. I knew from the day I laid eyes on you that you were going to be trouble. I told everyone that we needed to watch you closely. I knew you would get in the way." I recognized the quivering voice.

"So, you kidnapped us, Lamar? You brought us to this hole in the ground? Maybe I was just trying to help! Have you ever thought of that?"

"Liar!" Lamar's voice screeched through the silence of the storage building.

His rage silenced me. I knew there was nothing I could say to deescalate the situation. I needed to come up with a plan quickly because if I didn't, we might not get out of here alive.

Think Millie! Think!

Suddenly, a gun shot rang out and shattered the lightbulb above us, raining glass down. I covered my head, and beside me, Mickey did the same. "What the fuck?" I screamed into the darkness, my ears ringing.

A shadow held the gun, and they paced behind Lamar. Whoever it was seemed very agitated. If I could just get them to stand still, I could make my move.

"Yeah, we could have gotten you off of Gilligan's Island and saved everyone, including the Professor, Maryann, and the Skipper too," Mickey interjected, clearly trying to be helpful.

"I'm not sure who these people are but none of them have ever visited the island," one voice acknowledged.

"Well, there was one Mary but never a Maryann, so..." Another voice confirmed.

"Certainly, never a Skipper," verified a third man.

"Shut the hell up! All of you!" Silence fell across the warehouse. "You should have never come to the Island that night, Millie. You were never supposed to be there, but you came out anyway and almost drowned your damn self. Now you have seen our city, and we can't allow you to go free. You've seen too much." The voice shook with anger. "I took your brother, so you would stay in Seattle and look for him. So, you would stay away from the Island. I was going to release him. He would have never known he was down here. Then you showed up *again*, and I was forced to save you when you almost drowned." Juniper stopped pacing. I just needed her to lower the gun.

"Hey, I know you!" Mickey cried. "You were there the day those guys kidnapped me. Soda Pop, I remember now, she was the one who gave me the shot in the neck." Mickey pointed directly at Juniper.

My world collapsed. "Juniper, I thought you'd drowned." My heart started to race, but not in excitement because it was clear she wasn't here to save us. She was there to hurt us. "How could you do this to me? To my family?" I paused, staring into her eyes. "So, wait, none of this was Noble? You're the Body Goblin?" I was dumbfounded. This couldn't be true. There was no way.

I inched closer to Juniper as I spoke.

"For fuck's sake, would everyone please quit calling me that stupid name!" Juniper roared.

A huff of air released from her lungs as if she was laughing. "I told you one day we would look into each other's eyes, and you would have to make a decision. I was hoping you wouldn't have to, but here we are. Today is the day, Millie. And your decision is simple. You can come live among us or be buried six feet under us. Either way, you will never see the light of day again.

Although it was almost completely dark, there was enough light coming from behind the door to illuminate Juniper's silhouette, and I knew I had to take the chance.

I made Mickey a promise to be home for Thanksgiving dinner, and I'm not going to break that promise.

"Yeah, you just keep telling yourself that you get to decide if Mickey and I live or die. But I don't think so, Juniper. There is a third choice here. Do you want to know what it is?"

"Oh, please, do tell me! I would love to hear all your make-believe options, Mill—"

I took a running start and lunged at Juniper.

"Millie, NOOO!" Juniper screamed.

The loud pop of the gun went off and smoke filled my nose. My head slammed onto the ground. I rolled to my side, a stabbing pain in my shoulder followed by an intense burning sensation.

I've been shot. No... no... no, I've been shot!

Soda Pop!" Mickey screamed.

The room closed in, darkening while a jumble of confusing images filled my thoughts. Then, silence.

CHAPTER 39

*W*hen you've taken as many lives as I have, you start to wonder what it will be like when your own life ends. They say when you die, your whole life replays like a movie before your eyes for up to seven minutes. Physiologists say it can replay in any order, but all of them do happen.

Minute one, we see the moment we are born, our parents, and the doctors. I wonder if anyone truly finds this to be a beautiful moment as they are dying: watching ourselves put our mothers through such extra-ordinary pain.

But what about the children whose parents refuse them? What about the babies who go straight from the womb to a cold, dark crib in some lonely nursery where no one touches them again until a state worker takes them to a foster home?

Minute two is such a sweet one. When we see our first happy childhood memories, probably playing with your siblings or friends. But what about the kids who went from foster home to foster home? What if each *childhood memory came with a slap across the face, a burn on the arm, or a beating so severe that their first happy memory was when they escaped, even though it meant living on the street?*

Minute three is when we see all the people we ever truly loved, from the first to the last. A rapid fire of broken hearts, shattered dreams, endless streams of tears, and finally getting the courage to say 'I love you' only to hear silence in return. Then, one day you meet the one, the one who checks all your boxes. They are smart and funny. They make you blush and spin your insides with just one smile. They're beautiful, but they belong to someone else. Someone else gets to hold them at night, make them laugh, see them blush. Someone else makes their stomach spin with just one smile. Someone else is their forever and you get to die watching their happily ever after.

Minute four: this one hit hard—your most depressing moments. You crave a family like the other kids; you want a lover who someone else has. You watch the whole world fold in on itself while you watch because not one person understands that this world is worth saving. You sit in coffee shops and libraries. You visit what's left of our parks and forests, just to watch people destroy our Earth callously. She weeps.

Minute five is the miracle moment. Ha! I laugh. I laugh and laugh because our world is dying. There are no miracles. I'm curious what people witness as their miracles in this state of destruction. Being the single survivor of a plane crash or crawling out from under a thirty-story collapsed building seem like miracles. But what does the average, every-day person see as their miracle? What are miracles like for those people? For people like me...

Minute six brings judgment. Did I live my life well? Was I a good person or a bad person? Can I show myself compassion in this final minute and forgive myself for all my wrong doings? Or will I damn myself for eternity? No one else is here to let me off the hook—just me and my subconscious. I wonder, why wouldn't someone absolve them-selves of all their fucked-up ways? Make excuses to explain all their bad behaviors? What would you do if there was no one left to care? No one else left to listen? If it were just you. Are you strong enough to own your shit and forgive yourself? Or are you going to keep believing your own fucking lies?

Minute seven is the mystery minute. No one knows exactly what happens during this last minute of consciousness except that scientifically, all the chemicals in your brain start a frenzy of energy that some claim takes your soul to its next plane of existence without the constraint of the worldly body. Now this is where your belief in an afterlife or rebirth comes into play.

I certainly have my own beliefs.

CHAPTER 40

My hand stretched through the darkness, surrendering to the glow of a trillion radiant moons...

It's so bright... Mom? Aww... Mommy, cuddle me. All the babies in the nursery. I'm not alone. Aww, they put us together in the same crib to stay warm. Mommy, hold me, keep me safe. Daddy, hold me too! The light is so bright...

Mickey, you be the princess and I will be the dragon slayer; you make a better princess. You make me giggle, Mickey. I love baking Christmas cookies and decorating the tree, Mickey! The light is so bright...

Jenna, may I kiss you? I'm blushing. It's just you, Jenna. My first love, my only love. It's always only been you. Crawl under the covers with me, Jenna. I just want to hold you forever, until the day I die. Where is the light going? I want to go back to the light... It's so pretty... come back...

"Give her another ten cee cees and bring the paddles. Get me the goddamn paddles..."

I drifted into the silence, grasping for the alluring glow of a trillion radiant moons...

They are all dead. You wouldn't get dressed. You made me miss dad's call. You killed our family, Millie. The light is so bright...

Hi, I'm Trae. No, I don't want a drink. I'm gay-gay. Remember, Millie, I got you; you got me. I put the forever in your best friend. BFFs.

It's Cici. I don't go by Cinnamon. The two of you are my new family and this stupid private investigation business. The light is getting so bright...

Millicent, it's time. You are thirty-two and it's time, honey. You know, you might actually have a bright future in this line of work if you could just pass the test. I'm going to become a detective. No... no...

I floated toward the warmth of the alluring glow... I giggled. She's my favorite. I pulled her to my nose to breathe in every scent that creates her special magic: strawberries, baby powder, plastic, vanilla cupcake, leather, cotton candy, strawberries... strawberries... strawberries...

"Millie! Millie! Soda Pop! Wake up!" The sunlight was getting brighter as Mickey's silhouette waved a Strawberry Shortcake doll under my nose.

"Ohhh... ouch! What? What happened?" I took the doll from Mickey and tried to smile. "Is this the new version of smelling salts?" I looked around, realizing we were above ground and outside the Stone Water Games building. I was laying on a gurney in an ambulance with Mickey next to me and Trae and Cici just outside the rear doors.

Mickey was choked up. "You gave us a pretty big scare, Soda Pop. It was hit and miss for a minute, and we thought we were going to lose you. You took a clean gunshot to the shoulder. The bullet only grazed your arm, so only a few stitches, but then you fell and hit the center of your chest on a rock, which sent you into a heart arrhythmia. You seem fine now, but we are going to get you checked out at the hospital to be safe. They almost had to shock you with the paddles, Millie. You scared the shit out of us." He took the Strawberry Shortcake doll back and stuffed it in his jacket pocket, looking a little embarrassed.

"Thanks to whatever pain meds they gave me... my arm and ribs don't hurt so much. My heart doesn't feel weird or anything. I feel like I can stand up, if that's okay. I'm glad you had a doll to snuggle with while you were scared." I sat up on the end of the gurney, but still winced a little.

"You can try and get up, but you are still going to the hospital either way. And the only reason I have that doll is because I had been cleaning out the basement when I was kidnapped. I found it in one of your boxes, and I guess it was feeling nostalgic, so I stuffed it into my jacket pocket."

"Cute story but I learned a little something about you down under, and I think you just like to play with dolls." I started to stand up and everyone protested. "It's fine, I want to stand up. Tell me what happened because I'm obviously missing some pieces. The last thing I remember was Juniper in the storage building, and suddenly I was out here with Mickey's Strawberry Shortcake doll shoved up my nose." I took note of my bandaged upper arm and felt the bump on my head before I gingerly stepped off the ambulance step, feeling unsteady.

Cici rolled up beside me, and I nodded towards the revolving doors where a handcuffed Juniper was being escorted out of the building by two police officers. They seated her on the curb at the end of a long line of people, also sitting along the sidewalk. I recognized Beth, the entire Sheldon family, Lamar, his sister, and every other murder victim.

What the fuck? Ghosts?

"When you feel up for it, I can give you the full download," Cici offered, sensing my confusion.

"Give me a minute. I'll be right back. I want to talk to Juniper before they take her away." I walked over and sat down on the curb next to her. We remained silent for a few seconds, not sure which one of us should speak first. I was hurt and angry, but I wanted to be open to whatever she had to say. I needed to understand why she did this.

Juniper broke the silence. "I'm truly sorry I shot you. It really was an accident, but I know it may not seem that way given how angry I was. It's just that ever since you slammed your head into my mouth at Westlake, I've been a little jumpy when I see you coming at me like you did. I shot you as a reflex."

I nodded as I contemplated her apology. She sounded genuine. "Yeah, that tracks. Things like that tend to happen to me a lot. I don't mean getting shot but the part where people get jumpy around me."

"Your brother is kind of a wuss, you know. As soon as you went down, he started screaming and throwing up. I started CPR because you stopped breathing, then the police showed up like clockwork. They ripped me off you and dragged me away... I was so scared that I killed you."

"Thanks. I appreciate that you cared enough to help after you shot me." I gave Juniper a soft smile.

She shrugged. "It's the least I could do."

I wasn't sure if I should confront her about how used and betrayed I felt. She could have seriously hurt me and Mickey, but on some level, were we any different? I used her to get closer to Noble too, so I was just as guilty. Except, I really did care about her.

"Millie, just so you know, I'm not a monster. I only wanted to take away everyone's earthly pain and give them a place where they would feel love and acceptance. A place where all their dreams could become reality. Remember, I told you that the only protection we needed would come from the depths of our mother's womb, and we needed to die under the Saltwater Moon to be reborn again underground. In the center of the Earth, no one would go hungry or wake up sad. No one would ever find us. We made a home that was truly beautiful."

"I saw it, Juniper. It *was* beautiful."

"It's important that you know I never lied to you about my past. My parents and I were unhoused. They did go to prison for drugs, and my dad did abuse my mom. I love the color purple and pansies. Noble did take me in. But, Millie, I could never be the daughter he wanted me to be. He is not a good man. I will testify to that when you need me to. He's a murderer."

"I know you didn't expect me to turn out to be this amazing detective either." Juniper snickered, but I continued. "I'm sorry I tricked you, but I want you to know I did care about you and—"

"Stop, don't make this any harder than it already is for either of us, please. Don't say words you can't take back." Juniper's eyes fell to the ground.

I also lowered my head. "But why not just disappear? Why all the dramatics of these elaborate murder scenes?" I asked, so confused.

"Because I wanted to throw the police off the trail. I had been practicing killing," she air quoted the last word, "people for years, but no one cared or noticed because it was just a bunch of missing unhoused people. Then I met people like Darrin and Beth whose souls were tormented by others. People whose families actually cared if they went missing. Doing it my way, they would bury empty boxes and the cases would eventually run cold. Beth, Darrin, and so many others would have been forever free from the hateful, controlling grips society and their families had on them. I saved them, Millie." We paused when one of the police officers looked at us.

"I think we are running out of time. Millie."

My heart was breaking right in front of this woman as tears started to roll down my cheeks. "I know." I tried to smile.

She returned my sad smile. "Millie, we both knew who the other was. We could have avoided so much pain if you had just given me what I wanted. We used each other to reach our goals and in the process, we both may have caught some feelings. You could have been a part of what we built: no wars, no hate, no starving families, no divisive politics, no one class system. I was... no, I *am* a builder. A creator. An artist. I never hurt anyone. I gave them peace, you see? I was their savior. They were happy. Yes, I took their bodies, but in return, I gave them back their souls."

"What did you want from me?"

"You got to be kidding me." Juniper looked up at the sky in disbelief. "You don't have to keep playing dumb. You got me." Juniper lifted her hand cuffed arms into the air.

The cop was walking toward us, so I knew it was time to say goodbye. I'd been practicing this moment since I laid eyes on Juniper.

Juniper laid her head on my shoulder. "Millie, I was hoping to be holding your hand when I told you this, but, you know, the handcuffs and all. I want you to know that this wasn't personal. Sometimes we have to break hearts to save hearts." Then, with a tender kiss on my cheek, the police officer tugged Juniper to her feet and pulled her away.

"That did not just happen." I mumbled to myself.

I stood and followed behind them, not ready for it to end yet. The officer frisked Juniper one last time before placing her into the cop car. Juniper opened her mouth to say something but shook her head instead. She spoke no more words, the sadness in her eyes evident. Our story ended here.

The cop slammed the door shut, and we stared at each other through the glass, until the officer drove away.

I waved to Juniper one last time.

Until we meet again.

I turned my achy body toward the chaotic scene behind me. Trae was sitting next to Beth. I debated if I should give them privacy or snoop, and my curiosity got the better of me. I moseyed behind a police SUV within earshot of their conversation.

I'm, like, the sneakiest almost private detective ever.

"I just don't understand, Beth. You could have told me you were struggling. I would have been here for you. You left me, one of your best friends."

Cringe. One of his best friends.

I rolled my eyes and made a puking face toward the ground.

"Trae, you know my parents. They are a nightmare. I swear if I could have told you everything, I would have. It was too risky. This was like a dream come true. Juniper was giving all of us a chance to live a life where no one could ever hurt us. You have no idea how bad it was with my parents. They were going to send me away. As an adult, Trae. To another country where they had hard labor camps and conversion therapy. I needed help and that's when I found Juniper." Trae wrapped his arm around her shoulders.

Beth started to cry. "I would rather go to jail than to another country. I just wanted to be an archaeologist, but they wanted me to get that stupid technology degree. They hated that I was a lesbian, and were rude to every girlfriend I brought home." Beth paused with a wet sniffle. "Trae, does anyone know what happened to Mozzarella? I had her at work with me that night. I was going to take her with me, but the guns spooked her, and I couldn't find her. We had to leave; there was no time to search for her."

"We found her at the office. She was covered in blood and so scared. I took her home with me. We've created a pretty amazing friendship.

She's my princess. I promise to take good care of her and give her the best home possible." Trae sighed. "I swear, I had no idea how bad it was with your parents either. You won't be in jail forever. When you get out, contact me. I want to be your first call. Millie and I will help you get back on your feet, and now that we know your parent's plans, we can help protect you from them. We'll work out what to do with Mozzarella. I promise everything will be okay."

I peeked around the corner.

"Trae, you are one of my best friends ever. I love you so much." Beth leaned in, hugging Trae before an officer came to pull her to her feet and take her away.

"You can come out now, Millie. I know you've been behind the police car the whole time. I could clearly see your shoes."

Sheepishly, I inched into view. "Busted." I threw my arms up in surrender. "I just want to tell you though, I know I have been gone a long, long," I paused to take a deep breath, "long time. And I haven't been here to tend to your best friend needs. Fighting crime in the underworld has been hard on me too. But really? Beth? A Pisces? How could you, best friend, cheat on me with a fucking Pisces, Trae. What the hell?"

"Millie, I don't know if you can call it fighting crime in the underworld. I saw their little city. It was cute as fuck—just a bunch of tiny houses, gardens, and some starter trees. Not really the underworld. Besides, you know Beth and I have been good friends for as long as we have."

That comment sent a stab of pain straight through my heart. "I can't believe you just said that. You are not only belittling the very utopic city Juniper and Beth helped create, but you also won't admit that I'm your forever BFF." Swirls of crushing emotions began to bubble in my stomach.

Trae pulled me into one of his signature bear hugs. "Millie, we have such a unique friendship that I can't even put it into words. You and I happen once in a lifetime. We are two people connected on the deepest level, but not, like, in a romantic or even sibling-like way. We are beyond friends, beyond soulmates; we are something much more special. When the universe made you and me, they looked down at us and affirmed: one day they will put the forever in each other's best friend, and no one will ever be able to tear them apart."

"See? I always thought it was our trauma bond, but I like the way you tell it better. Now, tell me again about the part where the universe sprinkled us with the gay-gay glitter."

CHAPTER 41

Cici wheeled up beside us. "You two are so weird. I legit think you both need therapy."

"We should all probably go together. I will sign us up for a fall session." I smiled at my friends.

Cici shook their head. "It's not like baseball tryouts, Millie. It's therapy. You don't just sign us up."

"Cici! Cici!" Roy and Else yelled from behind the crime scene tape.

"Let's go, keep walking," Cici whispered.

"Cici, the rats are all gone. You can come home now. Roy shooed them out of your doorway. They are gone now. We miss you," Else called as we walked in the other direction.

Trae and I glanced at Cici. "I knew it!" I said, grinning. "You were unhoused. You know you could have just told us the truth. You will always have a home with us. We love you, Cici. I will get us therapy session tickets." I went in for a hug that was quickly dismissed as they wheeled to the right.

Cici shook their head. "Fine. You know the truth now. Can we please go back to focusing on the case?"

Trae picked up his pace and waved his hand in the air. "Oh no, no, no. This boy doesn't do therapy. This boy has his bot boys, who are the best listeners and tell him everything he needs to hear."

I watched Trae walk ahead of us, when I felt Cici take my hand. "I tried to tell you so many times, Millie. I tried to stop you from leaving the night of the storm. Do you remember the note written by one of the Sheldons?"

"Yeah, I remember. But the cops checked the whole basement and found nothing that made sense." I recalled that piece of evidence very clearly.

Cici continued. "That's because it had nothing to do with their basement, and it wasn't entirely a piece of junk mail either. It was a brochure for the Seattle Underground Tour. Mr. Sheldon, Sr., took a vendor order on it from Hans. That was the ten ct of BL, ten ct of BU and twenty cu of CH—a berry order: blackberries, blueberries, and cherries. But the 'help downstairs' was him telling us they were underground. He was giving us the ultimate clue, and no one could figure it out. And guess what else was on the front of the brochure? An eighteen-eighties bank vault door."

"Holy shit!" I threw my hands in the air. "Why didn't you tell me? I probably wouldn't have gone to the island that night."

"Really, Millie? I mean, I legit tried to tell you five thousand times, but you wouldn't listen to a fucking word I said. Anyway, once I figured out that the bank vault on the brochure was an exact match to the one on the map, I was pretty confident it was an entrance to the underground. I had a hunch something bigger was going on down there, so, I went back to the maps, and, sure enough, when I placed all the maps together, they told a story. Follow me to the detective's tent, and I'll show you the rest of the evidence that helped us solve the case."

Before entering the tent, I noticed Susan Spruce reporting live in front of Stone Water Games. "Susan Spruce, KRHG News, reporting live from the scene where the Body Goblin is being taken into custody as we speak. The police have not released any details at this time but have said that if it wasn't for the heroic acts of a small private detective agency, this case may have gone unsolved. We will remain diligent in following the story, and I promise to be the first to report back with any breaking news as details are released in the coming days. In other news, a local vibrator manufacturing company claims they can solve more than just your man problems. Their product can also solve your migraines. Join us tonight at ten o'clock to find out what all the buzz is about."

When we entered the tent, all the hustling came to a halt, and everyone turned to stare at us. Well, at me. Officer Palmer was the first to break the uncomfortable silence as she approached and folded me into a hug.

"Ouch! Ouch! Not so tight." I begged and squirmed out of her embrace.

"I'm so glad you're okay, Millie. Mickey told us everything he could remember, although I'm not sure it all makes sense. Anyway, we are so grateful that he fought off all of those tree huggers until the police arrived." I gave her a confused look and then my eyes darted over to Mickey, who was giving me a pleading expression.

"Uh, me too. What would I do without that big strong guy over there?" I pointed to Mickey, who waved back with a big smile. "In fact, Mickey, why don't you tell us all about how you took down all those tree huggers—"

"Millie, come on. I want to show you the maps." Cici pulled me along.

"Later, Soda Pop, for sure. I will catch you up later." Mickey waved, and I flipped him off behind Office Palmer's back.

Cici led me to a series of tables where multiple maps had been laid out. Some of the hand-drawn ones were placed side by side, while others were above or below one another. Looking at them all together, I could see that they did, in fact, tell a complete story.

"Are you ready to hear this? It's based on all the evidence we gathered, information from the police, plus details from Juniper."

"Yes, I want to hear it all. I need to know what we may have missed that would have helped us put a stop to this sooner." I sat in the chair.

"Okay, well, we all know that the Keepers of the Pines supported the unhoused. They fed them, clothed them, and even helped educate them. When some of the people were rehabilitated, the Keepers allowed them to join the cult by shedding their birth name and giving them a tree name."

"Yeah, I remember Juniper telling me about that." My heart dropped at the thought of her stories.

Cici continued. "Juniper was one of those unhoused people who joined the cult, leaving behind her birth name. Juniper, legally named Camila, joined the cult when she was just eleven years old, after her parents went to prison, and quickly formed a strong bond with Noble, who became like a father to her. Juniper never partnered with anyone until she met an unhoused woman nine years ago, named Aiko. They fell madly in love with one another, but Noble didn't approve and drove Aiko away. Noble was old-fashioned and didn't want Juniper to be with another woman. He wanted her to marry a man within the cult. Secretly, Juniper and Aiko continued to see each other when and where they could safely meet. They would meet in coffee shops, back alleys, and even store dressing rooms."

"Ouch! Ugh, go on." Cici gave me an odd look, and I waved for them to continue.

"Okay, one day Aiko was found dead in a back alley. Rumors around the island were that she overdosed, but Juniper knew better. It didn't take long for her to confirm Aiko had been murdered. With her heart crushed, Juniper, of course, didn't have proof, but she knew Noble had something to do with Aiko's death. Based on that new information and with everything that happened to Noble, Mickey said they would be taking a fresh look at Aiko's case."

"This must be why Juniper kept telling me Noble was a murderer. That is really cool of Mickey to look into this." I felt really proud of him.

Cici smiled. "We thought so too. Back to Juniper, who was obviously heart-broken over the loss of her lover and Noble's betrayal, so she decided to create a world where no one would ever feel that kind of pain. A world where everyone could love freely, be warm, be safe, be cared for, and go to sleep with a full belly at night. But Juniper knew that Noble would never let her walk away from the life he gave her. She also realized that it was possible that other people wouldn't let their loved ones walk away either. So, Juniper came up with a plan to create a paradise underground and to fake everyone's murder. She knew no one would look for them twenty-two feet underground."

"But what about people like the Sheldon family? No one would be out there looking for them. No one would make them come back to their lives? The Sheldons were a whole family unit." I leaned forward.

Cici sighed. "The Sheldons were hard for me because they were elderly, and they convinced their adult son to go with them. Jason told the police he had an older brother who was estranged from the family.

He had recently been coming around and threatening the family. They had no fight left in them, so made the decision to go with Juniper. In their will Mr. Sheldon left the farm to a nephew, so the other son wouldn't get a dime. As farmers, they were a crucial part of the future agriculture system of the city. Jason got spooked at the last minute, but couldn't let his parents go without him, so he wrote the note on the brochure." Cici was so proud of that guy because he left one of the biggest clues.

Suddenly, Trae pulled up a chair beside me. "Hey, you two! Mickey told me that Juniper shared with him that she was looking for someone with Beth's specific skill-set and knowledge of geology and map drawings. She invited Beth to help with the structural design of the rock formations underground. In fact, every single person in Juniper's community had a specialty or expertise that contributed to the city's creation and sustainability, including construction, medical training, tailoring, farming, pharmaceuticals, and more. You name it."

Cici added. "Exactly, and like Beth, other members of the group had similar stories. It wasn't that complicated, really. A lot of these people were choosing to walk away from discouraging and controlling families or partners, emotional and painful memories of abuse and trauma, or financial hardship and unhoused situations. Every one of them was walking away from a world who didn't accept them as they were, as humans. Juniper gave them a place to be themselves."

"So, did Juniper's city have a name?" I asked as I unsuccessfully searched the maps.

"Yes, they named it after the historic storm that was meant to serve as the final event to bring them all together, Saltwater Moon," claimed Cici. "They spent the first five years digging and stabilizing the area for construction. It was during the last two years that the city of Saltwater Moon really came to life."

"Hmmm, I should have known that would be the city's name." I was so invested now, although I knew a lot of people would see what Juniper and her followers did as horrible, disturbing, a waste of city resources, and so many other things. I bet one day Netflix will pick up Juniper's folklore and they will tell the story of the Saltwater Moon in such a way it will be up to the world to decide... were they the victims or the aggressors?

CHAPTER 42

My heart was twisted. I wanted nothing more than to believe in Juniper's mission, but I had to continue to follow the facts. "So, how did people get accepted into Saltwater Moon?"

"Great question." Cici was an amazing storyteller, so I could see why they were such a talented journalist as well. "Juniper believed there are no coincidences, and that it was fate that these people found her, always randomly meeting on the street or in a coffee shop. These people would share their stories, their dreams, their struggles, pouring their hearts out to her willingly. Then, she would make them an offer they couldn't refuse. Sometimes, they would bring people along with them who wanted to be a part of their new way of life, like Beth did with her team, the medical crew, and even the entire Sheldon family."

I pointed to a map with Hans's logo on it. "Is that the DeCafé? What's up with that?"

"You were right about the connection to DeCafé, Millie. They would often meet there because it was so close to Saltwater Moon.

It was also a place where Juniper would find a lot of her potential victims, all under Hans's nose." They wheeled over to the larger map and continued. "But this map over here? This beauty shows us the entire underground city of Saltwater Moon, from the bank vault door where they entered to the exit through the basement door at Stone Water Games. Beth orchestrated the secret door into the new building schematics so you wouldn't even know it was there unless you already knew about the city! That's how well this door was hidden. We all thought Saltwater Moon was a small town near Seattle somewhere."

"Brilliant! That's how the janitor and the unhoused folks only saw people leaving the building that night without ever coming in!"

Trae was invested in the story as well. "Crazy, huh? Yeah, the people of Saltwater Moon would sneak into the Underground Tour groups throughout the day and hang behind until no one was looking. Then they would enter through the bank vault door because too many people were working at the Stone Water Games building to use that entrance during the day."

I interrupted Trae. "That must have been the light behind that bank vault door I saw the day we were on the tour. We were so close to them and didn't even know it."

Trae nodded his head. "Yep, and the rats. Then, after working all day building the city, they would leave through Stone Water Games at night because the underground exit to the street was locked up after the tours were done for the day. Before Stone Water Games, these poor people had to exit through a manhole. Less than ideal."

I crossed my arms. "But where did all the blood come from at the crime scenes? Seriously, what the actual fuck? That part is still wild, especially because there was enough blood to indicate actual people had died and that was blood confirmed by the medical examiner as belonging the victims."

"Oh yeah, that." Cici chuckled. "The Keepers of the Pines held blood drives as a cover to save the victim's blood for their big bang sendoffs. Darrin, who was a victim from the network team, was a weapons specialist back in his military days. He used his training to make blood paintballs, which they shot from paintball guns to simulate violent murders. This tactic meant they could replicate the force of real gunshot splatter. Smart, but fucking gross!"

I sat back at the sudden memory of the blood donation machine in the hospital tent on the island. "Wow," I recalled, shaking my head. "Does anyone know what happened to me when I chased Juniper into the water on Blake Island?" I started to get teary thinking about that traumatic moment, thinking I was going to lose her in those swells. "But then I don't remember anything until I woke up in that hospital room with a drugged-up Mickey."

Trae stood up and pulled the island's map closer. "That part of the story is a bit fuzzy. We talked to Noble, who claimed he knew nothing of what Juniper and the others were doing, which Juniper corroborated. Noble told us that he was commemorating the rebirth into the Keepers of the Pines cult for a large group of people by blessing them with a sword. Noble did say he saw a few people and Juniper run into the water, then you after her, but the swells were too high and dangerous for anyone to attempt to rescue either of you, so he stopped anyone who tried. He claimed that the next morning, he sent someone to Seattle to alert the police; however, there's no record of such a call."

I shook my head in disappointment. "What an asshole. So basically, Noble didn't even attempt to save me or Juniper, who was like his daughter?" I sighed. "So Cici, how did you know it was Juniper behind everything and not Noble and Tim?" I still couldn't believe I hadn't caught on to Juniper earlier. I was so sure it was Noble because he's such an arrogant prick.

Cici nodded. "The real surprise for us was when I started going through all my pictures and realized what Juniper wanted from you all along was my SD card from the first crime scene. There are about a dozen pictures of Juniper behind the crime scene tape standing there, staring back at me. She had the creepiest smile. Everyone else looked shocked, scared, confused. But not Juniper; she looked gratified. Like she just pulled off the perfect murder. And you know forty to fifty percent of all murderers return to their own crime scenes to relive their moment, keep control or tabs on the investigation. Big mistake on Juniper's part."

"The perfect crime for people who needed help disappearing." I added and sucked in a deep breath as a wave of emotion came over me. I held back my tears as Trae's arm wrapped around my shoulders. "Juniper wasn't a bad person, Trae. She just wanted a better world for herself and her people." I dropped my head against his arm.

"I know, but there was better, and less morbid, ways than making it look like murderer. Juniper still stole them from their families and friends, baby girl. So, there was some bad wrapped up in there even with the good, a happy medium of sorts." Trae squeezed me closer.

I wiped the moisture from my eyes. "I disagree. They all were adults and left on their own. But you're right, less theatrics would probably have been better." I tried to smile. "So what happens now? Will Juniper go to jail for faking the murders? What's planned for the City of Saltwater Moon?"

We left the map tent and started back toward the ambulance.

"I'm not a hundred percent sure what will happen to everyone," Cici said. "What I do know is that they all have jail time coming. I also know that the structure they built wasn't completely sustainable.

The architecture book you had in evidence didn't address the specific needs for building underground and natural erosion. They had only a couple years at most before they would have had to come up with a plan *B*. Who knows, maybe Seattle will profit from another tourist trap and extend the Underground Tour and raise its prices."

We halted at the back of the ambulance as Mickey ran up. "Hey, do you two mind if I have a couple of minutes alone with Millie?" he asked.

Trae blushed and poked Mickey in the bicep. "Sure thing, detective. See you at home, Millie!"

We watched them rush away before I broke the silence. "Did Trae get a little more gay just now? I think you actually make him gayer, Mickey." I couldn't help but laugh.

Mickey shook his head. "He's always had a crush on me. Remember when he bought me flowers for Valentine's Day that one year? And then cried when I gave him a rose back from the bundle and asked him to stay for Sunday dinner?" Mickey smiled at the memory.

"Yeah, he still has the dried petals in a glass box with an "M" engraved on the top." I shook my head.

Mickey put his hand over his heart. "Aww, that's so sweet. I hope it doesn't break his heart when he hears that I'm getting married." Mickey looked at me sideways and clenched his teeth together while he waited for my response.

I wrapped my one free arm around him and pulled him in for a huge hug. "I'm so happy for you, Mickey! And I think I'm ready to talk about Mom and Dad. I went to the house after you were kidnapped and I found a box with a newspaper clipping. It was just the headline. It said something about our sister being a young mother."

"Looks like your ride is here." Mickey pointed to the ambulance.

"We are going to talk about our family, Mickey." I knocked on the back of the ambulance door. "I made you a promise when we were underground, Mickey. I told you that I would get you home in time for Thanksgiving dinner, and I kept that promise. I'll see you tomorrow."

The back of the ambulance doors opened, and the driver stepped aside to let me in. I stood there staring at the guy, waiting for him to realize that I only had one good fucking arm to climb inside.

"You ready to head to the hospital and get checked out, Millie?"

"One. Two. Three. Four. Five. Six. Seven." I recited my numbers so Mickey wouldn't die as I wrapped my free arm around my aching stomach. "One. Two. Three. Four. Five. Six. Seven." I recited my numbers so...

"Millie, you are having a completely normal response given the trauma you have just experienced. Let's take a couple of deep breaths together, okay?" offered the paramedic.

For some odd reason, the blare of the sirens comforted me as we pulled out of the Storm Water Games parking lot. What were normally the sounds of chaos were now my sounds of calm.

CHAPTER 43

The rich aroma of coffee and the sweet smell of Trae's coffee cake was enough to get me out of bed early. I tilted my head to see the clock and was surprised to see I was waking up at my normal time despite not setting an alarm. I threw my pillow over my head and nestled deeper into my warm blankets for a moment longer.

I better get up because I have a lot to catch up on today.

Plus, I had plans to go over to Mickey's for our Thanksgiving dinner. This was going to be the first time that it wouldn't be just the two of us because he invited Officer Palmer, I meant Nancy.

I guess I should start calling her by her first name now that she's going to be around more and not just as my boss but as Mickey's wife. My life is so fucked up.

Sitting up on the edge of the bed, I contemplated my arm, which was in a sling for another five weeks. That reminded me I needed to swing by the evidence warehouse to fill out my FMLA paperwork before I went to Mickey's.

I stared at my watch, waiting for the minute to turn from 7:59 a.m. to 8 a.m. At the top of the hour, I grabbed my phone from the nightstand and went to my recent calls to select Mickey's name; he answered on the first ring.

"Still kicking," Mickey mumbled with a big yawn. "You know it's Thanksgiving, so we can probably put the chat about Mom and Dad on hold." I knew Mickey just wanted me to be in a better head space.

I decided not to give his comment much attention. "Yeah, anyway, I was just making sure you're still alive. See you for dinner this afternoon." I tapped End on the call.

I exited my bedroom to find Trea and Cici already at the kitchen table.

"Hey! Hey! Look who's up and ready to fight another day?" Trae flashed a big smile at me.

Cici patted a chair beside them. "Come sit, we have some news to share."

I shuffled over and dropped into the chair with a dramatic sigh. I looked at both of them while I cut and scooped out a piece of coffee cake before plopping it onto my plate. I slid my fork through the layers of melted cream cheese frosting, moist, springy cake, and gooey, velvety cinnamon ribbon that cascaded across another layer. "Is it more important than this coffee cake? Or can it wait while I enjoy a slice of heaven?"

Cici shook their head and responded in a serious tone. "No, it can't wait. Trae and I have been talking this morning, and we have made a decision that impacts you. We want to make this private investigation thing into a real business. We want to get real clients and make money doing what we do—the whole nine yards. We can build on the publicity we are getting now from the Body Goblin case because the police named us in their press release." Cici threw down the Sunday paper. On the front page of *The Seattle Times* was a picture of the three of us, standing in front of Stone Water Games.

Where the Seattle Police Department fell short, these three unofficial and up-and-coming Seattle sleuths stepped in to save the day. Seattle Police Chief Tonya Warren gave thanks along with a stern warning for the contribution of these gumshoe detectives in his statement. "Although the Seattle Police Department is grateful for the hard work and dedication that it took for these courageous individuals to bring down the person responsible for causing fear and panic to our community, we urge amateur private investigators to refrain from assisting with future cases as one of their own members did incur an injury. We are very thankful that Ms. Myles will be okay." Police say it could be months before they unravel the full string of events that led to the motive behind everything that happened in the underground utopia called the Saltwater Moon.

You couldn't tell it was us, but that wasn't the point. The point was that we were recognized as being amateur private investigators by the Seattle Police Department. That was huge! I leaned over and hugged Cici tightly.

"This is amazing, Cici," I squealed. "I'm so proud of you!"

With a gentle push, Cici removed themselves from my arms. "Get off of me. We have hugged enough this year." They pushed back from the table and wheeled toward the couch. "The first thing we need is a name for our private investigation agency. Trae and I did discuss and want to pull you in for the decision. We would all own an equal share of the business, all equally invested in its success. But we do want you to lead us, Millie. Will you be our lead detective?"

I gasped and raised my fingers to my lips, thinking of the perfect response. "Yes! Yes! Fuck, yes!"

Trae squealed. "Yay! Okay, so now we need our name. What should we name our PI agency?" He tapped his hands excitedly on the table.

I grabbed my plate of coffee cake in one hand and fork in the other and skipped over to the couch to sit next to Cici. "Let's clear the murder board and start playing with some ideas!"

Trae meticulously plucked off each little knife magnet, tossing them into the blood splatter bowl that was on the table beside the board. "What should we do with all these pictures and clippings?"

Cici rolled over from the couch and carefully took them from Trae as he removed them from the board. "We are a business now and so we're obligated to keep our data and evidence for at least ten years, I think. We need to create an official case file and store it somewhere protected and secure."

My dream of starting my own detective business is finally coming true! I'm so happy!

I grinned widely at my friends. My thoughts floated back to criteria and options for naming the agency. "I'm flexible on a business name as long as we have an attractive business card. A card that will make people crack a smile and trust us at the same time. The name and the business card need to truly represent us. What do you think of rainbows and a magnifying glass?"

We sat there in silence as we considered the possibilities. Trae was the first to speak. "I'm not sure about the name, but I do want to paint the van with whatever visual we choose. I mean, what could be a better advertisement than putting our business name and logo on my VW van?"

Cici splayed out their arms. "None of us can quit our jobs until we can get a solid clientele and steady income from the business. You all realize that, right?"

We all nodded.

The couch made a loud scraping noise against the floor as I jumped up. "I got it! What about Two Queer Spies and A Gay Tech Guy."

Trae ran around the couch and lifted me in the air. "I love it so much!" My coffee cake flipped off the plate and onto my shirt as he pulled me in for a hug, squishing it between us. "Ugh, seriously! Every fucking time..."

We caught the rare sight of a smile creeping across Cici's face. "That is brilliant and sums us up perfectly!"

The pink bot rolled into the room and picked up Cici's fork and fed them a piece of coffee cake while Trae and I stared at the two of them awkwardly.

"Pink bot? What are you doing? I did not program you to feed Cici. You are a gay bot who only loves me." Trae put his hand on his hip.

"Pink. Bot. Boy. Love. Cici." The bot fed them another bite.

"Let me say this a little more clearly, Cici, I did *not* program *my* bots to fall in love with you. What did you do to him?" Trae sounded frustrated.

"Fine. I took a course during some of my free time. I need an assistant, and unfortunately, I screwed up the code somewhere, so instead of fetching my coffee or grabbing papers off the printer, he is placing cucumbers on my eyelids in the morning, trying to feed me, brushing my hair and whispering..." Cici paused and closed their eyes before continuing. "I don't even want to tell you what he's been whispering in the middle of the night."

I started to laugh. "What a shit show!"

"Great, pink bot was one of my best gardeners. I could tell something was up with him when he started to hoe hearts in the soil."

All this bot talk made me wonder what had happened to Trae's rescue robots. "Hey Trae, I'm not trying to knock your tech skills because those GPS glasses were amazing. But I thought your robots were going to come save me if I got into trouble on the island?"

Trae sighed. "Yeah, about that. Technically they did try to save you. I hooked them up to drones and flew them out to Blake Island, each equipped with a tiny sword and programmed to fight to the death. But, once they reached the island and saw all the gardens, the bot boys became confused and started to tend the crops. I should have removed that programming to avoid the internal conflict. It took me forever to get them to stop saying the tree blessing when they came home."

Cici handed me a beautifully wrapped gift with a blue bow. "Dang, Cici. What did I do to deserve a personally gift-wrapped present from you?"

Cici whipped their wheelchair around and retreated toward the kitchen. "Don't get excited. The shop where Trae and I bought it wrapped it for us. Now just open it."

I didn't even attempt to be careful. I tore off the bow and tossed it away. The wrapping paper, although beautiful, was ripped, crunched up in a ball, and strewn on the ground, which delighted Mozzarella.

Tears fell from my eyes before I could speak. When I finally found my voice again, I said, "You bought me a flip, dark brown, leather-bound detective's notebook case? And you had my name imprinted on the front of it. Oh wow, this is the best gift I have ever received in my life! I love it so much!" I ran my fingers over the burned inscription: "Millie Myles, Private Investigator."

Cici approached with a box of tissues and a bottle of water. "Millie, every private eye needs a notebook. Right, Trae?"

"That's right. This will make you the professional we always knew you were." Trae gave me one of his big smiles and made a heart with his fingers, which I immediately returned.

Cici rolled their eyes.

Suddenly a strange, loud cawing noise sounded on the patio. "Is that crow mad or sick?" Cici opened the sliding glass door.

"Definitely mad." Trae slid behind me and peeked at the bird.

A shiny little object dropped as the crow continued to caw before flying away. I walked outside and tears blurred my vision as I stared down at the matching earring that Missy had left for Juniper.

"Missy, you will always have a home with me," I whispered to myself, hoping that the breeze would carry my message back to the bird.

"Trae, would you make up a little salad for that crow? Her name is Missy, and she belonged to Juniper. It looks like she needs someone new to watch over her, so I want her to be a part of our family now." He could see the heartbreak in my eyes, so he didn't bother to argue.

"Ahh... sure, baby girl. I can do that." He gave my good shoulder a squeeze before heading back into the condo.

"You two are so weird," Cic snarked. "First a cat and now a crow. I can see how this is going to end."

CHAPTER 44

I stepped onto Lorraine's bus and took my seat behind her.

"I'm sure you've heard I'm famous."

"I might have read something in the paper about some young people solving the city's biggest crime." I could see Lorraine trying not to crack a smile.

"Yeah, that was me, Cici, and Trae. I'm actually the stand-out star though, but they were a big help. I appreciate them." I kept my head down but glanced up to see how she would respond. She had been telling me for years that solving crimes would never happen or be a real job.

"I swear I read something about one of those fools getting shot." She released a tuft of air.

Fuck. That was me.

Instead of replying, I pulled the line for my stop.

"See you tomorrow, Lorraine." I hopped off the bus.

"Get a real job, Millie." The doors shut in my face before I turned to walk toward the evidence warehouse.

I swiped my badge to get into the warehouse—business as usual, as if I hadn't even been gone.

"Hey there, Myles. Good to see you, pal." Eddie slapped me on the back, which sent a jolting pain through my shoulder and ribs.

I looked up at the big man, trying my best to smile through the discomfort. "Hi ya, Eddie. Sorry you all have to work on a holiday. How is the world of crime and criminals shaping up?"

"Eh' there are no holidays in the *world* of crime, but it's going good. I tell you though, I never thought the Body Goblin would end up being a lady; totally pegged the killer as a dude."

I was offended. "Why would you say something like that? Women can be serial killers too. Amazing, creative, and talented ones at that, so don't be so misogynistic, Eddie. And technically, no one died, so that makes this *woman was* the most skilled serial killer of them all."

I left him with a dirty look and walked over to my station where I found Phil working through what looked like a year's worth of evidence based on how high it was piled around him.

I picked up a flowerpot, and suddenly felt sad thinking of Juniper and her beautiful flowers on Blake Island. "Hey Phil, looks like you have your hands full here. How are you holding up?"

Taking the flowerpot from my hands, Phil replied in a controlled manner. "Please do not touch anything until you are wearing gloves. Thank you for asking. I'm doing fine. I obviously have a lot of work to do while you are out for a few weeks. But there will be plenty of work left for when you get back." I could tell he was stressed.

I studied a packet of seeds, which Phil immediately plucked from my fingers. "Well, I will get back to work as soon as I can," I said with a smile. "I start physical therapy this week but have some paperwork here to sign, so I will leave you to your duties. Good luck with everything, Phil."

Phil caught up to me as I walked toward HR. "Wait, I have something for you." He handed me a Shadow Workbook Journal. "I'm not sure what you're going through or have gone through in your life, but I have noticed that you count to yourself sometimes, which can be a sign of OCD. I've also noticed other rituals that I don't even think you realize you're doing. Anyway, I just wanted to offer this in case it helps. And just so you know, his name is Chad. The other day you asked me the name of my shadow, and his name is Chad."

A bit stunned, I nodded and smiled. "Chad is a really good name."

Phil gave me a small nod back before leaving me a bit dazed. I pulled his gift close to my chest and whispered, "Thank you," even though I knew he couldn't hear me.

The screen door slammed shut behind me and Mickey poked his head from the kitchen at the sound.

"Come in here, I want you to taste the sauce before Nancy gets here. It's kind of a special day having you both at my table for the first time."

I rolled my eyes and dropped off the computer bag in my bedroom before heading into the kitchen. All this new found fame had me fallen behind on my correspondence, so I brought my laptop to catch up on my life before dinnertime.

Walking into the kitchen, I smelled the turkey baking and when I looked over at the table, it was already set with my plate and tableware in the same spot, as always. I also noticed Nancy's additional setting, but something was off. "Why did you move your place setting?"

Mickey walked over with his palm hovering under a steaming spoon of spaghetti sauce. "Because I want to sit next to my future wife."

"Ummm... not good enough. You have sat in that same seat since the day I was born, Mickey. You can't just decide to sit in another seat because you suddenly have a future wife," I tasted the sauce and nodded my approval. It was good.

He walked back to the stove. "You're being ridiculous. You know that, right? It's just a seat at a table and someday, you might bring a plus one to dinner and decide to move where you sit too. And when that happens, you won't hear me complaining about it." With those unreasonable words, the screen door slammed.

Nancy strutted into the kitchen like she owned the place and went straight to the refrigerator, where she dropped off a store-bought pumpkin pie, swiped a cola, and then sat in Mickey's spot at the kitchen table. "How are you, Millie? Is your shoulder healing up alright?"

I sat across from Nancy, which felt so weird, but I tried to play it cool for Mickey's sake. "I have about five weeks of physical therapy before I can come back to work but otherwise, healing is coming along fine. Now that you are here, there is something I wanted to tell you and Mickey." I smirked because I could see the redness creep up the back of Mickey's neck as he stirred the sauce at the stove. He was nervous I was going to make him look like an idiot.

Nancy placed her hand over mine. "We are family, Millie. We will always support you, no matter what. Now Mickey, come over here and sit down so Millie can share her news with us." She made sure to say it with a bite, so he knew who wore the pants in their relationship, and I could tell I was melting her heart by including her in my announcement.

Mickey sat down and locked eyes with me, making it very clear that I was not to embarrass him. "My friends and I are starting a private investigator business." I left it at that.

Nancy lit up with excitement. "That is wonderful, Millie! Right, Mickey? Mickey, that is wonderful, right?" She hit him on the arm.

Mickey didn't speak or blink; he just sat there and stared at me. Then he stood up, went to the stove, and dished up our dinner. He returned with a platter full of turkey and our traditional Sunday dinner spread.

We sat together and Mickey asked me to say a prayer. We all bowed our heads. "From the rains to the roots, beneath the soils we grieve. We send our thanks to our fallen trees. Thank you for your abundance of love, warmth, security, and shelter. Blessings to the pines." I smirked and grabbed a piece of garlic bread.

"What the fuck was that?" Seriously Millie? You must have hit your head harder than I thought." Mickey shook his head.

I ignored his comment and piled my plate with turkey, bread, spaghetti, and salad. As I went to dig in, I noticed a pile of mail sitting by my plate. "What's this?"

Mickey stabbed his finger on the table, which meant he was gearing up to give me a lecture. "Okay. This is the last time I'm going to tell you this, Millie. I mean, it's like you just don't hear me when I speak. What did I tell you about using my address? This is the last time. Stop having your mail sent here. Seriously Soda Pop, you're an adult with your own address and mailbox. Quit using mine! And why the fuck did I get a bill in the mail for almost eight hundred dollars from an office supply store? I told you that card was for emergencies..."

I picked up the pieces of mail and began flipping through each of them one by one as I listened to Mickey's voice fade into the background. Most of them appeared to be junk, which I liked looking through.

Free training on how to advertise for our new business, I thought to myself.

I continued flipping through each letter as I stuffed a crunchy, buttery slice of garlic bread into my mouth. Mickey's tirade had started to ease up.

"I get mail at my place too, Mickey," I said around the garlic bread. "I only send the important stuff here. Like I told you before, no one is going to steal mail from a cop's—" my fingers started to tremble when I saw the return address: *My Private Investigator Official Test Results.*

"Soda Pop? Are you okay? What is it?" Mickey looked at Nancy concerned.

"It's nothing," I stuttered. "I just need a minute." I stood up, gathered all my mail and ran to my bedroom, slamming the door. Unable to wait a second longer, I tore open the envelope and threw it to the floor.

Dear Ms. Myles,

We would like to congratulate you on passing your private investigators exam with a score of 86%. Additional licensing details will soon follow. Welcome to the Washington State Private Investigators Association.

After doing some quick math, I realized that the questions I got right were the ones that I had just filled in randomly.

Welp, I guess that goes to show that I knew the right answers the whole time, and I was just overthinking everything.

I pulled out my new detective notebook to document this moment.

Detective's Log: Case# 7877554 / Under the Saltwater Moon. SOLVED by Millie Myles, Lead Private Investigator at the agency Two Queer Spies and a Gay Tech Guy in collaboration with Cici Haskins and Trae Michael.

I sat on my bed and leaned back, tossing the rest of my mail aside when I noticed my DNA results fell to the floor. I stared at the envelope for a minute then picked it up. I opened the letter and pulled out the single sheet of paper that had a code for me to access my results online. Maybe I had a rich old uncle in Italy longing to leave his fortune to his long-lost niece. I felt a small tingle of excitement as I logged into my DNA account and accepted all the disclaimers. I hit the last accept button and watched the double helix symbol spin as it built my DNA profile, family tree, and list of relatives.

When the helix stopped spinning, the room began to swirl in its place.

This can't be right.

I double checked to make sure it was my name on the profile. It was. My heart started to pound and my airway felt like it was collapsing. "What the fuck? No... no... no... no..." My laptop slipped from my fingers and hit the floor.

CHAPTER 45

I told you might love me a little by the end of this story.

Acknowledgements

Writing the book is the fun part. It's just you and your characters figuring out the world you're building. Then you write, "the end," and realize the real work begins. Creating a book takes a team of dedicated and hardworking people who collectively believe the story has a place in this world. I am forever grateful for these humans who helped me bring *Under the Saltwater Moon* to life.

Who is an author without their life partner? My biggest support system in the entire world is my amazing wife, Jenny. Jenny went through this manuscript as my first developmental editor. She spent hours continuously listening to all my different plot twists and ideas until I got them just right. I often say it's not what we as writers give up sitting on the couch writing for hours on end—the weekend trips, the date nights, or movie nights—but it's what our partners give up so we can live our dreams to write our stories. I don't take this lightly. My wife will always be my greatest love and my biggest fan. Thank you honey! I love you so much!

I am so grateful for my beta readers, Susan Brunow, Rae Taylor, Leetza Pegg, Skye Erikson, Joanne Marie Maloney, Reagen Dodson-Walls, and Chelsea Jones. They contributed hours to fine tuning everything from the smallest of details to the bigger picture, and that's not something I will ever forget. Millie and her friends would not have turned out to be the humans they are without each of you. Thank you for your honesty and especially for all the laughs throughout this process.

Big shout out to my photographer Kori Spencer at Irokimages.com. The way Kori was able to make me comfortable during a photo shoot was so special and unique. She sits with you and has these moments where she just smiles, and then, snap, snap, snap. Just like that, she captures the essence of your soul and every bit of your personality in the most beautiful way. When you find your people, don't ever let them go! Kori is my people. Also, a special shout out to her daughter, Avah, for all the laughs that day! Such a sweetheart!

I feel like the luckiest author in the world to have met two of the loveliest editors in the world, Sara Elisabeth and Laura Quill from Two Girls One Book Editing. I always say, "I am a storyteller, not an English major." I know editing is hard. It takes a remarkably patient person to sit for hours fixing all the things, making sure all my characters are connecting just right, and assuring that someone I killed off doesn't accidentally show up sixteen chapters later. It doesn't hurt that these women happen to be super fun to work with as well. Thanks for all the late night/early morning chats to get my plot nailed down. I seriously don't know what I would have done without the two of you!

This is my second book with cover artist Sarah Earnhart. Sarah never ceases to amaze me with her artistic abilities to pencil draw a picture, then layer in the unique pieces of different painting styles to create a dynamic piece of art that I can proudly call my book cover. Each cover that Sarah designs is a one-of-a-kind masterpiece that brings my stories to life. The artwork for this book features the Saltwater Moon's stormy water, a Jupiter tree, the city of Seattle, and Blake Island.

I want to forward a very special shout out to a very special reader, Moxie of Yearofqueerlit. From day one, Moxie has been one of my biggest supporters. She has created such an inclusive space for queer authors such as myself to shine and feel safe in sharing our stories. Without readers and supporters like Moxie, some of us indie authors might not have of ever been noticed. Thank you so much my friend. I adore you!

To all my readers, I am forever grateful that you picked my book. Thank you for taking a chance on my work and my dream. Without you, I am just a writer on a couch, but you made me a writer with readers. I love you all! Thank you! I hope you enjoyed reading this novel.

About the Author

Photography by Kori Spencer at @Irokimages.com

Moving from her Midwestern roots to the Pacific Northwest over a decade ago, Christa now lives with her wife, two golden retrievers and their pug. She enjoys everything the Seattle area has to offer, from the culture to the coffee, so there is never a lack of inspiration for her writing. When she's not writing, Christa enjoys supporting women's sports, nature, rock hunting, reading, and traveling.

Blurb

After years of dutifully waiting tables at the diner down the street, wannabe-PI Millie Myles is ready for a change. With a little help from her police detective, big brother Mickey, Millie lands the job of her dreams as an evidence processing technician with the Seattle Police Department. Her first day on the job, Millie is catapulted into the middle of the most brutal murder investigation the city has ever seen.

Against her brother's warnings and better judgement, Millie is drawn to action and proceeds with some unsanctioned, extra-curricular sleuthing with the help of her friends, Trae and Cici. The independent investigation introduces the trio to a group of local forest dwellers with a history of bizarre practices and societal beliefs. Things get complicated when Millie befriends a beautiful member of the woodlander community named Juniper and finds herself catching feelings, realizing that undercover work comes at a cost.

With bloody crime scenes piling up, the ever-curious Millie and her cohorts rush to uncover the clues that land Millie directly in the murderer's crosshairs. Her first unofficial investigation as an amateur PI could very well be her last. Join Millie, Trae, and Cici as they seek to uncover the dark truth of Under the Saltwater Moon before the killer strikes again.